Beside Turning Water

Edge of Empire Series
World Turned Upside Down

Dory Codington

Dory's Historicals Press
doryshistoricals.com

To the beautiful Percherons who work in
Downtown Boston.

&

The Mount Jewett Book club.

&

As always, to those who won and those
who lost
The American Revolution.

Preface

Breed's Hill, Charlestown, Massachusetts. June 17, 1775

"Retreat!" The command was given and repeated as men moved back and out of the redoubts. Cool rain might have been welcome on this implausabily hot day, but the order was not. Most of the Continentals couldn't hear the command through the cannon fire and chaos, the blood-red haze of battle. It had been a day of heat, of successfully repelling two British assaults on the Americans dug in on Breed's Hill. That was before reality hit - that they were simply out of everything, powder, musket shot, and really out of cannon balls. It was the third assault that was successful for the redcoats, causing chaos among the Americans and forcing their retreat.

The Continentals had, over the course of the long hot day, inflicted more damage than they themselves had suffered. The American riflemen, skilled at shooting vermin from afar, could see no reason not to aim at the bright red coats of the staff officers. So in technicality, the British won the Battle of Bunker's Hill, but it would go down in history as one of the worst single days for the British Army at war. In short, General William Howe's staff was decimated by what some had promised would be a ragtag bunch of farmers with old muskets and pitchforks, but instead had turned out to be local militias of undisciplined but skilled marksmen committed to a cause.

The General was not well pleased, but he was not surprised. He had fought with these militias against the French in the American wilderness. His brother George had died there, and was buried near Albany, New York. George Howe had been honored by the General Court of Massachusetts with a plaque in Westminster. The General gave up all notions of sympathy and called for his troops to charge the Americans, to work around them to the top of the hill – this was successful when the Americans' munitions ran out.

Alex Peele moved backwards in the hastily constructed earthen redoubt. He had been in this spot since just after sunset the evening before. It had been a long night spent digging this hole with walls into Breed's Hill. The heat had struck with dawn, before the British Army had made their clumsy way across the bay, making June 17, 1775 the hottest day anyone could remember. Certainly it was damn hot on the open land of the cow pasture where they had chosen to take a stand.

The spring had been like that, cold in the morning of the famous ride to Concord and Lexington, and brutally hot during the British retreat. That had been just two months before, when the town militias had come out that April morning to defend their lands and liberties. Now militia groups from all over New England had come to help, to defend Boston from British efforts to control the countryside.

Alex was one of those who had come to help. He left his schoolroom and students as soon as he heard, and arrived at Cambridge in late April. The commander had taken one look at Thorne, his magnificent gray, and decided that horseflesh like that should not be left moldering in the stable. So Alex had been sent straight out as a messenger to the Congress in Philadelphia.

He'd gotten back to camp just in time to have been

handed his musket and told to join the New Hampshire regiment, the reinforcement for the Massachusetts regulars. They had held their position, shooting at every advancing contingent, succeeding in holding off attempt after attempt, until after their third attempt the British pushed through and the retreat order was given.

He had probably killed a dozen redcoats as they held their line before the ball found his leg. Now he was bleeding, and barely half aware of being dragged behind a dirt wall. He could hear the low wail of the cannons, he smelled gun powder, and other more disgusting things, that stuck to his sweat - soaked clothing and skin. Like every man on that hill, he was hot and he was thirsty. He was keenly aware of this discomfort, more than of the wound in his leg. He hadn't felt the musket ball tear into him, ripping his pant-leg and pushing the filthy linen deep into the wound. Later, the misshapen ball would be placed in a wooden box and locked away with the other souvenirs from his travels. Gathering his wits, he crawled forward with the retreat and collapsed into the man in front of him, finally losing consciousness.

So Alex, and the rest of General Artemis Ward's small army, lost the hills in Charlestown, a glacially formed peninsula facing the Town of Boston. It had no real value other than for a clear spring and grazing cows. But the two hills rose over the larger town, making Bunker's or Breed's Hill strategically important. Charlestown was directly between American headquarters in Cambridge, and the British – blockading, occupying, and now suffering, in the water-locked Town of Boston.

The Americans' attempts to grab the high ground over

Boston was the idea of Joseph Warren, head of the Committee of Safety and the Province's great leader. Now he lay dead, the most famous casualty of the afternoon.

Alex regained consciousness on the way back to Cambridge. He looked straight up, into the bright blue of the June afternoon, and though it took a minute to realize that shouting men and hoofbeats did not belong in heaven, he understood that he was not dead. He was being moved away from the battlefield, but the man next to him on the wagon had a foul odor and most likely was. He dozed again, and woke in the field hospital set up near the college, the students having been removed west. He had a moment of sheer panic that they would take the leg, but someone pushed a bottle toward his lips, and after a swallow or two he found retreating to his own memories more pleasant.

He regained consciousness hours later on a dormitory cot. His head felt woolly and his leg throbbed. He touched it gingerly, hoping to feel flesh. The leg was there, swollen and aching miserably, but it was not ghost pain.

"Disgusting mess your breeches made of the wound. Sometimes well made clothing is the very devil. We got all the damn threads out of there. Probably would have been faster to take the leg, but the ball missed the bone." The doctor sounded disappointed as he loomed over him, checking his forehead for fever. "I'll change the bandage in the morning. In a few days, barring fever, you can go recover in your own tent." True to his word, Alex was back to his own quarters by the end of the week.

For Alex, being infirm was nearly insufferable, but to be a Yale man immobile in a Harvard dormitory had its own indignities. He wished himself well, and by the second week in

8

July he was able to tag along as a passenger on a supply run to Braintree Harbor, to the south. The doctor, a Connecticut man, had recommended ocean swimming as a way to heal both the wound and the muscles.

Chapter 1

Shipyard at Braintree harbor, July 14, 1775

Alex climbed out of the water, shook off and lazily dressed. Nothing would have been so nice as a nap on the warm sand. That was not going to happen, but the ocean swim had been good for both the weak muscles and the ragged scar. He vowed to swim in the river, given a chance in his schedule. It wouldn't have the healing properties of ocean water, but his leg would benefit from the swimming.

It had been a favor, this coming here early enough to get in a swim. His new friends had agreed to leave camp before dawn to give him time before the shipment arrived. He rubbed at his sore leg, a new habit that brought no pride. Above the strand he found a rock and sat. The wharf was busy now that it was full day. He watched as businesses and warehouses along the docks pulled back their shutters to the morning. The sandy beach on the side of the wharf was full of children running in and out of the cold water.

Lost in the warm sun and the lazy sounds of the ocean, Alex looked up as a horse whinnied. The fellow stood in the traces of a substantial wagon being loaded with heavy barrels, each one needing two workmen, who were carrying them from a small ship docked not far away. The men had been at it for a while, and they were building a sweat, though the early morning was not yet hot.

Alex moved onto an empty crate so he could put his leg up onto a granite block. He was absently grateful for the perfect height between crate and rock. The wind blew off the harbor. Alex noted that it snatched some bits of conversation away, and amplified others. He took off his hat and let the wind dry his still-wet hair. Watching the men and their horse was a pleasant enough diversion, a way to pass the hour he and his colleagues would spend waiting for their ship. The *Cardinal* was late, so he would no doubt endure some ribbing that he had made them wake too early.

Alex had been happy to leave camp, and not just for the chance to swim. Prior to his wounding, he had not minded the disorder of the American camp at Cambridge. He accepted it as normal, and knew that chaos was what he could expect as an enlisted soldier, but, since the injury he'd become less tolerant. He hoped the anxiety would pass with healing.

His fellows had chosen not to join him in the water and had gone into a small tavern for breakfast. Coats and musket balls, that was what was expected on the *Cardinal*. Considering the shape of the quartermaster's records, they would be lucky if it was a half shipment.

He was hungry. They had left camp before the ovens were warm. Smells from the tavern were good, but even the thought of hobbling the short distance was unpleasant. Sitting on this crate in the silence of sun and sea breezes was not. He enjoyed the bustle of shipyard activity, as he had when he first encountered it in New Haven. That young man, just arrived from the mountains of New Hampshire, seemed so alien to him now, but the fascination for the ordered chaos remained, no matter where he was. He had seen the same on his travels to London, Naples, Greece and Istanbul. But now, just beyond his hearing, another scene unfolded. He watched it with pleasure, since it involved a rather pretty young blonde.

The blonde's face, from what he could see under a

11

pleasing straw bonnet, was tightly drawn, showing frustration as she tried to explain something to the local cooper. Alex could not hear the words, so he allowed himself the luxury of silent eavesdropping. They seemed to be having an argument. The blonde gestured again and again, pointing to the man's barrels. Alex heard a squawk of anger. He wondered if he would go over to help if his leg were stronger. It was none of his business, but the maiden did seem to be in distress. His instinct was to rescue such a fairy tale blonde. Unfortunately, the aching leg telegraphed that he remain where he was. The sun had moved, and he now sat in the shade of the chestnut that grew upland of the beach. There was no reason now to leave his perch. Yes, it was rude to watch so closely, but since he'd been shot, he had had so little fun, and the blonde was so very nice to look at. Besides, he knew he would help if the man moved to hurt her.

***

Nina Bigelow was not shaded by anything more than a flat straw bonnet that was trying to fly off like one of those screaming sea gulls. It had not been an easy few months, and she was tired of Mr. Jones' excuses for not supplying new barrels or coming to the *Wheel and Hammer* to fix old ones.

"Mr. Jones, the *Wheel* has been buying your barrels for years, decades even. My father-in-law these past thirty and probably the Bigelows before that. I think it very wrong of you to ignore my needs." Nina bit her tongue, holding back her words. She was already known as "the alewife," and she didn't want to vent all her frustrations on this one older man.

It was not his fault if the maltster she had known since she had come to work at the *Wheel* patently refused to sell to anyone in the countryside, preferring to stay in town and supply the British. It was not Mr. Jones's fault that she wanted new gowns and her modiste was trapped at her shop with her goods. Marianne wrote that she could get a pass to leave, but her fabrics and notions had to stay behind. So she had remained in Boston, taking care of the wives and mistresses of the officers who had moved in over the past year.

Nor was it his fault that Newton, along with every other town in the Province, had agreed four years ago not to import or wear British made goods, so everything felt old and tired, even before the British blockaded Boston. Nina could brew good ale from apples and pumpkins, maybe even rocks, but she could not make window glass, plates or mugs. It was also true that she could not sew, or make or remake anything more than an apron, and the most utilitarian one at that.

If times were normal, she would find another cooper. But times were not normal. Too many local shipyards had closed, and the coopering with them. Mr. Jones had relocated from Boston months ago, and she had only yesterday uncovered his new location.

"Please, Mr. Jones?"

It was her brother David who discovered that Mr. Jones had set up shop at Braintree. David, the owner of a sawmill used by the shipyard for some of their lumber, found out only in casual conversation, and passed the information on to his sister. Nina had come to the shipyard as soon as she could, bringing David's son Davy, and her own young Jack. The boys had considered the short journey south a fine adventure, and were spending the warm, sunny morning, exploring the tidepools that flourished beyond the yard, but not quite out of sight. Though they both swam well and would stay together, she had made that one demand.

It took one more footstamp, but at last Mr. Jones, of Jones's Coopering, agreed to whatever the forceful lady was requesting. He lifted his chin and retreated back into his small shop. Alex nodded his approval. The removal of the gruff old man had improved the scenery nicely. He watched as gusts off the ocean pulled at her hat, revealing a mop cap and pale blond hair that looked too fine and silky not to jump and fly out of pins and ribbons.

The blonde was dressed in a plain blue vest, pinned in front, and a striped skirt of the same color - the plainest of clothing. No doubt she was a servant and these were her best clothes. But the tilt of her chin and her forceful behavior with the cooper said that was not so. Perhaps she dressed plainly as a uniform of sorts. She did seem to have a relationship with the cooper. She might be a maid, or the wife of the local fish monger putting pickled herring into barrels.

Alex felt he had almost puzzled it out, and then chided himself to stop this fancy. It was a bad habit of his, filling in make-believe stories with facts he had no business collecting. It had been a hobby of his since childhood. He did it rarely now, or it had been rare until that musket ball had forced him to sit still. As a boy, his family had become used to it and left him alone, always aware that he might piece together their private dealings and learn more than he ought. He had learned early not to let on what he'd learned. Often it was false, but too often it was true.

It was mostly innocent, and he liked to see how close he could come to the truth through observation alone. He had vowed, as a boy, that he would never read letters or diaries. Such activities did not amuse him, even if reading private things had been moral by any standard. No, Alex got his information by simple watching.

14

After the cooper went back into his shop, the pretty blonde, as he had named her, waved at the two boys at the water's edge jumping in the waves. They hollered back acknowledging her, but made no effort to join her. Alex was surprised when she laughed at their antics, seeming to enjoy their fun instead of insisting they return. Clearly she was not in charge of their welfare. Maybe they were all servants in the same household.

She went to her small cart to put her hat and cap under the seat, out of the wind, walking the cart horse to the trough to let her drink. She spoke to the horse and petted her neck, but he couldn't catch the one sided conversation. Alex pulled out a piece of wood he had been carving and contemplated the work. He looked up again as she turned back toward the water to watch the boys. Without cap or hat, the strands of her hair caught the light and danced in the wind. He sighed at the sight.

Alex considered himself an expert on women's hair and its color. It wasn't a topic that came up in ordinary conversation. Still, he marveled at the dark richness and airy lightness of different women's hair and how each styled it. Occasionally, he'd had the opportunity to remove ribbons and pins, and feel the various textures as well. The pretty blonde's hair, now floating out of her reach, was unusually pale. It would be false to call it colorless - it was, in fact, pale honey streaked with dark, rich hues. The effect was stunning.

Alex turned to see if the *Cardinal* had arrived. His cohorts were still not on the dock. There was no reason to leave the shade or his comfortable crate. He forced himself not to look back at the blonde. She was bound to feel eyes on her and he'd hate to make false excuses; he'd been having such a pleasant morning.

She moved toward the big tree, almost sharing his shade.

She turned again to watch the boys, clearly not yet anxious to leave. She leaned back against a boulder. Alex knew something about boys, having been one and taught more than a few. The older boy was thirteen, maybe fourteen. The younger one was smaller, no more than ten, maybe even a tall nine. The three had a remote family resemblance, a few features in common. The younger boy had her hair, pulled at this instant into an untidy queue, but he was too old to be hers. They might all be cousins, at the harbor for their errand, much like he was.

The blonde could be no more than twenty-six; he thought closer to twenty-five. He supposed a woman that age might have a child the age of the younger boy. But in his experience, if that were the case, there would be others, probably many others, all playing in the waves. He imagined the blonde, the mother of a happy family, babes in arms playing at the ocean's edge. He felt a tightening in his breeches and his leg wound pulled uncomfortably, reminding him that thoughts of pretty women and children were painful, and could not be his.

Nina felt appreciative eyes on her. It wasn't a new feeling; in fact there were times when it seemed like that was all she felt. At the *Wheel and Hammer*, a tavern at the Lower Falls of the Charles River, she expected it. She had always supposed it came with being a young woman working in a busy taproom. Most times she ignored the looker, and he'd become interested in something or someone else, usually one of the young tavern maids. He would turn away, and the feeling would stop. But the sense of being watched by the man under that spreading chestnut, sitting on the wooden crate with that interested look on his face and his longish, dark, ash-brown hair, didn't go away even when he turned. It was as though his concentration never wavered, even when he looked elsewhere. Mostly he hadn't tried to hide that he was following her with his eyes. At least he hadn't come over to say something ridiculous.

To acknowledge that she knew he had been watching her, she turned, nodded and smiled at him, thinking as she did that she would have tipped her hat if she had been wearing it. She had expected him to turn away embarrassed, but instead he grinned back at her, bright humor glowing in soft gray eyes as he returned her look. She giggled, happy that the wind whisked the sound away.

Alex wasn't surprised that his pretty blonde lady had a lovely smile. He appreciated that she hadn't come over to slap him across the face for being impertinent. She seemed to take being stared at in stride. He gave her credit for having a sense of humor. Most women, he knew, didn't.

Her smile was lovely, and the accompanying laugh chased away all the tension from those thoughtful blue-green eyes. It was one of those smiles and laughs that seemed conjured up solely for the recipient. Alex sensed he'd been extraordinarily lucky enough to have that smile bestowed on him just then, as though he had been granted a rare gift.

The pleasant reverie of the sunny morning broke when a barrel, falling from its precipitous perch on the end of the workmen's cart, made a loud, jarring sound. The men had gone into the tavern, and when their horse shied at a far away cry and stepped backward, a barrel shifted and fell. Alex jumped at the noise and watched it begin to roll down the slight incline. At that angle it was sure to roll harmlessly past the tree and down the hill toward the flat beach.

The small barrel gathered speed, which was not really a concern, but it changed course when it ran over a ditch and hit a small rock. Alex registered that it was very heavy, probably filled with nails from the nearby pig iron mill in Weymouth. The blonde, for whom he had no other name, stood in the trajectory of the barrel. She had turned back to the boys, and she strained to hear what the older one had shouted. It only took seconds, but Alex wasn't going to wait to see if the blonde noticed the damn barrel. It would break her legs when it hit. It was that heavy.

Nina started at the sound of the heavy barrel rolling directly at her. It rolled unevenly as its heavy load shifted inside. She knew she ought to jump, to move, but there was nowhere to go.

Terror hit. She could not move back into a granite boulder, could not have even if the rock had opened a magical door right next to her. Her feet were frozen to the spot. She shook her head "no" when the man shouted at her to move. She closed her eyes, hoping the horrible pain would be brief and praying that someone would bring the boys back to her brother.

The last thing Alex saw before he launched was the blonde shake her head and close her eyes. He propelled himself from his spot, stepping onto his good leg. He winced as he pushed, putting his weight on his injured right leg. He grabbed her around the waist and pushed off back to his original spot, keeping his weight on his left leg. He tried to balance, but the trajectory and extra weight of the blonde was too much. He put his right foot down to get his balance, but it crumpled beneath him as he knew it would. He fell backward onto a pile of leftover sail parts and bits of wood, pulling her on top of him, and knocking the wind out of him. A part of his mind acknowledged that the stitches in his leg had opened and he was probably bleeding.

Nina waited for the agony of the barrel hitting and crushing her legs, for the noise of bones snapping. She heard the barrel crash, and the sound of loose metal scattering over stone. She wiggled her toes, but pain did not come. Her breathing eased, and as she became aware of where she was, she realized she was lying in a pile of broken floorboards and sailcloth. She didn't know if it was better or worse, but she was on top of the man who had been watching her, and had grinned that silly grin at her - the man with the thick brown hair and laughing gray eyes. He had pulled her away from the rolling barrel, and it seemed she was lying on him, his arms holding her tightly.

She took a deep breath, taking a moment to let her head stop swimming, her heart stop pounding, and the taste of fear in her mouth go away. She closed her eyes and forced her breathing to slow. The man had not moved. Maybe he had injured himself saving her. She hoped not. Most likely he was in shock, and would get up in a moment.

Nina could not be found lying on top of a strange man, any man for that matter, no matter the circumstance of their meeting. She needed to stand, curtsy, and say a gracious "thank you." She needed to get the boys and rush away. She needed to open her eyes. She could not be seen lying on a man in a shipyard!

The gray-eyed man didn't seem to notice he was holding her in place. He hadn't yet moved or spoken. Pressed against him, she could feel every inch of him. It was most disturbing. He had not yet loosened his grasp - in fact, he was holding her very tightly in strong arms. She tried to lift herself up, but his grip was too strong. She wanted to get up and move away, but that would require opening her eyes. She was not ready for that. Really, it felt very safe here under these sails.

Nina wiggled her hips, finally trying to squirm away or get him to relax his arms. It did not work. She heard him moan in pain. She might have hurt him further. She stopped concentrating on her escape and sought to discover where he was hurt. "Have you hurt your head?" He didn't answer. She put her hands into his hair to feel his scalp, to hunt for a bump or a wound. Running her hands slowly through his hair and over his scalp, Nina was relieved to find there was no wet blood, and no large bump on his head, but he did moan again.

The leg was a low dull ache that Alex chose to ignore. He was dreaming that he was holding the pretty blonde in his arms, her body stretched over his, her firm breasts pushed against him while she moved her hips over his, her hands seductively in his hair. He moaned with pleasure. He breathed in her scent. It was unusual, and he didn't think that was because he had not been with a woman recently. If he was right, it was the smell of hops and ale. He knew he was dreaming. He'd had a good life, but a luscious body pressed against his, who smelled flowery clean, and of good ale? He must have hit his head, or died and gone to heaven.

He was proven alive when she spoke. It was barely understandable, and then she pushed strong fingers against his scalp and through his hair. He felt his heartbeat quicken and his body warm.

Slowly, awareness increased. The memory of what had happened hit him in a flash. He was mildly embarrassed to find that he was almost fully aroused - only mildly, as it had been a delicious few minutes, a wonderful dream. He shifted his hips away from the woman lying fully over him. He opened his eyes. Hers were staring back at him, pools of blues and greens, so much like the joint colors of sky and sea. A perfect way to remember this unusual day.

Her eyes showed concern. It felt unique to have anyone worry about him, sweet but unwanted. So, as much as he would have loved to hold her in his arms for a few minutes longer, he forced them apart. In seconds she was up, turning away from him, pushing down her skirts and fixing her short bodice. She looked up and smiled that magic smile at him. "Thank you for your quick thinking. You are unhurt?"

"Thank you, Mistress. Yes, I am fine, and you are very welcome. I am happy that you are unhurt." His voice was as lovely as the rest of him.

"Well," she pulled herself out of the reverie, "thank you again, goodbye." She gave a sort of desperate look in his direction, as if she wasn't sure what was supposed to happen next. Then she turned and ran down the beach to the boys. The little group of pale heads walked up the little hill to their wagon. The boys hitched the giant horse to the trace, and the three climbed onto the bench and, with the crack of her whip, they were gone.

Alex watched the little group drive away. He was relieved to have saved her, and honestly could not regret his leg collapsing or having her lounged for a moment on top of him. She truly had been a delightful armful.

He turned to wave at the wagon as they rode off. The pretty blonde - he would always remember her by that name - actually lifted her foolish bonnet in his direction. Then, just as suddenly, she plopped it back onto her head. The boy next to her took the reins, while she tied the ribbon and pinned it securely in place.

Nina had felt a deep blush from her eyebrows to her toes. It began that moment when the brown haired man's arms relaxed, and she had opened her eyes and gazed into the deepest, most lovely soft-gray eyes she had ever seen. Not finding any wounds on the back of his head, she'd insisted to herself that she had to keep checking. The truth was, she found his thick wavy hair irresistible. It smelled like fire and horse and some faint cologne he might occasionally use. It was shiny brown, like the sun glinting off winter trees. It was the same color as a nut ale her father-in-law had brewed, that time someone had brought Italian walnuts as a gift.

Nina was not naive. She knew what her thrashing, and running her hands through his hair, had accidentally done to his body. She was embarrassed to have made him uncomfortable, when he had been so kind as to save her from certain death. It would have been rude to point it out to him by apologizing. She had simply thanked him. She had been in the same uncomfortable state, being trapped in his strong arms, his firm body beneath hers. She understood how uncomfortable and unpleasant such reactions could be. Nina pushed these thoughts out of her head, yet the memory of his scent, the feel of that thick hair, and his small moans, stubbornly would not leave.

During the two hours in the wagon, she told herself that she had wanted that grey-eyed man to loosen his arms and let her go. She scolded herself that she could not possibly have enjoyed feeling a man's hard body under hers, that she felt sorry about his arousal, and had not been aroused herself in response. She let the boys chatter about everything they had seen and heard at the beach, not hearing a word.

She knew that later, alone in her bed, these tingly feelings would come back. She didn't like them. They made her uncomfortable, and she didn't want to be uncomfortable like that, not ever again. She had been married once. She didn't want to marry again. She would let the incident fade in her memory until she could forget it. In time, she would forget the man with the gray eyes - forget how strong he'd felt, how safe she'd felt in his arms. Even if that were not the case, she would never see that man again.

Near her own home, they stopped at her brother's sawmill to drop Davy. A large man appeared out of the workshop. He was followed by two little girls and a dark-haired lady with a big basket.

Nina waved hello while the boys jumped out of the wagon and ran toward their fort in the dark hemlock forest. After exchanging pleasantries, she had a private word with her brother.

"David, you should come with us to the wedding tomorrow. It won't take but the middle of the day. You know that Natalie would love to see everyone. Father should have at least a glimpse of Davy and the girls." By then, they had walked up the hill for a basket lunch under a giant oak. The little girls raced off after their brother with their mother following, a hawk's eye on her twins.

David Tyrie had the muscles of the sawmill owner, operator, and carpenter. He was a darker version of his little sister, having the same dark blond hair without the nearly white streaks, his eyes a dark brown where hers were sea green and the blue of a summer sky.

"I'm surprised you want to see the old fool, let alone let

him at Jackie." David huffed away, feigning to leave the picnic and go back to his work.

"David, he is old. Should we stay angry at him for the rest of his life?" Nina's raised voice followed David. She looked to Natalie, who shrugged.

"Maybe not at anything so public as a wedding, Nina. I will try to get over there soon." Natalie got up and ran after her daughters who were pretending to cry that their brother and cousin would not let them into the fort.

Later, as she mounted the wagon for the short drive along the river, her brother came out of his workshop. He leaned into her. "Nina, I love you. How often has it been that you and I are all we have? If you want to put yourself in direct fire by going to that wedding, you'll have to do it yourself. Natalie supports my decision - she doesn't want Davy and the babies hurt by their grandfather. You say he has changed, but I don't believe it, and I won't find out I'm right at someone's wedding. You know as well as I, he's as likely to pronounce the lot of us as 'lost beyond redemption' as he ever was."

"He can't be that bad. He can't." Nina mumbled the words under her breath. She was tired, it had been a long morning, and it would be a busy night at the *Wheel*. "Dave, tell Jackie to come home by dinner. I need to go." She got back into her small wagon, *ghe'ed* at the horse and drove the two miles down to the Lower Falls.

The *Wheel* was already busy though the sun was still high in the sky. Sukey and Dodi were serving the men from the forge across the road who wandered in as they finished their work, and those travelers who stopped to eat and rest their horses. Those were the regulars - easily identified workers and travelers. There was also a new group that had begun to come to the tavern in increasing numbers and regularity. They were the mounted troops from Washington's army at Cambridge. It had started when a horseman noticed that the distance from camp to the Lower Falls was just long enough to give the horses a good workout, but not so far as to tire them. So while the men ate and drank their fill, their horses grazed on grass kept soft and green by the spray from the falls.

Nina surveyed the taproom. It was well under control. Going to her house for a change of clothes, she took a minute to wash before reappearing to take her place as proprietress and chief brewer at the little tavern and inn. She laughed that what she called her work-clothes were so much finer than her day wear. The reverse was more common, but she'd found that evenings moved more smoothly if she dressed as a woman of substance.

Chapter 2

The *Wheel and Hammer* sat on the edge of the Charles River, a river named for a long-ago king who had never cared about this place. The main building was stone, as was the brewhouse that attached at one side. There was also a two-story wood ell that jutted off the side of the main building, with six guest rooms. An outdoor staircase used by the staff made it easy to bring water and clean sheets to the rooms.

Nina's little white house, which she shared with her son, stood up the hill at the head of the drive. Connected to the brewhouse by a covered path, it was separate in architecture and design. More modern than the inn building, it had symmetrical rooms upstairs and down, a kitchen connected to a well furnished dining room, and a staircase leading up, somewhat elegantly, from the front hall. She had fixed Jack's room in the attic when he turned eight. His room, and the unused one next to it, huddled around the central chimney, warmed in the cool months with fires in the parlor and in Nina's rooms directly below. The kitchen had its own chimney, a broad hearth with lots of room to cook, on an outside wall. The design helped keep the house cool in summer, and all the rooms warm in winter.

The inn staff lived over the taproom in rooms where Nina had spent her short marriage, and where she and Jack had lived until the little wood house was completed. Now it was a dormitory, overseen by Mrs. Cotton, her wonderful cook and good friend. The older woman kept as close an eye on the tavern girls as any mother could wish. This last was of great help to Nina, since out here in the country very few of her girls lived nearby. Two of the three main helpers lived right at the *Wheel.* She would have no staff if their mothers did not trust the inn to keep the girls safe.

John Bigelow, Nina's father-in-law, had built the inn, tavern and brewhouse some thirty years before. He had traveled in Germany and Britain, studying brewing at the oldest, most famous inns. He had come here first as brewmaster, hired by the first Bigelow, and then, after marrying the daughter and changing his name to match hers, as owner. With his son and heir dead, John Bigelow had taught his son's widow to read German, French, Italian and Latin so she might understand the long books and journals he had collected on the art of brewing and so that she might pass the tavern and the knowledge onto her son.

When his first wife died, John had left the name Bigelow to his grandson and daughter-in-law and reacquired his original name, Peddleman. His second wife and children had that name. Since his death last January, Nina and Joshua Peddleman, her brother-in-law, had improved the stables and inn yard. With Josh's help, Nina had hopes that the *Wheel and Hammer* would become a posting inn, but there had been no word from the General Court on that count. No great surprise - with the Province in disarray, the government's only concern was with the functioning of the army at Cambridge, and occasional reports from the local Committees of Safety.

Nina pinned her silk jacket, put a fine linen cap on her head, and checked herself in the small mirror that rested on the plain maple dresser. She fluffed her soft pillows and blew a speck of dust from between the framed miniatures on the mantle, hearing her mother's elegant South country voice, out of place in a world of hard 'a's and dropped 'r's. "It never does to look better than one should, or be better than one should be, Nina dear." And she could hear her father's deep voice, so used to delivering sermons, reminding her that she should not expect to find life easy or pleasant. She thought a retort as she looked at the pretty things she had purchased with her own money, things that made life pleasant and her surroundings pretty, but she would agree it had never been easy.

She wondered if her hard work, and the success of the inn, would finally earn his approval. She laughed at herself that she even cared. She knew most people considered brewing "men's work," but her father relished hard work, believing the effort it took to do something extraordinarily well was one's mission on earth. Nina shook off her father's voice, pasted her smile on her face, and went down to run her pleasant taproom, to try with good food and well-made ale to make her patrons' lives just a little bit easier.

Chapter 3

The Wedding, July 15, 1775

"Peele wake up, aren't you at all worried for your eternal soul?"

"No!" the sleeping man pulled a pillow over his head to blot out the bright summer morning, and his friend's chatter.

"You said you would come with me to my cousin's wedding. There'll be good food and happy women in pretty gowns to flirt with."

Alex growled something that might have been "alright." He rolled onto his back, rubbed his stiff leg, and stretched. "You have passes?" The first man waved a sheet of foolscap at him.

He had woken early to swim in the river and see if it felt as good to his leg as the ocean had. It hadn't, but moving through the water did seem to help. He hadn't been able to resist a few more minutes of sleep when he returned to camp.

It was just a few minutes later on the beautiful summer morning as the two men, now clean, shaved, and dressed in their finest, rode the few miles from the messy, chaotic army encampment at Cambridge to a world of well-built houses, farms, and shops at the old Meeting House on a steep hill. To Alex, the quiet village around Newton's First Church was a blessed silence. The difference shocked him. He likened his days at camp to being inside a pounding drum.

He was from a world of steep, rocky mountains, and prodding his reluctant stallion up the hill reminded him of his home and his family. He noticed that he had stopped his usual polite chatter only when Wythe stared at him oddly. He said something offhand to break the silence and shake off the mood, a kind of disquiet that he might not be made of the right stuff for the infantry, especially now that his leg did not want to quit complaining.

The men left their horses with the boy whose job it was to watch them. "Ah my mother, father and sisters!" Wythe grabbed his arm and brought him to meet his relatives.

Alex made small talk and generally enjoyed meeting the congregants gathered for the wedding. The bride seemed to be a daughter of a third cousin of Wythe's mother. He assumed friendship and proximity were the reasons for attendance, rather than familial closeness.

He let Wythe and his people move ahead of him and into the meeting house. It was easier to be a stranger if he came in late. Let them settle into their pews and finish their gossip and news before he sat next to his friend for the long and familiar service.

He wandered over to the tables. There were towels over the food, but he could tell the tables were laden with fresh bread, meats and pies of all sorts. There was a sort of frantic movement at the pie table, lovely ankles and legs stuck out from under, as a young woman strained at something. She was clever, Alex noted, though he was sure it was an intrusion to notice, at all, that she had rolled down her stockings and lifted up her skirts to keep her clothing clean as she rummaged under the table. Her knees, hidden under layers of gown, would be stained with grass and dirt. Clearly, that did not bother her.

"Is someone there?" The voice pleaded from under the table.

Another riddle, what a week! Alex felt inclined to solve

30

it. "Yes. Is there something I can do to help?" He should be worried about the beautiful pies that would be lying in the dust, but he wanted to see the girl attached to the ankles.

"Hold the table up, would you?" The voice was sweet, but the girl was clearly stressed. "The idiots set it up too quickly, and the pin wasn't pushed in properly. One nudge and the table will collapse. Can you imagine cream and fruit sinking into the mud? Ah. Thank you." He heard the wooden pin slip into place. "That will do it." The relief of having the task complete was evident in her voice. Alex was rooted to his spot, waiting to see the rest of the sweet voiced girl. "I don't eat pie, mind you, but the bakers would be heartbroken and we can't have that.

"Kind sir, would you mind turning away? I am rather in a state of disarray."

The girl must be part of the wedding party or family, to be so worried about the pie bakers. Alex turned away from the sound of the voice. "I am turned toward the meeting house, you have nothing to fear, but I think we must hurry." The churchyard was emptying as guests hurried to their pews. Alex almost stepped away to go in - after all, his short work was finished - but he stayed, keeping his back well turned. He heard the rustle of silk, petticoats and skirts, swishing into place. It was, he feared, an arousing sound.

Nina had climbed under the crooked table almost without thinking. It took a minute to realize that she would emerge a filthy mess and embarrass herself and her family if she did not remedy it. So with no one watching, she had lifted her skirts and untied her stockings. Now she had to pull herself together with a man standing not two feet away. No doubt he wanted to see what sort of woman was attached to those bare ankles, and

31

what sort of crazy woman went diving under tables to save pies. She pulled up her stockings and fluffed out her skirts, checking that all the layers fell neatly. "Thank you, kind sir," Nina laughed, "hero of the pie table." She turned and would have shrieked in surprise, but for the look of shock on the man's face. She burst into laughter.

Nina laughed until her laughter slowed to a smile, which he returned. He was about to speak, to ask her connection to the wedding, or marvel in her transformation from plainly dressed servant to a wellborn lady in layers and layers of fine silks. He wasn't sure if he was tongue-tied or if they were interrupted by Mr. Merriam's voice through the windows, open to the hazy blue morning, calling to the attendees, "Members and friends." They ran inside.

Alex found a pew at the back and sat. He watched his pretty blonde move down the main aisle of the church, opened the door of the first box, and lean over to kiss the cheek of a woman who looked enough like her to be her mother. Then she sat between an older man and some children. They stood as if expecting her, and neatly moved over for her. He watched her take a book from her small bag show the child next to her where in the book the readings would begin. She sat stiffly in the pew, fully concentrating on the words of the minister.

Alex looked over on the other side of the meeting house. There was Wythe with his family. They looked relaxed, whispering into their prayer books and trying not to giggle as the brothers nudged each other for space. He caught his friend's eye, and motioned that he would be staying in the visitor's pew in the back.

Alex let familiar words move him. He had been raised in meetings such as this. His years at school in Connecticut had required biweekly attendance. Now it felt like it had been too long since he had felt this calm. He had tried, but he had not found a likely Meeting since arriving in Massachusetts. Although the small local militias had been dissolved into the larger army, the men tended to find each other on Sundays. He had not come with a militia, and though he was from New Hampshire, he had only arrived there in time to settle in. Almost immediately, he had been called to the army in Massachusetts.

The minister began to talk about the importance of marriage and family to the institutions of the town and the new country. Alex let his gaze wander. The building and its surroundings were lovely. This was no rough hewn meeting house carved out of the wilderness, as the first must have been. No, in this time of provincial advancement, the Meeting House was well finished. Its many windows were clear, the trees and sky the only ornament. The box pews were white and freshly painted and the floor was slate, which felt cool underfoot. He looked down. The builder had allowed for braziers to heat the boxes on cold mornings, with notches carved into the floor in each pew to hold them steady.

The sounds around him pulled Alex from his reverie, and he stood as the families of the bride and groom filed past him and out of the Meeting House. He looked around for his blonde, wondering if there was a way to get a formal introduction. He didn't know her name, but it was obvious to him that they had been introduced, however informally. He found Wythe to ask him to present him to the blonde in the pink, ruched silk gown.

"No. No, Alex you don't want to meet her."

"Yes I do. It's fate. I have already met her, but I need an introduction." He would not mention how deliciously close they had been, or that his mind was already moving in directions that made knowing each others' names a necessity rather than a formality.

"Alex, I am double-related to the Tyrie family. Believe me. You don't want anything to do with any of them. My mother is a cousin of their mother, and her Aunt Charlotte, her father's sister, is my aunt through marriage on my father's side. Charlotte married my father's stepmother's son when he was over thirty and she was just out of school. Now she competes with her brother for head of family. Mather Tyrie is an old tyrant, a Puritan Patriarch doling out wisdom and condemning sin, and Charlotte Tyrie Whatever is an old battle axe. Truly, I vow I use my words kindly.

"I know Nina through family things, weddings, christenings, funerals. My mother never did like her mother. They didn't live here. But when they met" - he rolled his eyes mimicking his mother - "she said Caroline was too pretty, too perfect, never got in trouble. Mother said that as a good Christian woman, she did not like to dislike her cousin, so for the sake of peace she kept us away."

"Wythe," Alex felt the need to lecture the younger man, "I hate to disappoint, but they sound fabulous. I was raised by parents who believed that proclaiming the sins of their sons to be a God-given requirement. As for the aunt's attitude, and the mother's perfection, they will not be a problem, because I don't want to get to know the father, mother or aunt. I just want you to introduce me to the daughter. She is old enough to make decisions without consulting the father, mother or aunt."

"NO! Go back to camp. My brother met her. He came home saying she is just like the aunt. Said they call her an alewife, not a battle-axe. I don't see the difference. The shad we call an alewife is a fish of nasty countenance, named after a fishmongeress known for her harsh negotiations. Come away with me to my brother's table, where there is modernity and reason."

"You know nothing about her, you couldn't introduce me if you wanted to, tell the truth." A desire to strangle his tent mate was beginning to form.

"No, I know her. We grew up together, at least at church. I haven't seen her in ten or eleven years. She is Nina Tyrie. Do with that what you will."

Wythe headed for a group of young men sitting under a tree on the other side of the main table. The young man fell into their brotherly antics. Alex did not want to join in. He looked around. A gentle looking woman with graying blond hair and Nina's eyes waved him to an empty seat on her left.

Alewife? He stared across the lawn of people and watched her serve. She did not seem like a woman who could be described as a fish wife, or a boney shad. Of that last he could pleasantly testify. He accepted a plate of food and turned to see the supposedly imposing patriarch, baby on his lap, turn to his laughing wife, while, Alex guessed, a daughter or daughter-in-law spooned custard into the infant's mouth. After the meal and general conversation, he was asked about himself. In a short time he was talking about his recent journey through the classical world of Italy and Greece. Dr. Tyrie asked if they might talk while the babies finished eating. So for a delightful few minutes, Alex found himself talking of education and its increasing importance for the creation of the new nation. He was only slightly aware that other guests were finishing their meals and beginning to walk down the hill to the party.

Nina wasn't sure how it happened, but as soon as

everyone began to sit, her sister handed her a big apron and a pitcher and sent her off to serve. She didn't mind, but for one day it would have been nice to sit and be served. Servers always faded into the background of any event, and holding a pitcher of cold lemon punch gave her the opportunity to watch the eaters. She couldn't help it if her gaze kept falling on her knight errant.

She was a bit surprised that he was not sitting with the young men. He must have arrived with at least one of them from the encampment at Cambridge. She saw her cousins sitting together and having a riotous time. That was nice. She knew that the brothers had not been together since April, when the youngest had marched off with the town militia to join the Continentals.

Instead, her hero had done something out of character for a young man and eaten his lunch next to her mother, near Jack and the other grandchildren. Now he sat under a tree talking pleasantly with her father. She didn't think she had ever seen her father look so happily engaged. She wondered what they were talking about. She jolted slightly when she saw her father wave Jack over and include his grandson in their conversation. Nina had no problem spying where her son was concerned. She stood at a nearby table, refilled glasses, and listened.

"Thucydides - I think you'll agree that there is nothing like the original." Dr. Tyrie turned to Jack. "Have you begun your Greek studies yet, John?"

"No sir, but our school master says we may next fall, if the other boys catch up on their Latin."

"You look as though you don't believe they will, is that so?"

Jack looked crestfallen at having to admit he would not be learning Greek in the fall. Her father spoke before he could confess it. "Go off then and play, John. We will see what we can do about that Greek when the summer is over. Go have fun." Nina was surprised at his relaxed attitude, but it was the nature of grandparents to indulge.

"And you, Peele? For certain you will miss teaching for a while, but I feel sure you will have another chance. You must do what you must in this cause. But keep your mind sharp. No one said a soldier had to be stupid. Come back this evening, that house over there." He pointed out the house Nina had lived in until she was sixteen. A large but modest house, just within sight of the Meetinghouse. "Now, Mr. Peele, you go off and enjoy some music and dancing with the young folk. Don't be shocked, I'm not stuck in time as some would have me. We will see you after the party."

Nina quietly moved away before she could be noticed.

Alex took Thorne from the small paddock near the Meetinghouse. Wythe was certainly wrong about the father. That was no imposing, arrogant patriarch - just a well-educated man, willing and able to disseminate knowledge, probably too forcefully at times, as was so often the case. No doubt Wythe had been at the receiving end of that advice, and perhaps a switch. Alex chuckled at the thought. Wythe was a physical young man, given to racing and loud antics. He must have chafed whenever he was under the eye of the minister, his mother's cousin's husband.

Well, no doubt he was equally wrong about the daughter. Alewife or not, there certainly was a story there - a story that must match up with the one about a pretty blonde and two boys at a shipyard. Alex mused over it while he stared at her, his pretty blonde in pink silk, serving pie and pouring punch. He had noticed her stop and listen to their conversation. The fact that she was interested pleased him and added to his curiosity. He did love a riddle.

Nina visited with her parents after the ceremony, just before her sister had handed her that pitcher. It had been a comfortable conversation, and she couldn't remember ever feeling as much a part of her big family. In large doses it still might not be a happy mix, but she felt for Jack's sake it had been a start. It was her idea that Jack should eat at her parents' table, and he had seemed happy enough to talk to her father about studying Greek.

***

It had been just over ten years ago that she had left, married, and moved to the Lower Falls. She hadn't returned until one year ago last May, when her father had been honored on his retirement. Even for that occasion, it had taken all her cajoling to get David to bring his family to the First Church for the day. Their father had brought them all back to the house for a midday meal. It was then he had broken any vow of civility he might have taken toward his two youngest children.

Nina tried to remember that she had hurt her parents all those years ago, but when her father accused her of running away from them, it shocked her. She had never before considered that her parents cared. That accusation, a year ago, had caused some deep thinking about the last ten. Old John Bigelow had been a kind, generous man, willing to listen and to teach - things she had never sensed in her own father. But her father-in-law had never insisted she visit her own mother to learn to care for her child. Why, when she had felt most alone, had Mrs. Cotton, her mother's old neighbor and kind friend, suddenly arrived to care for her, the baby, and the inn? It had occurred to her, last year, that her parents might have been weary, and not ready to raise or restrain a headstrong daughter, their seventh child. She saw now that they had always tried to help.

She and Jack had driven over with Nina's team of matching Suffolk Punches, sisters named Bella and Jewel. The huge horses had no trouble pulling a wagon with only the few kegs of ale Nina brought to the wedding party. She had delivered the ale to a workman, left the horses to graze in the Parkers' field, and walked with the others up the hill. No doubt, the keg would be tapped before she could return. She was sure no one would guess who had brought the barrels for the party. It was strange to be incognito when her skills were well known not very far away.

Her natural shyness, something she had no trouble hiding when she was serving in a taproom of near-drunks and travelers, prevented her from doing more than making small talk and smiling gently at her old friends. She continued in that vein as she helped stack the pewter plates and mugs. She left the final straightening to the ladies of the congregation, and began her way down the hill, to her wagon and team.

She had little interest in reveling with the others, and would have grabbed Jack and taken him home if she hadn't looked over and seen how much fun he was having with the other boys. It had been a good morning. She nodded to herself. She had shown her parents that Jack was a wonderful child, that they were healthy and were doing well. The morning had also brought back bittersweet and confusing memories of her wedding and short marriage. These were thoughts she rarely allowed to surface, but the wedding vows, and the silence and solitude of the dirt road under her feet, led her mind to wander.

Having been dismissed from attendance at the afternoon service, Alex watched the happy throng walk as a group down to the groom's parents' house. He had intentions of joining the festivities, even though his leg ached and he would rather take Thorne and ride hard, away from chatter and polite conversation. But in truth he was curious. Wythe had mentioned music and dancing, things not normally found at a New England wedding, and he wanted to see how it would be done. The young couple had met in Charleston, South Carolina where, he gathered, dancing at weddings was *de rigeur* rather than taboo as it had been for so long in Puritan New England. He came from that same tradition, but had traveled in Europe and lived in England long enough to have gathered some skill on the dance floor.

The stallion was too high-strung to ride slowly in such a crowd, so Alex grabbed his reins and began to walk down the long hill, reminding himself that this was fun. The newly married couple looked pleased to be entering this phase of their lives, and he was pleased not to. Not that he didn't intend to marry one day. The state of marriage seemed as good a way to live life as any other, but right now he had a nation to help build, and, no doubt, an impending war to fight. There was no reasonable man or woman in the world who thought that Great Britain would give up her most valuable colonies without a fight.

Right now as well, Parliament was fighting over how harshly to punish the colonies. The Whigs proclaimed that the Americans had the right of representation, while the King and his supporters called the lot of them spoiled children who should be sent to their rooms. Alex supposed that if war truly came and the Americans lost, they would all be sent to their beds without supper.

Willing surrender was more unlikely every day. He had spent only a short time with the small army, a group of local New England militias really, but it was clear there was no man there who was ready to call it quits and go home. Some might leave, but even they intended to return when the fighting resumed.

It was going to take more than the King's rants, closure of the harbor, royal appointments of sheriffs and judges, and bans on Town Meeting to convince these men to quit. The new general had arrived in Cambridge. They would soon see if the blockade of Boston could be broken. It would be up to George Washington to find a way to send the King's men back to sea, if not back to their own beds.

Nina followed the revelers down the steep hill, keeping an eye on Jack and the other young boys as they ran through the fields and woodlots beside the road. Slowly, she became aware of footsteps catching up and then matching hers, accompanied by the sound of slow hoofbeats. She turned to her right, and found herself caught in smiling gray eyes. She'd been so lost in her own thoughts that she had no idea how long he'd been there. Her instinct was to flee, to trot after the boys, but that would be terribly rude. She had never been a coward, and as much as this man made her uncomfortable, he did not frighten her. He teased her with a look, had intelligent conversations with her father, and didn't flee when a ten year old boy sat next to him. She smiled politely, and may have curtseyed out of nervousness. "Hello. He is a beauty." Nina reached up to scratch Thorne's neck.

Alex hadn't noticed the horse had moved between them and was nuzzling at Nina's bonnet. Alex pulled him away before he began to graze on the straw.

"He's Thorne, and he knows he is beautiful. I'm Alex. Alex Peele. And you are Nina. I got that much from Wythe. He refuses to introduce us."

Nina fell in step with the horse and his owner. "Wythe?"

"My friend Wythe refuses to introduce us. Though he did blurt out that you are Nina Tyrie. It was mostly against his will, by the way."

"Yes. I'm Nina. Nina Bigelow," she didn't stop to explain. "But who is Wythe and whyeth doth he refuseth to introduceth us? that is - if he even knoweth me?" She giggled.

He could get very used to that. Alex pulled himself back to the conversation. "Why doth he refuseth? He sayeth thou were too quick- tongued for me, that he had knoweth thou well as a child."

"Oh Wythe. That is his middle name. I'm sorry, I hadn't thought about those cousins in years until I saw them today. His name is actually Eliphalet, but don't let on I told you."

"Oh I would never." Alex laughed. "The poor boy."

They fell back into their silent walking, the horse' chuffling and neighing, filling in where they did not speak. Nina wanted to shoo him off, make him join the others. It was ridiculous staying back with her when everyone else had hurried down the hill to punch and dancing.

"I should excuse myself and explain why I am so very slow. You see," she pointed to the boys in the woods. "I am trying to keep an eye on those boys who are climbing the trees and chasing each other through the fields on their way down to the Parkers' I did not want to intrude on their fun, but no one else has paid them any mind and well, someone should."

"Quite right, Mistress Nina. Someone should notice when they break their bones. It is good of you. We shall observe the hooligans together." He linked his arm with hers. Her hand rested gently on his forearm."But I don't mind being slow, I had a small mishap at the battle a few weeks ago, luckily nothing too serious." He pantomimed an exaggerated limp.

Alex noticed her reluctance, but was delighted there was no outright refusal. He recognized the gentle smell of ale and hops flowers from their unusual meeting the day before. The scent was intriguing, unusual for a perfume, but quite erotic, especially when combined with that face and an undeniably pleasant body. His "pretty blonde." He resisted the desire to pull her into his arms right there on the open road. He rarely felt so impulsive, but he would again be the gallant, this time escorting the last, lone female from meetinghouse to the home of his friend's family. All the while he would watch children at play. How delightful and unexpected at a time of war.

The Parkers' house was modern, with long, well-proportioned windows and Georgian columns. It had a low porch on two sides of the parlor, and multiple rooms for entertaining. The front of the house faced a new, well graded road, just west of the busy corner named for Mr. Angier. The gardens and fields at the back of the house faced back up the tall hill they had just walked down.

"Excuse me, I must see if they need my help with the refreshments." Nina lifted her hand from Alex's arm as soon as they entered the house.

Nina had felt the heat from their touch with every step of that slow walk down the hill. Now she turned toward the kitchens, anxious to leave, and at the same time reluctant to pull away. She was not used to such conflicts.

"Mistress Bigelow? I would complain that you did too much at the luncheon to be needed here. But alas, I must let you go." Alex smiled and graciously bowed over her hand, lifting it to his lips as if they had just ended a courtly minuet. His lips hovered there just a moment. Looking up at her, their eyes locked. He inhaled sharply, and wondered if she had noticed, as he had, that time had stopped. It had simply ceased to exist.

He had meant irony, a light flirtation to end their almost silent walk down the long hill. He had no time for anything other than light flirtation. Not realizing he had actually been holding his breath, he exhaled when Nina jumped, excused herself, and rushed off.

Alex cursed himself. He had gone too far with that look, that kiss. Not only had he frightened her, he might have wrecked any chance of continuing this pleasant flirtation. There was nothing else here for him; he might as well go back to camp. But he wouldn't. He'd promised Wyeth he would keep him company. And with the girl? He would do well to keep it light, but leaving her alone was no option. He was too bored and she was, by far, the best part of this day.

"Thorne, that girl is almost as skittish as you are," Alex said to the gray as he led him behind the house to the field beyond the flower gardens. "If she were a filly, I might wonder who saddled her too soon to make her so jumpy?" He pulled a small lump of sugar out of his pocket and let the horse nuzzle his hand before he trotted off the meet the other horses.

Alex watched two enormous work horses with matching white blazes come over to say hello. They looked like the water buffalo he had seen in Italy, but they had the grace of their own species, and Thorne greeted each as a co-creature. In minutes, they went back to their grazing. Alex watched the Suffolks. He wondered why they were here grazing when the food and ale had been delivered hours before. They gave him no useful reply. He watched the bucolic scene, relaxed horses grazing peaceably in the field, for as long as he deemed it polite to stay away from the party. Then, he walked up the shallow steps to the house.

Nina watched Alex talk to her horses from the drawing room window. She wondered what he was thinking as he stood there. She had almost walked out the open window to put her valise under the seat of her heavy beer wagon, but stopped in her tracks when she saw him at the field. So far, no one knew she was the guest who had gifted barrels of ale to the party. She hoped to keep it that way. These cousins didn't know her, and they didn't like what they knew. Most of what they knew was false, of course, but false or not they didn't like her. Hadn't Eliphalet's words to Alex confirmed that?

The barrels were in the kitchen ready to be tapped. She'd leave as soon as Jack could be dragged away. As if she'd conjured him, Jack and his new friends ran up to the paddock. Nina pulled him aside for a minute.

"Jack," she spoke softly, not wanting to intrude into his afternoon. "We need to leave just before sundown. There is a full moon tonight, but I'd rather not travel late."

"Sure Ma. I'll keep a lookout for the sun."

"Wise." She smiled and shook her head at his wisecrack, as he took off after the bigger boys. It was good he had his father's and his uncle's size. He had no trouble keeping up, even though he was clearly a year or two younger than the leader. Satisfied, she headed to the parlor windows on the side of the house. Unnoticed, she slipped into the room.

Alex walked through the fine house expecting to see his pretty blonde near the desserts or punchbowl. Nina! He must try to use her name. He found himself annoyed when she was not there. Wythe was, and the younger man handed him a glass of punch. He sipped at the sweet wine-punch, wishing they had supplied something more thirst quenching after that hot dusty walk down the hill. Even fresh water would have been preferable.

Surely Wythe could go on without him, finish with his family and then go off to pursue other plans - plans that included pretty women and kegs full of cheap ale. Alex watched resignedly as Wythe grabbed his wine and disappeared into a side room for cards and dice. Alex did not play; he supposed that was another of his faults. With luck, the young man would stay sober enough to return on time. General Washington had taken control of camp not ten days before, and discipline was finally becoming uniform across the units. It would be a shame for either of them spend the night in the stockade for getting drunk at a wedding.

Alex followed the sound of a fiddle toward the front parlor. Furniture had been pushed against the walls, and all the larger pieces had been removed. The tall windows facing the flower garden were open, and the smell of roses wafted into the room on the slight breeze. Guests were just beginning to take their first hesitant steps as the musicians began to play. Dancing at the Parker house was a surprise, even though it had been hinted at. As with the cardroom, he could see that tradition was fading, and old prohibitions were falling away. Still, he was happy to see a reel danced, and a fiddle and pipes played. Someone grabbed his hand and he was pulled into a line.

He bowed to his right, his left, and his partner in the opposite line. His feet barely needed his brain to remember these steps. The simple reel allowed his mind to wander, so he watched the dancers. Most were having to concentrate very hard not to fall over their own, or their partner's, feet. A general sigh of relief was given when the dancers began their promenade up the line and around. As the dance steps began their repeat, a woman giggled. The others caught the enthusiasm and laughed at their own seriousness. The second set was far more lighthearted.

In a few minutes they had gathered an audience. Some looked on, shocked and surprised at what the younger generation had gotten up to. Others tapped a foot in time to the music, captured by the beat, maybe looking for a chance or the courage to join the dancers. Alex realized with some surprise that he was having a good time. He liked the shocked look on some of the faces, and the admiration on others. The reel concluded, and the dancers reformed into groups of four. Alex took a moment to catch his breath. He stretched his back and looked around, taking a minute to make sure he hadn't done anything terrible to his leg. He turned, and there was Nina, standing by the window as if she had only just walked through. She was one of those tapping her foot to the opening bars of the next set. He reached out to pull her into the dance.

"You know I have no idea how to do this." Nina felt ridiculous as Alex held her hands and led her around the small dance floor.

"No one does. This is Newton. How many dance classes have any of the young ladies here attended? How many dance masters have set up shop nearby?" Alex was glad to make her laugh. It was a side of herself she had not fully shown, only hinted at with those smiles. "You are brave to attempt it, keep going and follow my lead. I may step on your feet, but in general, I know where we are to go next."

Nina had come in through the window to listen to the music, hoping not to be noticed. From the garden, she hadn't been able to see that there was dancing in the parlor. She was surprised, as were so many of the others. She watched for a while, memorizing the steps and enjoying the patterns in the dance. Most of the girls were dancing together, taking turns in the "men's row." All the men were in great demand, and not being allowed to take a set off. Nina was about to leave in search of a cold drink for them when Alex spotted her. He asked her to dance simply by taking her hand and pulling her onto the dance floor.

Really, it was fun, though she wasn't sure if she was or wasn't making a tremendous fool of herself. One time when she nearly tripped she looked up, horrified, only to see everyone else in a similar state. They were already laughing at each other and themselves. She kept going, and after a few minutes it got easier. Finally, it got easy enough that she could look somewhere other than at her feet.

She looked up, right into Alex's teasing gray eyes. She smiled back briefly, then looked away, and then down to check on her feet, although she didn't need to. She looked around at the other dancers, and realized that everyone was bare handed in the dance.

Gloves. When she hadn't been able to find gloves that morning, it had felt like a near catastrophe. It seemed that like her, everyone had given up mending their gloves. There weren't any good new ones to be found. They had simply disappeared from life, like so much else - new stockings, fire engines, dishware, and, of course, tea. Everyone missed tea, but right now, gloves - something between her hands and Alex's warm, strong ones - would be nice.

She was too aware of his strong body leading her in the lines of the dance, aware that they were only inches apart and had been for the entire set. She forgot to look past him when the dance turned them face to face and their eyes locked. He slightly tightened his hold on her hand, his other gently around her waist as they walked. She was afraid her legs would give way in a faint, and she would end up in Alex's arms again. She laughed to herself, shaking away the feelings which were gathering in her core. Finally the fiddler called a break, and they stepped apart.

She was wearing stays. Not that such an observation was remarkable - most women did - but Alex hadn't noticed till that moment that yesterday she hadn't been. At the shipyard, she had been dressed informally in a tightly pinned jacket over soft jumps. He hadn't thought anything of it, only enjoying her soft breasts pushed against him in that pile of sails.

He let his hand linger on her back as he led her off the dance floor. He hoped she was enjoying it as much as he. She gave no sign, but stilled for a moment as if relishing the touch.

Alex led them over to the punch table.

"You don't want to drink that, it will make you think you ate a bowl of sugary cherries. Wait here."

He was ready to object and follow her, when she reappeared a minute or two later with a tankard, filled to the brim with the heavenly tell-tale foam of thick ale, in each hand.

Alex took the one she offered. "Thank you, this is most appreciated. More than you could know." He took a deep draught, almost finishing in one swallow. "I'm afraid I had too much of that punch. You're right. I needed to wash it away."

Nina took a small sip and handed him her own tankard. "I didn't have any punch. Finish mine." She took his empty tankard and put it on the punch table.

He took a short swallow this time. The ale was good, better than most he had drunk, especially the swill they were serving in camp. Alex gratefully finished the second tankard. By then, a crowd had gathered around a large barrel of ale that had been brought into the dinner room. He joined them, and drank to the bride and groom's long lives and long happy marriage. By the time the music started again, and the slightly drunker crowd was listing toward the dance floor, his dance partner was gone.

Nina slipped back out of the long windows toward the rose garden. She found a bench in the flowers and gratefully sat. Her legs felt weak, she felt flushed and her heart was beating in a most uncomfortable manner. She blamed the dancing, but sitting there in the warm summer afternoon, she grudgingly admitted to herself that Alex, her intrepid rescuer, was the culprit. She had sworn off men so many years ago, vowing never to marry again. She assured herself that her short marriage inoculated her, had left her safe from the risk of future discomforts - physical and emotional - that being married would bring her. It was as well she would leave, and he would go back to Cambridge. This time, truly, she would never see him again.

She concentrated on the beautiful roses. In the warm dry weather of the last week, the flowers had bloomed early and now waited, suspended in glorious splendor, their petals open so far they nearly drooped. A few had already stopped trying to hold on, and masses of color littered the nearby ground. It was clear from some empty stems that the flowers that had been fresh and pretty this morning had been cut for the ceremony, or for the party here at the house. She scooped a handful of pale purple and yellow petals into her hands. She inhaled the heady scent.

Roses reminded her of that day, the summer before her marriage, when John and his sister Mimi had taken them all out to hear the latest preacher, an Indian with long hair and a booming voice. They had sat near the host's house and his wife's rose garden. Facing into the field with hundreds of other people, she'd been mesmerized by the speaker's enthusiasm. He had admonished the large crowd "to find Jesus in their hearts and not their heads." It was so unlike her father's church - no mention of, or careful reading of, the Bible, no edict to obey King and country. It was all new and exciting. The man spoke to possibilities, of a new world.

Less than a year later, she had married, and then Johnny left with his militia. At first she had been proud that her young husband was fighting for their King against the French. After his death, holding his tiny baby in her arms, she realized that she had never understood. Her head knew he'd had to go, but no one had asked her heart.

The world felt different this time. This "unnatural civil war," as the newspapers put it, seemed inevitable. She had read what the great men of Boston wrote, about the need to separate from Britain, and some of it made sense, just as she had moved from her parents' home to forge her own life, with marriage, a child, and an early widowhood. The Americans said the nation was ready to be accepted as a full member of the Empire with equal rights for all Englishmen. Parliament did not agree, would not grant them rights given to Englishmen, even as they agreed that the colonies were important members of their mercantile world.

Nina knew about that world, the cold world of money and goods. She had obeyed the agreements not to use British-made things like gloves and pewter, in order to punish Parliament and convince them to recognize Americans' contribution to the

Empire. Now she served ale in crooked tankards.

Gloves. She looked at her hands, remembering the way touching Alex on the hill and during the dance had made her feel. She wished she wasn't so uncomfortable when Alex flirted with her. He made her feel strange in ways she had sought to avoid. But the long day had been a pleasant one, meeting her hero, dancing with him, laughing. It was nearly sad that she would never see Alex Peele again. She could like him. She put her head back and watched swallows dart through the darkening blue sky.

***

Alex, too, had enough of dancing and polite pints of ale, good as it was. He had had enough too, of wondering where his Nina, the mysterious blonde, had gone. He found Wythe at the card table and wearily told him that after he picked up a book, he could be found somewhere between Angier's Corner and the encampment in a dark tavern, getting very drunk on what would probably turn out to be very bad ale. He expected to drink beer that had been sitting too long in a leaky keg. He discovered he felt uneasy and incomplete. He did not know why. It would seem to be a strange reaction to a lovely country wedding.

He whistled for Thorne, and synched his saddle into place. He gazed over the paddock. The two Suffolk Punches were still there. That was odd - he hadn't seen a workman or a delivery fellow. He didn't think the Parkers farmed their own land or if they did, he didn't think they would stable the work horses at the house. Well, curious as it was, it was not his mystery. He led Thorne around to the side so as not to trample on the flowers.

He stopped. Staying out of sight of the lady on the bench, he watched her drink in the scent of spent roses. He allowed himself a daydream. In it, he walked up to her, took her in his arms, and lay her back in the grass, so warm and open in the summer sun. Sweet and willing like those voluptuous roses, she would stare at him with the same rapt expression he saw on her lovely face.

Alex shook himself. He shouldn't think such thoughts about her, jealous as he was of those rose petals. She might be married. After all, she wore a small ring, and she had a name different from the one Wyeth told him. However, if she were well wedded, where was her elusive husband, and why had his name not come up? No, she would not be married. A woman that lovely, if she were wed . . . she would have the air of satisfaction, the roundness of a child or two. She had none of that. She would, though, if she were his wife. Not having a clue where or why such a thought arose, he shook himself again. It must be the smell of the roses.

He mounted Thorne and rattled the tackle, so he would not startle his pretty blonde. He rode hard, away from the house to the north road. In time his imagination, and these sorts of indulgences, would be the death of him. He was alone. There were battles to be fought, strategies to be made, a cause to fight for, and a nation to win. He would stay alone for a long, long time.

Chapter 4

"No Ma!" The child's singsong voice called out with a giggle from behind a row of kegs.

"Jack, the water is perfect and you need a bath," Nina called back while silently stalking her young son. She crept up on him from behind, picked him up into her arms, and placed a big kiss on his belly, to a howl of "unfair" and peals of laughter.

"Ma'am, I don't want to go to bed yet. The sun is up and it's a beautiful day!" He pleaded, knowing full well what the answer would be.

Nina sighed, "Jack Bigelow, you are going to Meeting in the morning. Don't complain to me, you're the one who told your grandfather we attended the West Parish." She pretended to sniff him. "You smell terrible. Into the pot you go."

Not every child was able to take a warm bath in an old beer kettle in a brew house. The pot had seen better days and leaked a bit now. Since it was no longer good enough for the precious brew, it was perfect for a good soak and scrub. The only victim of the leaks was the slate floor. And being an old hand at this, Jack threw off his clothes and, using a small step stool, climbed into the warm water.

His mother, politely averting her eyes from his nearly ten-year-old body, handed him brush, rag and soap. Leaving him to wash, she went to tidy up the brew house from their long day of work. And a good day it had been. It was one of those times when the maltster and the sacks of hops arrived within days of each other, something that had become increasingly less common with the roads watched and the nearest port closed. She couldn't complain. Jack was right. The weather was perfect. She had kept her young helper busy all day, and they had made six batches of strong ale, and the same each of dinner ale and small beer. The ales were now kegged and labeled; nothing to do now but wait for the yeasts to ripen.

Tomorrow she would taste her newest creation, a double brewed draft. She had started that one last winter, the day of the brewmaster's - her father-in-law's - funeral. The inn and tavern were closed, and after she and Jack returned from the Peddleman farm, she had felt edgy and sad, so had begun the last recipe she and John had worked out during his final illness. Weeks later, she woke up the brew by adding new yeasts and feeding it with molasses. It was the first time she had attempted the German brew.

The doppelbock was going to be a stupendous accomplishment or a tremendous flop. Either way, she was excited to discover the nature of her creation. She chalk-marked the special kegs, and the others they would need for the next day's business, and went back to her son. Yes, it had been a good day, almost better than dancing gloveless with a gray-eyed soldier.

Clean and rinsed, Jack climbed out, toweled off, pulled on his nightshirt and sat on a stool. Nina pulled a knife from the pocket of her voluminous apron. The boy dutifully offered first his toes and then his fingers. After his nails were trimmed to her satisfaction, Nina brushed his hair, pulling it back and into a queue. As always, she marveled at his thick, rich blond hair - so like what hers had been, before life and age had caught up with her.

She shook herself out of her willies, finished taming

Jack's short mane, and chased him down the flagstones into their little house. Nina waited patiently outside his door for him to call to her to say his bedtime prayers together. She knew it would be soon now that he would proclaim himself too old for a mother's help with bath and bed. She savored the years they'd had together, just the two of them, and reminded herself, as she often did, that it had all been worth it.

Alex Peele, had ridden hard on his way to Connecticut, only to have his horse throw a shoe a mere thirteen miles from his start. The day had been long and he had gotten a late start anyway. The conferences had gone on for hours. It was clear the Commander knew what he was about, how to organize and command men, but unfortunately the aristocratic Virginian could not understand that New Englanders' differing opinions did not mean disrespect. General Washington was not yet used to troops under his command thinking they had the right to speak their minds, even to put their ideas to a vote. Alex was sure that in time he would come to understand New England ways, and they to accept his.

He wished the morning's conference had not given him the kind of headache that required a long ride to cure. It should have been obvious hours ago that nothing on this day was going to turn out as planned. If it were, he would have left Thorne at the smith's, strolled along the river till dinnertime, grabbed some food, paid the smith and ridden till dark. Instead, the mercantile stood empty, the forge was quiet, and the blacksmith shop was closed. The smith himself had gone home to his dinner. When he had knocked, Alex was told that unless the good man was offered more than he had in his pockets, the smith was home and was going to stay there. Alex shrugged. He supposed, since he and they had no choice, the men in New Haven could wait another day.

The sign over the door said *Wheel and Hammer*, named for the forge across the lane with its large waterwheel and now- silent triphammer. The inn looked substantial, and would no doubt supply a decent meal, passable drink, and a soft mattress. As for Thorne, the stable looked well built, and as well cared-for as the inn. There was no stable boy at hand, so Alex took the reins loosely in hand and led the gray stallion behind the inn. He let him crop the soft grass that grew in the mist, while he strolled along the river in the long summer evening.

The falls were loud. The roar of water was a bit surprising, since what he knew of the Charles River was the bridge and dam at Watertown, and the fens and marshes of Boston and Cambridge where it was wide, tidal and somewhat smelly. He stood on the bank between the two waterfalls of the Lower Falls, watching water spill through raceways that split the river to power nearby mills. The first fall looked like it dropped nearly twenty feet, and the second, half that. No wonder there was so much noise, and no wonder there was so much soft grass, irresistible to a horse who had been subsisting on dry grain and over-grazed stubble.

Alex decided to leave Thorne to graze a while. He cobbled him and set off to explore this spot. No one was around at the back of the inn, and certainly no one would hear a footstep over the sound of rushing water. There were three semi-connected buildings. He recognized a kitchen and bedroom up the stairs at the back. The original tavern building was local stone, built with two chimneys on either side. A third was in the back of what was obviously the kitchen. The smells coming from that room were incentive for him to abandon his pleasant walk. The second building was brick and stone. It seemed newer than the first, probably built in the last decade or two. Someone had left a big wooden door partly open. It seemed to work on some sort of sliding mechanism.

Alex knew he was going to explore. He never could resist the temptation of a dark room behind an open door. He pushed the door to let some of the evening light into the room. The walls were unfinished brick, and a large hearth was built into the wall farthest from the tavern. Near the hearth were copper and iron kettles, scrubbed and neatly pushed aside, ready to be put away or used again. There was no fire in the fireplace, but the room was warm; one had been burning recently. There was an old wooden keg that seemed out of place in this room of neat, clean barrels and kettles - a small puzzle, until he noticed a bar of soap and a wet towel. Someone had taken advantage of the warm room and ready bath water. He smiled at the well-appointed room, realizing almost immediately what he had found.

Rather the spot Thorne had forced him to discover by throwing his shoe. They had found, he was delighted to note, an alehouse, not merely a tavern that brewed its own ale. He sniffed the air in the room. The sacks of hops might as well be rattling on the vine, they smelled so right. There were, as well, the sweet malt and yeasts that could be shared with the cook in the kitchen, but probably weren't.

He stilled. The heady scents reminded him immediately of the soft skin and sweet smell of Nina, his blonde. He could conjure her up, and might forevermore, whenever he smelled hops and good ale. He wondered where she was. If ales did that to him, she was likely to haunt him for life.

He shook that off and looked around. He supposed the ales fermenting behind him, in kegs lined up in neat rows with dates carefully chalked on their lids, might be inferior, but he rather doubted it. The room, kegs and even the cooking kettles were too well maintained for the brewer to accept poor quality. He was hungry and thirsty, but now he was excited to do more than fill his stomach and quench his thirst. He was going sample the ale brewed here at the *Wheel and Hammer*. He left the door ajar as he'd found it, whistled for Thorne and walked up the hill to the road and around the third building.

This was a small wooden house, built in a style traditional to New England. Symmetrical windows, like eyes, stared out at the post road. If the little house was connected to the other inn buildings, it was probably by a door into the brew-house he had not noticed in the dark. It did not face the small tavern lane as the other buildings did, but instead looked right out on the main road. It was surrounded on three sides with gardens of flowers, herbs, and vegetables. An old apple tree grew on the river side. The beds needed weeding, and the paths required pruning after the long hot days, but the residents of the little house were obviously connected to the inn, and the needs of the inn and its customers must come before a summer-shocked garden.

Alex paused at the side of the house. He heard voices coming from the windows above him, and stopped for a moment to listen. He resumed his walk when he caught the murmur of what sounded like the Lord's Prayer and intimate tones. Not wanting to tread where he was uninvited, he found a stable hand and a table in the taproom.

Jack was nearly asleep before they finished the last of his bedtime prayers. It had been a long day, beginning with first fires before dawn. Nina wanted to lie down and sleep or hide in her little parlor, and light a small fire against the chill of late summer, to put her feet up and read for a while. She opened her book, but she could not keep her eyes open. They felt dry from working over the fires all day, so she closed them.

Often these past weeks, her mind wandered to that strange weekend when she had twice encountered the gray-eyed man and his beautiful gray stallion. She could still see the happy surprise in those eyes when she had climbed out from under that table at the Meeting House. It was a look no woman would reject, and though she did not want a man in her life, it never hurt to be appreciated. He was a flirt and a tease. It was obvious that he recalled her flustered state at the shipyard. It was not her fault that she'd been worried he had hurt his head. She was very glad he seemed not to have suffered from rescuing her.

Before putting her head down, she prayed for all the men working to free Boston from the British occupation. As had become habit, she gave a quiet, separate prayer that things were going well for Alex at Cambridge, and that his leg was healing. She had gotten some news from the mounted soldiers who rode this way to give their horses some exercise. His name had not come up.

Those first days, she had thought he would come riding in, by another amusing coincidence, but as weeks went by it seemed less and less likely. She chided herself that she should be happy about that. His flirting left her disquieted, and made her recall the week of pain and aching discomfort she had felt during her marriage. Truly, she did not want to relive that experience. Still, she had enjoyed those brief encounters with her brown-haired hero. Not only had Alex rescued her at the shipyard, he had rescued the pie table and in more subtle ways by pulling her away from her shyness during the wedding party. He had made her dance, and he appreciated the good ales she had handed him. These little things spoke to his goodness.

It was good, too, that she'd had those experiences with Alex. They gave her something to think about beside the past. Her father-in-law's death had left her very alone. She and John Bigelow had grown close over the ten years since Johnny died. Now that her little Jack was growing up and needing her less, she found that loneliness sometimes overwhelmed her.

Once in a while she found herself almost saying yes to one of the men who kindly pestered her to marry him. There were two or three in any one week who'd ask, usually one of the regulars from a mill or the forge. She found that some men took only a pleasant word or two about the weather as encouragement. Whether any one of them wanted her, or just the chance to own a brewery, she was never really sure. Usually the man backed off when he found out that it was her son, and not she, who was the true owner.

But those few interactions with Alex had left her changed. It was easier to steel her will against ever marrying again. It was good she remembered the pain. The temptation to relieve her loneliness with marriage was gone. She was unsure how just standing near Alex had brought back those feelings deep in her belly and made her legs weak, but she was glad to be armed against them.

Early the next morning, Jack tiptoed down the stairs so as not to wake his mother. He was proud that he was able to get ready and leave with his cousins for Sunday school without disturbing her. He grabbed breakfast in the taproom, and Will, the cook's helper, handed him a cut-down flour sack with bread, cheese and a new apple for the walk home. Then Jack went outside to wait for his Bigelow cousins so he could join their group to catch a ride to the West Parish. His mother would be there later.

Nina looked out the window in time to see Jack run after a group of children, proud at the smart, wonderful child he was growing to be. The children took the path by the river that led upstream toward the Upper Falls and her brother's wagon. She was staring at the children when she spotted the gray stallion and his master's dark-ash brown head standing at the smithy, near the post road. She watched the magnificent duo as Alex paid the smith and mounted. His hat was tied to the saddle, he wore a gray cape of some animal's pelt which was thrown back over his shoulders, and his saddle bags looked full and heavy against the horse's flanks. Nina inhaled sharply, a strange reaction brewing in her gut as she watched horse and rider move as one up to the road and away.

She had a moment's madness where she imagined pulling on her boots and running down the stairs to tell him that this was her inn and that she had missed him, that she thought of him almost constantly. She stepped back from the window swallowing the words, and that queer notion. The coincidence had happened; she had been too tired to notice. No doubt it was just as well.

The smell of hops and malt had given Alex pleasant and disturbing dreams about his blonde. He could imagine she worked here, or somewhere like it. That would explain the gentle hops smell that hung over her like a seductive mist. He hated to think wanton thoughts of the very correct daughter of the learned reverend, but if she had anything to do with the fine ales, or that extraordinary doppelbock he had drunk last night, he would be right in thinking them.

He had woken early, anxious to shake off his dreams, and ready to make up the time lost to the thrown shoe. He was surprised that he had slept so well in the hayloft over the stables. A single penny had bought him a clean sheet for the night, and spread over dry hay, it had been quite comfortable.

He climbed down from the loft and checked the few sacks he had brought with him. As it had the day before, the importance of the task before him weighed heavy. He needn't have worried. His bags were intact. The correspondence from the Commander to the Connecticut Provincial leaders asking for more troops was exactly where he had put it, still covered with mundane things such as a fresh shirt and extra shoes. He'd found the privy and wash water at the back of the inn, and had a quick breakfast while the smith finished the horse.

As the smith worked, an excited group of children gathered across the lane. They were the same ages as the gang of boys, almost behaving themselves at the wedding. One or two looked familiar, but he wasn't sure. Once it had gathered, the group ran off upstream. He felt a stab of envy for their Sunday school teacher. Any teacher. He enjoyed teaching. More than enjoyed, he admitted smiling a little sadly. He relished it - every morning, energetically meeting the opportunity to open new vistas, helping children with deciphering arithmetic, and unraveling the secrets locked in books. He even liked knocking Latin, and a line or two of Greek, into the heads of a few of his brightest students.

It had been his skill as a tutor that had paid his way across Europe and for months in England, enabling him to stay long after he had planned to come home. A year on foreign shores had allowed him to acquire skills, and make acquaintance with people he would never have met had he stayed on the planned path.

His journey in through Italy, Greece, and his stay in England, seemed long ago already, as did his short time as the school master in the little school in the mountains. Now he had another role to play, as the newest courier plying the roads between Cambridge and the other provincial Congresses. He had to believe that carrying the General's message was of greater importance than teaching reluctant schoolchildren.

With new shoes on the horse, and a sack of food at his side, Alex turned the stallion south-west. By staying away from the traffic of the roads along the coast, he was able to let Thorne set the pace, and the young horse took advantage of the fine day and the dry roads and, once sure of their route, he let his thoughts go where they would.

Alex had never been able to say why one place felt right and another did not. He had traveled the world and noted the difference dozens of times, though most spots were neither pleasant nor unpleasant. The *Wheel and Hammer*, however small the taproom, was very, very pleasant. He had eaten well, slept well, and enjoyed the steady and gentle roar of the falls. He laughed out loud, for the beauty of the high summer day, a fine horse and the small mystery that was Nina, his pretty, but elusive blonde. It was good, as well, to have a cause worth fighting for.

Chapter 5

Alex rode hard and made Hartford late the next day. He stopped at the capital and then volunteered to take their memorandum south to New Haven. The extra trip didn't bother him, as it gave him time to visit with his old tutor at the college.

"So Peele, you have got yourself entangled in this rebellion?" The older man found most actions of the young somewhat amusing. They sat in the shabby but elegant front room of a large house. Carlton Peirson had rented these rooms for as long as anyone could remember. He handed Alex a glass and sat back with his pipe.

"Yes sir, I'm here hunting recruits. The General hopes to find a way to complete the siege and force the British forces to evacuate." Alex didn't know how to make light of it, since the siege fires had become his life since June. He felt a little like a student. His mind hunted for a Greek siege, perhaps in the Peloponnesian War, to compare to his life. He stayed silent and sipped gratefully at the wine.

"Your efforts seem to be successful." Peirson pulled at his pipe and offered Alex a refill on his brandy. "We have many men gone to Boston to help. Some of my own students in fact." He sounded like he would like Alex to return them, like borrowed books.

Alex changed the subject to that of the ancient world and his own travels. The men talked and drank far into the night while Thorne got a well deserved rest in the tutors' stable.

He'd made one other trip in the days before he could ride. Lying still on his cot waiting for his leg to heal had been boring, so he had insisted he be sent by ship around the blockaded harbor and south to Pennsylvania. He was to deliver coded papers to the Continental Congress from Samuel and John Adams, requesting aid on behalf of the Province and the Town of Boston. He had been smuggled south on various ships, the sea air probably saving him from terrible infection. It was interesting to see Philadelphia, a city bustling with revolutionary fervor. Subscriptions were being sold on every corner for shoes, clothing and weapons the local men would need as they went north to serve. Everywhere there was great patriotic energy. Alex found that his leg throbbed from the injury, and his head ached from the energy in the street. He'd wanted to pour water from a fire bucket to tamp down the flames of such rhetoric. Didn't they understand that dying men were putrid and covered with flies, that even the retreating enemy had humanity?

Alex understood, and believed strongly in the cause of independence, but it had been shown the price of liberty would be high. The King and Parliament had no desire to let their prize colonies go without a real attempt to stop them, and they would see no reason to compromise.

He wasn't sure that people in other regions yet understood what the citizens of Massachusetts had suffered and what they would suffer, in turn, if the British had the chance - the closure of ports, changes to local government, battles and deaths as at Concord and Lexington, fighting in the streets of Menatomy, the burning of towns as at Charlestown, to say nothing of major battles as the one in June, at Breed's and Bunker Hills. These might pale in comparison to what might yet happen to New York, Philadelphia or Charleston.

It would be a long war now that the Continental Congress had finally decided it would not be Massachusetts' own to fight. The British generals weren't stupid. They must know that they would have to occupy and hold every major town and city on the Atlantic coast, maybe even destroy them in order to win. Even then, it would be likely the fleeing residents would move inland, making it harder for the British to fight, and increasing death and destruction. Yes, Alex foresaw a long war. The classics had taught him that.

***

By early August, Alex was back in Cambridge, and back at picket duty. He lifted the flap of his tent one evening on his way to dinner. Wythe and two other soldiers were ready to saddle their horses and leave.

"Ho, Peele, get that skittish horse of yours and come with us to dinner."

".. tired, where are you fellows off to?" Alex stood at the well pumping water into a bucket for wash-water. He yawned.

"The tavern whose ale you couldn't stop talking about, 'Hammer' something. We heard the food is good, and it's perfect for a short ride. None of us've pulled duty first thing in the morning."

Alex finished dumping the cold water over his head. He grabbed his towel. "Give me a minute to change and I'll come along. You could use a guide. No doubt you'll get lost without me."

Alex saw no reason to mention Wythe's mysterious cousin. It was only a hunch, but there didn't seem to be anything more interesting to do, and mysteries never solved themselves. The worst that could happen was a pleasant ride and a good meal.

Within the hour they were seated in the public room of

the *Wheel and Hammer,* drinking ale and telling tales. They sat near the front where they could watch the pretty serving girls, while drinking the good ale and relaxing. While they waited for their food, the young men begged Alex for tales of his travels, especially of that woman he had met in Italy.

Alex generally did not enjoy telling stories of his wanderings through Europe, but the young men were hungry for something that did not reek of a military encampment. He decided to oblige, even to make up a scene or two if necessary, for added color.

"Her name was Charlotte, Carlotta if her husband was absent. She was a Romanian wife of an English aristocrat who functioned as an ambassador for Britain. Lady, I won't mention her last name or title, was the youngest daughter of a diplomat to the Court of St. James. He was of some high rank in his own country. She had grown up in London and spoke perfect English. I never learned if the marriage had been arranged, but by the time I became her son's tutor she found diplomatic functions at best routine and usually boring."

"I'll bet you were happy to supply the lady some diversion, weren't you Peele?" Wythe spoke loudly enough to attract attention from other tables.

Nina sat near the fire in the kitchen, just out of sight, but listening to the taproom and watching through a small hidden hole in the wall, as she always did. She had been doing the tavern's ledgers in the bright kitchen firelight.

"Wythe, hush. I'll tell you about the lady, but stop being an ass."

She recognized the voice. She stared at the open leger, but paid no more attention to her numbers. She swore that she would soon go over to them and introduce herself as the brewer and proprietress, soon. The men were out of sight, but she felt she had the right to listen discretely to her patrons. She sat spellbound.

"The family lived in Italy. They had since their last child was born. The ambassador had every intention of sending his son to Eton, but the boy's English was not good. He hired me to speak to the boy. I pointed out that he would speak like a Connecticut or New Hampshire Yankee, that I did not precisely speak the King's English. He didn't care and he was in a hurry to fill the position. He was pleased to have found an educated man who had time on his hands to teach the child.

"So right there, I was engaged in a full time position in this man's house, sort of as an upper servant. There were only a few short weeks to get the boy ready, so as we wandered through Rome, he showed me the sights, and I insisted he speak English. After a few days his mother started accompanying us.

"Carlotta was a natural tour guide. She knew the city like one who had lived there, and loved it dearly. She brought us to the most interesting places - ruins, cathedrals, the aqueducts, mausoleums, catacombs, she knew them all, including the best cafes and shops. Those weeks were enchanting to her son. Having his mother's undivided attention was very special.

"My young student was her fifth child. The others were quite a bit older and lived in England, Henry was the only one not raised there, but he was expected at school for the fall term. The father needed to continue his work in Rome, but he insisted that Charlotte accompany their son, and stay in their London home while the boy was at school. He would pay for my fare to England and back to America, if I would accompany them to London and continue to teach him until the

69

term began.

"Thorne was a gift from this ambassador's London stables."

Questions sprang into Nina's mind. Why had he begun his travels? How long had he journeyed? Carlotta? Alex certainly had spent many hours with the lady. Nina felt an unexpected stab of jealousy.

She pulled herself out of her thoughts just as Dodi walked into the kitchen to collect the plates of food for Alex's group.

"Dodi, I'll take these in, I haven't yet said hello, and now is as good a time as ever."

Nina picked up the tray that Dodi left next to the ledgers, and carried it to the group, all of whom were listening raptly to Alex. Now that she was close, she could tell his fellows were asking for information about the seemingly lovely Carlotta, information that he would rather not reveal.

Nina put the tray down and placed the food on the table. She motioned for Dodi to bring ale for the group, including herself. She felt Alex staring, his eyes seeking hers. She felt consumed by his look. She ignored her feelings, and turned to her cousin. She winked at Alex before she spoke.

"Eliphalet, it's nice to see you, how is your mother?" Wythe groaned, turning red from his ears down at the sound of his first name. He glanced at the men as if waiting for the jibes. They all held their words, politely waiting for their hostess.

"You see, Eliphalet and I are cousins, at least our mothers are." She rolled her eyes, refusing to recount the complicated family tree. "He never did like his name." She didn't say anything else, but she hoped he understood that she had not liked being denied and ignored at the wedding.

She turned to the table, addressing Alex directly. It was her standard welcome, but she had never felt so tongue-tied. "Good evening, welcome to the *Wheel and Hammer*. I am Nina Bigelow, brewer. The tradition here is that when I sit with my guests, the first pint is on the house." Dodi served the tankards and the men drank to tradition. She spoke quietly to Alex, who sat next to her. "I'm sorry I was unavailable the other day. Dodi told me you asked to meet the brewer. I had been cooking mash all day, and fell asleep instead of greeting guests. I hope everything was to your liking?"

"Oh, it was. I wanted to compliment the brewer on the excellent ale. If I'd known who she was, I would have insisted." Gently he put his hand on hers, and pulled it under the table. He drew soft circles on her palm with his thumbs.

Nina tried to calm her pounding heart. Men often made unwanted advances, often trying to hold her hand or even kiss her. Never had she stayed still for it, as she did now.

The men sipped their ale and began to eat. She stood, as if to leave the men to their privacy, as she usually did after her introduction. Reluctantly, she pulled her hand away.

"Nina, stop a minute." Wythe spoke through his buttered bread. "Is this where you have been hiding from the family? We heard you were an alewife. Is this what mother meant? Ale?"

"The fish?" Laughing, Nina sat back down, her hands firmly in front of her. "Wythe, this is hardly hiding. I live at a public-house, on a main road. I have for ten years." She included the other men in the conversation by glancing around the table and catching their eyes. It would do terrible things to the inn's reputation if she were known as a shrew, or an alewife.

Three of her guests, to whom she was just a pretty and

71

pleasant woman who made good ale and had some good gossip about their friend, smiled back and leaned forward to be included in her sphere. The other two men stared at her, their mouths agape, looking somewhat like the river-herring known as shad, and locally as alewives.

"Did you all think I had disappeared into the depths of a river pool? I'm sure that if any one of the family had missed me, information could have been found." Nina, sure of her audience, leaned forward and grabbed the tankard Dodi had placed in front of her, taking a short draught before continuing. "In fact, I have not actually left town, just moved a few miles west to the second parish. I don't wonder your mother has known for years. She never pretended she approved of me."

Alex listened to Wythe's strange accusation. He seemed to think it was Nina's fault that he had forgotten her. Her whereabouts and existence had not been secret. She was the hostess and brewer here.

He had met her parents. The minister of the First Church would never have sent his daughter off to run a public house. Her name was Bigelow, not Tyrie, she was married. The little ring was real. He wondered again where that husband was, how any man could leave this woman alone.

It had been weeks since he had first set eyes on her, and she had not been out of his head for more than a moment. If the husband had merely been traveling at the time of the Parker wedding, shouldn't he have returned by now?

Shouldn't he? Alex ate his meal, not tasting the good food. He was happier than he could have imagined. He had found her. He had not simply spotted her, as one does a bird on the fly, but found and fixed her in a place. With any luck, he would soon get the foolish cousin and his friends to leave. He excused himself to go to the privy, hoping the men would break up their evening and leave him alone with the lovely tavern owner. His pretty blonde was turning out to be very interesting.

Also, he was in awe that it was she who brewed this unique ale. He had not tasted the like since his months in England. It explained that wondrous hop's scent that hung over her. Even sitting at the table with the other men, he found it entrancing.

He came back in to find the men still there, but Nina was still there, as well. "Where did you learn brewing - this is not the average tavern brew?" He wanted to ask so much else, but bit his tongue, hoping for time alone with her. Lots of time.

Nina had heard from her tavern maids that a gray-eyed man had sat in the pub drinking ale "as if it were a fine wine." But he did not know she'd seen him the next morning; it would be bad manners to tell him now. "I learned from old Mr. Bigelow, my father-in-law. As a young man he traveled throughout Britain, the German states, and Austria, stopping long enough to learn brewing from the masters everywhere he went.

"He came to Massachusetts many years ago, and took a job here at Mr. Bigelow's tavern as brewmaster. When he married Joanna, the owner's daughter, he agreed to take her name, Bigelow, and to keep the tavern in the family. When it became clear that I was to be the next Bigelow, he set out to teach me everything he knew. He taught me to brew, and to read his extensive library in German and Italian. I also have deciphered some Latin notes on brewing written by French monks. I can't speak a word in any of them." She laughed at her own inadequacies.

Alex listened to the interesting and unusual story fixed on

only one fact. Daughter-in-law? She was married. He had been afraid so. But still, she didn't look married. She was too aware of his touch, and she was no trollop. He let the other men carry the conversation while he drank and thought.

The willing Carlotta had looked married. There was a certain confidence that married women had, even those bored and unhappy wives that young men found so interesting. Nina looked tired, as if she worked too hard. Now that he knew the quality of her ale, and had seen her spotless inn, he could understand why. If there was a husband, would he not be here to help with this work? He excused himself, saying he needed to stretch his leg, and headed into the kitchen.

A few minutes later he returned to the public room and his seat. He was not ready to call it a night.

"Gentlemen, anyone here want to exchange their picket duty for mine? I'm due at the redoubt, south of the lower fort, at eight tomorrow morning. Does anyone due on at midnight want to change?"

"Seriously Peele, you look like death and you want to switch? You haven't taken a minute off since that ball found your leg, and then those rides south. Fine, fine, don't back down now." He put his waistcoat over his shoulder as he stood. "Gents, I'm for my bed, I need to be on duty at eight, and I want to be well rested." Dan Ellis laughed, threw some scrip and a few coins on the table, and walked out to saddle his horse. Three men followed him.

Nina walked Wythe to his horse. "It was nice you found me here, Wythe. Don't be a stranger."

He kissed her cheek, and pulled her under his arm. "Nina, I can tell that Alex wants more from you than ale. I don't know you well, and I haven't known him long, but he is a bit of a wolf - foreign, from what I hear. Learned far too much from those London rakehells, and that woman Carlotta. Be careful."

"Darling cousin, I am nothing but careful. But I will keep your words in mind. Stay safe and come back soon." She hugged him good-bye, trying not to laugh at such a serious warning.

Alex stood at the end of the row of buildings, leaning against the corner of the stable. He watched Nina with her cousin, deciding he had no interest in anything that young ass had to say to her. He had lost that right at the family wedding when he forgot her, or he chose to deny knowing her. Both were despicable, and Nina deserved better.

He wondered if he were too drunk to think clearly. Maybe he should go right back to camp. He did volunteer for duty in a few hours, and he would have to ride out before eleven. The sun had just set, so it couldn't be much beyond eight. He would just speak with her for a moment or two. If he had known, he would not have drunk so much of her fine ale. One of life's strange ironies.

Nina waved off the riders and walked toward him. It felt like a moment of discovery, a moment of tremendous possibility. She was frightened but felt compelled to loop her arm though his. She rested her hand in his. She could feel Alex's heat through his linen sleeve. She reminded herself this was just a walk by the river with a charming man. They reached the river. He gripped both her hands in his. They were warm and strong, sure. Sure, that was what he was. He seemed certain that he was present at the right place, at the perfect moment.

Nina wondered how he knew that. She never had. She watched, removed, as Alex took her hands and moved his strong thumbs in deep, slow circles in the palm of each hand.

Her focus dulled, and she stepped back into herself, and closed her eyes, letting her muscles weaken, forcing herself not to be afraid. He traced along each finger with his own, and lifted her hand to his mouth. He pulled one finger into his mouth, letting his tongue tease at it. Nina heard herself moan.

The grass was warm and dry from the sunny day, and they were very alone in a cluster of old apple trees that grew by the banks. Nina sank onto the grass and Alex sat next to her. She put one arm behind him and instinctively moved her fingers into his hair.

He kissed her lips gently as a butterfly, and feathered kisses across her cheeks and neck. He pulled her head onto his shoulder and put his arm around her, holding her close, feeling her breathe. The sounds of night insects, the crickets, katydids and cicadas crying for their mates, filled the air. The rising moon was large and nearly full, it took up most of the sky.

He lifted her left hand to his lips and kissed the top, seeing, but ignoring, the small ring on her finger. Then he slowly turned it and kissed the arch of her palm, trailing kisses from there to her fingers.

Nina did not understand how being touched and even gently kissed along her palm and fingers could cause such a reaction in her. Her breathing changed and she felt uneasy, almost queasy. She shook her head, but nothing changed. Surely she wasn't scared or nervous enough for her heart to beat a tattoo. She held herself still and tried to calm her panic. She stared at the huge moon, then she turned instinctively, and looked into Alex's eyes.

It was almost full dark as the moon rose above the horizon, but his deep gray eyes seemed to have a light of their own. He nipped at the flesh of her middle finger. Nina jumped and tried to pull away. Gently, he held both her hands, and softly kissed one palm and then the other, thinking, as he did, that she really did remind him of a skittish colt. Why he felt the need to concern himself with gentling her, he was not sure, but he could see that the task could easily become irresistible. Her scent alone would make the effort worthwhile.

He lifted her by the waist and gently put her on his lap. He left his arms around her, but loosely in case she wanted to flee. She didn't. Instead she turned her face to his and opened her lips to his kiss.

Nina had been kissed before. She was quite sure she had. But she had never had a kiss render her so weak and needy. She had a passing remembrance that she found these sensations unpleasant. She had long ago decided never to explore this aspect of men and women.

She heard talk all the time from the other women; even her tavern girls occasionally told her of the lovely times they had with men. Nina was sure they did not feel as uncomfortable as she did. If they had, they would not talk of it with a gleam in their eyes.

Alex wasn't sure when his skittish colt would return, but he moved slowly. Maybe she was a lonely wife whose husband had absconded. That scenario did not quite fit, but no matter. He moved his hands into her hair. Carefully, he untied the string and removed the cap. Her soft hair fell out of its pins and over her shoulders. Slowly he kissed her, letting her respond before cupping her breasts through gown, stays and chemise.

Nina hushed her worries and enjoyed the feeling of her fingers in his glorious hair. She drew her hands over his strong back, feeling his strength. His body stiffened as he touched her. She could feel his arousal, but he was slow, not insistent.

It was so different from what she remembered, so soft and gentle, mesmerizing. She fell back on the soft grass, grateful she didn't have to sit upright. She heard herself moan as he pulled up her skirts and touched her leg.

She was so soft, so sweet. Her hard, tired face melted and became beautiful as she relaxed in his arms. Her cheeks were flushed, her moans soft and welcoming. Alex felt he had entered another plane of existence. She was everyman's dream, nicely formed, and willing and responsive in his arms. He ran a finger over her cheeks, neck and breasts, lingering at each to extend the touch and echo each with a kiss.

She moaned and opened to him, limp and needy. He felt the urgency of his own arousal. He pulled himself back and carefully untied her chemise, releasing her sweet nipples from inside her stays with a practiced move. She thrashed beneath him as he suckled her breasts. He pushed her skirts up, again slowing himself so as not to startle her. He reached to her softest core to feel her sweet moisture. She was so moist and ready. He kissed her as he fumbled with his breeches, springing free the moment the last button was undone.

Nina held her breath, waiting. She daren't move in anticipation of the searing pain. She didn't want to do anything that would hurt Alex's feelings. He was nothing but kindness. He was doing things to her she'd never imagined. She willed herself still, ready to try, to endure, whatever was to happen here on this dark night. She heard him unbutton his breeches and felt him rise over her. She felt his kisses, opened her lips and kissed him back, her tongue twining with his, their breath mingling.

Alex was lost in the moment. It took all his effort to hold himself over her, and wait for an acknowledgment of any kind. It was past full dark, but moonlight filtered through the apple trees. She smiled into his eyes. His anxious cock was more than ready, and he moved to enter the warm, soft sheath that his body ached for.

It was not there. She was not there. In a split second she had turned away, onto her side, and curled into a little ball. Her sobs split the dark night. Alex jumped up, fisted his hands in frustration, his hot blood and hard cock angry at him for the deception. He limped over to the side of the falls and let the cold spray cool his body.

Poor Nina! Whatever physical discomfort he felt was momentary. Whatever secrets she hid were far more long-lasting. There was a story there, one she must have carefully hidden. He took a deep breath and let it out in a whoosh as he repaired his clothes. Already, she was his irresistible obsession. He couldn't abandon her as he found her. The fates had given him this unusual gift, so she was his to unravel and to repair. Unfortunately, he was due at camp for picket duty soon, and Nina's story would likely take the rest of the night.

"Nina?" He pulled his waistcoat which he had slung over an apple branch before they had sat down. Fully covered and contained, he pulled her into his arms for what he hoped was a comforting hug. After a long moment, he pulled away and helped her trembling fingers with laces, drawstrings, and jacket. He picked up her cap and handed it to her.

"Nina, I spoke to Mrs. Cotton during dinner. I hope you will agree to join me, but I intend to eat lunch by the bridge below the forge tomorrow. I will be back just before lunchtime. Please say yes.

"Please?"

Tomorrow? it seemed too soon to think. Nina stayed still, safe with his arms around her. She couldn't explain what had happened, but she supposed she owed Mr. Peele an explanation or even an apology. She nodded shyly, agreeing to meet him the next morning.

She sat in the shadows hugging her knees, hearing him mount Thorne and ride off. Her clothes were neatly arranged as if nothing had happened. She could have gone back into the taproom to work. She didn't.

When all was quiet around her, she started crying again. She cried for her short marriage, and the young love she had lost. Then she cried for her loneliness, and her fears.

In a few minutes her crying eased, and she listened to the inn at night. She heard her brother-in-law Josh check the horses and climb to his room above the stables. She heard the girls call out from their attic rooms, picking the unlucky tavernmaid who would wake and help Mrs. Cotton in the morning. Then, when it was very quiet, she walked soundlessly down the short dirt road to her house. She went in by the front door, away from all things brewhouse and tavern. She checked on Jack, who was asleep with a book open on his pillow, his candle burned down to the stub under the glass chimney. She slipped a mark into the book and put it on the table.

Down the short ladder to the second floor, she walked through her staid, polished parlor, and unlocked her quiet room. On the other side of that door was her sanctuary. Turkish carpets, silk-covered pillows, sandalwood boxes and unusual candlesticks from around the world decorated the room. These were the things she had collected since her widowhood, bought with her own money during trips to Boston, to the harbor and marketplace, some of them gifts from sea captains who thought there might be a chance.

Chapter 6

Those were sweet times, the days she spent with her son and his grandfather, buying crops of fresh hops at the haymarket, and taking the time to visit coopers and their maltster. After their work was done, they would spend the rest of the day exploring the overflowing stalls of the marketplace and buying whatever appealed. She never bought what was fashionable. Things for the inn and tavern were the only exception. Instead, she brought home items that would shock the New England sensibilities of her neighbors - if ever one saw her room. Her purchases were things that simply pleased her and nourished the senses: silk ribbons in outrageous and beautiful colors from Italy, tiny bells of bronze and silver from China and India, rugs from the Orient and her favorite, long and wide lengths of silk in bright colors which she used for summer sheets on her bed. In winter, she changed to thick Portuguese flannel, her other indulgence.

This room was her favorite place, and mostly her secret. The girls at the tavern and her son knew of its lavishness, but they rarely entered. The rest of her little house had domestic goods, made locally or donated by friends and family. Even there, there was a kind of excess, and Nina knew it. She didn't need to save China teapots and plates, saucers, and cups from England, or the wood plates, pewter bowls and mugs that the tavern could no longer use, but she did. She liked having shelves in her dining room crowded with pretty things.

She opened a small box that sat on the table. The heady smell of sandalwood rose from it. The box was where she kept her special things: Jackie's first lost tooth; a thin braid of her hair from the day she married; and a miniature St. James Bible that her father had given her when she turned ten. She picked up the tiny book; it fell open to the psalms. She recited her favorites by heart, relishing the sensuous language, and the glory of life offered in the words. Calmer, she returned the little book and closed the box.

Nina lit one small candle and blew out the brighter lantern that had been left. In the half light of her room she unbraided her hair, dragging her own fingers close to her head, remembering the feeling of strong fingers in her hair and on her scalp. Slowly, she untied the laces of her chemise, forgetting how gentle he was when he retied them after, and remembering how it felt when he delicately traced his fingers over newly bared skin.

She tried to imagine what it would be like not to be afraid. Failing at that, she shed the rest of her clothes and fell asleep on her soft feather bed, on silk sheets, wearing nothing but the warm summer air.

Chapter 7

The morning, after a brief summer shower, was perfect. Alex wished he had gotten more than a couple of hours sleep, but since Thorne seemed to remember the way, he let himself doze in the saddle. His time on duty had been uneventful. Even with the bright moon in the sky, no redcoats had fired in their direction. The inaction made it hard to stay awake, but he had, until it was clear that not much was going to happen. Then the men had taken turns sleeping in short naps until the duty change.

He got back to headquarters in time to wash and dress, putting on his last clean shirt and leather breeches. He brushed and tied his hair into something resembling a respectable queue, put a tri-corn on his head, and went off toward the Lower Falls. Somewhere around the old cemetery in Watertown, he realized he was "going courting," so he stopped at the wine seller to buy a light Riesling for lunch, and picked flowers when he passed a garden with vines spilling blooms over a fence.

Nina woke to the rat-a-tat Jackie used to knock on her bedroom door.

"Jack, it's early, tell the girls to get to work."

"They are working, Ma. Mrs. Cotton says to wake and dress. She said that you're having company and she says she won't tell him to go away." Jack heard his mother growl something she wouldn't want him to hear. "Ma, I have hot water. I'll leave it out here for you." And with his errand completed he was gone into the bright day, before she opened her door.

Nina brought in the bucket of hot water, pouring some into a washbowl and then standing in the bucket to wash her legs and feet. She always said this was one of the great luxuries of owning her own inn and brewhouse. The nature of beer making, and even making coffee for the tavern, required unending hot water, and she had become used to being clean.

Washing reminded her of Alex's strong, yet gentle, hands caressing her body, and his taste when he kissed her. She also tapped down her embarrassment at her reaction. No, she might feel like the lowliest fool, but she would not hide in fear. She dressed in a light-green linen gown, with a matching striped petticoat, and short jacket. She was ready. She called to Sukie from the tavern to help her with stays.

Alex handed the stallion to Josh in the stable yard, and went inside. He looked around, marveling at clean windows, spotless floors and polished tables. He had never been in a tavern so early in the morning, but he would not imagine they were all this shiny. His pretty blonde might be a taskmaster, making her staff polish windows when the tavern wasn't busy, but he imagined her with her sleeves rolled up, working hard right along with her staff.

The Brewmistress was not in sight, but Alex had business with the cook first anyway. He walked past kegs that were marked for tapping at lunch and dinner, and then through a small door into the kitchen. It was a wonderful room, with a large hearth and chimney on the back wall. Shiny pans and kettles hung from the rafters. There were three tables with people cutting and stirring. Mrs. Cotton looked up and smiled at him.

"Here you go, Mr. Peele. Jackie's been up, and told her to come down and meet you. If she had a notion to skip her picnic, she was warned that I would send you after her. I'm sure she will be right down." She handed him a half barrel with jute handles. He peaked inside, and tucked his bottle of Riesling between the meat pies and fresh apples. "The plates and things are in there under the pies."

"Thank you so much, Mrs. Cotton. The food smells wonderful."

"No problem, Mr. Peele, Nina works too hard. It'll be good for her to get away for an hour or two."

Alex nodded his good-bye and left by the back door. He stopped to look at the falls, watching the mist rise into the moist August morning. It wasn't hot, and it probably wouldn't be, but he wouldn't be surprised if it rained again later when what heat there was built up. After a few minutes, Nina appeared over his head at the top of the outdoor stairs. She was laughing with someone on the other side of the door.

Alex looked up at the sound. "Morning, I hadn't noticed those stairs." It was clear he was curious.

"We use them mostly for housekeeping," she called down to him as she descended. "That way, the guests don't see us hauling sheets out to the wash bucket." Nina stepped onto the ground. She breathed a sigh of relief. The first question was easy. Maybe he wouldn't demand answers for her bizarre behavior. "I know the perfect place, far enough away so I can't see the *Hammer*, but close enough so I can hear the bell if they really need me. Cook never uses it, but it will let me relax if I can hear it."

"How did you go to the wedding, if it makes you nervous to be away?"

"We closed the kitchen. Mrs. Cotton's son insisted she go

home that weekend. The girls served cold meats and ale."

"Nothing could go wrong with young tavern maids, cold meats and ale?" Alex was nearly giddy with the pleasure of simple talk.

Nina started to explain about Josh and the blacksmith being near, and then realized that Alex was teasing, and that no explanation was necessary. She laughed. It was so easy, talking to him. Maybe this wouldn't be a terrible day.

She led them over the river on a footbridge and up, away from the roar of the falls, to a clearing. She chose a spot under a tree, near some grazing cows. Alex seemed satisfied with the place, so she shook out the old blanket she had carried from the inn, and sat down to spread out the food.

"Alex sit. I'll serve us some breakfast. I don't know about you, but I am famished. I'm sure you haven't eaten yet today, and Mrs. Cotton's pork and apple pies smell wonderful."

The blanket was old and faded, but had once been a beautiful blue and white candlewick bedspread. The pattern of pine tree and leaves was faint but still visible. Nina arranged her skirts, not realizing till that moment that her pale green gown and the blue, faded though it was, would work to bring out the aqua of her eyes. She hoped Alex didn't think she had planned the combination.

Alex tried not to stare at the tableau as it presented itself to him. The bucolic setting was so different from the smell of men, gunpowder and the occasional wound or death that the siege presented. Here he was, barely ten miles away in this other world, with a lovely woman with eyes that matched the blanket, her gown and, most of all, the summer sky.

He knew how shy she was, how afraid of intimacy. He would try not to frighten her. But after some food and wine, he hoped she would tell him why she was afraid of sex. Saying it aloud might help her. It would certainly help him. He was almost completely sure he had done nothing to scare her last night, but he needed to be reassured.

He poured sweet wine into cold pewter tankards, and handed one to Nina. She served the small pies that cook had just pulled from the oven. They ate until the feeling of having eaten replaced the gnawing hunger of a late start. Alex refilled Nina's tankard.

"Alex, I confess to listening to your stories last night. I hope you don't mind my eavesdropping. Which parts of the world have you seen?"

He finished chewing and nodded, swallowing some wine. "Turns out quite a bit. I set out from college in Connecticut to see the ruins of the ancient world. You see, I had taken an abnormal liking to Classical Greek and Latin and I wanted to see the ruins. I hadn't enough money to go south directly, so I established myself in London with a distant cousin of my mother's, and tutored boys in mathematics, Greek and Latin. When I'd saved enough, I set off for Greece, with stops in Spain and Portugal. The architecture there is remarkable for the Moorish influence, so that was instructive.

"My goal was always the classical worlds of Greece and Rome. In Greece, I learned that being quite literate in classical Greek was very little help in modern Greece. Everyone was kind enough, though I suspected they had a good laugh behind my back. I must not be a truly great scholar, because in mere months I was able to see enough to satisfy my curiosity.

"After I'd finished my wanderings though the Grecian Isles, I went to Turkey to see Istanbul and the ruins of Constantinople. After that I was nearly out of money again. And to be honest, quite ready to speak English. So I signed on to work a trade vessel that was heading to Naples. From there I walked to Rome.

"I love to claim I walked because I wanted to drink in the land and people. Italy in the spring is beautiful, which is undeniable, but really I had no money in my pockets, and worse, no way to make enough to get me home, or even to England. I'm not one to mope, so in Rome I reentered the world and looked for employment. That was when I saw the advert, in English, for a tutor. It seemed too good to be true."

He had such a lovely voice that Nina felt she could listen for hours. It was good to hear the rest of how he had met the beautiful Charlotte, Carlotta. Nina felt jealous, not for the woman's relationships with young men, one of whom was Alex, but for the ease with which she must have moved from one lover to another. It would be pleasant to find life so easy, love so easy.

Nina knew that soon it would be her turn. She would have to tell the story of her short marriage. It had none of the drama of traveling to Istanbul. Her tale had no beauty, and as soon as he heard about a child, he would ride away on the magnificent Thorne and not look back. Dismayed, she realized she would miss him.

Alex served himself another helping, Nina felt tongue-tied about her own story and decided to postpone talking until they had finished eating. She would hear more of his stories, about his childhood, how he had gone to school, and how hard it had been to leave America to travel. She would hear the story of the places he had seen, the people he had met, even Carlotta.

Nina would have loved to travel. She sipped at the light

wine, "My father-in-law used to tell me about the different places he traveled in his youth. His were stories about dark wood churches and oak barrels. I always had a vision of dark woods and dark little men." She shrugged. "I know that's wrong, and for the south I have visions of hot light and bright colors. I've seen the ships come into port from Marseille. The men are sun darkened, and look, hmm, happy. In port, they smile and sing."

Alex knew precisely what she meant. He was also from this land of rocky fields and long winters. Sunshine was often swallowed by clouds or haze, if not by an unexpected storm. On most days the brightest colors were paled by the grayed sky. He drank wine and listened to her tell John's stories.

Nina was happy to retell stories about learning to brew. John Peddleman had been an entertaining man, and those stories were part of who she now was. She was equally happy not to talk about John Bigelow's son. She owed Alex the truth, but she put it off.

Alex listened to retold stories about the man's travels in Scotland, Austria and Germany - the capitals of brewing. He understood now how she had become so expert, able to use available plants even when hops and barley were in short supply.

He felt warm from the good food and sweet wine. Nina's voice melded with the muffled sound of the falls. Bees worked some nearby daisies, their steady hum mixed with the other sounds. Alex was relaxed, comfortable and wine-warm. He fell asleep.

Nina was telling the difficult story of her marriage. She wouldn't recount the details of the six days and five nights. "I moved in with Joanna and John the days before the wedding.

My parents came, of course. I don't remember being sad not to marry from the first parish. I was just in a happy daze." She looked down and saw that her audience had fallen sleep.

She understood how tired Alex must be. He had stayed with her till late, and then he had picket duty from midnight. She wondered if he had slept at all. He looked uncomfortable lying on his arm. Careful not to wake him, she lifted his head so he could rest in the pillow of her lap. Jackie had napped like that often when he was very little, but this did not feel in the least maternal. She arranged her legs so she would be comfortable, and sat back against the tree to enjoy the quiet of the early afternoon.

Watching someone sleep often brings temptation to poke or rouse the sleeper, but that was not Nina's instinct. She had been a mother long enough to understand the value of sleep, but even so, she itched to run her fingers through Alex's thick wavy hair. She stifled the urge to touch, but it got harder to behave herself as a few minutes turned into an hour, and the sleeper barely moved. What they must be thinking back at the *Wheel and Hammer*, she could only imagine. They would never believe that a tired soldier had used this lovely afternoon, and a widow's comfortable lap, to sleep.

Her own legs were now soundly asleep and she could feel neither leg nor foot. Nina unpinned her short jacket, carefully shrugging it off and rolling it into a pillow for the still-sleeping Alex. It left her in stays and chemise, but she needed to stretch. Carefully she lifted his head, and placed him right back onto the jacket pillow. Then she got up to stamp her feet and stretch her legs.

The afternoon had turned uncomfortably moist and warm.

Nina was not at all sorry she'd had an excuse to shed the jacket. She walked a bit away and watched Alex from a distance as she reached to stretch out her back and hips. He really was a beautiful man, sort of the fairytale Prince Charming she had imagined when she was very little - a knight come to rescue the maiden locked in a tower, or her father's woodshed.

He had lost some of the sun-kissed cheeks and brown skin he had had at the boatyard. He must be sleeping days and taking night shifts on the lines. That sort of pattern always made one tired. She knew that when they had extra-late nights in the taproom, simply sleeping late the next day fixed little. Looking at him with an expert eye, it looked as if he weren't eating as well as he needed. She wondered how well that leg wound was healing. He did not seem to favor it too much, but one never knew. Her knight, come to rescue a maiden, who wasn't a maiden, or even a willing widow. She sighed, disgusted with herself.

She tried to shake off some of those feelings. She never spent this much time without some occupation. If she'd known she would have brought some knitting or needlework. There were so many things, she rarely found the time to finish them all. She leaned backward against an enormous oak to stretch. The huge tree was ready to drop its acorns in the next wind. In fact, the first batch had already fallen ripe and fat from the old tree. She picked up a few and aimed at another tree some yards away. The first one missed, but second hit with a thud. She turned to see if the unexpected noise had roused her sleeper.

Alex barely noticed the noise that woke him. He turned and stretched like a cat, feeling more rested than he had in months. He had dreamt that he lay in Nina's lap sleeping the sweetest sleep. He smelled her, but it was only her light linen jacket he was using for a pillow. He pulled himself up onto his elbow and tried to remember how he had fallen asleep. He hoped Nina would forgive him. If she were insulted, he would have to find a way to make up for that.

Looking around for her, he spotted her leaning against the trunk of a big oak. She wore only plain summer stays and a thin linen chemise, her pale green skirts blended with the background of grass and of wild flowers growing just beyond the shade of the enormous tree. She was lovely, and he needed to help her. He took a minute to himself behind some bushes, and walked down the path toward her.

Nina heard the crackle of crunching acorns. She looked up. It wouldn't do to insult a hard-working soldier by making him think she was angry that he had slept away their picnic. In truth, she was relieved. She smiled at him.

Alex stood in front of her and put his hands on either side of the tree. He caught her eyes and leaned over, lightly kissing her lips. Nina thought she should feel trapped, but Alex made no effort to snare her or deepen the kiss. She surprised herself when she reached up and put her hands around his neck. She pulled him down to her for a real kiss. He pulled her close, covering her mouth with his for a moment, then gently kissing her eyelids and cheeks. Nina put her hands in Alex's hair, pulling out the leather ribbon, and running her fingers through the thick waves. "I have been wanting to do that for an hour." She cradled his cheek in her hand.

Just touching his hair and breathing his scent began a tightness in her belly. It was becoming a familiar sensation, but still not one she liked, or even understood. She pulled back, twirling the leather thong.

Alex needed to hear her tale; there would be no going forward without it. Without asking if she had more time to stay away from the inn, he led her back to the blanket. He pulled it into the shade, lay on his back and pulled her down against his side. She curled her legs under her skirt, sitting rigidly upright. Her hands pulled and twisted the leather thong she had taken from his hair.

"Nina, tell me, you are married? You talk of John Bigelow, your father-in-law. How long have you been married, and where is your husband?"

Nina spoke as if from a great distance. Alex almost had to strain to hear. "I would have been married ten years last March. The truth is that I was married one week, ten years ago." She made almost no sound, forcing the words out on air.

Alex ignored her distress, although he wanted to let her stop. "How old were you when you married?"

"I was sixteen. The wedding was on my birthday." She heard Alex inhale sharply, but stay quiet. "My parents said I was too young, but I was angry at them for telling me how to live my life. I think I'd been angry at them for most of my life, and Johnny's sisters, who had always been my friends, wanted me to marry their brother. I must have whined long enough, because my father gave in, saying that I would grow up as a wife more quickly than as a daughter.

"I did not understand. I thought he was telling me that it was all the same, that being married would be the same as living at home with them. I believe now that he was offering me the chance to stay a child for a while longer." She leaned backward, her weight on her hands behind her. She stared at the sky through the leaves of a young birch, watching the dappled shade move over her. She noticed how the young tree did not supply the shade of the old oak.

"That must have been a while ago. How old are you?"

"I'm twenty-six. It was ten and a half years ago."

"So you said. Where is he? Where did he go?" Alex saw this was hard on Nina. It was likely she had never told the entire tale to anyone before. He wished he could let her stop, just hold her in his arms and feather kisses over her tempting decolletage, but he could not.

"I'd better tell you the whole story. As I said, I was sixteen, he was nineteen. He was everything to me. We were married six days, Saturday to Friday, when the militia was called. Other towns had already left, and it was Newton's turn. The treaty was signed in Europe, but there was still trouble in Canada, in York. Lord Geoffrey, General Amherst needed troops. One last battle in a war that lasted well over the seven years they'll write about in the history books.

"Our militia marched west to Springfield and then into the mountains. They told me he was the only one to fall that day. That somewhere in the dark woods of Canada, he took an arrow in the chest, probably rolled in dung the way it festered. He died the next week. He's buried somewhere out there." She pointed northwest with practiced skill.

She seemed to take strength from telling the story, so Alex only nodded. "To answer the question you're too polite to ask. Johnny was delighted with me. With sex." Nina sat back up, stiff as a ramrod, she spoke very softly. "I was like a new plaything and he couldn't get enough of it. Every morning, every night, sometimes at lunch. For that whole week. I knew he was leaving and didn't want to hurt his feelings, so I never told him that it hurt me, or that it left me fuzzy. I don't know any other way to describe it.

"Now I hear women talk about their husbands, and they elbow each other and giggle. They consider me one of them, because I was married. I have no idea what they are talking about. Certainly not why they are laughing." Nina sank. All the strength she had gathered to tell her tale had drained from her. She put her head in her hands, trying to stem her tears. Alex said nothing, just let her cry, combing her long loose hair with his fingers. "I never cry, it must be your fault." She laughed as the tears rolled down her face.

He wanted to comfort her, but more than that he felt a duty to help her. This wasn't the time in his life for a love affair, but the poor girl would never marry again if she wasn't helped over this. Wasn't he the man who saved her from rolling barrels and tipping pies? He would make it a project, and it wouldn't be onerous to teach her to enjoy the pleasures possible between a man and a woman. He pulled her up, out of her despondency and into his arms. She hid her face in his chest. Slowly the smiles overtook the crying.

Nina rested her head on Alex's shoulder. She would have liked to run away now that her embarrassment and humiliation were complete. She had confessed to him that she was a complete ninny, and then she burst into those childlike tears again. She expected to see the back end of him and the horse as soon as she turned around. It would get worse. She hadn't even mentioned Jack.

She looked to her right, and into soft gray eyes. The sun brought out tiny flecks of green and brown in the gray. He didn't look angry or disgusted. He looked like he cared.

"Nina, except for this, you are a very brave woman, am I right?" Nina nodded, she had always thought she was. Alex went on. "From your clothing, I suspect you like to feel comfortable and enjoy pleasurable things." She thought of her bedroom with the pillows and the silk sheets. She nodded again. "Good. I wonder if I might propose a challenge?"

"A challenge? What sort of challenge?" She was wary of agreeing to the unknown with this man. He made her feel things she didn't understand - strange feelings that left her confused.

"Nina, The challenge is this: you will allow me to show you the pleasure your body should enjoy with sex?" Nina blushed from the top of her head to well into her chemise. Alex wondered how far the color spread; it would indeed be grand sport to find that out, as Carlotta's British husband would say.

"If I say yes, what will happen?"

He thought for a moment to frame his answer. "A fair amount of skepticism, very good. First, I will not simply rip off your clothes, or expect you to do so. I will not scare or hurt you in any physical way. I can't possibly put it into words that will make sense - those are the things I will not do.

"Second are the things I will do. I can't explain it all in words you will understand yet. But, I will touch you slowly, to rub you with oils, kiss you in places you did not know you wanted to be kissed. I will help you fly and shatter as you lose control in what the French call a *petit mort*, the little death.

"And, I absolutely promise, I will not to engage in any act of coupling unless and until you beg me. But when, not if, but when you beg me, I will insist that you follow through. I would survive the rejection, but I will not allow you to be a coward."

"Allow? How would you make me?"

Alex could see her interest and her ire were piqued. "I will seduce you into compliance."

"What if I curl and cry again? I couldn't endure being that cowardly. Even thinking I might makes me afraid to try."

"I won't let you."

"How?"

97

"I just told you - kisses, soft feathers, warm oils, lots and lots of kisses." He reached for her and feathered kisses on her eyes and over her cheeks. Instinctively she tilted her mouth to his, and he covered her lips for a gentle kiss, pulling away and pulling her head onto his chest. He breathed in the essence that was Nina, feeling her full breasts pressed against his chest. Oh, it would not be an onerous task at all, teaching Nina to love her body and the pleasure it could bring her.

***

"Hey, Peele, aren't you a bit late getting back from your *moment* with my cousin last night?" Wythe greeted Alex when he rode into camp. The younger man followed him to the stables.

"Now she is your cousin? You didn't show much interest before this."

"Well now that I have, maybe I want to protect her from wolves like you."

Wolves? That was interesting. That was what Carlotta said he was. A wolf. She even had that leather cape lined with wolf fur made for him. It had been his wolf skin, carried in a box since he was a boy of twelve. The animal and he had come face to face one frozen winter morning near his parents' farm. The ground was as hard as the granite boulders that peppered the fields, and there had been a thin layer of snow, just enough to preserve the beast's footprints, when he'd snuck out to track it.

It was hard enough keeping animals alive over the hard winters of New Hampshire's White Mountains without a wolf eating what was left of the winter herd. His father, and some other men, had planned a hunt for the lone wolf that had wandered too close to the town, but Alex had an idea about where he might be, and had tracked him for hours though the

98

winter woods. He shot him just as the large male lunged for him, his teeth ready to grab at Alex's neck. He had lain with the dead animal nearly crushing him for what seemed like an eternity, until he was finally able to slide out from under. He remembered it as a disgusting and humiliating experience and was glad no one had seen him. To thank him, the town had collected coin from residents, and paid for the tanning of the fur.

He knew something about wolves, and mostly he liked them. He liked that they were fiercely loyal to their pups and their mates, and didn't kill indiscriminately. To be a wolf was no insult, and if Wythe was suddenly going to be foolishly protective of Alex's "pretty blonde," the fool boy would likely do more harm than good. Just one more obstacle to overcome.

"Wythe, lay off. It's none of your business." Exhaustion hitting him full force, Alex turned to walk away, hoping to find a cot somewhere and get some sleep. He felt a hand on the back of his shirt pull him around. He ducked just as Wythe's fist headed toward his chin. Alex ran at Wythe and knocked him to the ground, and he was just going to finish it and find his cot when he was picked up from the collar by a large man.

Henry Knox, bookseller of Boston and the largest man Alex had ever seen, pushed Alex against the brick wall of a college building and grabbed for Wythe.

"What is the meaning of this? Do you fools not know to save your energy for the real fight? Is there anything I should know, or should I put you both in the guardhouse?"

"No sir." Alex would just as pleased to sleep in the barrack's guardhouse as anywhere else, as long as he could put his head down.

"He didn't come back for duty last night, spent it with my cousin, . . . close enough to be my sister, we are . . . " Wythe

99

kept talking.

Alex rolled his eyes, as the young man droned on. "Sargent Knox, I was at the redoubt on Menatomy from midnight until eight. The rest? I have no idea what he is on about." Alex saluted the large man, turned his back on the confused Knox and the rambling Wythe, and found his bed.

Nina had guessed Alex was a scholar, probably a schoolmaster, since she'd overheard his conversation with her father, but if she had harbored doubts they flew away with that challenge. Although it might be a very imaginative one, it was presented in a very organized way. Threatening to ensure her obedience with gentle kisses added to its intrigue. She should refuse his offer - it was unladylike, to say the least. Perhaps she should vow to herself that she would never plead or beg. Then she would never prove herself a coward, but she would never know the truth.

In days, the picnic and that challenge seemed like a strange dream. Her cousin and his friends continued to come to the tavern, but Alex was missing again. She told herself not to be concerned at his absence. Soldiers did not own their time. So at first she merely missed his appearance at the tavern, but as the days tuned to weeks, worry of rejection turned into worry about his leg and then his life.

Maybe it was good that he was gone. The inn was her life, all that was left for Jack from his family, something no one could take from the Bigelows, no matter who Nina might be worried-over or miss.

Work at the *Wheel and Hammer* had a way of being as never-ending as the water going over the wheel, so she found herself again wedded to her routine and pushed thoughts of Alex to the deepest corner of her mind, to be explored only when alone, in her soft silken bed.

Chapter 8

"Peele, the General would like to have a word with you. Two o'clock this afternoon, Vassall House. Yes?" Washington's aide de camp found Alex eating breakfast and spoke to him quietly. Such a request wasn't really a question, and neither man expected an answer. The General never dealt with personnel issues, so this could have nothing to do with Wythe or Knox. Curious, Alex spent the morning polishing Thorne's tackle, and his own boots.

He knocked on the door of the outer office at exactly two o'clock, expecting to be ushered in by another aid, but Washington himself opened the door.

"Mr. Peele, have a seat, I have a request or two for you." The man sat on his desk, his long legs dangling in front. He sat still, but like a cat, full of energy waiting to spring.

"Yes, General, how can I help?"

"I understand that you've only recently joined the militia, that you have been away in London?" His voice was strong, but with the soft vowels of his native Virginia.

"Yes, sir, I have. I returned from England last year. Before that I had been traveling through Europe."

"They tell me, during your time in London, you were a bit of man about town, gaming hells, salons and whatnot?" Alex did notice a trace of a smile on the man's face.

"Yes, sir. That is true, but it did rub against my grain."

"That's probably true. You're from up here, old Yankee stock?"

"Yes, sir, New Hampshire, Yale man."

"Would you have any real objection to playing at your London self? Getting down to it, I would like you to go into Boston as a man who lived in London and loved it, loved the life you enjoyed there. You've returned to live in Cambridge at the College. Make up your role, you'd know better than I. Of course, your neighbors have made your life unpleasant, and you seek refuge in Boston. Stay there a while, learn what you can. We'll find some way to get your information back to us.

"Peele, we've got to find a way to break the blockade. I need better ears in there."

Someone must have told the commander about him. Of course he would go.

"But Peele . . . " Alex nodded at the General. "Before I let you settle down as a man about town -" he smiled slightly at his rhyme - "I must ask you and that lovely stallion to take on another errand to Philadelphia. The papers will be ready this afternoon, if you please."

"Yes, sir, I will be ready." Alex saluted and left, pleased to have been given roles he could play in this cause. He certainly wouldn't be marching with Benedict Arnold and Daniel Morgan along the Kennebec to Quebec.

Alex had, in fact, tried to volunteer for the mission. He met the requirements, at least the first few: woodsman, familiarity with the small bateau used on inland waterways, greater than average height. But there was the problem that he couldn't walk more than a few steps.

It was likely he and Thorne would be carrying the report of that mission to the Congress in Philadelphia. When he returned, he would be using his various life experiences, moving into Boston as a spy for the Americans. That afternoon, Alex set off for Pennsylvania, carefully avoiding the

103

distraction at the Lower Falls.

***

It bothered Nina that she couldn't go to the Boston docks to watch the ships and browse goods in the marketplace. She knew that was petty, that Bostonians had been chased out of their houses when the British Army moved in, and there were constant rumors that the residents were being shot on the Common. Probably that was untrue, but certainly times were hard in the Town. Firewood would be scarce, and food, no doubt, was hard to come by. Her life might be more dull than others' in these changing times, but rather than crave adventure, she felt blessed to be safe.

Life at the Lower Falls and in the countryside had changed less drastically than that in the capital, but had changed nonetheless. One of the most striking changes Nina noticed was in the Sunday liturgy. It happened around the time of the "Destruction of the Tea" that led to the Port's closure.

At Meeting each Sunday, her father and every other minister in the country, for as long as anyone could remember, had preached loyalty to the Crown as well as subservience to God. Part of every sermon had been a prayer for the King and his family.

At some point, that had changed. Nina was unable to say precisely when prayers for the royal family had stopped, or when the ministers had stopped speaking of subservience to King and God. But one day, they had stopped preaching subservience and started lecturing that liberty and freedom were gifts from God.

Another major change occurred because there were no sheriffs. Under the new laws imposed with the Port Act, sheriffs were to be chosen by the Royal Government. As soon as that passed, no one wanted to be chosen. The few that were found themselves tarred and feathered for betraying their neighbors. Committees of Safety, which operated in every town of the Province, replaced the sheriffs and maintained safety and order. Not all, but some of the Committees began to monitor opinions as well as behavior, making sure people signed pledges to the Cause. Even those who were neutral, happy to be left alone, and willing to support whichever army won and whatever government came to power, were forced to declare their loyalty to the Cause or risk having their property carted into the street.

Nina didn't know who bothered her more - the occasional information seeker or spy sent out by the British Royal Governor to examine the countryside, or the local Committee of Safety, who felt they had the right to involve themselves in everyone's life, even hers.

"Ma?"

Nina was in the brewhouse sorting apples for a mash to replace the rotten, sprouted barley that had been delivered. It was one of those September days that made one wish the seasons stood still. "Jack, don't you think you are too old just to be calling me 'Ma' - can't we think of something better?"

"Mother." Nina groaned but did not stop him since it was obvious he had something to tell her. She looked into worried blue eyes. "There are two strange men at the stables asking about a horse. Ma, they are really insistent. Josh told 'em there is no such gray horse. Not here. But they keep arguing with him.

"Did I tell you that there was this other man here last week asking the same thing?"

"Another man, last week? Asking you about a distinctive gray stallion?" Nina put an apple back in the bucket. This was going to be a problem.

"Yeah, that man, the first one, he wore a suit of all black. It was too fine for out here - you know what I mean?" Nina nodded. "He made me feel like snakes were crawling down my back."

"And all they wanted was a gray horse?"

"Yes'm. Josh convinced them to stay and eat. The men were ready to leave. But now they've sat for dinner."

"Have they seen you?"

"Maybe? But they weren't the type to notice a kid."

Nina rolled her eyes at the slang. "Stay out of their way. Better yet, go into the house and stay there. I'll tell Mary to bring you dinner from the kitchen. I don't like it. I don't know why, but I don't want them to see you."

"Yes, Mother." Jack always understood when his mother was serious. This was one of those times.

Nina kissed the top of Jack's head, and sent him off to safety. She wiped her hands on a rag, and pushed her hair back into the cap. Seconds later, she was ready to go into the tavern room and see about these curious strangers. There had been so little trouble here. Maybe she had gotten too used to the peace.

Were all these men looking for Thorne? They must want to find Alex. Why? It must be Thorne they were looking for. Was there another gray horse of such distinction? Alex had not been around in weeks. He must be in trouble, but she had no way to know.

The men were seated, and enjoying their ale. She moved over to their table. It was obvious from the way they moved and ate that they were not Americans. Foreigners did occasionally come through, but not often and not lately. Their accents were contrived, and increasingly slipped with the strong ale.

"Hello. I heard you were looking for a gray horse. If you knew more than a horse-color, perhaps I could help you."

"Are you the host?"

"Yes, I am."

"We are looking for a fellow on a gray horse. Heard he comes through here. Have you by chance seen him?"

The man was working hard not to sound British. So many New Englanders sounded like Englishmen, the man would have been better off using his real voice. "No, I'm sorry there has been no one on a noticeable gray horse. Did you ask at the stable?"

Nina felt precisely what had Jack worried. She also got a bad feeling from these men. She wished she could find out why they wanted Alex, and how they knew about Thorne.

"Yes, we did. Josh, nice young man. He said he remembered seeing you with a man who had a gray horse. You don't remember him? Probably because you know lots of men, pretty young tavern owner like you."

Nina didn't react to the insinuation woven into those nasty words. She didn't need to defend her reputation and she wasn't going to try. She said nothing. It was better to pretend not to be insulted than to put Alex and Thorne in danger. Let the men assume the worst of her. The truth was that she had no idea where Alex was, but she wouldn't admit to that.

"I'm sorry I can't help, but no, I don't know anyone in particular with a gray horse. My brother Josh would remember the animals better than I. Do you have a name? I am better with people."

"No, just the look of him and his horse." The first man turned to his partner. "Manning give you a name?"

"No. Just the horse and this location. He said the boy

Josh would help."

"Manning? Who is that? Should I know him?" She took a deep breath to keep her voice even. "Gentlemen, I cannot possibly help you if I do not understand you. You said Manning, is that the fellow with the gray mare?" She waited to see if they knew the sex of the horse. Neither man corrected her.

The first man, a tall thin fellow, who looked like he had never done a day's work, spoke. "No. E.P. Manning can't ride. Sits. Needs someone to chauffeur him around in his fancy carriage." He pushed out his 'h's, and tried not to sneer at the mention of the mysterious Manning.

So there was no love between these men. She needed to think about what to tell Alex, if she ever saw him again.

"Can I get you gentlemen anything else to eat or drink? I'm very sorry, can't help you with the bay horse." She went back to the tap to refill their cups, making quite sure these men paid their tab. She smiled at the image of a pretty bay mare, wondering what she would name her imaginary filly.

The men rode off. Nina went back into the brewhouse to finish the apple mash, her head full of Thorne being hunted, and Alex in danger. Jack was there waiting for her.

"Mater, I saw those men ride off."

"Mater?"

"It's Latin. Ma, stop worrying about your name, I was worried about the men."

"Not your worry. But yes, they rode off, and are gone. You know, Jack – I think I might like 'Ma' better.

"If it helps, they made my skin crawl, too. If anyone like that comes here, I want you to stay in the house, or run off to Uncle David's or Aunt Merry for a visit. I don't want them to know there is a child here."

Jack nodded, fully serious. His mother had never asked him to do such a thing before - never had that tone of voice before. Always, he had been allowed to go anywhere in the inn, and help in any way he could. But clearly this was different. He hoped he never saw those men again.

Nina didn't want to scare Jack, but there was something wrong with those men. And now she had to deal with Josh Peddleman, her young brother-in-law. He must be made to understand that being a Bigelow and a Tyrie would not save the tavern if the Committee of Safety thought they were helping British spies. She hated to limit the young man's friendships, but a situation like this could be more serious than he would expect. She found him at the paddock looking over a mare he had recently acquired.

"Josh, who were those men asking about the gray?"

"Englishmen, from the sound of it. I've got nothing against them asking if they're curious. They offered me money for the new stables, if I would help them. I couldn't, so I didn't get paid. Shame."

"Yeah, shame. They didn't bother you, or threaten you, did they?" Nina usually tried hard not to sound like Josh's mother. The lady was still very much alive on a farm not two miles away. Sometimes when she was about to sound motherly, she actually bit her tongue.

She had married his older brother, the baby of the first family, when Josh was just nine. Johnny died that year, and she had stayed and worked at the tavern with his father. She had been fond of Josh, but she had never been part of the Peddleman family, remaining friends with her husband's older sisters and their families.

When old John Peddleman died, he left the land across the road to Josh so he could develop a horse farm, his long-term dream. The will of John Peddleman's first wife, Joanne Bigelow, stated that tavern and inn had to stay in the Bigelow family. Because of that, it would go to Jack, or his cousins if he were unable.

Nina understood that Josh resented that will. He had spent his youth here while his brothers helped their mother on the farm. Of course, he had never met Joanne Bigelow. It made sense to him that he should inherit his father's tavern. She had explained that it had not been his father's to leave. It had been only his employment, as it was hers. That she worked at the inn, just as the cook and the tavern-girls did. She paid Josh what his work was worth, but she understood the temptation of ready coin to someone who was hungry to improve his life. It would be tempting for Josh to help the men, simply for the company of rich strangers, and a bit of coin. He must be made to understand that it would risk all their livelihoods to cross the Committee, but did he care?

Nina considered Josh. What did he believe about this conflict for the great cause of liberty? What did she believe? Until the shots were fired at the North Bridge last April, she had simply wished for quiet. She had listened to, and appreciated, the forceful arguments the rebels - now called Patriots - had made in the tavern, even joining in as they raised their cups to an end "to taxation without representation, liberty, and the end of tyranny." But she did not understand why the tea had been destroyed.

It seemed a foolish way to complain about tyranny, to pour crates upon crates of good tea into the harbor. She missed tea. Hot and sweet, it woke you up in the morning and soothed the long afternoons. She had drunk it at home as a girl, though her father had not approved of her mother's tea things - the strainers, and the pots, cups and saucers, needed to properly prepare the drink.

The capital had voted, just about the time of her marriage a decade ago, to support the non-importation agreements, and all the Town Meetings in the Province had voted in support. Since then, there hadn't been tea. She understood that these things needed to happen, but now what she needed was for Josh not to put them in danger from the British, or from the Committee. She needed to find a way to protect Alex and Thorne as well.

"No, *Aunt* Nina." He so rarely used the title that she cringed. "They didn't threaten, they were just insistent, like they wanted me to tell them, even if I didn't know."

"Josh, I know they offered money, but listen, I think they may be working for the British in Boston, and if you help them the Committee of Safety could punish you, or even take the tavern."

"Jewett and his guys never come out here. Nina, you worry too much. I don't know the horse - how could I answer?"

Nina prayed that would be true.

Chapter 9

The last days of August had Alex repeating his journey in reverse. The trip to and from Philadelphia was successful. Congress had been slightly better than its slowest self. The late summer weather had lasted, the roads had been better than expected. Now, with a new set of papers, letters and orders, he was on his way back north. He made a stop to rest the horse in New Rochelle on the Sound, and then at New Haven, where he again visited Carlton Peirson. As before, it had been a good visit. They shied away from current issues, and delved into literature and philosophy.

For a fleeting moment, he thought he would like to shed his responsibilities and stay in the old college town with its scholars in their black robes running to class. The rhythm of the academy, and the idea of another day or two with his dear friend, was tempting, but by dawn he was on the road, concentrating on the task ahead. He gave Thorne full rein, and they made good use of the nearly empty roads of the early morning. Occasionally they were joined by farmers, their slow wagons overloaded with harvest bounty. Alex looked over their loads each time he slowed, taking a moment to remember, and to offer a silent prayer for the health of the people of Boston, who lacked such plenty. Even on the misty morning, he could not forget the blockade or his sackful of dispatches.

When Alex woke in the woods of western Rhode Island the next morning, the mist and fog that had surrounded him in the evening had turned to drizzle, and wind was whipping branches high in the trees. Chilled from the cool air, and wet, he pulled his leather cape from his bag. He could tell from the direction of the wind that he was going to have to try to outrun a storm.

Roads in New England were rutted and muddy at the best of times, and now light rain was turning the mud to the slippery goo of smooth clay. Thorne almost went down. That one slip was enough for Alex. He had a sense of where he was, even with the fog. He headed off the north-south road and traveled cross country into the rocky woods. He headed north - northwest as much as possible to avoid the natural detours of Narragansett, Newport Island and Cape Cod. By the dim light of late afternoon, he was following the paths of the two rivers from Dedham northward. This route would take him right to the *Wheel and Hammer* and a diversion he craved, but had avoided.

Alex thought occasionally about his challenge, but had convinced himself it was a poor idea. Nina would no doubt become attached, and she should never choose to have another soldier in her life. She had been widowed once. His own path as a courier and spy tread too closely to the edge. If he proceeded, it would only cause Nina pain. He hated to renege on a bet, but better to be labeled a cad than to hurt his pretty blonde.

He turned this over and over, as he and the horse fought the increasing winds and rain. By West Roxbury he could barely tell the river bank from the downpour. They were near the tavern, the well-built stable of the *Wheel*. Thorne badly needed rest. A mere hour or two of shelter, and he, Thorne, and the dispatches would be on their way to General Washington.

***

Like the river, the *Wheel and Hammer* was near to overflowing. There had been three days of dispiriting drizzle, which just that afternoon had turned into gales and driving rain. The deluge showed no sign of letting up. Travelers who had been seduced onto moist roads by the light mist were drenched to the bone and looking madly for shelter. The roads had turned to a morass of deep mud that seemed alive, grabbing and holding hard to carriage wheels and horses' hooves. And the inn, which on rainy days was usually not particularly busy, was suddenly full of nervous patrons, crying children, and the smell of wet wool and leather, as people hung cloaks and carriage blankets over chairs and pushed their boots close to the fire to dry.

The inn yard was busy with traffic from carriages detoured by the rush of rain and river. The carriage horses were wet from the storm, and tired and hungry from fighting the bad roads. They needed food and a dry stable as much as the passengers and drivers needed warm food and good drink.

Nina was in the thick of it. She had dressed in her brother's old waxed-linen greatcoat, its collar turned up over her head, leather pants, and heavy boots. She stood in the center of the inn yard, rain pouring off her, directing riders and drivers and passengers into the inn and stables. She helped with luggage and horses, handing them off to any able-bodied person who was willing to towel-dry and feed a tired animal or help tired, stiff passengers over the mud and into safety. She had begun the afternoon with seven helpful boys who thought it great fun to be out in the rain and mud, but now she was down to three, and she did not have the time to investigate.

She reached up to take a horse's bridle, turning to exchange a word or two with the rider, but instead of a greeting, he dismounted quickly, and ran back down the road, disappearing around the buildings. Curious, she stared after him, but her attention was called back to the storm-soaked guests and their animals. She handed the familiar gray to one of her helpers without taking a minute more to think that he needed food and a good drying. Poor mud splattered Thorne - he was so tired he was almost shaking. Immediately, she reached for the lead of a carriage with four wet beasts. She hoped the inn and stable had room for them all.

Alex had ridden those last miles with visions of hot coffee, a stew of some sort and dry clothes on his back, encouraging Thorne with kind words and promises of a dry stall. He would have wanted to avoid the *Wheel and Hammer*, having convinced himself that Nina would be far better off without him. The weather dictated otherwise, so he'd had to follow the western side of the river or deal with rutted and slippery roads.

As he turned down the lane that led to the inn, he was waved at frantically by a colored scarf. He left Thorne with the small, odd man trying to create order in the unexpected chaos of the stable yard, and ran back to investigate.

At the corner of the building, he saw that the scarf was actually a hat. It was waved by a young boy who, as soon as he spotted Alex, ran away toward the inn kitchen. That first boy was then chased by a battalion of wet boys. Thinking that the boys were engaging in a foolish chase in the rain, he turned, anxious to get back to dry and warmth, when an odd movement at the river caught his eye.

Any sound the boy made was swept away by the wind, and overwhelmed by rushing water, wind and rain. He looked to be about ten years old, and at that moment he was clinging to a fallen tree, his feet dangling, nearly touching the rushing and quickly-rising river. It was clear the child could not pull himself back onto the big dead tree. Maybe his arms were too tired and weak, or he was caught on something.

Alex threw off his cloak. He was immediately struck by the cold rain pounding at his shoulders. He ignored that, and ran to the river, frantically trying to see through the rain. He knew he had to act fast or fail. Carefully, moving as quickly as he could, he climbed onto the wet trunk. He thanked an unruly childhood for teaching him how to deal with dead, wet, barkless trees. It seemed to take an eternity, but finally he was close enough to see and hear the boy.

The boy's small fingers dug into the wet trunk, gripping at small branch ends, but with the pouring rain he would not last long. Alex was right. He was caught, held in place by his shirt that was stuck on a broken branch. The wet linen had stiffened and strengthened, and it showed no inclination of giving way. Alex pulled out his knife and cut the shirt, catching the boy as his fingers slipped. He pulled the child into his arms and held him to his chest till their heart beats calmed enough to talk.

Holding the shivering boy close, he spoke below the storm. "I'm Alex." He thought he recognized the boy, but it would take a better look than this. "Son, why are you out here?"

"The boys dared me." He rubbed his nose with the back of his fist, as though something could be dried while still out in the storm.

"A reasonable explanation." Alex had been a ten year old boy once himself. "I understand that. Um, what did you say your name was?" Alex knew the boy had not told him, but he suspected it might be necessary to get them off this tree before the river took it, and them.

"I'm Jack."

"Well, Jack, we need to back off this tree before another tree comes and knocks it out of here. Do you understand?"

"Yep, I seen that." He nodded in childlike agreement, calmly assessing the river and the tree.

Alex started to crawl backward along the length of the tree. As if by prearranged choreography, Jack stayed right in front, never more than a hands-length distant, until Alex reached solid ground. He reached forward and grabbed Jack off the dead limb.

Alex couldn't tell if the shift in weight caused the oak to fall. Perhaps it was the river's rising, but just as they moved away from it and back under the kitchen roof, the tree was taken by the river. The noise was deafening as it crashed into the falls, and was whirled away. In seconds they heard it smash into the bridge.

They looked at each other, grinning as if a marvelous joke had been told. Then Jack shrugged and started to laugh. Alex allowed himself a moment to enjoy the child's laughter and joined in, simply for the joy of being alive.

They caught their breath, and Alex put a guiding hand around Jack as they walked sedately back, ignoring the water cascading over their faces, and clothes stuck to their bodies. Alex picked up his cape, and they shook hands in a silent agreement that what had transpired would never be spoken of, especially not to mothers. "Thank you, Mister- em-Alex." Jack stood with his shoulders back and feet planted firmly on the ground, once again a young man in charge of his world. "I think I better help my uncle with the horses." He turned back. "You were at that wedding with my grandpa, right?"

Alex must have nodded, understanding why he looked

familiar, but not why he was here. He mulled that over while he watched as the boy ran through the drenching rain back toward the stable yard. Alex pulled his cloak over his shoulders and slowly followed, relieved that Jack showed no ill after-effects. Then, remembering Thorne and the precious saddlebags, he trotted quickly toward the stables.

The strange little man in heavy linens and leather was still in the center of the yard dealing with the unceasing traffic moving toward the inn. There may have been attempts at conversation, but the constant wind made understanding impossible, and the frequent gusts nearly knocked the small fellow over. Alex's natural sense of concern made sure he checked the fellow again after seeing to his horse. Thorne was well cared for, however - toweled dry, and fed, in a stall by himself.

"You gave them a bit of a time, didn't you fellow?" Alex talked to his horse, giving him a sugar cube from his pocket. The head groom came over to join him. They heard the boys welcoming arriving horses.

"He's a beauty." The young man, who was no more than twenty, spoke to Alex over the top of the stall.

"I noticed he got a spot to himself. I'm sorry if he was a pest."

"Well, he had a few bad moments, telling us he didn't want to be here, but then, young Jackie just walked in said somethin' to him, and he calmed right down. He's dried and eating. He's a pretty unusual color, ain't he?" Josh seemed to be considering something. Alex nodded.

Alex slipped the man a crown coin and told him to share it with his young helper. He spent a few more minutes with the horse, pleased that his new friend had cleaned the mud out of his hooves as well as the basic tasks. "Behave yourself,

Thorne. We leave first thing in the morning."

He collected his saddlebags and crossed the yard into the taproom. He looked over his shoulder. The last horses and carriage had been cared for, and the yard was now empty of everything but the wet and mud. Even the strange wet fellow was heading into the taproom, his task finished. Alex held the door open. Catching a glimpse of escaping blonde hair, he suppressed a grin as he pulled the door closed.

He was hit with the smells of wet bodies, drying leather, and wool. All of that was overpowered by the noise of uncomfortable people trying to maintain their composure in an uncomfortable situation, and of crying, screaming children. He found a hook for his cape on the back wall, and was grateful for it. He hid his bags on the floor below, and made his way to the hot fire at the front of the room. The girls were busy taking orders and dealing with a distraught woman and her wailing children. Alex didn't know much about babies, and he wouldn't guess what this one needed, but she was surely exercising her lungs. The young, frustrated mother did not know where to turn, and if there was a father nearby, he was in hiding.

In seconds, Nina came out of the kitchen. She had taken off the greatcoat and wore a man's shirt with ruffled collar, leather breeches, and boots. The laces of the shirt were loose, and the sleeves were too long. Suddenly dizzy, he could see her curves and soft skin through the laces. The leather breeches hugged her hips. The room quickly became unbearably warm.

Nina took the baby out of the arms of the frantic mother. The youngster abruptly stopped crying. She silently motioned to the mother that she and the other children should follow her. They took the path from the tavern room through the

119

brewhouse. The silence they left behind was palpable, and everyone heaved a collective sigh of relief.

Alex wondered at the illusion of masculinity from the long coat, breeches and mud, and how that was reversed so totally by the sight of her in that ruffled shirt. He had vowed not to pursue this woman any further, but it took all his control not to make a fool of himself and follow that little parade out the door. At that moment, Sukie handed him an ale. He went back to a corner bench near his cape, to think. This was not the night for seduction and pleasure, so he assured himself that Nina was safe from him. He would bed down, right here in this public room, away from temptation.

***

Nina was wet. Tim's old coat had done well enough for a while, but once it was thoroughly wet there was no hope. The warm sweater was better, but the chill day was not cold enough for thick wool, so she had been uncomfortably wet and hot, and grateful to shed her things in the kitchen. She didn't expect to be devoured by Alex's gaze the moment she stepped into the room in that old shirt. She pretended not to notice.

Luckily, the screaming baby needed quiet, and she'd had an excuse to leave the taproom immediately. She brought the young mother and her other children in her private parlor, the cozy room outside her locked bedroom. Then she'd sent Mary to the attic for bedding, and got the family settled. She sent Mary back to the taproom and she went into her own rooms, tiptoeing past the tired children and their grateful mother.

"Hi Mr. Alex." Jack sat down and placed a plate of buttered scones between them.

"Thank you, Jack."

"The kitchen is very busy, dinner will be a while, but

120

cook made these for me."

"Well, I am grateful for your sharing." Alex took a bite. "So Jack, where do you live? How is it that you are still here? The horses seem settled."

"I live here. My Ma and I live in the white house on the other side of the brick brewhouse." He spoke slowly, carefully weighing the information.

Alex had good instincts about children and their stories. He had no reason to pry information out of the boy. Jack no doubt had been instructed not to tell strangers too much, as all children are told. That must be doubly true if you lived at a tavern. But Alex was greedy for information, and the best way was to play the role of school master. "So Jack, what are you studying in school?"

Jack's face lit up and he started listing his studies and the books he had recently read. "...and Mr. Conway says I may start Greek early if I continue to study Latin as carefully as I am now."

"Ah, I believe you mentioned that to your grandfather." Alex's thoughts made quick connections. Mather Tyrie's grandson, Nina's son. Ah. The boy at the beach, and the youngest child running with that group of boys through the fields and down the hill. Being carefully watched by Nina, by his mother. Oh.

"That is wonderful, Jack. I have done some Latin teaching myself."

"Really? Would you help me with a translation?"

"Of course." Jack was already across the room, and out the door toward the brewhouse. He was back in short minutes. His book was opened before he sat down.

In no time, the men were entranced by the writings of Tacitus. Alex listened to Jack's translation, making him recite the ancient words out loud as if the language still lived. "I have always believed," he said as Jack packed his book and a rough stylus back into his sack, "that we should attempt to speak the words of the writers, not merely consign them to the silence of history."

"Mr. Conway says the same things, but most of the boys ignore him, and do very poorly."

"I suspect you do better. Are there any girls in your school?"

"Yes, sir, there are. But mostly they don't do Latin. That's for the older boys."

Alex knew precisely what Jack meant, and nodded. It was clear that Jack had been singled out to learn the subject at his young age. The boy was unlikely to brag. It pleased Alex to meet a child so interested and enthusiastic about his studies, even if he didn't yet have the sense to avoid stupid dares.

Jack excused himself when Mary came over with a hearty stew, and Alex waved him off, letting him go. He hoped he would have another chance to talk to the boy. Nina Tyrie Bigelow certainly was full of puzzles and mysteries. There was no doubt that the core was getting more wonderful as he unraveled the strings. The stew was good, and he had not eaten since the day before, so he put his head down to avoid distractions and ate. Or so he tried.

He held his spoon suspended in the air, as Nina crossed the room toward him, a tankard in each hand. In spite of his intentions, he had known she was there the second she walked in. She worked her taproom like the perfect host, greeting people and checking on their dinners. The girls never stopped serving, but Nina seemed to have all the time to listen, and every diner had a story. She must have finished, because finally the only sound in the room was contented people eating.

He had dreamed of it, seeing her like this, coming toward him in the taproom. She was wearing a gray gown. It was long sleeved and rather plain, but her fichu was bright yellow with white embroidered daisies. She conjured up visions of sunshine coming through gray clouds.

"Hello." She smiled at him, put a fresh tankard on the table, and held out her hand to his, shaking it very competently. "It's nice to see you again. Alex, isn't it?" She smiled sweetly at him.

Alex felt like a toad and thought he must look like a hooked trout. He slammed his mouth shut. "Hi Nina, I've been traveling." He left unspoken that he'd thought of her, and dreamed of her.

"I noticed that you and my Jackie seemed to be lost in conversation. Somewhere in ancient Rome, if I were to guess. I was also told there was something I wasn't to ask about."

He almost asked a string of questions: Nina, did you think to keep a ten-year-old secret? Did you think I would turn and run at the sight of a child? Instead, he answered her question. "Yes we were quite lost in Tacitus. A vice of mine, he seems to have the same inclination." He had realized when talking to the boy that he was Nina's, but suddenly the enormity of having saved the child's life made him dizzy. This was Nina's son, the delightful product of that sad, brief marriage.

"Yes, mine." Nina nodded, acknowledging that she had not spoken of her child. "Alex, my nephews were unable to look me in the eye when they came back into the lane. And Jack, who tells me most everything, carefully avoided telling me what happened at the river. And then you use Tacitus to avoid answering my questions.

123

"True, you are quite correct. I'm afraid I am guilty as charged. Jack was reciting Socrates when I found him on that log. It was not a monologue I would wish for a ten year old."

"Ah, I've lived with these boys for a long time. So, I am going to posit that Jack, being the youngest of many boy cousins, took a dare he should not have, as he often has done. Considering the enormity of this storm, I suspect I owe you thanks for saving my son." She looked at him gratefully, thinking that pies could be damned, she would be dead or have, at best, two broken legs, and Jack would have been washed away, without this man.

Alex didn't want or need thanks. Actually, he felt embarrassed that he had helped the mother understand what the boys had been up to. He looked into aqua eyes, the only warm spot on this gray, stormy day. He was happy to save her. He felt he would rescue her, and hers, into eternity. He had never felt this way and did not understand it.

He had spent weeks trying to convince himself that dreams of Nina were products of simple desire. Given time, he would get over her. He would simply release her from his challenge. She would be free to live her own life, marry or not.

He pulled himself back into the taproom. "What happened at the river this afternoon was simply a dare. What older boys will suggest to tempt the younger ones into mischief. I did very little, just herded him back onto dry land." Alex gently took her hand in his, and looked into those summer's day eyes. They were as he remembered them, aqua and azure, but now glowed dark with concern. "Nina, why didn't you tell me about Jack ? You told me so much else."

"I don't really know." She smiled a little and shrugged. "I think the answer lies somewhere between not letting you get too close, and not wanting the existence of a child drive you away. That's not very clear, is it?"

Alex knew precisely what she meant. He felt closer to Nina than he should. It could break her if he died or was sent away. Yet he was unable to stay away from the tavern, from her. He admitted that if he owned his time, he would not stay away at all. He pulled her hand to his lips. After a kiss, he let his cheek rest in her palm. He expected her to pull away, as soon as the intimate moment ended. They were, after all, in a public place. She didn't. Instead, she took his hand from under the table and moved it to her cheek.

In a few moments, Nina took Alex's hand into her own and held it. It felt good to leave her hand in Alex's. His hands were warm and solid, and with hers nestled in his, she felt safe. All day she had soothed the frayed nerves of travelers, smoothed sheets on newly made guest beds, helped cook in the kitchen, and poured cold ale into cold tankards. On those rare occasions when someone did take her hand, it was to receive comfort from her.

She was used to it. She had helped care for her father-in-law during his last days. She had always been strong for Jack - now, it seemed, this man who appeared and reappeared offered more than an interesting challenge. He offered safety and comfort as well. Her instincts were to resist him. She managed well on her own. To take him up on the challenge would require only a sense of adventure, perhaps some bravery. But to accept comfort, she might find she needed it. What then?

"Alex, have you eaten?" He nodded and patted his stomach. Well, I haven't." She called to Dodi, and in seconds, a fresh plate of food appeared for the famished hostess, and two empty tankards were put on the table.

Nina disappeared, and reappeared holding a large bottle. It looked thicker and heavier than most bottled ales. He realized he had never seen bottles here.

"My latest attempt at a doppelbock." She poured the beer into the tankards, took a sip to sample, and smiled. She took a long draught and swallowed.

Alex followed suit, and before they knew it, they had finished most of the bottle. Nina motioned to one of her girls to bring another, and soon Alex was sure he would not mind sleeping on the floor, in this very corner. He took her hand and kissed her palm, breathing good wishes into it. It had been an extraordinary hour of comfortable silence.

The room was already changing into sleeping quarters, as many travelers pulled out their bedrolls or blankets and made-do on the hard floor, simply glad for the dry room and a strong roof.

"Sleep well, Nina."

"Thank you, Alex, you too." She squeezed his hand good-bye. She went into the kitchen to check on fires and servants, all of whom had given up their beds for a few coins and were sleeping in front of the kitchen hearth. Then she went into her house, tiptoed past the sleepers in her parlor, unlocked her door, and found her bed.

Alex woke to the sound of men's voices, the scraping sound of shovels, the smell of bread baking, and good coffee. He ran into the rain to the outdoor privy, finding the continuing bad weather a great incentive for hurrying. Then he dressed quickly in the taproom, now the bastion of men. The women, it seemed, had found beds in rooms elsewhere, presumably bunking together in the rooms upstairs.

He stayed in the taproom only long enough to learn that the bridge had been washed out when a huge tree had hit one of the pilings. The noise he heard was the local men at work.

They didn't expect to repair the bridge until the storm abated, but they wanted to salvage as much of the remaining bridge as they could. He downed his coffee and pulled his damp cape over his shoulders, then he went into the wet, to help the men remove bridge parts. They worked in a steady drizzle and light wind. Someone said the worst was over and pointed to blue sky overhead. An old man said the worst was yet to come. Alex knew enough to believe him.

Working as quickly as they could, they found bridge parts downstream and collected whatever could be reused. The larger timbers were completely gone, washed away during a deluge, after the initial hit. Someone had already sent to David Tyrie's mill for replacements. Hopefully, David either had the lumber or could make the cuts, but no one had hopes that the saw mill was open with the river this high.

The men set to clearing the broken tangle of bridge timbers, and the tree limbs, rocks and sand that had collected below the falls. It wouldn't do to have the debris causing further damage to the bridge or the wheels. When they had done all they could, they went inside for coffee and whatever else Nina Bigelow's kitchen had to offer.

From the men's chatter, Alex learned that most of them were related to each other and to Nina, either by marriage or blood. The Bigelows and their various in-laws seemed to make up most of the group, while the Tyries farmed to the east and worked at the sawmill.

There was an ongoing argument in the town about whether it was worth the time and expense to build a very good bridge. Big storms washed it out every year or two, no matter the quality. The issue had been brought to Town Meeting, but no money had been appropriated. So far, the town fathers had left the repair to the local farmers and mill owners who did the work.

He listened to their arguments. They had been made before, and did not require his attention. It seemed that at least three of the men he had been working beside were the husbands of Johnny Bigelow's sisters - the women who had been anxious for the sixteen year old Nina to marry their brother. Alex imagined strong arguments had been made for that, too.

By late afternoon, wet and tired, the men had salvaged what they could, and cleared what they could. Nothing could be finished until lumber and good weather, but a temporary bridge could be constructed with daylight the next day, if the storm abated. They were finishing their work when the storm came back with a vengeance. Tree limbs cracked like twigs; suddenly, the air was filled with bits of building. Most of the men ran back to their own homes. Alex and some of the others sought refuge back at the tavern.

A few travelers whose destinations were to the west had braved the afternoon's lighter rain and moved on, but those who had been heading to points east, north or south had stayed put. Now, with the second wave of the hurricane hard upon them, they were relieved to be indoors and safe at the sturdy, comfortable inn. Alex knew there was a route north of the river over marshy farmland to the post road. He looked out the windows into the increasingly gloomy evening. He wouldn't make a horse ride in such weather. He would likely break a leg in the wet ruts. The General was too good a horseman to ask that of him in exchange for paperwork. Tomorrow would be soon enough to get the dispatches to camp.

He was happy to spend another night at the *Wheel and Hammer*, even if it meant another night sleeping on the floor of the taproom. He left the shelter of the inn once more to check on Thorne. Crossing the muddy road, he slogged through a muddy stream that had formed in the lane, connecting the curves in the river. The wind pushed sheets of rain. Hit by leaves and twigs, he dodged larger bits of trees and building.

The short walk over, he slammed the door behind him, closing out the roar of rain and wind.

"Thorne old boy, sorry to have ignored you all day. But you do look better for a day off the trail." Jack must have been here again, and had done a good job on the stallion. Weeks of dirt were brushed from his coat, his hooves were clean, and there was fresh food in his trough. It was clear the boy was not afraid of either the storm or the skittish horse. On his way in, he had looked briefly at the other horses in the stable. They were all in fine shape, but none had been so favored. He expected young Jack had found a way to show off to his cousins that the high-strung stallion favored him, as he'd found a way to pamper his new friend.

"Hey Mister, mind if I take a minute?" Josh appeared from the tackroom where he had been working.

"Of course, what can I do to help?"

"You mentioned days on the trail - sorry, I didn't mean to eavesdrop, but I was just in the other room. Mind if I ask where you were?"

"Down the coast a'ways, and then back up north a'ways." It was Alex's standard answer for those who had no stake in his journeys.

"I see. Not going to be specific. I understand." Josh nodded at Alex and spent a moment staring at the gray stallion before he returned to the tack room with the stirrup he had been polishing. Alex shook off a strange feeling, as he had shaken off the chill rain. He gave Thorne his lump of sugar, and went back into the storm for the peace of the taproom.

Nina finished her day by making sure there was food for the last of the bridge crew. The stranded travelers had already eaten their dinners. She looked out the window for Alex, as she had done every few minutes. She didn't know if he had eaten, but she knew she was pretending she cared only because he had worked hard all day. It was more than that. Her staff tried to get her to rest, reminding her that they would be in the taproom to serve any hungry worker or straggler. Nina laughed at them. They had once again rented their bedrooms above the tavern to women stranded by the storm. The barmaids were happily expecting to sleep on pallets and blankets in the kitchen for a few extra coins.

"You girls are awful happy about sleeping on the floor. All these years I've been proud that I had quarters for you. If I'd known how happy you were to bed downstairs, I would have saved you the trouble and required that you sleep in the kitchen." Nina teased Dodi and Sukie. Mary had gone the short distance to her mother's house, during the lull in the storm.

The young women laughed at Nina's tease, understanding that she was the kindest mistress, and knowing that it was her kindness that allowed them to keep the coin they were getting for their rooms.

"Good night girls, I am for bed. Could one of you carry those buckets to the brewhouse for me?" Nina picked up two large wooden buckets of hot water and followed Dodi to the building next door. She thanked her and placed the buckets near the huge hearth and a small fire she had started there earlier. Then she pulled the old barrel she and Jack used as a bathtub to its spot near the hearth and poured hot water into it. She brought an empty bucket to the pump near the back door and mixed hot and cold in the tub till she was happy. Then she undressed and climbed into the warm water.

Nina bathed quickly. She was too tired to indulge, sure that she would fall asleep in the tub if she did. The day had been long. Tomorrow promised more of the same, and no matter how she felt about it, the problems were hers to handle. She soaped and rinsed before the water could cool, then washed her hair using the extra water in the kitchen buckets. She looked over the puddles and dirty clothes, sorting in her mind what needed to be cleaned away immediately and what she could leave till morning. Then, with a towel wrapped around her hair, and wearing only her shift, she went to the little house she shared with Jack and the small family now inhabiting her private parlor - a mother, two young children and the mewling, screaming infant.

Nina settled onto her bed, her eyes closing the minute she lay down in spite of the family on the other side of the door. The banging of a shutter woke her with a start. She rose to see if she could fix it from inside. As she feared, the only quick fix was to close the shutters and lock them closed, making the room unbearably stuffy. She could open the door to let in the windy air from the parlor, but if she did, she would disturb the small children and their mother, who were restless after spending a stormy day indoors.

Feeling like she would scream if she tried to lie still, Nina decided that she might as well finish her chores in the brewhouse as stay trapped in her bedroom. She tiptoed past the giggling children, and gave their mother a wry smile on her way back downstairs.

***

Alex waded through the rushing water that had once been a small path between buildings. He laughed back as the rain and wind whipped the hood from his head, and grabbed for his hat. He opened the door of the taproom. It was warm with the moistness that cooking and storm's dampness brought. The tables were filled with travelers who had been trapped inside for over a day, and although all of them were glad to be indoors and safe, the energy of the storm, combined with lack of activity, created high energy and a boisterous, mildly unhappy crowd.

As had become his habit, Alex scanned the room before stepping inside. Taking a last breath of the cool moist wind, he pulled the door closed hard behind him. He found his table, shook off his cape and hat, and hung them on the hook he had used the evening before. Although the room was smokey and still, it was a relief to be inside, away from the lashing wind. With the evening in front of him, he relaxed into his chair. He hoped the storm would have spent itself out by morning so damage could be assessed and repaired. So far the buildings here seemed to have withstood the worst of it, but even if everything stayed the way it was, there was going to be significant work to do.

Alex wished he could stay and commit himself to helping Nina with repairs. They both understood that previous commitments must supercede. He put his foot down on his bag beneath the table, reminding himself of his purpose. Reminding himself, he was here at the *Wheel and Hammer* entirely because of the hurricane.

An ale, and a plate of stew and cornbread, was placed in front of him. He nodded his thanks. The girls were busy, but Nina was nowhere to be found. No doubt she had gone to her bed and was soundly asleep. He wondered how long the food and drink would hold out if the storm did not let up. He had no high opinion that this rowdy group would have any sympathy, if the innkeeper found herself in short supply. Her girls were dealing easily with a room full of people who had decided to get as drunk as they possibly could. Alex noticed the staff were carefully collecting the coin before any ale was served.

He sipped his drink and turned to musing. He daydreamed of Nina sitting at this table with him, as for a while the evening before. He would put his arm over her shoulder and remove her fichu from her neck. He'd tease the soft skin over her neck. She'd turn to gaze into his eyes, lowering her lids and sighing with pleasure. There was no tension, no fear. The dream continued, and in a flash they were in a comfortable bed, Alex resting his hand on her hip as they lay on their sides. He imagined he could feel her soft skin and taste sweet lips.

His delightful daydream was interrupted by the crowd breaking into song. He had accepted that he would spend another night under the tables in the dark corner of the taproom. He had put his head down on his bag as he had the night before. The raucous crowd grated on his tired nerves, bringing on an exhausted tirade he almost let out.

Alex had found he could sleep anywhere. In many ways, it was the only thing that had made the last months bearable. Tonight that was not to be. It might have been the storm, but hard as he forced his eyes closed, he could not relax. In a minute, he would have to make a choice to either toss and turn, wide awake under that table all night, or punch that fellow who was singing and raising toasts to the General as loudly as he could.

Alex grabbed his saddlebags and eased out of the taproom toward the door leading to the stone brewhouse. The short passage was dark once the door was closed behind him, and he walked forward in silence following the dim light provided by a small fire.

He entered the cavernous room. A fire burned inside a great hearth that took up most of one side. He remembered the enormous brass and wooden fermenting kegs from his first peep. That day already seemed like lifetimes ago, and yet if he hadn't drunk Nina's fine ale, he might never have had the good sense to recognize that the alewife was his pretty blonde.

Somewhere in his lonely nights she had become "his Nina," but by morning he knew she wasn't his or anyone's. No matter his somewhat interesting skills with women, acquired in Italy and England - the last thing the young widow needed was to tie her life to another soldier.

Alex found a spot between the wall and a row of empty barrels to spread out his bedroll. He lit his travel lantern, and pulled out a book of Greek poems he had been translating. He left it open on his bedroll for later. He looked around and realized that alone with his lantern, he could explore the large and fascinating room. He assured himself that he could be very careful and would not knock anything over.

He jogged in place, working out the stiffness in his wounded leg. He walked over toward the shadows on the far side of the small fire. He smelled the soft scent of flowers and soap, quite unexpected in a brewhouse. In front of him was a large half barrel, full of water. It was still warm; it had been used very recently as a bath tub. On the floor within reach of the tub were wash cloths, a jar of soap, a brush and a few dry towels. There were wet ones too, neatly piled on one side.

Alex inspected the water. It felt warm and did not seem particularly dirty. He was a child of the country, fourth son among many children, and as such felt himself to be an expert on bath water and its reuse. He filled two empty buckets with water from the barrel, carefully skimming only the surface, where soap and dirt collected. He tossed the dirty water out a small door on the river-side of the building, into the rain. Then he poured one bucket of clean water that was sitting by the hearth into the barrel. He left another for rinsing.

He stripped and climbed in. Ah, pleasure! He rubbed his leg in the warmth, and injured muscles eased. Alex would have sat happily in warm water forever, and he relaxed into the water, rousing himself just enough to wash. When that small effort was over, he lay back to enjoy the rare treat of solitude, safety and warm water. The only sound was the rain on the roof of the brewhouse. He woke to strong fingers moving soft, sweet-smelling suds through his hair.

He smelled her. The sweet scent she wore, and the earthy and flowery perfume that was her essence and her work permeated his being. He inhaled her, felt his body react and harden. He didn't move, and just lay there trying to breathe, reveling in Nina, her hands on his scalp, her fingers in his hair.

He relived that morning at the shipyard, when she'd run her fingers so innocently through his hair, looking for blood or some other wound. She had been unaware, or seemed to be unaware, of the reaction that pushing her lovely body against his, running her fingers through his hair, had caused him. He didn't think she was unaware this time. He reached back as she ran a comb through his chaotic waves, took her hand and brought it to his lips. He lingered over her fingers with a slow kiss. He let her go and stepped out of the tub. The room was so dark she could not see more of him than the firelight caught. He dried himself with the towel she handed him, giving her time to utter a simple goodnight and leave. She didn't.

"Nina?" All his good intentions - his vow that he would

not hold her to his ridiculous challenge, that he would leave her free, would not interfere with her decisions or stubborn convictions, let her grasp at fate, all of it - simply flew away.

She said nothing, but simply stared back into his firelit eyes. Her hands still held the comb in front of her. What little light there was from the small fire haloed her hair and body in the gentle glow. Alex swallowed. He could not see her face now, could not read her eyes. He heard what might have been a deep sigh. He found his breeches, pulled them on and lay down on his bedroll between large wooden kegs, and waited.

Nina lay down next to him. He kissed her softly. She lifted her lips to his and relaxed into him. Alex put his arms around her, pulling her close. He could feel her soft curves molded into him. She put an arm over his chest, her head on the indent between ribs and shoulder, her fingers on the back of his neck.

Alex lay on his back, enjoying the feeling of Nina's body close, curled into him. He was exhausted. Days in the saddle and nights on the hard, wet ground, and then a day battling the river to save whatever they could for the rebuilding, had worn his injured body to the edge. But he would do whatever she wanted, or needed.

She must also be exhausted as well. She had spent two days dealing with the storm and its effects. She had been in the rain, helping travelers off their horses and into safety. She had cooked and helped serve. She had mopped the wet off the stone floor so no one would slip. She had soothed nerves and quieted screaming babies. He moved over as far as he could to make room for her, but she did not uncoil from his side. Slowly, he felt her drift off, her breathing becoming deep and even. Alex smiled, happy that she slept. He knelt, climbing onto his knees, ready to carry her to her bed. He stopped when he remembered that he had no idea where that would be.

In other circumstances he would explore her little house, but Nina had moved mothers and babies there as a way to keep the children away from the cold, wet and noise of the inn and taproom. It would be comic and dangerous to climb over sleeping children to find her room – carrying a half dressed woman, asleep in his arms. He lay back on his narrow bedroll. Nina curled back into his side, her head gently pillowed on his chest. He wrapped her in his arms, holding her against the storm that raged around them, against whatever fears and loneliness haunted her dreams.

Alex lay on the hard stone floor, loving the softness of Nina softly curled along his body, the soft murmurs of sleep and the gentle rising and falling of her breathing. She hadn't shown a moment of weakness since he had met her - the pillar of strength to her staff and her son, keeping all the facets of her life functioning perfectly. She wouldn't want him in it, creating disorder in her organized life.

He stared upward into the dark shadows. Her staff was good, but it was Nina who held this tavern and inn together, and it was not just her skill and willingness to work hard. There was a depth to her. It pulled people to her, it made her staff want to do the hard work, just as it pulled him to her. She was responsible for so much; it would be terrible if his presence, or absence, became another burden.

He thought about the brilliant and compelling man he had met at the wedding. He wondered if Nina knew how like her father she was in that quiet, commanding way. He had spoken with Dr. Tyrie only during that brief luncheon, but Alex knew it was the hard skills learned from the parents, not the kindly ones from the father-in-law, that benefitted her here, and kept this lovely inn afloat against all tides, and against all deluges and rushing rivers.

He had been raised in a world as secure, and safe against the storm as this one, in these same hard New England ways, deep in the White Mountains of New Hampshire. His parents had farmed their piece of the tiny mountain valley and raised five sons and two daughters to adulthood, losing only one babe to the measles that swept through, when he was five.

The boys had contributed by hunting and fishing the dark woods and quick streams, the girls by sewing, cooking, gardening and teasing their brothers. The region was too steep, and the winters too long, to create surplus or ease, but life was good.

Like all New England towns, no matter how remote or sparely populated, there had been a school master beating knowledge into children, as stone cold and hardheaded as the granite mountains around them, or so Elihu Davenport had said. He was a Yale man, and so when Alex showed more promise than most, "although not as much as he'd need," his parents had agreed to let him travel over the mountains and down the Connecticut River to New Haven, to complete his education. After Yale, he had worked and traveled through a world newly safe at the end of seven long years of war.

He had enjoyed France and the southern countries, where he traveled as the most raw tourist. In England, his base during his travels, he had felt alternately at home and alienated - happy to be a part of a great empire, but a lost, angry, lesser cousin of it. There were days he dressed as a gentleman, and days when he, like many young Americans in London, dressed in deerskin fringe and homespun breeches, a worn leather tricorn jauntily set on his head.

He returned to America in 1771, a year after the event dubbed the Boston Massacre. He had settled back into the mountains, to a teaching position at the new Indian College in Hancock. It had felt like a good fit. He reveled in the students' expectant enthusiasm, even their recalcitrance. But the call to the cause of liberty had been too strong to resist after the battles in April, so he'd abandoned his students to other teachers and come to Boston to fight for a cause larger than his own. So far, that decision had left him with an aching leg and a bag of damp dispatches.

In time, the wind howling against the shutters and rain assaulting the slate roof created a backdrop to Nina's soft breathing. Alex closed his eyes and allowed himself to drift off, warm and comforted by the woman, his pretty blonde, Nina, curled against him in the dark, stormy night.

Alex wasn't sure what actually woke him. It was dark, hours before the late summer dawn would even begin to lighten the clouds. Nina's legs were wrapped around his hips; her breasts, through the thin shift, were near his mouth for kissing. It was a delicious dream, her body rubbing against his, soft purrs and moans coming from the sleeping woman. By the time he woke fully, he was suckling her breasts. His hands gripped her buttocks, holding her hard against him.

It was hardest thing he ever did - harder than firing on unknown redcoats or hunting a wolf in deep snow. Careful not to wake her, he lifted her gently, and put her chastely back on the bedroll. She turned, and her arm fell across his chest, instinctively caressing hard flat muscles and smooth flesh. He lay back to relish the moment, a wonderful way to be awakened. He felt alive and happy. He almost turned and put her away from him again, but remembered a promise and a challenge he had offered on a hot summer's day.

He thought about how to make sure she would not be frightened, or curl into a ball like those little curly bugs he and his siblings played with, in the spring. He pushed the image of the sow bugs away, smiling at the funny thought.

Sweet Nina, so beautiful and soft. She lay entwined in him, her arm over his chest, touching him. He let his hand wander to her hip, learning the feel of her, smelling her essence, absorbing her. Gently, he rose. He'd dreamed of pillows, feathers, even silken rope, but none of that was available in this hard workroom of wood, brass and iron hooks. In the dim light he found a small bottle of oil he had purchased in New York, optimistic for this very moment. He went to the hearth and put the glass in the dying embers, blowing on the kindling to make a small flame.

Nina was dreaming. It was wonderful, more vivid than anything she had dreamed before. She felt a drop of something hot on the skin between her breasts. The smell was exotic and heady, spices and orchids. Alex pulled her chemise from her shoulders, released her arms, and placed more drops on her stomach. The heat grew. He kissed her breasts, suckling and kissing, tonguing until she stiffened and relaxed into him. He did the same to the other. Nina felt strong hands spread the scented warmth over her neck, her shoulders, her breasts, her stomach.

She heard herself moan, and felt her breathing quicken. With each breath she inhaled the spicy, musky scent. In her dream, Alex was suckling at her breasts. No one had touched her there since the baby was weaned. Johnny had kissed them once or twice - she had liked it, but it was never like this. Nina lay back, lost in scent and sensation.

Nina felt loose, like a rag-doll, as Alex rolled her over. She felt deprived, needy, but then she stretched out, her arms over her head. She felt warm oil dropped onto her back, along her spine. This was no dream. She realized she was wide awake, and she had no intention of stopping this amazing night. She imagined Alex, his granite gray eyes, and warm smile, and how he must look, very pleased with himself, if she had the strength to turn around and look, if there was light enough to see. He might be very pleased - his challenge was moving along well. Certainly she had no will to refuse him. She had no idea if she could beg, or what she would beg for.

He rubbed warm oil onto her inner thighs. She lifted her buttocks, rising on her knees in response.

Alex was lost in her moans and little sounds as she cried out for completion. He wanted to join with her, replace his fingers in the worst way, but his torture was glorious. He understood, knew at his marrow, he would slay dragons for this woman. His pounding cock was nothing.

Nina wanted to die - she was so overwhelmed with sensation, all the discomfort she had felt and remembered. She squirmed to make him stop, make him understand that she hated these feelings.

Then he turned her toward him, holding her body close to his, his hand still between her legs, teasing and rubbing needy moist flesh. He leaned to her and suckled her breasts, scattering kisses until he reached her mouth. Nina opened her eyes to his, and her mouth to his kiss. She fell back as he used her moisture to rub the center of her sensations, murmuring that she should fly. She did. Alex held her, continuing to speak softly to her as she cried out, and then shattered into a

141

thousand pieces, her body wracked with pleasure.

Nina woke at dawn's light in Alex's arms. For a minute she thought again that it had been a dream. She had dreamt many times of Alex in her bed. This one had been very different. It hadn't ended in the undefined pleasure he promised on that dry summer day, but in dramatic sensation.

She was covered by Alex's linen bedroll. She peeked under the linen; she wore no clothes. Alex still wore his smallclothes. He had fulfilled that strange promise he had made in the seductive warmth of summer. She smiled over at him, remembering his soft words, reminding her of the soft summer breeze of the Parkers' rose garden. He'd murmured in her ear, of heavy fecund roses so like her breasts, of sweet petals opening in the sun, as his mouth worshiped her flesh. She blushed with the half memory. She had floated in pleasure and scattered like wind swept rose petals. She didn't understand it - it was a new and raw feeling, but certainly not a horrible one.

Nina stretched, and looked into Alex's eyes, smiling over at her in the half-light of the still stormy dawn. Lightly she kissed his lips. "Alex, go back to sleep, I need to check on things." She climbed out of their nest. He felt the cold and empty space where she had lain, but closed his eyes for a few more minutes. He hoped she had not noticed the passion and need in his eyes. He hoped that the night's interlude would allow her to move on, to take the risks that life requires, to find and love a man. Not him, not a soldier. He groaned, and put his arm over his eyes to block the thought, and the day.

By the time he woke there was a strong fire spread along the large hearth, and his clothes were clean and drying in the heat, neatly hung on a line. He found a shirt and breeches that were at least half dry, and dressed. He remembered wearing linen breeches when he held Nina in his arms. That same pair was now hanging near a barrel, drying at the fire. It was too bad, really, that he didn't remember Nina pulling them over his hips. He checked his bag for his papers. They were untouched. He threw the saddlebags over his shoulder and headed toward Nina's house. He smelled maple syrup and fresh ground coffee beckoning from the direction of the kitchen.

"Good morning, lovely lady." Alex walked into the room. He looked around quickly, taking in all Nina's treasures, and smiled.

"I thought it would be nice to eat over here instead of in the crowded inn." Nina scurried around the room, putting out hot coffee and warmed syrup and then ran back to flip the cakes on the grill.

"You are absolutely right, the quiet is a treasure." He listened for a minute. "Has the wind actually abated? I thought we were in for forty days and nights."

"Yes, I think it's moving out of here, but don't jest. My grandfather Tyrie used Noah to threaten us. Said our behavior was just this side of debauched. He became so involved in it one time, that Father and Mother actually rolled their eyes at him." Nina laughed as she put out cups and silverware.

"Whatever sinning you may have done as a youngster, you have done penance. And speaking of that, thank you for my laundry. That trail-soiled, muddy-mess should secure your place near the throne." Alex sat at the table and took the mug of hot coffee. Gratefully, he drank. "You have, as well, saved me the untold misery of having to wash it myself."

"Happy to help a lonely traveler." She nodded at the saddlebags. Her face dropped into seriousness. She hadn't

143

looked inside those bags. She hadn't needed to guess where he had been these past weeks, to know his work was important. Her problems and desires were insignificant. "Alex, you know it is always nice to see you, as you pass through on your way. You are always welcome. I would like to ease your burdens. I hope I don't present one to you."

Alex looked up at Nina over his coffee. She had quickly busied herself around the room, setting things out, the milk the sugar, the syrup. He was speechless. "No, you could never be a burden. You are a port in a storm. This week more literal than metaphorical."

He was connected to this woman, he wouldn't deny it. Under any other circumstance, he would say the things that should be said. He could tell her that she was beautiful, that he desired her tremendously, would love her forever, happily kill or die for her. But these were not such circumstances. He had a saddlebag of papers that could change the course of the British Empire. And he had agreed to move into a town occupied by a force that would be happy to hang him, if they discovered who he was.

He could not promise to be alive, not in a month, not in a year. That was the nut. A normal infantryman might promise to try to stay alive. He might not succeed, but he could try to be smart and careful, do his best to keep his musket clean and his feet and powder dry. Not him - he had volunteered for an assignment for which there would be no forgiveness asked, or granted. He was going to assume a role, and as that person he would steal and connive information from his enemy, as he pretended to be their friend. Then, against all known law he was going to give it to his real friends - those on the other side of the armed boundary.

He could not ask any woman to wait for him, to worry about him, especially not Nina.

He ate the syrup-covered corncake, each bite weighting him to the chair, pulling him toward safety, reminding him of home. "I'll need to leave soon, the rain is finally stopping. I can't wait for the bridge to be finished. As soon as it's dry overhead, safer for the horse, I'll head north around the lakes to the Post Road."

He wished he could stay and help engineer the new bridge, help with the shutters and roof shingles that would be missing after a storm like this one. But that would be wishing for a different life, one that was not his, just as Nina could not be his. He would never forget the feel of her in his arms, her voice, her kindness, her strength.

"Alex, you can take that route," Nina's voice interrupted Alex's thoughts, "but remember, the water level is going to be very high in the swamps around the lakes. I would take the Weston Road straight north to the Post Road. It makes a detour to the west, but the river will be less of a problem that way." She looked out the window. "You don't need to leave yet, do you?" She sounded almost frightened.

Alex groaned from simple animal need. He pulled her onto his lap, covering her mouth with his. Quickly, Nina's hands pulled at his queue, running her fingers though his hair as if to memorize every curl and unruly wave. His head pounded that this was a mistake, that he should let her go, stake no claim on her. He had fulfilled his promise. He had to let her go.

He could not do it. There had been a plea in her voice, she had almost begged him to stay, yet she was too wise to ask him for promises he could not give. They sat at the table, staring into coffee cups.

145

These last minutes together, Nina wanted to talk to Alex, to savor simple conversation, something to remember in later years, when the memory of his touch began to fade. She hunted her mind for a topic that would not cut too close to their parting, remembering something she had meant to ask about when she had first learned his name. "Alex, how is it you're named for a warrior hero? Alexander is not very common in New England."

He smiled with the memory and looked up from his cup. "My father got tired of the names my mother was using for us. My brothers are Tobias, Abe, and Sam. He told me he wanted to use something from another part of the world. He chose Alexander. I always thought that was why I gravitated toward the classical world, and had to travel.

"What about you? Nina is not exactly common outside Italy or Spain."

"I am not named for a person." She giggled, a sound he had never heard her make. It bubbled up naturally. A delightful noise. "I am named for a boat, Columbus's ship. Remember? The 'Nina, the Pinta, and the Santa Maria'? My father teased me, he said I was a Roman Pagan, a Papist. I redeemed myself by naming my horses Arbella and Jewel. Ships' names, but Winthrop's Puritan ships." She smiled at the notion. "But I do think the name Nina inspired me to explore when I was young." Alex nodded that there was time - she should go on, and please tell him the stories that had made her.

"I am the youngest. The boys were all given biblical names, and my sisters are Verity, Prudence, Constant and Mercy. The day before I was born, my mother was helping my older sisters with their reading on Columbus's voyage to America. She says that I kicked her especially hard at that section, so she chose the name Nina. If I'd been a boy, I suppose I might have been Nino or Cristoforo. That would really have been a shock to Father's congregation at the First Church."

Alex laughed, recognizing outright the surprise that would have caused, and the unlikelihood of those names in a traditional New England family. "Maybe my mother guessed that her youngest would never sit still, or maybe the name cursed me, but whenever I could I would grab a musket and go adventuring. I didn't go far, but I was often out for hours, pretending I was voyaging to distant lands, with strange people and animals. I didn't hunt, but I did see a wild dog one time. That was why I had the musket. It was David's idea that I should know how to shoot. He taught me when I was eight."

"Not too many girls learn to shoot here in civilized Newton. I assume Verity, Prudence, Constant and Mercy are all conventionally happy? Do they live in the area? Did I meet any of your sisters at the wedding?"

"I imagine you did. Pru and Connie were there. Pru had the baby you sat near at lunch. Verity lives on Cape Cod. Mercy, her husband Ben, and their babies died of fever when I was eighteen. They had moved to Vermont, so their loss was not so painful." Nina let her story trail off. There was no need to finish, it was a story too common, and understood by all. Alex gripped her hand, sharing her grief for a moment.

Nina got up and refilled their coffee cups. She poured more of the corn mixture onto the hot griddle to cook. Alex noticed the cakes' sizzling was finally louder than the rain, but it was still wet enough outside to make travel unpleasant. Nina followed his gaze out the window. There was still little to see but streams of endless water.

He sighed, sitting back in his chair. "Nina, I should go back to the inn. I shouldn't be here alone with you. I know the

147

weather has kept the neighbors away, but what if the other guests talk, your tavern girls? They must gossip. Will they know where you spent the night?"

"No one will care and if anyone did, he could never guess where I spent the night, in my parlor, kitchen, or the extra room in my attic. My reputation can't be harmed, you see. I should explain - can't be harmed further. No one knows what to make of me no matter what I do. The Bigelows know the truth. Neighbors don't care, they know I am a good person. But some people, folks who don't know me, don't stop by for an ale or dinner, believe that my Jack is old John Peddleman's son, not Johnny's. Newer folks never met Johnny, they don't believe he existed, don't see how I could be a widow. They see a young woman alone with a child, practically living with an old man.

"I don't blame them for what they think. I should have gone home to my parents after Johnny didn't return. I waited and waited, insisting that he would come home. Then I started brewing for my child's inheritance. Anyway, I just couldn't go home. I'd made such a statement about wanting to leave and be married." She got quiet and her thoughts seemed to drift. "It's lucky that Jack takes so strongly after me, and Johnny's sweet, blue-eyed, blonde mother, Joanna. Lucky, he has none of that dark Scots in him. Johnny was not pale, but he did have his mother's eyes." Nina kept talking.

Alex wondered if she had she really kept all this to herself, this anger at being thought a loose woman, widowed at sixteen. The tension was well hidden. Had she had anyone to talk to all these years?

"Of course I won't remarry, and that makes folks uneasy. The forge-boys think I've a man somewhere. They just haven't seen him. Otherwise, of course I would have said 'yes' to one of *them* by now. That's part of their vanity." She shrugged, feeling lighter for the telling.

She served the corn cakes and more syrup. They ate and drank for a while in a silence, heavy with everything they could not say. Finally Nina spoke into her cup, her words almost completely drowned out by the lighter but still-steady rain. "Alex?" She sounded so serious, he looked up from his plate. "I needed to tell you that I wished I had been the willing widow you expected that night."

Alex almost choked. He wanted to pull her back into his lap, to whisper into her ear. Finally he found the air to speak. "Nina, I know, and cannot blame you. I know, this morning I might have seemed disinterested, but please, never confuse restraint with lack of desire." He moved away from the table and sat on the low bench along the wall. Nina sat next to him, letting her head fall onto his shoulder, her arm around his chest.

Nina was sad she had dozed through so much of this morning's pleasure, and had not taken the time to touch him, really touch him, to learn him. She craved that knowledge. He was a beautiful man, but he was not the healthy man she had met two months ago. Camp food and weeks on the trail had taken their toll on him, and he had lost some bulk since she had first met him.

Nina didn't know if such feelings toward him were maternal, or something equally primal. They made her want to care for him, to feed him, to help him regain the strength he had lost since his battle wound. He had become dear to her, she would admit that much, though she knew she might never see him again. His gray eyes, still as granite, jumped with energy. He was ready to undertake his next task. She must never make her longings his burden.

The door banged open, letting in a stream of mist and light rain as Jack flew into the room.

"Ma! You in here?" Nina pulled away, as Alex dropped her hand.

"What's wrong, Jack?" She read fear and anger in her young son's eyes.

"Josh is showing Thorne to those Englishmen, the men the Committee told him to avoid. They just rode up now that it's mostly stopped raining. He has Thorne out of his stall. The stallion is nervous, and the men are examining him. Ma'am, it scares me." He shuffled his feet, trying to keep his words polite in front of company.

Alex looked from mother to son, seeing the same look of concern in the same eyes. "What is going on that I don't understand about my horse?" A jolt of fear passed through him.

Nina spoke before Jack could confuse the man with ten-year-old logic. "I was hoping it wouldn't amount to anything. Alex, a few weeks ago, Josh was outside talking to two men. They seemed intensely interested in discovering if he had cared for a particular gray horse. When Josh had only a vague memory, they asked Jack. Of course he had no idea, and honestly said so. When they caught up with me, I told them we had seen many grays here and told them to leave." She looked at Alex, wanting to plead for his safety, but unsure where that would be.

She looked away. The second round of corn cakes were brown at the edges. She focused her full attention on the fire as she put the cakes on a plate and brought them to the table. She let them cool, trying to think how to explain to Jack that the men were trying to catch Alex through his horse.

"Alex, why do those men want your horse?" Jack poured syrup on a cake and took a bite.

"It's Mr. Peele, Jack." Nina was glad she could find something to correct.

Jack turned to his mother with a nod and a shrug.

Alex watched the interchange between mother and son. It was healthy and affectionate, reminding him briefly of his life long ago. He nudged himself to leave before he lost his resolve and stayed forever. "Jack, those men were hired by a fellow who is trying to stop the Americans. They think if they destroy my work it will help the King win this war. Do you understand?"

Jack nodded. "Yes, sir. I think so."

"Do you think you could get Thorne to come to you, and lead him around to the back of your house, here" - he motioned to the back door - "away from the inn? If you can't find his saddle without Josh noticing, I'll ride without it."

"Yes, sir, I can do that." Jack was off at a run, his mouth full of pancake.

"I have more maple syrup if you want." Nina reached for a clay bottle and handed it to Alex.

He poured syrup on his corn cake and another drop on his finger. He licked it and pulled Nina to her feet, covering her mouth with his. He tasted of sweet maple and Alex. Nina pulled him to her, thinking she must never forget the feeling of him.

The sound of hoofbeats reminded them that their interlude in the midst of the hurricane was now over.

Alex didn't want to say these words, but he could not ride off in silence. "Nina, it may be months, it may be forever. Don't expect me. Don't worry, I have chosen this path, and I must see it through. He brushed her lips with his as he turned and stepped out the door. He raised his head and shoulders, assuming a military bearing. "Jack, you found my saddle, thank you so much." He mounted the gray, keeping his eyes on the boy and not the silent mother. "Keep studying your Latin. I expect great improvement when I see you again. If you have any questions your schoolmaster cannot answer, ask your Grandfather Tyrie, I expect he knows as much Latin and Greek as anyone in the Province." He wanted to admonish the boy to take care of his mother, but that was presumptuous. Of course he would. He always had.

Chapter 10

The ride from the Lower Falls required pulling Thorne out of puddles they both would rather have avoided. The destruction was enormous, and Alex felt quietly humbled to be alive. He passed more than one house that had simply been lifted off its foundation by the wind or the gushing water. There were random roof shingles and clapboards lying everywhere in the road. Church steeples lay tipped and broken, sometimes blocks from their churches. Streets had simply turned to streams and flooded houses, fields and stores. Autumn crops ready to be picked, and hay fields ready to be harvested, lay broken and sodden.

The destruction was bad at the falls, and on his way down the Post Road, but it became clear, as he headed east, that the destruction would be worse - much worse - near the coast.

Nina went back to the brewhouse to clear away the remnants of her night with Alex before anyone else noticed the disarray. She needn't have worried. The linen bedroll was gone with its owner, as were all his washed clothes.

Chapter 11

Alex returned to camp, as ready as he ever would be to move into rooms in Boston and assume the role of himself, the American in London, now seeking safety in the British-run town. He pushed the days of storm spent safe at the *Wheel and Hammer* out of his mind, along with those persistent questions to which there were no answers. To become that man, he'd need a new wardrobe. That meant he'd need the means to buy one. He set out to gamble just enough to win what he needed.

As so many had before him, he won when he did not drink. He did not drink. By the time the order was given to leave camp for his new life, he was ready, heart and wardrobe, with some extra cash in hand.

For those last day in camp he avoided Wythe and all the young man's friends. He had no intention of leaving hints of where he had been during those days and nights of the storm. The only exception was a note he left with a quiet man whom no one knew well. The soldier, older than most, kept his counsel and could be trusted to keep secrets. The note gave instructions for delivering his horse, and a large wooden crate full of memories he would not wish on his mother, to Nina at her inn – if he should fail to return.

Secure that his things would be safe, he said a silent good-bye to camp life. He would not return here. At the end, this project would have succeeded or failed. If it succeeded, the camp would be packed up and gone by the time of his return. If he failed, he would have been hanged as a spy. He explained what he could to Thorne, asking him please to behave for his next owner. A sense of finality hung over him.

His waiting came to an end when verbal orders to report to the checkpoint at Roxbury came through. The trip in the back of a wagon around from Cambridge though Brookline was good, and he was able to shake the feeling of despondency that had come with inactivity, and from missing a woman he was steadily trying to convince himself he had no right to miss. Warm, moist air from the end of summer had been replaced with cool autumn air, as always happens in war or peace. The brisk northwest wind gave him the jolt he needed.

Soldiering was alien to Alex. He had not joined the local militia because of his youth at the time of the last war. At the right age, peace had come, and he had gone away to school and traveled. As a schoolmaster, and then as a teacher at the college, there had been only small, local militia, nothing that constituted what he considered soldiering. The task that lay before him was different, and would be interesting. Being a displaced scholar? That was real. Becoming a social chameleon? That was close to what he had been all those months in London. As for collecting information from men who did not know they were giving it, ferreting out secrets had been his hobby since boyhood.

He caught a ride on a wagon delivering firewood, and was dropped in Roxbury at the *George*, a small public house not far from the former governor's mansion. It was right where the Americans – guarding the countryside from British attempts to break out of Boston – met the British trying to control the neck and keep an American invasion out.

The tavern had a few tables in the public room, and rooms upstairs for the owner and his family. In the main room, Alex met General John Thomas, commander of the American line at Roxbury neck. The General used the tavern as his field office. Thomas was a physician who had begun his army career as a surgeon, but during the last war he chose to assume command and had given up his surgery. As the men shared a meal, Thomas gave him an idea of what sorts of information would be most helpful.

"Mr. Peele, we pretty well know what is going on in there. The rumors of mass execution that brought half the countryside to the neck were easily proved to be false. But let me tell you, getting people to believe their instincts are false, once they have hold of the tail of an idea, is very difficult, and we had a devil of a time getting them all to go home.

"The young redcoats on the inside of this line are jumpy because of it, and that does not make our life easier on our side. Forgetting that, we need to know the mood of the high command - when they plan to make a move, what maps they are using or requisition, when, and if, they intend to evacuate, if they would burn the town, and so on. I heard you have some experience with uppity British aristocrats?"

Alex smiled and nodded, remembering his months in London, his life with Carlotta's family, his experience at horse races and gaming hells. "So, you'd like me to convince them that your men are here in the hundreds, and they are ready to pour over the neck at the least provocation? Or should I hint that you and your men generally lack ideas, that you and General Washington are frustrated with the countryside, that you command morons and dullards?" The General laughed. He seemed to enjoy the break.

They spoke long into the afternoon. Whichever story he chose to tell would be fine. It would be his job to count troops and document activity within Boston, to become familiar with the high command at their leisure, in the coffee houses, and at the gaming tables. If possible, he was to finance the project with his own winnings, but he should never be perceived to be a pauper. If necessary, he could go to Cambridge for additional funds. He should, if possible, help patriots trapped by their activities in the town. And most important, he should be careful not to get caught. If he were, no one on the outside would ever have heard of him. He nodded that he understood.

Before he joined the throng of refugees waiting to enter Boston, he walked around the small town of Roxbury, to breathe the air of the countryside one last time. The area had fine houses and rich farmland that in good years supplied the large town with its produce. Now, the harvest was in, and the fields were cut and bare, ready for next spring's crops, ready for the snows of winter. Alex laughed, almost surprised to realize that not all life stopped because there was a military conflict, with battles, war and death only feet from a corn field or pumpkin patch.

But just beyond these fields were signs of battles yet unfought. The Americans, ready for a British attempt to break out and overrun them, had built redoubts into the hills that surrounded the town and into the bay at the south of the neck. With these, and the redoubts he knew so well at Cambridge and further north along the coast, the little peninsula that contained the town of Boston was truly surrounded.

The British had created their own boundary to keep the Americans out. Men 'o War, the enormous vessels of the British Navy, blockaded the harbor. A series of mudwork and brick walls had been constructed by Royal Engineers to keep out an invasion from the countryside. Alex counted three of these imposing fortifications and entrenchments, from Roxbury to Boston along the neck, as he followed the crowd trudging down the long road. To his side, he saw armed flat boats in the bay and along the river banks. So not only was the town under siege from without, it was well armored from within.

Alex was one in a long line of walkers, riders, carts and wagons, all waiting to pass through the gates into the security of the well-guarded town. All were refugees from their local "Committees of Safety" and Patriot neighbors who were ready to burn or seize the property of a suspected Tory. He pushed their fear and misery out of his mind, and concentrated on becoming the false, new Alex Peele.

Getting through the British line was even more onerous than the American. The American checkpoint, set up to prevent the British Army from marching into the countryside, had no real interest in preventing loyalists access to Boston. A bribe of money or semi-valuable object was all it took to get through. The British Army didn't care that the refugees were loyal Englishmen. They were all just hungry mouths. Food lines were nearly impossible to maintain with the Americans blocking the roads, and the navy could not get enough money or support from Parliament to bring in enough food by ship. But even among his enemies he saw that kindness prevailed, and as long as these refugees could prove their distress, they were allowed to enter.

Alex had prepared his story. A tutor at the college in Cambridge, he had lost students when his political inclinations were discovered. Later, someone had tried to burn his small house. After that, he packed his few books and clothes, and here he was seeking refuge in a town already overburdened with refuge seekers. He understood, and was very sorry, but he had nowhere to go.

Once they let him past the interview, he fell in with some fellow walkers from Milton. They had sold their house and most of their belongings at a forced sale to neighbors, and were going to stay with family. They had cousins with property in Barbados and intended to sail as soon as they could book passage.

As the last of his group went off to meet family or long-lost friends, Alex found his way to a list of rooms to let, and by evening he was living on Queen Street near the Revere Hardware Store. He had met the father a few days before his first courier ride south. The generous man had given excellent advice about long rides. He would not tell Revere Junior who he was, but he was sure he would need a new key, a blade, or perhaps a friend, before the winter was out.

***

Nina was weary after days of wind and rain - days and nights of finding food and caring for scared travelers, crying children and anxious parents - and saying what felt like a final good-bye to Alex. After the storm moved north and away, the rain and wind stopped, and the inn and stables had emptied out. Nina took a long breath and closed the *Wheel and Hammer*. Later she heard that thousands had perished in boats, and along the coast from Georgia to Maine, during the storm. She said a prayer of thanks that her hostelry had held and had kept all her staff, family and guests safe.

With the taproom and inn closed, Nina and the bar maids spent days cleaning every bit of mud and clay from the floors, walls and windows. They washed every sheet, aired every blanket and wiped the last thin layer of dust from the tables. When the inn, outside and in, met with Nina's approval, she was ready to confront the low supplies.

"Sukie and Dodi, come with me to the fermenting tanks, we need to see what we can bring up. Even if the brew is closer to small beer than table ale, we'll have to bring it up.

There is almost nothing left." Nina was afraid her reputation might suffer, but after the week she had just had, she was ready to laugh that off. Hadn't she told Alex she had no reputation to worry about? Of course, that was of a different sort.

The three women climbed down the ladder that led to the fermenting room below the brew house. Nina heard her helpers whispering as she stepped off the ladder. She lit the lanterns along the wall, but it wasn't necessary. The room was nearly empty. The kegs had already been brought back up to the brewhouse, chalked and tapped. There were only a few barrels of small beer in the corner, and nothing else. The men working on the bridge repair - men from the forge across the road - were so used to bringing up the large kegs that they had done so many times over the past few days, without telling Nina. Bridge crews and the thirsty guests hadn't any interest in drinking the small beer, and few drinkers wanted cider. It would have been nice if someone had thought to tell her.

She led the way up the ladder, mumbling something Sukie and Dodi heard as thumbscrews and nettles. She turned to them as they walked back into the tavern. "You'll serve cider. I know it's not hard yet, not even slightly. I don't care." It sounded to the young women like she might cry, but they simply nodded. "Just feed anyone who complains. That's assuming we can get food to serve." They rolled cider barrels to the front of the room, then Nina sent the girls off help Mrs. Cotton in the kitchen.

The day was close, hot and sticky, one of those early autumn days that can't shed the heat of summer, not a good day to heat the brick-lined room with the fires necessary for brewing. She forced herself to accept it. She unlocked the storeroom off the brewhouse where the precious hops and malt were kept. She stepped inside and examined her stores.

Rainwater ran out of drenched bags and along the floor. What should have been crisply dry hops and perfectly malted barley was molding, sprouting hops and wet barley. She groaned, collapsing into the wet on the hard, polished fieldstone floor.

It was unfair. She had done everything she could to keep the inn running. She had poured all her energy, poured her life into it for over ten years. Now, after keeping strangers fed and safe during the worst storm in memory, after hosting the community of local workers as they put a washed-out bridge together, after saying good-bye to the only friend she felt she had in the world, watching him leave to pursue what was undoubtedly to be a very dangerous mission, she was left with a leaking roof and soaked-through supplies.

She lost track of how long she cried. It must have been a while, because she was tired and hungry when she was finished sobbing herself out. Resolved to do something more than just cry, she went to her own house, grabbed some food and washed her face. She left a note for Jack to meet her later at the inn. She put a mop cap on her head to look respectable, and took a hat and cloak for the short walk to her brother-in-law's house behind his feed store. There she would find Miriam, older sister of Johnny Bigelow.

"Mimi, you pushed me into this eleven years ago. I know you were glad I was there to help your father, and not you. I know you never wanted one of your sons to come home smelling of the brewhouse. But now, unless you want the inn to fail, you are sending Henry to help me. He is fourteen, the harvest is in, and after the storm last week I need his help. If he hates it, he can quit once we have good ale in the barrels."

Miriam Turner, six years older than Nina, glowed with the good fortune that healthy children and a friendly marriage

161

had provided. She had been sure of herself as a young girl. But now in matronly success, she ruled her roost with no less assuredness than a queen. Hair that had been rather plain, and a figure that if anything was over-lush, had both found their calling under the starched cap and well tucked-in fichu of this mature, successful good-wife.

A young man's face peered round from the dining room. "Mother, I would much rather do that than go back to school. You know I need a skill. You said so yourself. I've heard you and father talk about an apprenticeship. Please?" Fourteen year old Henry tried carefully not to plead or let his voice crack.

"Wait a minute, Henry. Let me think." Miriam put her soft hands on her lap and considered for a minute. "Alright Henry, I will let you go, but I don't want you living at the inn until we decide it's an apprenticeship. Right now, you are going to help your aunt. Do you understand?"

He nodded at his mother, smiling with unrestrained glee in anticipation of something new in his life.

"Mimi, I will make sure he leaves every day in time for dinner." She turned to her nephew. "Brewing starts at dawn, Henry, I will expect you there early mornings. Most brewing days we are finished before dinner. Days we don't brew, you can help in the upkeep of the inn or stables, yes?" She spoke to both mother and son. Both nodded agreement." She turned to Henry, "Come with me now and I'll get you acquainted with the process. Mimi, I will send him home after lunch." Henry almost jumped with excitement. Her sister-in-law nodded her agreement.

"Mother, I am going too." An adamant voice attached to seventeen year old Marty resolutely walked into the room. "If Aunt Nina could learn to brew at my age, I can too." Martha Turner was the near opposite of her mother. Slender almost to the point of boyishness, her brown hair hung in a long plait down her back. Her large brown eyes showed her excitement. "And I am not coming home at night, if Aunt Nina has room, and she doesn't mind." She looked hopefully at Nina, who nodded that she did have room and did not at all mind her niece joining her staff.

"Martha, your aunt had no choice, since her husband died leaving her in that circumstance." Miriam tried to be strict, but her eyes welled at the memory of her younger brother's death.

Nina shook off the mood. "Mimi, you're right. But the truth is that I did learn from your father. He wanted me to teach the children, at least some of the children. It was you who kept them away. He loved beer and the art. It is his legacy. You know that.

"Now that the inn needs the help it's a wonderful time for them to start. If, after we catch up with the stock, either of them wants to leave, I won't stop him, or her." She pointed with her nod, first to Henry and then to Martha.

"If you're wondering where Marty will sleep, it will be under Mrs. Cotton's supervision with Dodi and Sukie. The third girl, Mary, lives out." Nina smiled at her niece and nephew, fully appreciating their desire to move away from their wonderful but overbearing mother.

Nina could tell that Miriam wanted to object to letting two of her children go to the inn, but it was her family's enterprise, after all. She waited for the next objection. "What about Jack, isn't this his to decide?"

"Mimi, he is too young for such decisions. And I did say the inn needs help immediately. If I wait for Jack to grow up and make such an important decision, the tavern will be long gone."

"Why?" Miriam wasn't above being suspicious.

"The increase in traffic from the storm and bridge repair left us almost down to the bottom of the barrels. This morning I discovered rain water in the grains. I need to use the lot immediately or lose it all to mold, and I need to see about fixing that leaky roof."

Miriam might be the worthy wife of a hard working storekeeper and farmer, but she had grown up helping at her parents' tavern. She understood the urgency of wet grains, especially with the chance of warm autumn days when mold could grow, and the coming cold when the damp cold would supply little chance of drying. "Okay children. Martha, pack a few things. Henry, I expect you back in time to wash for dinner. Brewing is sweaty, hot work and I won't have you smelling at the table." She put her nose up in the air, reminding the trio waiting to leave that she knew what was what, and she did not approve.

Miriam had given one past piece of her mind before she let them follow the path of the river back upstream to the inn. She reminded them that Joshua would be unhappy that his Bigelow cousins would be living at the inn, learning the workings of the brewhouse. "Marty, Henry, you need to understand Josh. Right now he is angry at the world. Many of his friends have gone to enlist, but his mother is too ill and anxious, so he will not leave."

Nina thought how that was half true. She did not speak her mind and say the young man desperately wanted money to open his own stables. Or that he might do anything to get it, including letting those men take a gray stallion hostage. She also kept to herself that Josh seemed to sympathize with loyalists, the Tories who were trooping into Boston, rather then with those friends of his anxious to enlist and help the Patriot cause. He might be considering enlistment in the King's

American Volunteers, who were recruiting in New Hampshire and New York, for all she knew. If that were true, Josh would be wise to keep those plans to himself, not let on to the Committee of Safety that he did not support his neighbors. Josh Peddleman was young, and he certainly was not wise. Nina did not say any of this to her new helpers.

Busy days over the next weeks were helped enormously by the fact that Martha remembered helping her grandfather when she was young.

"Why don't I remember working with you, Marty? You certainly remember a lot."

"It was when little Jack was born. You were exhausted. Mother came to help you whenever she could. I hated staying home to help in the store, so I came with her. She didn't like me underfoot, always saying I would wake the baby, so she sent me off to Grandpapa. I was seven, and I loved it. The magic of putting handfuls of hops and malt into the boiling water. Grandfather sniffing at it until he liked the color and smell. I remember nearly all of it. After you and Jack were stronger, Mrs. Cotton came, and my mother made me go back to school. But Grandpapa kept giving me things to read on hops and brewing. I miss him."

Nina put her arm around Martha's thin shoulders and squeezed her close. "I know sweetie, we all do. I didn't realize he had taught you so much, but I'm glad."

"Me too. He didn't tell, said it was our secret, because Mother pretends not to approve. She insists she wants her children to have nothing to do with the inn, but I don't believe her. I think it's that she loved Johnny so much, and she doesn't want us to be jealous of Jack. She feels it should be his inn and brewhouse."

165

"That's very sweet of her, but she needn't have kept you away. Brewing is a skill, useful even without an inn to inherit." Mimi certainly doesn't mind the money I send her from the profits each month. Nina kept that last comment to herself, having just decided to pay Martha for her work above what her family got for their shares. "You should work the taproom with the other girls, Marty. It's fun. You'll get tips."

She looked stricken but excited at the prospect. "Really, Aunt Nina? Won't my mother object?"

"She might, but she waited tables in the tavern before she met your father. We all did. Before we built the extra rooms for the inn, it was simply a small tavern. Your grandfather's family still lived at the farm, you know, where your Uncle Nathan lives. When it got busy here, everyone stayed and worked. There was no time to go back and forth - later, after Johnny, he hired an innkeeper and concentrated on brewing. When I got old enough to be the innkeeper I took over, and now with him gone, I do both."

Martha looked at her young aunt, seeing through her lighthearted chatter, as though anyone would believe doing both jobs was easy. No, it was three jobs. She was keeping her own house with Jack at the same time. She was happy, almost giddy with the possibility of learning the secrets of brewing. She even loved the smell of hops and malted barley. Brewing was something she had been around all her life, yet it had remained just out of her reach. It was going to be good, helping her cousin and aunt, her favorite aunt, and learning to brew - to do more than study the theory in her books. She might, she thought, even be able to stand her brother, if they were both busy.

Nina got the young people settled in, and soon they were

boiling malted barley in spring water to produce the wort. Nina explained how she used color and smell to tell when the wort was ready to be poured-off. She knew it would take a while, but Martha especially was eager to learn, and Henry was big and strong for his age. With extra hands the work flew, and in just a few days all the dampened barley and hops were brewed and fermenting, using every barrel they could find.

Chapter 12

October 1775

Nina had watched riders approach the *Wheel and Hammer* since she had moved to the inn at sixteen. There were a few persistent patterns she had learned to associate with personality. Most riders slowed down on the main road before they reached the narrow lane, turning into the unknown path carefully, and cantering to the stable. Others kept their speed up; they slowed after catching sight of the stables, and trotted to a halt. A third pattern emerged when mounted soldiers from the encampment at Cambridge discovered the respite at the *Wheel and Hammer* for themselves and their horses. These fellows did not slow down before, or immediately after, but rode hard and pulled up short just as they passed the inn. They stopped at the paddock, where their horses could graze in the constant mist. Nina had come to expect it from them, and the style of their entrance announced their arrival. It wasn't long after she first observed it that she noticed others arrive in the same manner.

On afternoons when there was little work at the inn between lunch and dinner, Nina worked in her own house or rested. Because of that, she was not at the tavern when she heard hoofbeats bearing down hard into the lane. She was moving to the window to see who might be in such a hurry, when Jack ran into the room.

"Ma, that man from Meeting and some others are in the yard. They are looking for Josh. They're angry."

"What man from Meeting?" She hurried down the stairs, calling back over her shoulder. She stopped just inside the tavern door and turned to Jack, who had followed on her heels.

Jack shuffled his feet. This had something to do with a friend. He was fiercely loyal.

"John Mather Tyrie Bigelow - tell me what happened before I hear it from Martin Jewett." Nina looked at her small son sternly. An expression she used so rarely he squirmed again, this time for another reason. "Jack, now!"

He spoke softly, still shuffling his feet on the step. "It was at Meeting two weeks ago. Remember how we always blessed the King and asked God to keep him?"

"Of course." Nina nodded, encouraging him to go on.

"Micky said that."

"He blessed the King?"

"Uh huh."

"And..."

"That man," he motioned with his chin to Mr. Jewett, "he grabbed Micky after Meeting, and started giving him a licking. He had no right. He ain't his Pa, or teacher or nothing. So we pushed him off 'a Mick, and ran away."

"You and some other boys pushed *him*?" She looked over at the large solid mass of man in the stableyard. "It must have been quite a push."

At that very moment, Martin Jewett felt eyes on him and turned. He spotted Jack standing with his mother. He nodded at Nina as she shoved the boy behind the door and out of sight.

There were four men standing with their horses. They surrounded Josh and were talking to him. They had serious expressions on their faces, and their voices were low. The young man looked defiant and nervous. He shuffled his feet.

Abruptly, he left the group and walked into the stable, returning a few minutes later with a sack, a powder horn, and his musket. He handed them to the large man.

The men pointed to a horse and Josh mounted. He turned the black, and led the men out of the lane - they turned west, toward his mother's farm. One of the men stayed behind. He swaggered into the public room.

Nina moved sideways into the shadows and around the tavern to the back. She reappeared, coming in from the kitchen to welcome the man and take his order.

"Is it acceptable to ask what you men want with my husband's nephew?" She served his ale and waited for a response. He was seated in the small alcove they used as a private diningroom. He had asked for the room, although he was alone. Nina assumed he was waiting for his compatriots to arrive.

"Of course I can tell you. Such cases are not private. It is highly likely the young man would wish for it to remain so. You may tell him that you heard something about his case, but that is up to you. As I am sure you know, we are the Committee of Safety for the second parish district of western Newton. Right now we are waiting for a representative from North Dedham. Mr. Jewett and the others have gone to interview Missus Peddleman." He fell silent. Nina guessed that she was allowed to know who they were, but not the particular charges. She left orders that the men were to be served whatever they wanted, to take their money if they offered to pay, but under no circumstances should anyone insist on payment.

Later, she called everyone together in the kitchen to explain. "Such committees can cause a lot of trouble, and we want them to be our friends. I know Mr. Jewett, seen him most of my life. He is a good man, but full of himself. The kind of man who might cause trouble if he was convinced he was in the right." Everyone nodded that they understood.

Jack was sitting on a log near the river, throwing rocks into the water, when Nina found him a few minutes later. He turned away to wipe his face. He had never liked to be seen when he was upset, so she waited. She had relied on him to do the right thing, and he always had. Being honest came to him so easily that her life as his mother had been easy. She had a queasy feeling that might be changing.

She sat down next to him on his log and threw a rock into the churning water. It broke apart the red leaves' pattern on the water's surface, but they quickly resumed their journey. "Why does Martin Jewett frighten you so? You said that you and the other boys pushed him to help Micky?" Jack nodded, his lips tight together. He wiped an unruly tear from his cheek. "Jackie, let us go and make chocolate biscuits, then you and I can figure out how I can help you."

"He'll shut the tavern, he said he would, if I told you." Nina pulled her son by the elbow, down the path and into their cozy kitchen. She put some coals and kindling into the side oven and let it burn. She handed a brick of chocolate and a grater to Jack. For a few minutes the only sounds in the room were the sounds of chocolate being grated, eggs being cracked, flour being measured and sugar being scraped off a cone. Nina combined her ingredients and waited for the oven to reach an even temperature.

Calmly, she spooned even amounts onto metal trays, and put them into the oven. She poured each of them a glass of small beer while they waited. When the first batch was done,

Nina put in the second, handed Jack a biscuit, and settled to talk. It had been an hour.

"He'll shut the tavern if you told me. Why? Jack, no one can hear you but me."

"He tried to tan my hide. He grabbed at us after we pushed at him. Said he knew my father, and I wasn't getting beat enough. He said something about me being a lazy good for nothing, defending a Tory like Micky. Stuff like that. I tried to forget it, and I almost had until he saw me today. He made me scared he might hurt you."

Nina didn't want to know. These were the changes she had tried to ignore, as she tried to pretend nothing had changed since everything had changed. She had seen Martin Jewett at Meeting on Sundays, and at Town Meeting when there was a reason for her to go, but she never to spoke to him and he didn't know her at all. He had no right by friendship or authority to touch her son. "Jack, did he actually whip you?"

"Yup, took a belt to my butt. Only the once though, cause the boys came back, and said Dr. Jackson was coming. We ran away fast after that."

"Listen, I don't want you to get in the habit of flaunting authority, but you did right to run. The only thing you did wrong was not tell me. But *fili mi*, I understand why you didn't." Jack smiled at her use of Latin to cheer him. Nina took the other tray out of the oven and sat to eat a biscuit. They finished, and put the biscuits out of reach of mice.

She left Jack to his homework and went back to her work. The Committee was still in the alcove, eating and drinking newly fermented ale. She wondered if she would have to prove to them that she was a loyal Patriot. Suddenly the sound of galloping horses made the whole inn jump. The men in the private room ran out to see who had come, increasing the tension; a sense of danger and chaos. Nina pulled Jack into the kitchen. "Run back to the house and stay there. There is no reason for you to be involved in this."

He looked relieved, but like he would like to watch the exciting happenings. "Ma, I'm gonna be bored - can Henry come and stay with me?"

"Better yet, I'll send him by, and you and he can go to the Turners. Have a visit with Aunt Merry. Take your things for school tomorrow and stay the night." She hugged him close, knowing that he would sleep far better in the farmhouse behind the store than he would wondering if Martin Jewett could make good on his threat. "And Jackie, don't worry. I'll come by Mimi's later, to tell you what happened. Promise."

Pleased that Jack was safe, she glanced out the window to see a group of five Continentals ride to the sweet-grass meadow and tether their horses. She turned back into the room, prepared to answer any questions Martin Jewett might have. Jewett stood and looked over to her; it didn't seem as though he had planned his words.

Nina approached the little dining room. The men looked relaxed - even Josh had the look of the others. In front of them the table said it all – dinners half eaten and cups well used. "I'm glad you've found the *Wheel and Hammer* to your liking, Mr. Jewett. Is there anything more I can do for you? I'm Mrs. Bigelow." She presented her right hand, but he did not.

Instead, he looked stunned and almost stumbled, stepping back. "But you're nearly a child yourself, how can you have that...boy?" He stopped himself from saying anything more, as a group of Continentals walked into the room. They were loud and laughing at something one of them had said.

The soldiers had the look of men in control, of themselves and their space. They had changed in the months since the battle at Charlestown. They were less green, more of a cohesive group. They moved with more poise and operated with less bravado. They had become serious, especially as their comrades, their friends and members of militia had left on various missions. Wythe, she knew, was gone on some task. Where, she had no idea. She hadn't seen him in weeks, just as she hadn't seen Alex since that day after the hurricane.

Then men entered and called a polite, if boisterous, hello. Nina got them settled with ales, and sent Mary to take their orders for food. Then she turned back to Martin Jewett. Happily, the Committee of Safety for the west district of Newton had adjourned, paid their bill of fare, and left without another word.

Nina left her staff in charge and walked down the river path to the Turner house. Jack and his cousins were sitting in the parlor reading their lessons when Nina entered.

"Hi Nina, Jackie said he was going to spend the night, something about a committee?"

"I don't need him home, but I wanted to let you know that the Committee of Safety left without incident." She quietly told Miriam about Josh's having to hand over his powder and musket, but was otherwise fine.

"Miriam, their chairman scared Jack at Meeting last week, threatened to whip him for defending a friend who had insulted the Cause, so I sent him down here before it got worse for him."

She turned to the scholars, their heads in their books, pretending to work. "But Jackie, guess who came into the yard right after you and Henry left? A whole group of Continentals,

I think they scared the Committee, and that should be enough to prove that the *Wheel* supports liberty." Nina knew that no one, not even Jewett, would think of accusing her of Tory leanings, but that wouldn't mean he thought she was a good mother, or strict enough with her son. Jack should continue to avoid the man.

Chapter 13

Over the next weeks, as the days shortened, the temperature dipped and iced the edges of the river, and travelers became more scarce. It was probably because the roads were hardened from the autumn rains, making it easier to travel long distances to bigger inns. The cold weather had also hardened the grass along the river into crisp, frost-bitten reeds. With no fresh forage, the mounted soldiers stayed closer to Cambridge or were riding elsewhere.

She would have liked to see them, feed them warm food, and ease at least part of their task. Word had gotten out that the men were in tents and lean-tos, cramped together on the town green. If something weren't done to end the siege, it would be far worse next year. Food for the men was scarce, and their firewood had to be delivered from farther away each week. Support for Washington's siege was nearly universal, but no one wanted his woodlot stripped for someone else's need.

The partially vacant inn and tavern meant time to brew and catch up on her ales. Alone in the brewing shed, Nina had time to miss and worry about Alex. As she worked, she would pull out memories of those brief moments, like pieces of stained glass, wondering if they fit together in a mosaic - a shipyard, a pie-table, a country dance, one dinner, a sunny picnic at the river, and two stormy days and nights. And if the pieces did make a whole, what did it look like, and why had it become so important?

***

It was a mid-December afternoon when Martha walked into Nina's room to find her aunt flinging clothing over her bed and floor. "Aunt Nina! What's wrong?" Jackets, skirts, and gowns were strewn about, and Nina was jumping around in chemise and stays, clearly upset. She collapsed on the edge of the bed, and put her head in her hands.

"Marty, I haven't been anywhere important. I need to dress tonight. Every gown is out of fashion. And not just that - they are old, used." She picked up a yellowed petticoat and threw it back on the pile.

Martha, who had grown up around shop goods, took a good look at the various pieces. She lifted a few and moved them out of the way. Finally, she picked up a quilted petticoat, heavy jacquard jacket and a golden velvet skirt. The gold color of the velvet was repeated in the birds' wings in the pattern of the jacket.

"Marty. I never thought of those together. It's wonderful, oh thank you!" Gratefully Nina slipped the skirt over her head. Marty began tying strings and smoothing fabrics.

It had been two weeks before - a rider from the camp had brought a note asking Nina to join a dinner party to be given for Mrs. Washington, just arrived to join her husband at the Vassal House. Nina guessed that Alex had somehow sent the invitation. Maybe he was to be there and they would eat together. She was nervous and anxious to see him. She was nervous about the formal dinner as well, but there was nothing to be done about that.

Nina harnessed Bella and Jewel. She packed warm lap robes and a heavy cloak with a hood that was guaranteed to destroy her carefully constructed coiffeur, planning to pull it on for warmth on the way home. As always, she placed her two firearms, a riding pistol and a musket, in the box under her seat. She packed a small barrel of triplebock as a gift for the Washingtons, and an extra large barrel of dinner ale for the men of the camp to share.

The ride felt long, even though she had driven these roads many times before. The moon was already in the sky, full, its edges rimmed with cold. Nina shivered. Even through the thick wool cloak around her shoulders and the warm gloves she saved for driving, the chill crept in. She took deep breaths of the chill night, reminding herself that the invitation had to have come from Alex. He would be there, or least send some word to her.

The hour it took to drive the team over roads, still rough and rutted from the damage of the September storm, gave her time to think. She hadn't liked to admit to wanting a man, but weeks of worry had made her confront it – he was not a mere friend. When she thought of him, which was nearly constant, it was as a man, one who had so casually come and upended her ordered world. He had also insisted she was not to expect him, and demanded that she spend no time worrying about him.

She had promised herself and him, and she had tried - tried not to worry, tried not to expect him to ride into the stableyard or walk into the taproom, his gray cape over his shoulders, his saddlebags slung casually over his shoulder, his eyes smiling as he scanned her taproom and lighting up when he found her. During the day, she almost succeeded in not worrying, but alone at night, when the chatter and activity of the day stopped, she worried and then acknowledged that her feelings were deeper than worry. They had changed to longing, yearning for warmth, and of a loss of something she barely understood. These new feelings rose from her deepest center.

There, on the road, she forced herself to do something she had steadfastly refused to do: remember her short marriage. In all the years since her widowhood, she had reasoned that one short week was all there would be for her - six days. She had found the experience wretched, tried to forget about it, hated when she was goaded into remembering, as on that first night with Alex by the river. After that night, she had coped by pretending to move beyond those memories, to become someone else, a person who could learn to enjoy those things that frightened her.

Her world had shifted with the storm, after she brought Martha and Henry into the busy world of the brewhouse. It was watching Martha with her brother and cousin, with the girls in the taproom, seeing how she threw herself into learning, devouring everything she could about brewing and running the inn, that made Nina realize she had been a child when she married, younger even than Marty. She had been a silly girl, all excitement and expectation, far too young to understand, but with the energy that was youth.

What would she counsel her son, her nephew, niece or any young person? She had been taught to forgive and to find peace in that. Nina knew she had to find forgiveness, first of all for Johnny, nearly as young as she, who did not understand what she needed. She had been angry at him for not understanding her pain. It was time to let the anger go, time to let Johnny go.

It was time, as well, to let go of the guilt she'd held for ten years, to stop thinking that she should have been wiser, or more able to guide him. She must forgive herself for the shock of their first lovemaking, and the pain and horror that had lived so vividly in her memories – of being married and widowed so quickly, so young. She must also forgive him for dying, and never coming back.

She had been speaking aloud, talking to Johnny, to the wind and the rising moon, telling him that he should have come home to her, older, wiser and more patient, that he should have come home to love her. Tears fell down her cheeks. In the middle of the road, her team obediently trudging on, Nina sobbed, realizing that she had never cried for herself, for the end of her youth.

She had sat with Johnny's family and mourned the loss of his young life. She had cried for the father who would never know his son, when little Jack was born. But once her lying-in was over, she had resolved to work hard, and she had never looked back.

Unable to see through her tears, Nina steered the team to the side of the road. In a while, she stopped crying. A feeling of peace settled over her. She recognized what she was experiencing. She had been raised to recognize it. Growing up in an Old Light Meeting, she believed that cathartic experiences were necessary for redemption, that God's love and forgiveness entered one's body as a physical force. This experience was not only encouraged, it was required for membership in her church. Nina had never expected to experience such overwhelming emotion herself, certainly not on the road to Cambridge.

Nina knew that such forgiveness was the greatest gift she could be given. She felt newly born into a grown woman. It was good that she'd had these weeks to herself. Better that Alex had been away as long as he had. Maybe now she could be his true partner, the helpmeet she been raised to become - not merely the willing-widow. She laughed through the last of her tears.

Light snow-flurries danced in the moonlight. She was anxious to tell Alex what had happened. It felt wonderful and necessary to let him know she was free, ready to begin again.

Chapter 14

Cambridge was a world transformed, but not the chaos Nina feared. She left her team at the horsebarn with a groom she recognized from his visits to the *Wheel and Hammer*. She spotted Thorne in the barn, but there was no time to check on him, or say hello. She had taken too long on her trip, and needed to rush so she would not be late to the dinner. She walked from the horsebarn to headquarters as fast as was acceptable. It was not far - someone else would bring the triplebock to the dinner party and the barrel of ale to the mess tent.

Nina looked around in spite of being in a hurry. She had not been to Cambridge since the town had become a camp. Lit only with campfires, she could see that everywhere men were eating, shining boots and playing various musical instruments. There were wives cooking and mending, and children as well. From what Nina knew of long campaigns, the number of families would increase as husbands stayed away, sometimes for years at a time. It was not yet so dire that farms had been lost, or families become homeless, not in the few short months these men had been here. Nina fervently prayed it would not become so.

"At least now the camp is calm and the men have achieved harmony. Most observers had no faith that such disparate groups could coalesce as fast as we needed them to, especially during such a long period of inaction. A story, a story." The man raised his glass to General Washington. The rest of the table followed suit.

The man continued. "Tradition dictates that Massachusetts-men celebrate Guy Fawkes Day, which here they call Pope's Day. The celebrations consist of going from pub to ale house and getting drunk, very, very drunk. Then, they gather in the streets to parade a burning straw effigy of the Pope dressed in a long robe and pointed hat.

"The General heard about the tradition, and he saw a problem. He understood his New Englanders, but he also understood the newly arrived militia from Maryland. You see," he held the audience with his voice, "if the Catholic Marylanders felt insulted, we might have had a war within the camp. Washington brought in the New Englanders. He spoke to them in private. And they did not parade the burning fellow through the yard. No one cares how much they drank.

"So, let us drink to General George Washington. A man with patience and wisdom, may he keep them. He is going to need them." Everyone raised their glasses and the man telling the story sat back down. He was seated on Nina's left. She sipped her wine with the others, scanning the room as she sat. Alex was not here.

She had been ushered into the crowded dining room, just as the fellow raised his glass. The room was large. All the parlors had all been converted to offices, and this dining room had papers and uniform-parts stuffed into corners, out of the way of the large table and many chairs.

The food was excellent. Nina concentrated on it, trying to look as if she belonged. The gentlemen on either side of her talked over and around her. She felt silly, until between courses she quietly traded places with one of them. It undid the careful seating plan, but it allowed her to concentrate on their speech without turning from one to the other.

She tried to conceal it, but every minute or two the door would open and she would look up. Sometimes it took ten minutes or more before a uniformed soldier would come in with a message for one of the men at dinner. The dispatches were not always for Washington, which seemed not to surprise him at all - in fact, he looked delighted when a messenger singled out some other diner. The chatter was that Henry Knox had been delayed again. Deep cold had not come, and the ground around Albany was still too soft for the heavy wagons. She must have looked confused, because the gentleman to her right told her that Knox and his brother had gone to New York to retrieve cannon left at Fort Ticonderoga.

Nina had thought the surrender of the British fort had sounded heroic, but the real story, told by the man on her left, was that the British commander had been awakened from a deep sleep and opened the door in his night clothes. Surrender was inevitable. The man had not even worn a sidearm.

The heavy cannon and the ox handlers were now on their way back to help end the blockade. Knox hoped they would be back by New Year's, but now it sounded as if that wouldn't happen. Nina could feel the whole room sigh with wearied sadness. The blockade of the capital had gone on over a year. Two battles and many smaller skirmishes later, the British still held the town – captured within its watery borders by the American siege. Nina felt sure Alex was somewhere in Boston.

As dinner ended, the ladies rose to take tea in a separate parlor. Nina imagined the room being prepared by papers being swept off tables and hidden under tables and chairs. It seemed war took an awful lot of office work.

She said good evening to her two dinner partners, and stood to move with the ladies into the adjacent room. Out of recent habit she turned to look as the door to the room opened. She inhaled sharply, and realized that she had been holding her breath for hours. The room and people in it moved in a blur and almost disappeared. She stared at the newcomer. They locked eyes. In a moment he broke his gaze - dipping his head slightly, he headed over to Washington to hand him a folder of papers.

Nina followed Mrs. Washington into the next room where she was introduced to Abigail Adams, wife of John Adams, who was then in Pennsylvania at the Continental Congress, and Mercy Warren, the poet, writer and wife of James Warren, who worked on the General's staff. Politely nodding and smiling at the uniquely female yet passionately political chatter, she sipped false tea made from steeped herbs.

She was used to listening to her patrons pontificate about their political ideas, getting louder as they drank. All the while she stayed neutral, never expressing herself. In the world of innkeeping, opinions were bad for business. Now, when she had a chance to speak, she found herself with nothing to add to the talk of these accomplished, educated women. Happily, no one expected her to wax poetic.

"Most Americans have not bothered perfecting their replacement teas." Mercy Warren complained, trying to effect a light note. Nina knew how hard it must be. The drink in her hand was terrible. "We women around Boston have gotten so used to the faux tea, we now prefer mint, chamomile, and coffee. There is nothing that can replace real tea." The women added agreement, though most confessed they had lost the taste for it.

"I've brought a small keg of triplebock. It's a very strong ale, good for sipping." Nina offered. The women looked at her with surprise. Then collectively their eyes lit up and they nodded, expressing their hope for something better.

Mrs. Washington asked one of the servers to retrieve the keg from the kitchen. The ladies anxiously applauded as Nina expertly tapped the barrel and poured the dark sweet beer into small glasses. They saluted their hostess, and then Mrs. Adams stood with her glass. "We ladies here in Boston know the pain British law can bring. I believe our message has reached to the far ends of the colonies so that everywhere we clamor for justice. Let us drink this one glass to Independence and successful revolution."

Nina turned just as Abigail Adams finished her toast. One of the servers had slipped out of the room. The man seemed familiar. She felt goosebumps when she recognized him as one of Joshua's friends, the ones who'd expressed interest in Thorne. She realized with clarity that he had been staring at her, trying to place her. The keg had sealed his memory. Her stomach fell.

She pasted a smile back on her face, trying to think of how to warn Alex. Even in the relative safety of a group such as this one, she was unsure if it was safe to announce what she had seen. She allowed herself to be distracted for a few minutes by a young woman playing a spinet that the Vassals had left behind in their hurried desire to get into the safety of Boston.

By the end of the girl's playing, a few gentlemen joined them, and were now drinking the beer. Nina saw that Alex was one of them. He made no move, but raised his glass to thank her. She nodded in return, thanking him for the compliment. She needed to think of a way to be alone with him, to tell him that there were British spies living at or near the camp.

"Mrs. Bigelow, you must meet our handsome young friend." One of the officers' wives, Nina could not remember her name, took her by the hand and dragged her to where Alex was leaning against a desk in the corner. "We can't get him to talk more than a few words; maybe you can." The woman was old enough to be a grandmother, but Nina sensed she wanted an excuse to flirt with the handsome young man. "Mr. Peele, I make known to you Mrs. Bigelow. She brought us the most delightful and delicate ale."

"Brought a delicate ale? Wherever did she find one?" He sipped his drink and then gulped the rest in a wholesome swallow. He grinned happily at her. He looked as though a good laugh might exhaust him, but his eyes lit as he put out a hand to take hers. "Lovely to meet you, Mrs. Bigelow. Always happy to meet the bringer of delight." He lifted it to his lips and delivered the hint of a kiss over her knuckles.

Nina gasped, blushed and gave him a fierce look. She took her hand back. "Thank you, Mr. Peele. It is always nice to meet someone appreciative." She felt the piece of paper in her palm, and hastily put it in her pocket. Perhaps she didn't need to warn him after all. The three chatted for a few minutes, and then the older woman moved as if to drag Nina off to meet someone else. Alex took her hand for a second, holding it hard in his until he had to let go.

As soon as it was polite, Nina snuck off to read her note.

N. I will find you afterward. There is danger, be careful.
It was unsigned.

The moon was high in the sky, announcing the middle of the night, when Nina headed back to the horsebarn for her wagon and team. She was almost there when she heard rustling in some bushes by the road. "A..." she turned, expecting Alex, she almost said his name. She'd stopped herself in time, it was the server, the man she recognized. He grabbed her arm and put a knife to her throat.

"W-what do you want?" Cold fear grabbed at her. She stumbled as he pulled her along into the dark growth and bracken.

"We wanted the horse he seems to care so much about. Bastards won't let us in the barn, but the pretty brewer will attract his attention."

Nina almost laughed with relief. "You don't know him, do you?"

"We will in a minute, then we'll have a name to hang on the noose when he tries to return to town."

Return to town. So he had been in Boston these weeks. That had to be dangerous. All sides hanged spies during war. This man had no British accent. He spoke with a flat tone, not a New Englander, but as American as anyone. Too bad he was intent on the death of a fellow countryman.

Nina could almost understand not wanting to support independence. The inevitable war would bring chaos and death. But to wish for the hanging of a man who had done you no harm, and whose face and name you did not know? That was plain wrong-headed and evil.

The man pulled her away from the camp toward the marsh at the edge of the river. Right now with his hand on her, there was no way to escape. She remained passive, hoping he would let go. They had created a camp hidden in the midst of the tall grass. There was a canvas lean-to, and four men sat around a small fire. The man pushed her toward it. He was greeted silently.

It was dark. The light of the bright moon barely penetrated the tall rushes. Nina shivered cold and a deep fear at what they might to do her, what they would do to Alex. She backed out of the circle. It was too bad to move away from

188

their fire, but she had hopes they would forget she was there.

The men spoke softly, she heard only a word or two. They seemed not to have any real plan, just an idea to capture the man they were sure was an expert agent working against the Crown. Nina did not believe Alex was such an expert that he could single-handedly bring down the Empire, as they seemed to imply. She knew she did not want him captured or hanged. She stilled her rapid breathing so she could listen.

The cold crept from her feet up her legs. It was probably foolish of her, but she felt safer in the shadows. After a short time, someone new came and said something to the group. Nina could not hear the words, but suddenly everyone was on the move. The man who had dragged her now grabbed her wrists and pulled her back toward the main road.

They stopped just west of the horse barn. The fellow pulled out a pistol and pointed it very dramatically at her head as he backed away into the undergrowth, making it clear without words that if she moved he would shoot her.

Alex waited at the horsebarn, standing by Nina's horses. He needed to ask her to store a box for him. He had given up waiting for death to send it to the *Wheel and Hammer*. The box contained the sum of his treasures collected in his travels. Lately, he had dreams of the men pawing through it, sampling oils, examining the gold chains, jewels and pot shards. He found talking to the large horses surprisingly easy - they really did seem to answer. He could sense their unease. None of them knew where Nina had gone off to. He looked in the wagon.

Alex lifted the bench top to see if there were any clues. None, but inside were the warm wraps for her ride home, a carriage pistol and rifle. He hated to steal, but instinct told him his own sidearm would not be enough. He primed the pistol

189

and put it in his pocket. Then he wrapped the rifle inside the warm cloak and returned them to the box. There wouldn't be time to ask permission. He lifted his crate into the wagon, and tied it down just behind the bench.

He whistled low for Thorne, who trotted over, anxious to move. Poor horse, he had probably shied away and bucked anyone who had tried to ride him. No doubt he'd spent these months in the barn, fed and ignored. Alex patted his side and promised he would do better for him.

He led the horse into the road and stopped to look and listen. There was nothing back toward camp, but west, toward the curve in the road, there seemed to be someone standing. Whoever it was, was looking back in his direction. It was hard to make out the shadows, but he saw movement at the side of the road. It was a woman standing. It had to be Nina. She was not alone. Someone was in the scrub.

He suspected it was the gang of deserters that had grown too interested in him. They had to be in the employ of someone, but no one had been able to find out just who. Just this afternoon they had gotten word that someone or a number of people were in the camp, and working on the British side. That was not unexpected. After all, many Americans still harbored favorable feelings about the old ways. He could let others deal with those things, but holding Nina hostage was intolerable. He was ready to kill the man in the bushes.

He moved deliberately, working in a white rage. Just out of sight of the gunman, Alex reached down, grabbed a handful of pebbles, and put them in his pocket alongside the pistol he had taken from Nina's bench. His other pocket contained his gun, a finer, more precise tool - useful when one could sight and aim.

A childhood with brothers, snowballs and long winters

had taught him patience and good aim. Shooting a pistol from a horse into the dark might be a hit or miss proposition, but he was very likely to hit something with a good round rock, about the size of a healthy snowball. He kicked at the edge of the road until he found what he was looking for. Then he whistled, Thorne trotted over. Still out of sight of the scrub bushes, Alex mounted and started the horse at a steady and gentle canter, heading him between Nina and the man. As he neared the bushes he threw the pebbles, hoping for some sign of surprise that would help with his aim.

Nina saw Alex in the road. Thorne was just behind him. She didn't think the men to her side could see either of them. She watched him kick at the road, curious as to what he was doing. The whole night had seemed so odd, she felt as if she were in a dream. She couldn't be sure if the man in the road was Alex. If he was, she should try to warn him. The man mounted, and horse and rider started toward her. She needed to warn him. Use a name the men couldn't use.

"Johnny! Don't come closer!" She wasn't sure where that had come from. It surprised her as she said it.

Still at the canter and almost at his target, Alex heard Nina shout "Johnny." Of all the names to shout at him, certainly that was the last name she would use accidentally. He threw the pebbles and heard the grunt and "what the . . .?" he was listening for. Then he let the rock fly at the source of the sound. He heard moans as he slowed and lifted Nina onto the horse behind him.

Nina leaned her body into Alex as he rode them away from danger. It was only minutes before they stopped, but she could feel him relax at her safety. She felt his strength and warmth, even through their layers of winter wool. She wanted so badly to hold him, to look into his gray eyes and tell him that she understood, that she loved him as she had never loved before.

Alex reined in the horse and jumped to the ground. "I have to go back and deal with this." He pulled Nina's pistol and checked the flint and powder before putting it in his pocket and checking the other."Take Thorne, I'll make sure someone brings the Suffolks to the *Wheel* in the morning. Nina," - he dragged air into his lungs as he drank in the sight of her, putting loose hair behind her ears, pulling the hood over her head and securing it with the pin - "it was wonderful to see you. These moments remind me why I am doing this."

"Alex I..."

"There will be time, I promise. But not now." He lifted her onto the horse, cinched the stirrups and turned. As she lifted the reins she heard him. "If you find a way, it's fifteen Queen Street, upstairs from the back."

Alex ran back to the spot in the road. His pistols were out and he burned with anger. These fiends had held a gun on Nina, his Nina. The road was now crowded with soldiers from the camp who had come to investigate the sound of pistol fire. He would do no good here, and as much as he'd love to shoot someone, it was more important to use the low tide to get back to the gaming tables, where a few of his friends would be waiting for him at midnight. He went by the barn to tell the grooms where to bring the team in the morning. Then he walked past the college to the river, where a flat bottomed canoe and an oarsman were waiting for him.

He had been working just off the room they were using as the diningroom. He had yearned to go in and have a normal

192

meal with the laughing people. At least he had been able to look up occasionally to catch a glimpse of Nina. She had sparkled as the men tried to impress her with their stories of the camp and Washington. She hadn't even noticed their flirting. He supposed that as a tavern owner she was so used to it, it barely registered. He couldn't help but be pleased.

He wasn't supposed to be here at all, but he had found a minute between the beginning and the end of the low tide to hand over some papers, and grab a moment in the drawing room after dinner. Someone had warned him that he was being watched by whomever had infiltrated the camp. He hoped it was those men they'd caught, but nothing was ever as easy as was hoped.

Nina had tried to talk to him. She had something important to tell him. He wanted to crawl after her, to hear what she had to say. It would have to wait. He would conjure her image to keep him warm in the lonely, soulless room he used as the false Alex Peele. If he were very lucky, she would remember that address and find him on Queen Street. He did not think it would be possible, but he would dream anyway.

Fifteen Queen Street. She even knew where that was, up the hill from King's Street, near the town house. She recited that address to herself until is was memorized.

She rode Thorne north, following Menatomy. Along the way, she realized that she was following the route Mr. Revere had taken to warn the countryside the previous spring. She passed through Arlington into Lexington, before turning and heading south, toward home. It was on a high hill coming down from Waltham, toward the lakes that made a portion of the river, that she realized that she had not been at all cold. She had been cold earlier. She felt her arms and realized that she was wearing Alex's fur lined cape. He had slipped it over her shoulders. She had not noticed. She buried her nose in the soft fur, smelling scents of leather, the animal, and the wonderful essence of Alex. She felt safe, even loved. She pulled the soft warmth closer. She would find a way to Queen Street. She didn't know how, but she would.

Nina had not ridden more than once since she was a girl. She had her team of Suffolks and the inn's light cart. Now she was astride one of the biggest, most high-strung mounts she had ever met, and enjoying every minute. She knew the stallion could be difficult. At the inn, he had allowed only Jack to curry him. She wondered if he had kicked or bitten the grooms at the camp. Stubborn fellow, had he even seen blue sky since being left in Cambridge?

The moon was low in the west as she dismounted on the far-side of the main road at the Lower Falls. They had ridden hard, the frozen fields and bright moon supplying a wonderful night to work out her worries. She walked the horse across to the inn road to cool him. Lanterns were lit at the door supplying the only light, but Nina could see that Joshua was there with his friends. Her heart sank, but they had not seen her or the horse. Nina thanked heaven for the incessant roar of the falls, turned Thorne, and led him out of the lane. She worried about his feet on the uneven ground of the deep rocky woods, so she held the reins and walked him across the bridge to the narrow path that followed the river to the Upper Falls. Keeping in the woods on the west side of the river, she led the horse to the thick hemlocks. She found some fresh grass at the edge of the evergreens and left him to graze. She looked into his eyes, "Thorne boy, you stay right here. I'm sending your friend Jack." The horse went back to his grazing.

David's mill was right there on the other side of the river, but she did not want him involved. Big brothers had a way of helping that disrupted delicate situations, and right now she had to get Thorne somewhere safe, a place neither Josh nor his friends would think to look for him. She could take care of herself, she hoped.

Chapter 15

In her dark house, Nina climbed the ladder to Jack's room. The dawn was a pale pink line at the eastern edge of the sky. She could hear Mrs. Cotton starting the fires for her coffee, but even her helpers weren't up yet. There was no good reason to start the day too soon this time of year. It was not as though cows needed milking or chickens their feed. She felt sorry about it, but "Jackie wake up!" She nudged him gently but firmly till he grunted.

"Mama, what is the matter?"

"Listen, wake up. I need your help." She packed some of his clothing, his favorite books and an extra sweater in a sack. "Thorne, Alex Peele's gray horse is in the hemlocks above David's. You are going to ride him to your grandparent Tyrie's farm. You have to leave now. You've got to be gone by daybreak."

Nina could not believe she had thought of this plan. Josh would never imagine she would ask her own parents for help. That it was out of character would protect the horse. Jack could use a break from life at the inn. "You know the way to Tyrie Farm, don't you?"

"Near the first Meeting House? Sure, I know how to get there. But now?"

"Yes, now. I'm sorry to have to ask you to go out in the cold and dark."

"Ma, do you want me to cry and say how scared I am? Or do you want me to tell you the truth?"

Nina laughed at her little man. "The truth, why not?"

He pulled warm breeches on under his nightshirt, and pulled it off. Nina folded it and put it in the sack with his other things. She found a linsey-woolsey shirt and handed it to him.

"I'm excited. Mr. Peele told me things might happen and to be prepared for anything. He said that wars call for men to do extraordinary things. He also said if I ever had a chance to learn Latin and Greek from Grandfather, I should take it. Mama, may I stay at the farm? I'll ride Alex's horse and take really good care of him."

"Jackie, it's horrible for a mother to say, but I think staying with the Tyries is a good idea. I haven't felt right about Jewett and the Committee meeting here so often. I've felt like I can't keep you safe. So try it. Maybe you'll be happier with Uncle Seth and your grandparents. I will be at First Church for meeting, I promise. Please explain that I can't write a note to send with you. It would be dangerous if Josh were to see it, but I will come to the farm as soon as it is safe."

"Mama, what happened? I know you went to Cambridge. You looked so pretty, now you look very tired. What is wrong?"

"Jack, if you can get Thorne to the farm and away from the Falls, nothing will be wrong. It's those men, they are still trying to find Mr. Peele, and we must not let them. Tell your Uncle Seth to bring Alcea and have dinner here. My treat. It's time we all started acting like family. He can tell me what a wonderful help you are to him, and how hard you are studying with Grandfather."

Jack pulled his mother's face down to him for a kiss, something he had always done and couldn't imagine stopping. He rarely noticed, but his mother gave him the strength to go off on his own. He was very proud of his mother and how hard she worked. "Mama, I don't want to worry about you. Take

197

care of yourself."

"Yes, and you too." She swallowed her tears as she watched out the window as her son made his way through the woods toward the hemlocks.

***

"Ma, I wrote a whole story about my trip from the Falls to the farm. Actually I wrote it as Hercules traveling past wolves and over raging rivers, but Grandfather said that might frighten you, so I rewrote it, and told the truth." Nina was seated in the family pew in the First Church. Jack, sitting next to her, handed her a sheaf of papers. She glanced at them. His handwriting had improved in a week with her father as his school master. What would happen to her son if he stayed the winter? She would discuss that with her parents during dinner.

Nina put the letter on top of her prayer book. The minister was talking to a few people before he began, so she took the time to start reading. Jack sat quietly but expectantly, waiting for her to read his story.

The boy moved silently up the hill from the lower to the upper falls. The route was familiar. He followed it each day on his journey to school, and his feet knew the rocks and slippery spots, even in the dark of the pre-dawn.

He came out into the hemlocks, and breathed in the fresh breeze of the grove. The trees there were ancient, and he always felt the awe of the place, even as he and his cousins played hide and find in the thick brush. He spoke softly calling to Thorne, telling the high-strung stallion that he was near. Then he whistled, and waited for Thorne to whinny back. In a few minutes he trotted over, his bright gray coat appearing out of the river mist like a ghost rising in the early dawn. The boy untied the loose laces, mounted and headed toward the bridge that crossed the roaring falls. The sun was just brightening the pink sky, as the boy headed southeast toward his grandfather's farm.

The early morning was cold and the boy was not sure of the shortest way. He knew it from his home, but not from this south bend in his river. He started following the southern road, but then he realized he needed to go north before he went too far east. That meant heading into the hills.

The Newton hills were famous for being too rocky to farm, and except for some grazing land, the townsfolk had left the rocky area wooded. Now the boy needed to cut east over the hills and through those woods. His mother had told him that there had been wolves in the area when she was young, wolves coming after deer, wild turkey and other prey. The ground was hard, and covered with just enough early snow to make coming near humans worth the risk for a wolf. He picked his way over rough, narrow tracks, hoping not to see one.

It took the boy longer than it should have. The winter sun was slow rising over the horizon, and he lost his way more than once in the dark woods, forced to retrace steps on trails used by wild animals more often than people. Finally he saw morning smoke rising from a farm house and recognized his grandfather's house and barn.

Nina finished reading, just as the minister said good morning. She put her arm around Jack's shoulders and smiled at her son. They rose with the first hymn.

Chapter 16

He was not meant to live alone. At the moment Alex thought this, he was sitting at the British Coffee House on King Street, drinking brandy. He was feeling lonely, as he often did, but he was surrounded with men who thought he was their friend. He never had actually lived alone before he took those rooms on Queen Street, not as a child with siblings, not as a student in a community of scholars, not in London with various flatmates, not even on the long travels he'd taken through the ancient world. There, he was always accompanied by someone or other. Certainly he had not lived alone at the camp in Cambridge. No, he didn't like living alone, and he didn't like lying. He lifted his glass a quiet inch, and silently pledged that if he lived through this, he would never again, purposely, tell an untruth.

Boston had become a world of men and gaming hells. He didn't suppose Boston had much gambling before Gentleman Johnny Burgoyne's army arrived, but these new places were where he did his best work, and collected most of his information. Sometimes he got an IOU printed on the back of an important memo. He never redeemed those.

He thought about other games, even that ridiculous challenge he had made with Nina, but that no longer felt like a game, and he wasn't sure where the players stood.

There had been a second wager the men had made, behind Wythe's back and without his knowledge, that Alex would bed the pretty alewife before summer's end. He had ignored all attempts to question him. He didn't give a damn who won or lost that stupid wager. He chalked it up to boredom during wartime. But games they were, and although he'd rather have seen his last card table, he had become an excellent gamester.

Now he gamed with officers of the famed British Army, second and third sons with money to burn and too much time spent in this tired town. He laughed out loud at his strange predicament. His fellow drinkers at the coffee house turned in his direction. He hoped he looked sufficiently bored. He'd like them to believe he had nothing to live for beyond the next night at the tables.

He swallowed the last of his brandy. He hadn't been able to bring himself to drink ale at any of the pubs. No ale - he couldn't imagine a more perfect metaphor for this ridiculous situation. He wondered if he should laugh, cry or begin writing maudlin love poetry. He couldn't drink ale because he was in love. Love, what a perfectly damnable time to discover it. He'd realized that he loved her those days at the inn. He'd vowed to slay dragons and all sorts of manly things. But he hadn't actually admitted it, until he sat here alone.

Nothing could be less romantic than sitting in a cold, muddy and blockaded town while the woman you have just become aware that you cannot live without is a mere ten, maybe twelve, miles away, on the other side of two, three, maybe four checkpoints, armed by opposing armies. He pushed away a recurring vision of Nina driving her team into danger, his horse tied to her wagon and a gun held by an unseen man, aimed at her heart.

Later that night, after winning at dice and losing at cards, he went back to his rooms. Solemnity overwhelmed him. He stared at the dark windows of the early winter night, not really sure why he was here anymore. He had given the Americans enough information to prove what everyone knew, that townspeople were not being executed on the Common. He'd added a few juicy tidbits which, though unexpected, would not be unappreciated. He had carefully spread the word, "having read it in a letter from an old friend, who heard it from one of the soldiers he knew," that the soldiers at the neck below, and the heights above, were not going to storm the gates without warning. He couldn't imagine how his staying on through the long winter would help move ten thousand British soldiers and sailors back onto ships and out of the harbor.

***

The wooden crate, along with Bella and Jewel, arrived the next day. Nina had the men leave the large box in a corner of the brewhouse. It would be safe enough, and Alex could deal with it when he got back. A week later her curiosity was piqued, and she had Dodi help her move the crate to her own parlor.

That was the day Nina found the note tacked to her front door. She wasn't quite sure when it had been left or by whom, but she had no doubt who had written it. The note was a rebus. Nina sat in her kitchen to decipher it. The art was small and precise. She stared at it a few minutes to interpret the meaning of the letters and the pictures.

There were a few standard symbols and she did those first, filling in *I*'s for the eyes, and you for the yew bushes. There was a clock, that always stood for time, a key and box for safe, a well for deep. It took a minute to work out that the galleon was the Nina, but then the rest fell into place.

Dearest Nina,
Time is too short. I leave this small token with you to

hang hidden deep and safe. The way I feel when I am with
you. Nina, if the gods are kind, and fates allow, I will return,
and if you will have me, I will stay. You have my - it was
signed with a heart, drawn, not as two half circles that dipped
in the middle, but as a human or other mammalian heart with
valves and veins - and a simple *Alex*.

Nina wiped tears. He must have left something for her in
that box. Perhaps he wasn't sure he wanted her to have it until
now. She wondered if something had happened to him in
Boston. She resolved to get in there and make sure he was all
right, but first she had to see the token he had left for her.

Carrying the rebus and her translation, she went upstairs
to Alex's box, hidden in the corner of her parlor. She pried
open the heavy lid. Right on top was a small, lacquered silk
box. A little gaudy and painted in an elaborate design in red,
with gold etchings, it opened stiffly as if it had been closed for
a long time. The top and bottom were nearly fused together.
Inside was a small, blue velvet purse. Nina pulled the strings
open and poured out the contents. In her hand was a large
aquamarine set in gold filigree.

It was nothing even a young widow should own, not one
raised in the New England church. She lifted the chain. It, the
stone, and the gold surrounding it shimmered in the morning
light. The chain was soft as silken thread, made with three fine
chains, each braided, linked and intertwined. Nina slipped it
over her head. It was unusually long. Perhaps the maker had
planned that the stone would be hidden. What had he written?
Nina picked up the little piece of paper and read the rebus
again. 'Hidden deep and safe.'

It hung nestled between her breasts. It was small enough,
and the gold chain fine enough, that it would hang around her

neck unnoticed. It was large enough that she would never forget it was there. She wondered how Alex could have planned such a gift. How could he have known all those years ago that such a stone would match someone's eyes - her eyes? It was an unusual gem.

The bottom of the silk box had the remains of glue and another fabric. It had been stuck to something else, probably for a long time. Nina saw no reason to pretend she was not going to follow the clues to the end of this mystery. Of course, she was going to discover where in the wooden crate this little box had been stored. Carefully, she lifted out the things that Alex had left behind. Most of the objects were less than glamorous, but he had obviously traveled with this wooden crate for many years.

There were notes on the walls of the crate saying where he was, a diary of sorts, with a few words about what he had found. There were exotic fabrics and ribbons, Nina ran her fingers over silver bells and silken tassels. Smaller boxes lined the corners, but she ignored these. Along the back wall, under books and boxes, at the bottom left corner, was a tiny square of space left behind when something small and square had been pulled away. In the square was a note. Nina peered in to read it. It was in Italian. Nina had learned to read enough to translate. "Pull this from the glue when *tre importante* aqua eyes come to you, not a moment before." It seemed to be a message from Carlotta, the lover who seemed to see the future.

***

The men of the army, even those high in command, liked Alex Peele. Night after night, he carefully established himself as their friend, someone who was always ready to listen to sad stories from soldiers, men far away from family and loved ones. It wasn't a complete lie. He did feel sorry for men sent far from their homes to fight and die. If they wanted to talk, he was willing to listen, and since General Washington wanted him to stay in Boston until something could be done about the blockade, he set out to do more than merely absorb their chatter, to collect whatever bits of information might help him protect his home.

Thanks to that "friend, who had a friend in the American Army," he quickly became known as the fellow who had real knowledge of what was happening in the countryside. Because of that, or in spite of it, he was a much-requested drinking buddy among enlisted men and officers, the latter often asking, as if it were a joke, whether the countryfolk were ready to storm the gates. He was happy to reassure, calm anxious waters, and tell them the country was at peace. At the same time, he spread whatever misinformation might put the British off their guard - troops heading to Canada, establishing fortifications in New York - whatever he could make up based on their curiosity. He discovered he was good at it.

It didn't take long to get to know many of the officers by sight and even by name. He never let slip that he was an energetic, athletic man, always assuming the affect of the bored man-about-town. Mornings, he took a daily walk by the Common, saying good day to the camped soldiers there. He chatted with the men while quietly observing irregularities, and noting if, by chance, they seemed to be preparing to leave the town to harry the countryside.

By mid-December, when the deep cold moved in, there was little troop movement in or out of the harbor on naval vessels. Washington's orders had been to concentrate on the people of Boston, the troops, and the loyalists moving in for their safety, not the river or harbor - those could be observed from other points.

It was assumed that the British had spies in the countryside, and the General wanted to know when these men, or perhaps women, returned to Boston with their memos. That night near the river had surprised him - Alex had not expected coming so close to capture while outside the town. He understood the risks living in Boston, but to be accosted in Cambridge was unsettling in the extreme. More than worried about himself, his concern for Nina and Jack increased as the days wore on, and he desperately sought for a way to discover if she had gotten home safely.

Across from his rooms on Queen Street stood the small hardware store run by Paul Revere, Jr. His father and family had fled to the country, and were then living in Watertown, not far from Angier's Corner in Newton, and Nina's parents. Paul the younger had been left behind to care for the store. Early on, Alex had decided not yet to make himself known to the young man, for the safety of both of them.

Alex decided that it was finally time to make the young man's acquaintance. He went shopping. The sign over the door showed a hammer hitting a nail, and the bell on the door clanged as Alex opened and closed it behind himself. He pulled out a door hinge he had wrenched off and broken that morning.

"Mr. Revere, I wonder if you have a replacement?" He handed over the hinge. The boy - he might have been fifteen - was already taller than his famous father, with what must be his mother's light hair and thin, narrow face.

"I have a few that might do." His voice hadn't yet settled into its low range and cracked a little. "I'm afraid stocks are low - it's not like the British are bringing in goods for the local stores."

"Not likely you would sell many. Have you had any luck getting supplies from the other direction, the countryside?" Alex asked softly, not sure if the young man would consider such words an affront or an attempt at humor.

"No. We hadn't had shipments of fine hardware for some time. We always agreed to the non-importation agreements." He eyed Alex carefully. It did not do to be open or generous with his words. "As for the countryside, what would your interest be, sir, in goods from there?"

Another customer paid and exited the store, leaving just the two of them. Alex waited as Revere walked to the door, locked it and stood in front of it, a pistol out and pointed at Alex. He was very assured for one so young.

"I should ask you to leave. No one is fooled by me. My family is known, my father is wanted for high crimes, but Gage and Howe have the decency to leave me alone. But you, you are not what you seem. Who are you and what do you want?"

Revere walked back to his workbench, took Alex's hinge and some plyers, and bent it back into shape. He picked up the pistol from the counter. With his left hand he held out the black hinge. "Here! Leave or speak."

Alex leaned against a pillar. He found the young man honest. He was almost ready to be honest in return. "I am a refugee from the country, enjoying the hospitality of the British. In other words I am precisely what you see."

"Fine, then take the hinge and leave."

"I'm Peele by the way, my friends call me Alex." He put the hinge in his pocket, unlocked the door and left. He returned the next day for a lantern wick, and the day after for a bellows he'd spotted in the corner the day before. As he was leaving, he turned.

"Revere, I have a friend I may have put in danger, and I

207

wondered -" Alex slowed down his speech so as not to sound demanding. "I should like to discover if she is well. It occurred to me you might have regular communications with - " Alex jutted his jaw to the west.

The lad sighed looking tired. "Peele, obviously you are not the first person to ask that. I will tell you what I tell everyone who asks that question - no. I have no special way of talking to anyone beyond the town borders."

"That's a shame." Alex didn't believe him for a moment. He turned with his bellows to leave.

"How did you put this person in danger if you have been in Boston since, when did you say?"

"I hadn't, but it has been since autumn."

"Then I expect your knowing or not knowing can no longer matter."

"You have me there, except if I am to be completely honest, the incident occurred more recently. I had something to give to a friend, and I may have rowed over the back bay during a low tide. I need to know if the lady made it home safely."

"Tides were low during the full moon. I don't suppose you could just row back over and ask?"

"No, someone might be waiting for me."

"Specifically you?"

"Afraid so, yes."

"I see. My sisters sometimes run over the flats. They think it is fun. You may as well tell me who, and what. I will find out what I can. Where is she to look?"

"No further than the First Church in Newton, just up from the bridge at Watertown. Her name is . . . " The men spoke in hushed tones too quietly to be heard through the walls and too slurred to be understood. Alex felt better asking for help, even if the boy was little more than a child. Clearly his father believed that his son was ready to endure the rigors of running the store during such times.

Chapter 17

It started when little Fanny, a child with a round face and reddish brown hair, peeped her head over the Tyrie pew at the First Church.

"Who might you be?" Jack was concerned the unrecognized girl was alone and nudged his mother.

"I'm Fanny, Frances Revere. I'm to find Nina." Jack pointed out his mother who was carefully reading along with the minister in the prayer book.

She motioned for little Fanny to come and sit by her side. After the morning service was done, they strolled outside to talk. Once they were out of the building, an older girl appeared.

"Someone was worried about you getting home safe."

Nina thought no one could get in or out of the town. "How am I to tell this person I am fine?"

"It's best to go over the mudflats at low tide. If you're light enough you don't sink, and I bet with it frozen you could get a cart over. See, the soldiers don't really care what you bring in, as long as it isn't contraband or maps. They're more worried about people coming to stay and eat their food. It's the Americans on the outside who care about making life too sweet for the Redcoats."

Nina went back inside for the afternoon, formulating a plan for getting into Boston to see Alex on Christmas. There would be a service here with the family, then dinner, then a second service. She would explain she needed to see to the inn. Travelers often needed help in the winter. It was dishonest, but would hurt no one. Christmas was not a particularly important day to her family. They wouldn't mind if she left early.

The next day, Nina visited Deborah Revere to ask her advice for getting into the closed town.

"Best to go by the Neck from Roxbury. My daughters think running over the flats is fun and easy, but only if you are ten years old. Get a pass from someone at Cambridge for the American line. The British only care if you are supplying the rebels. From what I hear, if you have something they want, and you promise not to stay, they will let you through."

So there she was on Christmas afternoon with a wagon full of greens to exploit the British fascination with decorating at Yuletide. For days she had been in the woods cutting greens from the pines and fir. Under the floorboards she had hidden as much firewood as would fit, a tin bucket full of roast turkey, cranberries and mincemeat pie, and two bottles of ale.

It had been easier to accomplish than she could have guessed. The officer at Cambridge was happy to help his friend Alex, winking at her most inappropriately. The Americans at the neck were happy to help once they read the letter from Alex's friend, and the British were happy enough that someone got through the line with Christmas greens, especially when she explained that she was needed back at home as early as possible.

Nina stopped on Common Street, where she told a sentry that she had greens to sell. She did not overcharge, but saw no good reason not to ask a penny or two for her trouble. Happily, the men were delighted with a few pine boughs, and more than paid for her time. Finally the wagon was empty of all the fir, pine boughs and holly leaves. Nina continued north from the Common to Treamount Street and turned right onto Queen Street. Number fifteen was on the second block. The whole area was quiet - quieter than it should have been on a Monday, even on a day when the British Army and Anglican Tories went to church. She left her boxes at the rear entrance to the house and found a nearby livery, explaining that she would be leaving very early in the morning.

At Alex's door, she grabbed a box of wood and balanced the tin of food on the top between pieces of firewood. Carefully she climbed the stairs and knocked gently at the door.

Alex had accompanied his friends, the young sons of families with connections to the previous governor, and officers who had the bad luck to be stuck in Boston on Christmas Day, to church that morning. Many of the current residents were of a mind to celebrate the birth of the Lord, but the town did not have a festive feel. Not only was it warm enough for the snow to have turned to mud, but few homes had bothered even to hang a pine bough in the window.

Before the occupation and naval blockade, the townspeople of Boston had begun to enjoy the celebrations around December the twenty-fifth, but it was always complicated for them. First, the Puritan edicts ran contrary to celebrating just one day for the birth of Christ, conflating the winter holiday with the pagan solstice of the north, and the Saturnalia, the Roman celebration of the new year which was both pagan and raucous. Traditionalists argued that any celebration around the winter solstice was Popery, or even paganism. Others understood that it was important to celebrate the birth of Christ, even if the day had not been a significant holiday in the previous century. Everyone, it seemed, had begun to agree that it was unkind, in this cold, dark place, not to have some celebration at the dark end of the year.

Now, however, the occupied town was dreary and sad on the best days. Roads had not been groomed or cleaned, wooden walks had not been repaired, and lights that were scheduled to be hung near the market were either broken or had never been set up.

Alex spent as much time as he could in forced jollity with his friends. If he could have attended a service at the nearby New South Meetinghouse, the day would have had some meaning, but to have gone to New South would have attracted the wrong kind of attention. He had worked very hard to be the man everyone liked and nobody noticed. It wouldn't do to have notice made of him now.

Ruefully, he acknowledged that this life was exhausting him. He lied so often about who he was and what he was doing that he had lost his energy. His life had no zest. Every night, he dressed and went to whichever club next was on his list, living the charade of the well-heeled Tory looking to entertain himself until his army won back the colonies. He played his role so well that he had been invited by the young officers to spend time at the Province House drinking with them and their superiors, officers of the highest ranks. Lots of inadvertent information had started coming his way. Now was not a good time to be noticed in any capacity, certainly not for the stupid mistake of going to the wrong church.

It was at the Province House that he became acquainted with the small ash girl. Twelve, though she looked eight, Maryann Bickerstaff had been sending papers, carefully transcribed from Generals Howe, Clinton and Burgoyne's notes, to her father at Cambridge. She was so small and insignificant Alex had almost missed her. To a British aristocrat she was less than noticeable. He had been reading the London newspapers when a raised aristocratic voice from another room caused him to look up.

"Damn! What is this nonsense doing with my notes?" General Howe was angry, his voice carrying through the house. He picked up and then threw a piece of foolscap with Greek lettering printed in a student hand back on the table. He had accidentally picked it up with some other papers and glared at the student work that made no sense.

Alex picked his head up from his reading. He could see the men through the open door, and carefully lowered his gaze. He knew those papers. It would be nearly impossible to decipher the Greek words written by the girl because it was not written in Greek. Of course, General Howe and his staff had all had at least a rudimentary classical education. The student who had carefully written Greek letters that could be deciphered phonetically into English words had done an excellent job of making General Howe's notes and memos look like childish gibberish.

The General exited, trailed by his staff. The small insignificant girl, the girl who tended the fires in the mansion that was the Province House on School Street, picked up her foolscap with the Greek letters and carefully put it on the cabinet top, with other, similar papers that were stacked with Alex's London Journal. She didn't turn or look at Alex, only curtseyed briefly in his direction and left the room with her kindling and ash bucket.

His head too full of memos and newspapers, Greek letters

and small children who should be more careful, Alex left his fellows' company as early as was polite and went home, ready to spend Christmas alone with a book. Once he was as warm and comfortable as possible, he set a bottle of fine cognac next to him on the table and began pouring the warm wine into a crystal glass. He had a copy of Seneca open on his lap, but right then he found the wine more interesting than Stoicism. It wasn't that the Stoics weren't compelling - it just seemed redundant to him. What he needed was to get very drunk.

He remembered Christmas a year ago. It had been his first in America after being in Italy the winter before. Music ringing from the churches and halls echoed in his memory. He never expected his New England homeland to celebrate with the elegance of Florence, the abandon of Rome or even the chiming of London, but he had put holly and mistletoe in his parlor and a candle in the window. Now there was nothing.

Alex looked at his glass and realized that it, and the bottle on the table, were empty. He had been making up for a week's work of staying judiciously sober. He tried to stand to find another bottle of wine. He grabbed one and sat back hard when he heard footsteps on the stairs. He briefly considered throwing off his despond before he was asked to go out to a another boring evening. He rejected the idea, and was sitting with a full glass of wine and a new bottle when the footsteps retreated and reappeared, echoing in the hall as they moved down and then back up the stairs.

The steps went down and came up a third time. This time they knocked on the door. He had already decided he would say "enter" rather then getting up to answer it. He had achieved the perfect state of inebriation, and didn't want to wreck it.

He might have grunted, but it didn't matter if he made no sound. The door just opened. Boxes of firewood were pushed from the hallway through the door by a lady's foot in dark burgundy boots. Even in boots, she had a lovely ankle - very pretty legs from what he could see. Alex sat back. This was either going to turn out to be a drunken hallucination, or else he was asleep and having a fabulous dream. Ladies with nice legs who brought firewood could only exist in dreams.

Alex smelled food. Now he was sure the lady was a hallucination. Roast turkey and cranberries. Food that shouldn't be here. He swallowed deeply from his glass. The mirage with the pretty burgundy boots threw off a burgundy cloak and revealed a green gown with a purple striped petticoat. The gown was low cut and revealed more than it should have to a man as drunk as he was. He reached for his glass to prolong the hallucination.

In this dream, Nina was building his tiny fire until it gave off heat. Other firewood was lined up in boxes near the door. The vision moved near him. She leaned over him, exposing a lovely neckline and the tops of full breasts. Carefully he did not move or speak, careful not to wake himself or shake the apparition away. He swallowed hard.

Nina knew when a man was drunk. She took her tin camp kettle and unpacked it on a small table near the fire, setting up a plate of turkey and stuffing. She sat on the floor at his feet, and handed him a piece of turkey on a fork. "Alex, you need food, eat." He blinked at the plate of good food and the fork in her hand. Obediently, he took the fork and ate the food. When the plate was nearly empty, he reached for his wine. Nina replaced the glass in his hand with a tankard of ale.

"It doeshn't sheem right to eat. I have made a polishy of not eating." Alex sat back in his chair. He took a long drink of Nina's ale. He could feel his head shrink and mind clear.

"Why don't you eat? You are very thin." All sorts of panicked worries began swimming around Nina's head. Terrible things happened to people when they began to starve. She wished she could hold him, drag him away from here and care for him, but she was sure he would refuse.

He spoke quietly, almost needing to force out the truth, as though he was not used to simple speech. "There is little food. Most townspeople are here because they have nowhere to go. The redcoats are only holding warehouses and store goods here, not people - they are free to leave. I don't mean the Tories, the refugees, as they call themselves, but the locals. Food is smuggled in for them. I don't deserve their food. I eat with the Tories, but I can't eat much."

It was nonsense, and yet Nina understood. She would never fault Alex for a lack of discipline, or of lacking a clear sense of doing what he believed. It would be foolish to try to change his mind on such matters. "Seneca?" She picked up his book from where he had dropped it. "Don't you think this ascetic life is punishment enough?"

"Punishment? I am not being punished. I am performing a necessary task."

"Yes, I know." She turned through the pages of the book.

Alex relaxed back into his drunkenness. The food was nice, and it was very good to be warm, and having Nina or her apparition here was good. He was sure he would wake in the morning, cold and hungry, and with a terrible hangover. His mouth tasted of ale. He hadn't thought he could conjure the taste of Nina's ale. He hadn't had good ale since that night in Cambridge, when he had lost Thorne and Nina. The false Alex Peele had completely stopped drinking beer. He turned to find that his apparition was talking to him. He fought to focus.

"How is it you are here? You are here, yes, not a hallucination?"

"Deborah Revere said I should come to town. No, that's not the truth." Nina fumbled, trying to find words. "The truth is I wanted to come - she told me how." She stumbled over her words, thinking of nonsense, but was not ready to tell him. She looked up at the man in the chair. He was as familiar and dear as could be, but she had seen him only once in the last four months, and that was five minutes on the back of a horse.

Alex poured some cognac into his empty tankard and handed Nina a glass of the wine. She sat close to him on the rug near the fire. He rested his hand in her hair. "Start at the beginning. Nina, I'm afraid I can't focus, but I will try." His slight laugh gave her courage.

"Alex, it was the night of that dinner party. I tried to tell you – after – when we were on Thorne."

Alex remembered being afraid for Nina's life, afraid there would be no reason to carry on with his own. Was there a way to explain all that? "I remember a terrible need to shoot the bastard who held you hostage in the road. I recall you trying to tell me something. I remember that the gunshots interfered."

"Yes they did." Nina took a deep breath. Sitting very straight, she put her hands in her lap. "The next week I made a confession at Meeting. They voted. I'm a member of the First Church now."

"Yes, congratulations. I know your family must be relieved. But, I am sorry. What does that have to do with what you need to tell me?"

Nina started speaking before Alex finished, before she lost her nerve. "My confession was about Johnny. That I had stayed angry at him for ten years. I confessed that I had never forgiven him for leaving me, and dying before we could make a marriage. Then I told the elders that someone had come into my life. And that I had asked God to help me forgive Johnny. I needed to make room in my heart to love this person. Because I love him."

Alex held his breath. He had been present at many confessions. Some people had begun to take them lightly, but Nina wouldn't. Such public confessions were required in the Old Light tradition for church membership. Dr. Tyrie was strictly Old Light. Confessing a sexual love was unusual, but nothing was unheard of.

"You'll understand." Alex nodded that he did. "It happened on the way to the dinner party. I had been screaming - howling louder than the wind - at the unfairness of my life, at Johnny. I guess I was screaming at God. Suddenly, I felt all my anger leave me. I cried for a while, and then I wasn't scared anymore.

"When I finished my story, the ladies in the Congregation started to cry. Their husbands looked a little uncomfortable. But the wives all ran to hug me.

"Alex, I am not afraid anymore. It may be wrong to say, but after that night I feel reborn."

Alex pulled himself out of his chair and walked the few short steps to the window. He pushed his head against the cold glass and looked at the growing dark of the late afternoon. Clouds blocked the moon, making the evening as dreary as the day had been, until now. He thanked the gracious God for bringing Nina here, bringing her just for a moment, into his complicated life.

He, too, had had the moment when he realized that he loved this woman. Like hers, it had happened during these long weeks alone. But the false Alex Peele could not be here with this newly reborn and clean Nina. He could not love, or make love, to Nina when he was this man. Unfortunately, there was no way out of this that she would not interpret as a rejection, a rejection that might do untold damage to such a delicate woman. There was no way - but there was one. Dishonesty was his new name. He might hurt Nina by telling her the truth, but he wouldn't hurt Nina by being a sloppy drunk.

"Darling," he carefully slurred his words, "you may be sure. But I am afraid that you find me in a bit of incapacitation." That was a hard one, and he made the most of it. His gait wobbled as came back and sat next to Nina on the warm rug. He didn't need to fake that, nor that his head swooned as she leaned into him, false. Her kiss was very sweet and brief - his mouth must taste like cognac. He took just a minute and closed his eyes. He felt her head on his shoulder, her hands in his hair, greedily pulling out his queue, her fingers against his scalp.

In a few minutes, Nina stood. There was a short corridor to Alex's bedroom. She went in and set the fire. It was clear from the cold ashes there had not been many fires in this room. Again she was aware of wanting nothing so much as to drag Alex back to the *Wheel and Hammer*, feed him well and let him rest. She could see the weariness in his eyes. Even the fact he was long in his cups couldn't hide the profound tiredness.

It felt good to have Nina here, good to stop worrying about her. Perhaps the recurring nightmare - where he stood watching Nina dragged away and held at gunpoint, while he, so afraid to expose his identity, did nothing to save her - would cease. He hated himself in those dreams. He had lost his heart that morning with a kiss. Nina's strength and beauty held him in awe. That kiss had nearly cost Washington his eyes in Boston. The enterprise was only saved by Nina's young son walking in the kitchen door. For all he knew, young Jack had saved the American cause that morning.

He had lost his heart, though it had taken some time to acknowledge it, lost, just as Carlotta had seen in the strange way of hers, to a woman with aquamarine eyes. He remembered when she had given him the bezel and told him to give it to the lady whose eyes matched the stone, the one who would own his heart. Carlotta should be hanged as a witch.

He watched through the open door. Nina had set the second fire and shed her shawl. She looked magnificent in the green and violet gown, the colors like a spring tulip. He summoned his energy to bank the fire and put the screen in front of the hearth. He forced himself to drench his desire in the knowledge that she would be better off without the false man he was that winter.

He half crawled into his room and climbed onto the bed. He let his head fall back into the soft pillows, and closed his eyes. These pillows were the one extravagance he had allowed himself in this strange, false life. It was his one delicious moment per day, letting his head sink into softness. The room was warm, which was a pleasant shock. He kept his eyes half closed and watched his Nina take off her boots and socks in front of the fire.

That simple act was breathtaking. He had seen the veil dancers in Istanbul, and sat in the salons of courtesans in Paris. Nothing he had ever seen on his travels compared to watching Nina step out of thick boots, warm socks and thick, quilted petticoats. He swallowed. He willed his body to be as inebriated as he needed it to be.

Nina fiddled with the strings and hooks of her gown. Her heart pounded in her ears. She wished it was with excitement, but she knew that she was afraid. She hated to retreat, afraid of humiliation and of hurting Alex's feelings if she failed. She breathed, telling herself it would be perfect. She would not curl into a frightened little ball. Her heavy, quilted petticoats fell to her feet. She stepped out of them, and turned to the bed.

Alex was soundly asleep, his head deep in the nest of pillows, a smile on his lips. She had felt him watching her until just a minute before. Quietly Nina tiptoed around the two rooms. She snuffed the candles and checked hearths, banking coals so that they would be alive in the morning. She washed her teeth in some clean water and braided her hair. Then she pulled back the covers on Alex's warm soft bed and climbed in next to him, snuggling against his hard back. She put her arms around him and drew him close, breathing his scent deep into her lungs. It felt familiar. At the same time she felt warm, a tingly feeling that had nothing to do with the temperature in the room. She had not expected to feel physically connected. It was almost sinful and wonderfully right. Nina sighed with contentment.

Alex felt Nina press her delicious body into his back. He cursed himself for the necessity of deception, but he was smiling as he fell into a not-drunken slumber.

It was before dawn that Alex woke to Nina's gently climbing out of bed. He remembered enough of the night to understand what had and what had not happened, and why. Alex fixed the fire in his parlor and set water on the hearth to boil for washing and coffee. He ran out to the privy, only slightly surprised to see Nina's Suffolks, harnessed and ready to leave. He greeted the horses and wished them a good new year, then he pushed a leather pouch under the bench and went back into the house. He climbed back into the warm bed, his head splitting.

"I have to leave." Nina, dressed in a warm wool gown, leaned over to kiss him good-bye. Alex pulled her into his arms. He rolled her beneath him and covered her mouth with his, deepening the kiss when he felt Nina fingers dig into his back and run through his hair.

Nina opened her lips as Alex demanded, lost in the whirlwind of sensation, his fabulous hair loose in her fingers. Her feet struck the floor as the clock struck its second charm. Alex let her go, picking up her fingers and kissing them one by one.

"Thank you." Nina heard the sweet words as she went down the stairs and home. Alex watched out the window as she hawed at the horses and headed south down the neck.

Chapter 18

The day had dawned cloudy and warm, but it chilled during the drive west, and by the time Nina arrived at the falls it was raining, with the promise of turning to snow. She walked the big horses into their shed, and unloaded the few things stored behind the bench. She found the leather pouch as it rolled backwards and dropped onto the ground. It was long and slim, shaped like a small log with two ties along one side. She put it deep into her pocket before tending to her horses and going back to the stableyard and inn.

Nina heard the loud, angry voices before she rounded the corner. She was glad to have spent a day away, but she wouldn't wish this anger on her staff, either. She took a deep breath and moved forward, ready to prevent any escalation.

"Joshua, you must stop fraternizing with those men. You know the Committee has suspicions that they are spying for the British. We can't prove it, but it would be safer for you if you dissociated from them." The speaker was Martin Jewett.

Nina stopped to listen to Josh's reply. He was unrepentant, even petulant. Neither attitude would help. "Look, Mr. Jewett. You've taken my rifle and told me to stay out of trouble. I don't know what else you want." He turned his head and spotted Nina standing at the corner of the inn. His gaze and stance shifted. He looked oddly triumphant as he gave her a look of deep loathing. He gave the men of the Committee a vicious smile as he turned his back to them and went into the stable. Nina felt she had missed something, but knew she had

224

to let it go. Whatever Martin Jewett and his men decided to do about Josh, she had no time or inclination to worry about it.

She did worry and then recalled the conversation she'd had with Josh the day before her Christmas journey. It was one they reargued often. "...but Josh, how can we stay connected to a foreign government that will not allow us to grow, but to which we are required to pay taxes? We cannot build manufactories. They barely let us build our own ships, and you know we can't trade freely even if another nation is nearer, or will pay a higher price for our goods."

"Aunt Nina." Josh spoke slowly as if talking to an idiot. "We are subjects of a great King and empire. I am surprised you don't realize and respect it, but I will not be bullied into feeling differently."

Nina sighed. She knew arguing wouldn't help, but she feared for Josh's safety and for that of his mother and her farm. Josh had always felt strongly about his father's heritage, his youth in Dumfries and London, and how proud he was to be from England and Scotland, and "not this provincial backwater," as he would moan and complain. Added to that, Josh had idolized his older brother and could not square Johnny's dying for the King in one war and now fighting against the Crown in this one.

Nina understood his view, but her ancestors had been in America for over a hundred years, and if that wasn't enough time for Massachusetts and the other colonies to grow into nationhood - to be fully represented in Parliament - to have the rights of Englishmen, then how long should it take? She had tried to convince her young brother-in-law of the right of the colonists' cause against the Crown. Alternately she had tried to explain that it might be safer for him to remain quiet about his beliefs. Certainly, it would be better for them to send away those English boarders his mother had taken on. Josh insisted his mother liked the two well-behaved gentlemen, Nina had let the issue drop.

She said nothing, but knowing that those men lived nearby frightened Nina, even though they had not been seen at the *Wheel* for weeks. In fact, she had seen neither since that morning she had nearly ridden Thorne into their trap. Josh had told her that they remained interested in buying the gray stallion for stud.

Nina pretended she had no idea which horse they had in mind, there were so many. Their interest in Thorne, and of course in Alex, remained a secret she shared with Jack and no one else. Even if she could have gotten word to Alex that the inn was unsafe for his horse and his friends, what could he possibly do about it?

Later, in her own kitchen, she pulled at the long shoulder strap of the case she'd found in the wagon. She untied the two leather strips and unrolled the little round box. She pulled out the documents and laid them on the table. The lettering was in a child's hand and the symbols were Greek. She did not read Greek, but she had helped Jack with the alphabet last spring. Those few months seemed like a lifetime ago.

She put her mind back to the document in front of her. Carefully she sounded it out. The words were not Greek - phonetically, the sounds were English. Nina read just enough to know that these papers included maps and lists of names. She'd had no idea why Alex was in Boston. These papers surprised her and showed that someone was copying the highest level of planning in Gen. Howe's offices. If that person was not Alex, he was closely connected to the person who was.

Nina felt a shiver of fear that the case might have fallen where Josh could have seen it. One document had names of men and women who had signed their property over to the Crown as a pledge of loyalty. The information was priceless to the Patriots. At the same time, possession of such a document was enough to cost any patriot his head. The code was confusing and brilliant. The Greek lettering would slow anyone who was trying to decipher the papers quickly, and anyone expecting Greek would be oddly confused. The lot needed to get to George Washington as quickly as possible.

***

Alex rose late in the morning. He hoped Nina would not believe him to be the debauched libertine she had seen the night before. He would not look back at these months as his finest work, but horrifying as it was, it needed to be done. Late in the night, his loneliness a raw scab, and his head fuzzy from cognac and heated desire, he'd told Nina more about this work than was safe for her to know. He had confessed that without winning at the tables, he could not support his work in Boston, where he could do some good. Foolishly, he had told her he was nearly broke. At least he hadn't told her about the child, the girl with dark hair and equally dark eyes, who set the fires and cleaned the grates, whom the men, in the arrogance of military honors and aristocracy, ignored.

Alex had to chuckle over their ignorance of New England ways, that they saw no reason to hide their notes and maps. In their world, it was impossible for the cinder-girl to read and write. So little Maryann was invisible and harmless. But she had learned that and more. Like all New England girls, she had attended school, no doubt a well-run Dame-school. Someone else had taught her the phonetics of the Greek alphabet. If Alex could guess, it would be older brothers who had created a

227

family game.

He found her strange notes and scribbled maps wrapped in the well-read newspapers. These were the papers she used for firestarting, and were generally ignored. No one noticed Maryann's very early arrival, and of course no one cared. The rooms were warm and the hearth swept. She did the job that was expected of her. They missed the rest.

Alex stripped and washed, enjoying the last warm fire he would allow himself this winter. He then dressed in what he considered his disguise for an afternoon of elegance, wine and gaming. Nina had left one small holly bough on a side table that had so far avoided the fire. He smiled at her small attempt at holiday cheer for his gloomy world. He lifted a stalk to look at the bright red berries. Hidden from first sight under the branch, Nina had left a pile of coins. It had to be all that she'd earned selling pine and fir to the soldiers on the Common. There was enough mixed British coin to make him look like a rich American libertine for days to come. Alex laughed at the many ways Nina amazed him.

Chapter 19

The next week brought one small crisis after another, so it was impossible for Nina to leave the tavern and bring the papers to General Washington. One day the midday meal burnt, and only the proprietress was able to serve extra cider and ale to placate the regulars' meal of bread and cheese. Then the girls got sick, one at a time, with sneezes and coughing, so that she had sent them home and done the work herself. And finally it was Josh.

Two days into the new year, she walked into a nearly empty taproom one morning to find Sukie crying and Dodi in a furor.

"Girls! What on earth?" Nina looked around the room, nearly empty at this hour on the dreary day.

"It's Josh. He stole the pot money. Now Mrs. Cotton is outside trying to make him give it back." Dodi stomped as she spoke, giving her sniveling friend a hard look. "Sukie, stop crying."

Nina ignored the squabbling. She pulled a heavy cloak from a peg and threw it over her shoulders. Then she reached under the long counter at the front of the room, taking the long rifle she had inherited from Johnny, and the pistol she always carried when she made deliveries. It had been a while since she had fired either, but that did not mean she had forgotten how. She loaded both with powder and ball. Stuffing the pistol in her pocket, she stepped outside.

A storm had dropped nearly half a foot of snow the last few days, ending with fog and rain. Now, there was a light, almost-frozen drizzle falling from the skies, and the ground was an icy, muddy mess. Josh stood near the stables. Five horses, their reins in his hands, waited to move on. They shifted anxiously as Josh and Mrs. Cotton battled with words.

"Joshua, I have known you nearly your whole life, now go put that money back. You have what you came for."

Nina stepped out of the shadow. She held the rifle to her shoulder and aimed it at Josh. Her heart was pounding and she fought to keep her hands from shaking. "Josh, tell me what is going on here. Maria, go back inside." Mrs. Cotton gratefully ran through the open inn door.

Josh looked up. He seemed surprised that someone else had entered the scene. "Nina, I've had enough. I am taking what is mine and moving on. Those men, the committee, harrowing me, bothering mother and my younger brother, it's gone on long enough. If I leave, they will leave mother alone."

Nina lifted the rifle just slightly. "That's fine, you should do that, but what about the pot-money you took from the kitchen?"

He looked slightly chagrined. "I need money."

"Where is the coin you've been saving all these years to start your stable?"

He kicked at the muddy ground. "I lent it to those boarders of my mother's - to help with their rent. Mother has it now. I can't take it from her."

"Well you can't take it from me." Nina thought of the inn without that bit of coin. A week without custom would bring the already nearly-desperate situation crashing down. She thought of the three girls whose families relied on the tips and pay they received here, the rooms over the taproom, their only home. She also thought of the generations of Bigelows who had worked the brewhouse and tavern, building it into the prosperous place it was now, and how Jack, Martha and Henry would have work and a place to live, no matter what, in these uncertain times.

"Josh, I can't let you leave with my money. I'm sorry, but I can't. Put the sack down and get out of here." She tightened the grip on the gun, sure that the light, icy rain had wrecked the black powder, but hoping Josh was not thinking so clearly.

"Nina, you wouldn't shoot me." He started to mount the one horse that wore a saddle.

Nina fired at the branch over his head, twigs fell around him. He brushed them off. She pulled the pistol from her pocket and held it in front of her, her arms outstretched, both hands clasped around the weapon. "Josh, now!"

He dug his heels into the horse's sides, shouted 'haw' to signal the other animals, and threw the bag over Nina's head into a pile of wet, muddy snow. Relieved, she let the ball out of the pistol, picked up the rifle from where she had let it fall, and retrieved the sack with the coin from the snowbank. Nina put the coins back in the kitchen, and confronted a future without horses or a stableman. The incident with Josh had made her realize, more than ever, that the Americans would need all the little nudges possible along the way to win the war.

She walked from one end of the stable to the other. The nearly-empty building echoed with her footsteps. It was past time to get the strange Greek documents to Washington. The inn's small cart horse was the only animal in the stalls. Her Suffolks were safely in their shed. She had never tried to ride one of the big horses. It might be possible with a side saddle, but that was not an option. She saddled the little mare, hoping she didn't mind a ride. The ground was simply too muddy for cartwheels.

231

Dory Codington

Nina arrived at the camp at lunch time, and sat in the anteroom of the General's offices, jealously smelling cooking food. After a while, one of the secretaries brought her a piece of roasted turkey and a slice of bread. Nina was grateful, but as often as the men offered to take them, she would not leave her documents with anyone but the General.

It was much later when he was able to see her. She nodded awake, and was ushered into the room by a suffering secretary who rolled his eyes and shrugged his shoulders at her. Nina smiled back sweetly and swept by him into the office.

"General, I will be brief." Nina responded to his query, sitting where he offered. "I had occasion to be in Boston on Christmas afternoon." The General's eyebrows lifted in surprise. He nodded that she should continue. "Our line recognized that I had dinner for Alex Peele and a cart of firewood for their friend, and let me pass. I brought in some green boughs for the British troops on the Common. Their guards seemed to believe it was Christian charity and allowed me to pass. As I was leaving before dawn, Mr. Peele put this in my wagon. I did not discover it until I returned home. I'm sorry circumstances did not allow me to hand this to you sooner." She handed the cylindrical case to him and moved to leave the room.

"General, it seems to be English written phonetically in Greek letters. Someone working for you, us, is very clever."

"Yes Mrs. Bigelow, she is very clever. One hopes she is as careful as she is intelligent." He sighed, worry written on his face. "These were written by the daughter of one of my commanders. She looks far younger than her years, and playacts as a servant in the Province House. She was trapped in Boston, living at her aunt's home. Please understand this was completely her idea. Neither her father, nor I, approves in the least. However, to be honest, we do not regret her contributions."

"Yes General, I can understand that. I suspect it comes with parenting." Nina moved to the door as Washington bent over the papers now open on his desk.

He stood and walked her to the door. "Thank you, Mrs. Bigelow, your coming out on such a dismal day is a gracious act." He took her hand, bowing gently over it.

Nina looked up, "General Washington, if there is anything I can do for you, or even if it is just that you and Mrs. Washington need an hour away from camp – my tavern, the *Wheel and Hammer* at the Lower Falls, is not far. Most of the local men know the location. I would be honored to have you as guests."

Nina went back to Goldie and took the blanket off the little horse. She was just about to mount when she felt someone behind her and hands put over her eyes.

"Guess who?" She heard the man laugh.

"Eliphalet! You're safe! When did you get back?" He stepped to her side. She stared at him hard in the almost dusk of the winter afternoon. He looked haggard. Clearly the expedition had not gone well.

"We lost too many good men, Nina. We just weren't ready for such a trek through the wilderness to Canada. The nicest way to put it is that they were ready for us." He sighed "Maybe some years from now, I will tell you about it."

"You know, Wythe, I would be happy to listen whenever you are ready to tell it. I wish I knew what Johnny's trek through Pontiac's land was like. I am no summer bloom who needs to be protected from such stories, much as you might think I am."

"I don't think that way, I'm sorry if I did. But now the sun is low, and you have to ride if you are heading back. I will come by when I get leave, and you can tell me about your life these months. I think I need stories of normal happenings."

Nina chuckled that there was little to make Wythe happy about the state of his cousin's life, but that would have to wait. He kissed her cheek, pulling her into his arms for a life-affirming hug. He lifted her onto the horse and waved his friend on her way.

***

In spite of winning regularly, Alex was known as an easy mark, and he found it amusing. Thanks to Nina's coin, he became the fellow who was happy to lose, who paid for a round, gambled easily, and laughed when he paid his IOU's.

"Peele, you have to have a pint, this is good."

"Thanks lieutenant, but you know I don't drink ale."

"I recall, someone said that it was because you proclaimed that all the ale in Boston tasted 'used'. Did you say such a thing about the local brew?"

Alex recalled the less polite word he had used to describe the carelessly made swill. He nodded as he carefully sipped his wine, always pretending to drink more than he did.

The perfectly turned out lieutenant pulled on his pint, grimacing as he did so. "My brother has written of perfection, the perfect ale. Brewed, he claims, of clean well water, and aged in a river-cooled cellar by a waterfall. He is most poetic when he says it is the best he has tasted in America. He is a mariner and has visited many ports. Therefore, one must suppose he had tasted many ales.

"He is a year older than myself, and I trust his judgement. I'd like to wager that if we can get some of that ambrosia here, you will drink it. We need the distraction of the wager, so I will consult with the quartermaster as to how we can get a barrel or two past the lines. Perhaps the experiment will alleviate the tedium for an afternoon."

Men lined up to put their names in the betting book that sat on a table in the public parlor of the Province House. True to form and proof of ennui, they did not care on what they were betting. Alex tried to look bored, but he guessed this might have something to do with the *Wheel and Hammer* and wondered what the outside world was up to. "How did your brother come to mention this ale?"

The blue-eyed lieutenant's voice got low, as though he was revealing a dark secret. "My sister-in-law needed cambric. I don't quite understand it myself." He shrugged, helpless at women's requests. "A gown she had seen at a local event - the wearer said the fabric was woven in the center of Newton, south of the first church. Locally-woven fabrics make her giddy, Jason tells me, so they traveled from their home in Salem to meet the weaver." The man's indulgent smile made it clear that his brother was not the only one fond of this sister-in-law.

"My brother is recuperating from some injuries and cannot yet work, so he indulged her and off they went looking for the weaver. I realize how unlikely it is that my brother is here, but it has nothing to do with me. The love birds met in Boston before I arrived.

"Jay remembered a particular tavern that had extraordinary ale. They had a luncheon, and now Jason demands that I discover a way to bring in a barrel or two. He implies that there may be a lack of fine ales in the future. He wants me to feel guilt for the shortages rampant in the countryside. I will not assume that guilt, but that is another story.

"Perhaps, if they send all that is left, we can get the countryside to surrender in order to stop the ale shortage. Without ale, the colonies will surrender and I can go home." He laughed at his joke, and even Alex smiled that it might be that simple to avert a war.

"So what will the bet entail? You can't bet that I won't drink it? That leaves nothing to chance."

The lieutenant nodded, agreeing with Alex's assessment. "We will all crowd around you and watch for the obvious pleasure on your face. It is hard to hide a look of heavenly delight. Though I have observed that you Peele, very rarely look pleased with anything."

Alex chose to ignore that. He was sure it was true. He tried to paste a smile on his face at the thought of this wager. "Fair enough, Simm, and if I do smile and look appropriately heaven-bound, I will do a penance and dance a minuet with the barmaid." He looked over at the manservant serving drinks and pointed him out. "If no barmaid is present, I will dance a jig with him." The men agreed. None of them had seen Alex Peele so much as tap a foot to music, let alone dance. It went without saying, that if no look of delight flitted across Alex Peele's face, the men would pay the lieutenant, leaving Alex as they had found him.

Chapter 20

February 1776

It had been a typical February - days of heavy snow, rain, and finally, at the end, the hopeful signs of tapped maple trees, the scent of wood fires, and the wonder of boiling sap. Nina and Martha worked on recipes that replaced malted barley with maple syrup. Martha suggested they simply ferment the syrup like mead. Nina reminded her young niece it was not good business practice to cause such inebriation that their customers lost sight of their wallets and fell off their horses. They would create a new ale, not a fermented syrup. This was something they had done again and again since shortages became the norm.

At the end of the summer, Nina had used apples. In the fall, she and her helpers used pumpkin in the mix to some success. Both those ingredients had been combined with malt, but now they needed to work without the standard malt-barley mix, and the maple seemed possible.

Constant work had kept her mind from the siege and the problems caused by a blockaded harbor. There was persistent worry over Josh and his friends. She hoped they were long gone to Nova Scotia, but she had no idea if that had really been his destination.

Alone at night, her daytime problems fell away and she dreamed of Alex. She contrived dozens of ways to slip into Boston but kept herself from acting on them, remembering that it would be risky, and could endanger him by cracking his carefully-constructed veneer as the careless royalist dandy.

One afternoon, a small carriage with a beautiful team drove into the stableyard. Henry, who now had double duty as assistant brewer and stableman, helped the man get the horses situated while his wife found a table for lunch.

"Oh my, how nice! You're Jason who traveled with Michael Goodiel. How nice to see you again." Nina recognized the man's glowing amber eyes as soon as he sat next to his striking wife. Nina had remembered him telling her the story of his grand love. She wondered if he could tell that she had changed.

Jason FitzSimmon introduced his wife, and the women exchanged pleasantries, Mrs. FitzSimmon finally asking for directions to a certain linen weaver. Nina took their order for lunch. When she came back, she had their food and a map to the workshop. It was not far. At the same time, the door opened again and a familiar elegant man and woman entered. Their driver sat at the fire while they found seats at a table.

"Mary, Sukie, find out what that young man at the front wants to drink, and take this order in to cook. I will see to the General and his lady." Nina smoothed her apron and hoped she presented at least a small amount of Martha Washington's poise. "General, I am honored. What can I get for you?" Nina took their orders, and introduced the Washingtons to Jason and Oona FitzSimmon, who were seated nearby. The people at the two tables were soon in deep conversation. Nina watched throughout the afternoon, pleased that her customers were so clearly enjoying their food and talk. She knew that General Washington enjoyed meeting new people, but she wondered what they had found to talk about for so long.

"Mrs. Bigelow, if I might speak with you for a moment?"

The tall General stood and pulled out a chair, helping her sit before he sat back down. The young couple had left on their errand, and the taproom had drifted into the calm after dinner. He was not a man who needed long introductions. "I have a task I must ask you to fulfill, and there is no other option that won't put the child at risk. Mrs. Bigelow, you recall the young girl I told you about who lives near the Province House. The one who translates the generals' papers?"

"Yes, of course." Nina nodded.

"Her father is increasingly concerned that she be removed from her situation, and soon. We expect the siege will break through with Knox's team's return. The girl should be out before that."

"I agree. If I were her parent, well it must be frightening for him. What can I do to help?"

"Do you have any traditional ales available? And can you deliver it in a very large barrel?" Again Nina nodded. " Good. I need you to make a delivery of your excellent ale to our estimable friends at the Province House. "

Chapter 21

Boston, March 4, 1776

With a letter from General Howe's staff officer, and a pass from General Washington, the trip down the neck was easy. Rebecca and the Suffolks made good time. The roads were finally frozen solid, a good thing for her and for Henry Knox and his Ticonderoga cannon, who were one day ahead of Nina on their way to Dorchester Heights.

Maybe, she thought, the added bonus would be that her ale would distract the officers from the work taking place almost directly over their heads. As requested, she had brought the empty and overly large barrel, clean and ready for hiding a precious and precocious twelve year old.

Nina pulled her team up to the Province House and pointed out the barrels that were to be brought in. The military governor, General William Howe, did not live in the old governor's mansion in the center of Boston, but at his headquarters on Castle Island where the barracks were located. Province House was a meeting place for his staff officers, and the parlors were often used for entertaining. It was to one of these parlors Nina and her ales were to go.

She was shown into the large kitchens, and someone pointed out where to leave her things. She kept an eye out for the cinder-girl and a way to let her know that she was to be her way out of Boston. Nina remembered being a strong-willed girl herself. She hoped Maryann chose to agree to come with her.

As she started to tap the first keg in the large parlor, she

240

spotted the young girl adding wood at one of the two fireplaces in the long, narrow room. Nina imagined that if Maryann was kept busy in this room, there should be a way to talk to her.

It was a pleasant space, furnished with small tables and chairs, and a few chaises placed near the windows. Nina could imagine a time when someone might sit and read for an hour or two, occasionally glancing out the window at the passing world. How odd to think of a normal day in the middle of what was anything but.

Alex was sitting in a coffeehouse drinking coffee when a messenger ran in to tell him that "the moment of truth had arrived." He jumped, thinking someone had found out his true motive for being in Boston, but then he realized that the doomsday message was from John FitzSimmon. The ale had been delivered. He took his time finding his coat and hat. The weather was turning wet and icy. It would not do to get sick now after making it through the entire winter.

The room was already crowded with men drinking the good ale. They seemed so happy with the brew, Alex wasn't sure if he would be needed for the Lieutenant's bet.

"Peele!" He heard his name shouted from across the room. "Sit down and I'll bring you a pint. This beer is as good as Jason claimed." Alex sat, put his hat on the table and slipped his greatcoat off, draping it backwards over the chair. In seconds, a pewter mug was put in front of him.

Knowing what he would taste before he opened his mouth, he breathed in the fine blend of yeast and hops, took a long swig and swallowed. He knew the Lieutenant would win, and that he would have to do a jig with the groundskeeper or a minuet with the barmaid. He looked around to see what his forfeit would be.

"Peele, I saw that look of heavenly delight." The man looked at Alex with the glee of one who had won a wager. Alex turned to the voice and turned away quickly, hoping to hide the look of shock on his face. The Lieutenant had turned away and was chatting up Nina. His Nina. What the devil was she doing here?

Alex covered his shock with a long pull at his ale, shook his head to show nothing was wrong, stood, and fixed his waistcoat, "I think I am due for a jig or a minuet with the lovely barmaid." He looked at her. She wore a pale green water-silk gown. He had heard rustling, but the sound was common in these drawing rooms, so he had thought nothing of it. The low cut was filled in with a pale pink fichu of a gossamer silk, so thin a breeze might whisk it away. He sighed, thinking of the warm breezes and soft skin. He shook his head, pulling himself out of memory and expectation. Neither one was helpful at the moment.

Nina was tapping the third keg. The crowd had quickly gone through the first two. As a policy, she tried never to let anyone else tap her ales. She had perfected the craft, and she hated seeing good ale spilled due to a careless tap. The rather beautiful Lieutenant had come over to flirt. It was obvious he was very skilled at it, and she was having fun. When, a moment later, she felt eyes boring into her she ignored the feeling, as she had taught herself to do, but she wondered who would stare at a strange woman so intently.

She had a silly thought that it might be Alex, but she couldn't imagine he would be here in the Governor's mansion. When the tap was in, she looked up to follow the hard gaze fixed on her. Storm-gray eyes bore into her. His angry flares were carefully hidden as he approached the beer table. At the same moment, she heard music start and tables and chairs moved aside. She moved to the side of the table, making room for the dancers.

She jumped as Alex stepped in front of her and bowed over his leg.

"I am to dance a jig or a minuet with the barmaid if I lost the wager, and you, pretty barmaid, are the victim. I apologize. May I have this dance?" A fiddler began the well known minuet in three/four time. In his eyes, she saw her cousin's wedding party and the generous partner who patiently partnered the novice dancers. At the same time, his eyes glowed with confusion and jealousy.

"Yes, of course, sir. But tell me, what sort of a wager?" Nina was keenly aware they were on stage. His jealousy must be diffused before anyone else noticed.

"The wager was that I would enjoy the ale."

"You don't generally like ale?" Nina was really curious. She had seen him down flagons with his friends.

"I am not a beer drinker. I have shunned ales since I removed to Boston."

"I see." She was afraid she squeaked. There was nothing she could add to that. She understood his reasoning perfectly well. She took his offered hand, and he led her onto the makeshift dance floor.

He bowed as she curtsied. He looked up into her eyes, silently asking why she was here. She ignored it.

"I'm afraid I don't dance very well. I'm sure everyone has heard that New England girls were never taught to dance." Nina spoke a little loudly for the benefit of the watchers, hoping they would get tired of watching so she could exchange a quiet word or two with her dance partner.

The steps were no harder than they had been the summer

243

before. She tried to remember and match his feet, while trying to find words that would explain her presence. She needed him to understand that the ale was part of the greater plan.

"You know, sir, it is so nice to be in Boston after all this time. The town has changed less than I thought it would. Being able to come was such a fabulous opportunity to see the sights, you know." She gushed and giggled as he turned her in the dance.

At first Alex assumed he was the "the sight" she had come to see. He would put her over his knee and spank her for putting herself in harms way, when her words surprised him and he listened carefully.

"My Uncle Vernon has been very strict about traveling in these dangerous times. But when the Lieutenant's letter came our way, asking if someone would deliver the ale, Uncle thought it was a good idea, and as he very much needed something from here, the timing was excellent." Nina mused and stressed the words "Uncle Vernon" hoping Alex would understand that "Vernon" meant George Washington, whose estate, Mt. Vernon, was named for his brother Lawrence's commander and friend, Admiral Edward Vernon.

By now Nina's false steps had caused the watchers to find other activities. Alex nodded and turned her again, holding her tight for a second before moving away as the steps dictated. "And what sort of thing does he need you to find for him?" Alex kept it light, hoping the small crowd of loyalist refugees and off-duty soldiers were drunk enough so that their chatter would not be carefully analyzed.

Nina spoke very low, under the melody and normal speech. Alex leaned in. "Your cinder-girl Maryann. It seems her father is intent she not remain with her relative here in town any longer. My Uncle agreed that it would be better for her to find employment elsewhere, or go back to school."

The music ended a minute later. Alex bowed as Nina curtsied. He lifted her hand and kissed her knuckles, lingering politely. He bowed to the Lieutenant, and then, reluctantly, he turned and walked out of the room.

Alex walked around the Province House till he found Nina's wagon and her two matched Suffolks. There was an exceptionally large barrel well secured to the wagon. Upon checking, he found it had two heavy wool blankets lining the bottom, and a small brazier ready to be filled with hot coals. He covered the blankets and took the brazier into the back door of the house.

It didn't take much work to find Maryann in the kitchen stairway, her ear to the conference room where the Generals and their staffs were now meeting. He had barely registered the men leaving the parlor and the party. It was a good thing the cannonading from the north was increasing. He hoped it was a signal that his false life was coming to a close.

A cannon ball hit somewhere nearby and shook the house. Maryann turned to face him. She put her finger to her lips and motioned that she would follow him downstairs. They stopped at the bottom of the stairway. Heavy closed doors separated them from the next room. Alex listened at the door before he spoke.

"We have orders. You are to take this brazier," Alex opened the door and led them into the empty kitchen. He knelt at the kitchen fire and shoveled a large handful of coals into the small brazier. "Gather whatever you want to take out of here, and hide in the large barrel on the alewife's wagon."

"Alewife?"

"That's what they call her. Nina Bigelow was sent here

with the ale in order to bring you home. Your father insists, and General Washington worked it out so she could come into town and make sure you got out safely. I don't know how that was done. You and I will have to wait to find that out. But those are our orders."

"I have nothing else I need, sir. I am ready to go." It was clear that she wanted to object, but she understood orders when they were given. She took a rough wool cloak from a hook by the door, grabbed the brazier by the wooden handles, and carried it out the kitchen door to the wagon in the yard. Maryann assessed the large barrel that was to be her hiding place. She opened the top, saw two blankets and a tiny brazier, one that was big enough to heat the small space but not large enough to start a fire in there. Carefully she transferred a few coals from one to the other, and placed it back against the iron plate supplied for the trip. She was pleased that her rescuer was thorough. She felt safe knowing that, and immediately liked the woman she had not yet met.

Alex knew that obedience was not actually part of Maryann's personality. He was impressed that she was willing to walk away from a job that had been important to her. He made his way back into the house as silently as he could, following servants' corridors toward the parlor to tell Nina that Maryann was ready. Nina's voice, determined and angry, was coming from an anteroom at the front of the house. He stopped. Staying out of sight, he put his ear to the door to listen.

"Josh, I'm surprised to see you here, I would have thought you would have ridden your herd north. New Brunswick is not too far."

"I was offered a good price, but more important, *Aunt*

Nina" - he sneered the words like they were dirty to him - "What are you doing here? Something to do with that man you whore with?"

Nina felt as if she had been slapped in the face. She'd known her brother-in-law was angry with her, with the world, but this was his attempt to be cruel. "I received an invitation from one of General Howe's staff to bring ale. I asked permission from General Thomas at the neck and was allowed in. It is that simple." She turned as if to leave the room.

"Nina, nothing is simple and I think you are here to cause trouble. All your friends are patriots. Why would anyone ask you to come? There are other brewers." He spit out the words and then spit into the hearth. It hissed.

"Joshua, I am telling the truth."

"Oh, I believe you have that letter Aunt Nina, but there is something else. Something I think the Generals upstairs would like to hear. Come, I will take you up." He pulled a pistol from under the table and aimed it at Nina.

"Josh, I will just leave now. Let me go. I won't yell or scream to let anyone know you are insane - I will just quietly leave." Slowly she pulled her own traveling gun from the pocket at her side. She aimed it back at him.

"Nina, you won't shoot me. You can't. You already proved that the day I left."

Nina said nothing. There was no reason to defend herself against such nonsense. She felt a presence behind her and put out her left hand to stop him from moving closer. She felt a strong warm hand cover hers, grasping it tight behind her skirts.

"Ah, I see I was right. And I also see why I remembered the gray. It was not really the horse." Josh stared into Alex's gray eyes, now angry and threatening. "Move. I will take you both upstairs."

"I don't think so." Nina spoke as Alex gently pushed her behind him. If Josh could, he would force the two of them upstairs to talk to the General. It could not be allowed to happen. Not only would Alex and she be arrested as spies, but the child would, too. There was no way to prove they were not, and Josh would do his best to see them hanged.

"I am not moving." Nina stepped back in front of Alex. Lifting her hand, she aimed her pistol. The second she moved, Josh raised his gun at Alex and fired. The ball hit Nina in the upper chest, just above her right breast. The sound of cracking bone broke Alex's control. As she screamed and fell to the floor, her left hand clutching at her right shoulder, Alex drew his gun.

The roar of the cannonading from the north, supplied a backdrop to the altercation in the small anteroom. Occasionally a cannonball hit the town somewhere near the wharfs, rattling any building within the shockwave. At the moment a distant cannon roared, Alex calmly shot Joshua Peddleman through the heart. He gathered the man's cloak, wrapped Nina in it, and ran, carrying her out to the wagon, his own heart pounding fear, while his mind ran icy cold with planning.

Maryann saw him coming out the side door of the Province House, running to the wagon with someone in his arms. She helped him get the unconscious woman onto the wagon bench and wrapped her in one of the blankets she had packed for her refugee. Maryann put the large brazier at Nina's feet and climbed into the barrel. Alex lightly sealed the lid on the barrel and took the reins.

Chapter 22

He had not expected to make this trip. It seemed obvious to him, now that he had a minute to think, how this had been arranged. Nina was offered a chance to bring her ale to town as a nice respite for bored soldiers and a few of their friends. From Washington's point of view, it was the perfect opportunity to get Maryann home to her anxious parent while she was still safe. It had been easy to keep her safe those first months. It was different when the new Lieutenant on Howe's staff arrived after January. Since then, Alex had been getting nervous.

The girl was good, but as with all such operations, a huge part of that sort of success was knowing when to stop. He was glad she was now safely in a large beer barrel, being driven south down Orange Street to the neck and freedom. He prayed Josh's body would not be discovered, and that they would not be followed.

For Alex this false life was over. It wouldn't matter if the redcoats evacuated or stuck it out for another year. He wouldn't miss it. Oddly, he had come to like the tall, sandy haired Lieutenant with the bright blue eyes. An honest discussion of philosophy and politics would have been most interesting. He supposed that was one price of war - friendships that might have been. He roused himself from maudlin thoughts and drove, concentrating on the one life, the one woman he would give his own life to save.

So far she was still alive. He pulled her as close to him as was safe, trying to share some of his heat. He wished he had time to care for Nina's wound. But as with everything else in their time together, outside elements were getting in their way. Now it was the weather, worsening with every mile. The more important goal was to get her home where someone could care for her – out of this damned rain. He blessed Nina's Suffolks. They had needed no direction once they passed the last military checkpoint, and seemed to sense that time was important. With barely any guidance, they raced over wet, muddy roads, now getting thick with freezing rain and snow.

The horses raced to the kitchen door and stopped. Alex wasn't sure how they knew it was the right place. He had been busy keeping Nina from slipping down to the wagon floor. She had stopped shivering, and he was getting increasingly worried about her and the girl who was still in the barrel. The winds were picking up, and an icy rain pelted them from the northeast.

Alex shouted to Maryann that he was leaving the other blanket for her right next to the barrel, and she should grab it but stay hidden. Then he picked up Nina and ran for the kitchen door, screaming for Jack.

"He's not here. Hasn't been for months now. Who are you, and what's wrong with my Aunt?"

Alex had never seen this girl before, and right now he never wanted to hear Nina called anyone's aunt, not ever again. "There is no time to explain. Have to get out of the rain. I am bringing her upstairs to her room. She has been shot and needs immediate care. I need to leave. I am sorry. When she wakes, tell her I promise to come back as soon as I am able. Can you remember that?"

Martha took the stock of the man and decided she had better do as he said. She nodded yes. She would remember the message. She went to find Sukie, whose mother was a well-known healer. It was mumbled that she might be a witch, but nearly everyone needed her herbs and care.

Alex carefully carried Nina up to the room he was sure must be hers, through the small parlor and just above the kitchen. That girl, Nina's niece, said Jack had not been here for months. He shook his head, trying to clear the confusion, and hoped there was no problem. There was no one to ask, and there was no time. He lay Nina on the bed and removed her cold wet clothes. He covered her with blankets and tucked them under her feet. Then he knelt to start a fire in the hearth. He could look at the wound, but she seemed calm and the bleeding was not excessive. Heating the room was something he could do until help arrived. While he waited for the kindling to catch, he looked around the room. He was not completely surprised, but rather delighted with what he saw.

Just outside this door was Nina's personal parlor. The parlor had two wingback chairs, set decorously before the hearth. Between them was set a small round table, positioned to hold a book, tea cup or a reading lantern. The walls were covered with shelves. There was a small selection of ladies' novels, but most were books and journals in various languages concerning brewing. Near them was a desk with open notebooks, work on the rudiments of the art. It looked like she had been helping someone learn.

At this point in her brewing, Nina might consult one of the journals her father-in-law collected in his travels, but she would not need this level of illustrated instruction. He used this moment of reasoning to calm his mind, and nodded to himself with a certain understanding. It was not important to him who Nina was teaching, but felt right that such skill should be passed along. He understood that need to teach. He had missed teaching since the moment he stepped away from the college in the mountains.

He added a larger piece of wood to the fire and turned to Nina's bedroom. In a dark corner he saw his wooden crate, the one he had placed in her wagon the time she had ridden away on Thorne. He wished he had a moment to find his horse, but he must leave. He looked toward the door - help had not yet arrived. He pushed his box back into the corner, thinking that someday, if there were a moment, he would open it and remind himself of his own past.

He looked around Nina's bedroom. There were tapestries on the walls, and one used as a bed cover. He had barely registered how lovely the room was as he'd hunted for soft blankets to cover his love. The floor had a braided rug of warm soft wool. It reminded him that he could take off his boots. How long it had been that he had gone without stiff boots, he could not remember. He wiggled his toes, then reminded himself that as soon as anyone came in the door, he had to get Maryann back to Cambridge.

On the floor next to the bed was a leather elephant, no doubt from India or Siam. On a shelf were a series of wooden dolls from Russia, arranged large to small, carved so they could fit inside one another. Next to them were other unusual trinkets. Sketches of Jack at different ages, each framed in a different exotically-carved frame, graced the shelves around her finds. It was clear she would have loved to travel to collect the world's treasures, but it was also true that she had enjoyed her short trips to the nearby port to find them. Most people who walked through the marketplace did not purchase the most extraordinary things on sale there. The young Nina was not most people, however. Widowed before adulthood, she had used that unexpected freedom and coin to buy the unusual and extraordinary.

He heard voices and wondered if Nina might be more comfortable in her bed with the heavy blankets pulled over her instead of on top of the stiff tapestry. He gently lifted her to one side of the big bed and pulled back the blankets on the other, one layer at a time.

First he pulled off the oriental tapestry, folded it and put it over a chair. It probably had a solid crate for storage, but he didn't want to waste time looking for that. The next was soft wool made of knitted squares, crocheted together. Like the first one he had grabbed to wrap her in, it might have been made by a young Nina practicing stitches.

Waiting for help to arrive was turning out to be more pleasant than Alex had expected. These moments spent contemplating the things this amazing women had chosen for her room, and for her bed, were showing him visions of her deepest longings in ways that moved him beyond imagining.

Beneath the soft wool squares was a pieced quilt in a triangle pattern reminiscent of flying geese. Some of the pieces were worn and faded. This one had been pieced from fabric left over from what looked to men's clothing - perhaps young Jack's or even her long dead husband's. Alex wondered at the importance of clothing that rated being remembered. He pulled back the quilt.

Nina's sheets were red silk.

Alex grinned as he put Nina on her soft, luxurious bed and covered her with the blankets. Muttering, "Nina, these sheets tell me that the pleasures we began in that storm are only the beginning. I look forward to exploring that." He spoke softly. He had no idea if she could hear him. She seemed to drift in and out of consciousness - maybe it was blood loss, maybe it was pain.

He checked her wound briefly, leaning over and kissing Nina's forehead. She was warm. He wished there were no fever, but not all wishes came true. Nina woke enough to smile weakly as he whispered again that he would return to her. He stepped away, relinquishing his spot to the battalion of healers, a small gray lady with a bright lantern leading the way.

At the foot of Nina's bed was a familiar gray leather cloak lined with the fur of a wolf in winter. He was glad she had slept with it, and he silently apologized for taking it. He threw the cloak over his shoulders, thinking that the real Alex Peele, the one who wore such things, had returned to the present.

The wagon was facing the way out to the lane. The space was narrow, and he could not see how Maryann had turned the horses. He leaned into the barrel to ask, and told her they would be underway in a minute.

"I felt the horses pulling the wagon around, but I didn't hear anyone talk to them. Wasn't it you?"

"No, I was inside. No matter," Alex was curious, but there was no time to worry it out.

The girl was shivering. He could hear it in her small voice. The few coals she had in that little brazier were long out. He stopped for a second, aware of the roar of the falls in the melt of this late winter night. He had spent little time here, but still the sound was striking and familiar. Alex took a moment to listen and absorb the power of it. His mind was full of unanswered questions. He understood why Nina had been sent to Boston. Sending her into a dangerous situation had not been anyone's intention, but shouldn't the command have found a way to let him decide how to get the girl out? It was after all, his project.

He climbed onto the wagon bench, dragging his leg

behind him and cursing it for stiffening up every time it rained or snowed. As they set off, he offered up a prayer that Nina recover and heal easily – that when he finally returned, or crawled his way back to this falls if that was what it took – she would be well. He would not mind a good Alewife's scolding about how he had been away too long. Now he concentrated on getting the team, wagon and his important cargo over the river and off to the side of the road.

Maryann had been trying hard not to fall into the sleep that freezing brings. Rubbing her hands and feet together in the cramped quarters was not easy, but she kept at it until she heard Alex call to the team and felt the wagon stop. She pushed at the top of her barrel prison, relieved to see a friendly face staring down at her, happy when strong arms pulled her out.

Maryann ran around the wagon a few times to get circulation and warmth back into her arms and legs, while Alex kept a careful watch on the road, both of them stubbornly ignoring the increasing storm. Once she could feel her feet, Maryann climbed up and sat a respectful distance from him on the bench. Alex shook the reins and the Suffolks began a hopeful trot east, toward Cambridge.

They had worked together for months, but purposely had not spoken more than a hushed word or two. Alex smiled at the girl, hoping she was not afraid of him. He had maintained an aloof and slightly nasty persona while in Boston, but now, for her safety, he needed the girl to agree that he was really just a comfortable old school master who meant her only well. He opened his warm fur cloak, motioning her to climb over and sit next to him. "Maryann, you look frozen. I don't think that blanket over your thin cloak is doing a good job."

The wagon rocked to the side as the horses kept their pace, and Maryann almost fell into Alex as she cautiously moved down the bench to sit next to him. He pulled the warm cloak over her shoulders, relieved as she settled next to him.

"Mr. Peele?" Her voice was slightly uncertain and she seemed like she might bolt if he was not careful.

"Yes Maryann." Alex tried to sound relaxed, all the time sick with worry about Nina, and trying to concentrate on the road. No reason to take that out on the girl whose life and health had hung in the balance all day.

"Can I put my cold feet under you? Papa lets me do that on long drives."

Alex laughed with relief, as he stood slightly and helped Maryann get comfortable and warm, cuddled like a kitten next to him on the bench. Once she was warm enough she fell asleep, leaving Alex alone with his worries and thoughts.

He pulled into the courtyard of the camp and called Maryann's father's name. Col. Bickerstaff was found, and ran over just a few minutes later. Alex handed the still-sleeping Maryann over to her father and had begun to turn the horses, when a group of twelve men approached.

Chapter 23

Suddenly Alex was glad Nina had help enough without him. He had hopes that his role was over for the day, maybe even longer, but he hadn't counted on an all-out battle at the edge of town. Again, war had a way of interrupting plans.

"Peele, so glad you are here with a wagon. Excellent. These men need transport to the Heights." Alex turned around. Men were already seated in the wagon, shovels and rifles stacked neatly against the hinged tailgate. They were bundled in their greatcoats and covered with sailcloth tarpaulins. They were ready to leave. Alex took a deep breath, readied himself for another long night, fixed his cloak and hood over his head, and shook the reins. He turned the team and wagon and headed back the way he came, turning south in order to join Henry Knox's cannon on the hill.

The wind howled. Alex pulled his cloak closer. He could have missed this, back in his small rooms in Boston, completely unaware that the tide of the siege was about to turn. It would have happened that way if that idiot Josh had not appeared with his pistol in a civilized parlor in Boston. Perhaps even General Howe was unaware of what was happening on Dorchester Heights, almost directly over his quarters on Castle Island. He might be hunkered down, riding out the storm, staying warm and slightly drunk on his favorite brandy. As for Alex, he wasn't missing this important moment. He felt alive and ready.

He had heard snippets of Henry Knox's project during

257

that one moonlight trip to Cambridge. The night that had been the most frightening of his war, that is until this afternoon, when Nina blocked the bullet meant for his heart. He reminded himself that she was alive, and she had help. He dragged his mind back to the men behind him. Planning for this mission had started last November. Henry Knox was to bring sixty cannon from Fort Ticonderoga in New York, across the long southern border of Massachusetts, and position them on the Heights, the last undefended hill looming over the closed town.

The warm, wet winter caused Knox trouble from the first. In many places, the snow was not thick enough to support sledges carrying the cannon. Roads were not frozen, and then, too often, the ice on the rivers cracked. More than once the men had to drag a cannon out of freezing water. Conditions were so unusual that the mission, predicted to take three weeks, took nearly nine.

Now, with the help of every farmer and militiaman in Roxbury, the materials were ready to be moved up the Heights and positioned on the hill facing the harbor. The goal was to shock the British with cannon aimed at their ships and redoubts built into the hill, manned and ready to repel any assault from the sea. Washington was ready with terms. The British were not to further loot or burn the town, but to hurriedly pack and leave, to simply evacuate. Under the terms, the Americans promised not to blow the masts off or sink the British warships.

The townspeople, men, women and children, had built large numbers of fascia, the bundled sticks that would cover redoubts and make them look deep and permanent. Each redoubt would be armed with a cannon staring down at Howe's headquarters, or at a Man o' War anchored in the harbor. The storm that was battering the region would only help the Americans, adding needed cover to the dangerous operation.

Alex pulled the team to a halt at the base of the hill known as Dorchester Heights, in the little farming town of Roxbury. The roads were covered with hay-straw, muffling the racket made by the heavy wagons rumbling through. The *George* beckoned, and the men went in for orders, an ale and some food before they climbed the Heights to work. Already, men were bringing barrels of heavy sand to the summit to arm the holes built into the side of the frozen hill. These would be ready to roll down on any invading force of Royal Marines should they attempt to take the hill. Alex climbed off the bench and swore at the storm, as his leg buckled under him and he grabbed the wagon for support.

He'd hoped the weeks of semi-rest as a loyalist fop might have hastened the healing, but inactivity had only made the leg weaker. He pushed aside the thought that the leg might never heal and stomped around the wagon, trying to get some feeling back into his cold feet. He looked around to see who might be in charge of the ordered chaos.

After a few minutes he saw the tavern keeper's daughter, and asked her who might direct him. She pointed to a small shed partway up the steep hill. Hidden in the apple orchard, a small puff of smoke rose from its chimney. Alex wasn't surprised to find that General Thomas was using the little shed. Out of the back, it had a view of the men working on transforming the hill. He knocked at the door.

"Come in. Oh, Peele, what are you doing out in this weather?" The man had obviously just walked in himself. He was covered with ice and drenched to the bone. He laughed at his quip.

Alex brushed snow off his shoulders and closed the door behind him. "Evening Sir, I ended up in Cambridge due to a small errand, and was sent here with a wagon load of supplies and men. Wondered if there was anything I could do to help."

Thomas, who had gotten to know Peele slightly from their talks, watched him rubbing the same spot on his leg he had favored months before. "We can always use help, fill in where there is an opening. No digging possible, the frost is two feet thick on that side of the heights. We are camouflaging the redoubts. Move to the forward lines and see if the field commanders need anything."

"Yes sir, I will." He made as if to turn and leave, when Thomas's words stopped him.

"Son, do you mind if I speak out of turn?"

Alex nodded.

"Peele, I haven't been a practicing doctor for some years now, but I know a problem when I see one. If it was my choice, I wouldn't want you in my regiment. I could just about guarantee that you would be trampled in retreat or worse. If we were to send you as a refugee into the next city, doing there what you did for us here, like as not you'd get caught by someone you diced with at the Province House. They'll happily hang you.

"So go do whatever you can find to do around here tonight. Then take that leg and go build this nation. Leave the fighting to the men who haven't got shot yet."

"Yes, Sir, thank you, sir. General Thomas?" the old soldier looked up, "It's not going to be that easy, is it?" The old soldier nodded acknowledgment as Alex got up to leave.

"No Peele, I imagine someone will need your unique skills again before this war is over. Could be sooner, could be later."

The General went back to his work. Word was, this engagement would be the last one of John Thomas's long career, and he wouldn't leave his Roxbury farm to move on with the Continental Army. Alex left him to complete his victory. It was going to be a hell of a morning for William Howe, and Alex felt an urge to be back in Boston to see it. First, he would do what he could to help here at the Heights, and before dawn he would make his way back to his rooms in the town. As for his skills being unique? He doubted they were, but he was a good observer, a fine rider and could usually find a way to do what needed to be done.

Behind the *George*, Jewel and Bella were picking at some shoots that the March sunshine had coaxed out of the ground. Alex knew they, like most intelligent animals, knew their way home and back to their warm shed. Hadn't they done the trip with him just this afternoon while he was worrying over Nina? He didn't want Nina's beautiful Suffolks yoked and sent up the hill with men and planks of wood. He wanted them home and away from this mess before it got full dark, before the snow got thick on the ground. Every horse he had ever known hated running in the snow. If he was to keep them safe, they needed to leave now. Alex looked to see if anyone was watching him.

"Jewel and Bella?" He kept murmuring to them as he tied the reins loosely to the wagon and released the hand brake. He unyoked them, and put the heavy wooden yoke in the back. If there were a problem, it would be far safer for them not to be connected by the thick board. The horses whinnied, seemingly telling him they understood, "I need you to find your way back home. Can you do that? Home! To your warm shed!" Again they whinnied. This time they shook their manes free of snow, turned their heads to say good-bye, and then together, in tandem, they trotted west toward their home at the *Wheel and Hammer*. Alex was jealous of those horses.

Alex looked around at the men busy with carting armaments, wood and supplies up the hill. Over the hiss of rain and sleet, he could hear shovels hitting frozen ground as men dug into the tall hill to fix the fascia into place. Alex shook the water off his hat and pulled up his hood against the weather. He picked up a shovel someone had lost in his rush to get to work, and climbed up the hill after the supply cart that had started a few minutes before. It was the first of many trips up and down the steep heights he would make that night.

Much later, he called it a night and decided he was ready to cross into Boston through the silent checkpoints. The American guards had no reason to care who went north. Their only concern was to watch for redcoats who might be ordered to storm the gates toward the Heights. The British guards at their checkpoints were so tired of being trapped by circumstance and bad weather, they didn't even look out to see who might be walking through their gate. Filthy, cold and exhausted, Alex was glad conversation was unnecessary.

Hours of slipping through mud and ice on the slick trails leading to the eastern edge of the hill had him bone weary. Yet in spite of that, he felt elated to be once again involved in the physicality of preparing for battle. More precisely, he would have been elated if there were no steady drum beat of worry pounding "Nina", incessantly in his brain. He limped one last time north to Queen Street.

***

As with countless battles over time, the Americans were helped by the atrocious weather. The storm probably came across North America from the west, and struck the cold moisture of the Mid-Atlantic coast. Hitting the ocean air, it changed direction and pushed north toward cold Atlantic waters, gaining strength and moisture as it moved. By the time it hit New England, the northeasterly swirl of the winds caused it to be caught in the bays and harbors, blocking itself from moving quickly eastward, or north and away. For hours, it battered the town and harbor, reducing visibility to inches, and turning roads and fields to ice and mud.

In Boston, it started in late morning as rain. By afternoon, the rain had turned to an icy mix, slowly turning to snow, sleet and rain in competing sheets. It battered the workers on the eastern slope with raging, incessant ocean gales, broken by stronger gusts and icy rain. At the coast it brought high seas mixed with the abominably high tides of the March full moon, assuring that the British Marines headquartered just below Dorchester Heights would be unable to make landfall without risking a watery, rocky death. The roar of the wind was such that for the first time in days, the cannonading from Phips Farm on the Cambridge side was muffled.

March 6, 1776

Alex pushed away all thought of the previous day and night, and dressed in his urban finest. He would be glad to see the last of these clothes. He was wretchedly tired of dressing like the foolish, foppish refugee. He hadn't much enjoyed dressing in fashion when he'd lived in Europe, and now that these had been the clothes for the false Alex Peele, he would be happy to put them in a case and never see any of it again. One afternoon and night as himself had served to make this morning's charade considerably harder.

He sat in his regular seat at the coffeehouse, sipping

strong coffee and listening to the news around him.

"Word is that Howe is as angry at the weather as he is at the marines for being forced back from the Heights. The strong wind and the high tides, we didn't have a chance. We heard they got cannon up there! Cannon!"

By late in the day, word got out that evacuation would be immanent, but no official word or directions had been issued. Alex wondered how information was getting in and flying around so fast. Soon, loyalists and redcoats were convinced their days in Boston were over.

"Washington says they won't cannonade the Admiral's fleet if Howe agrees not to burn the town." A fellow rushed in with this news and announced it over brandy in the Province House parlor.

"Losing the fleet would trap us here for months like rabbits in a snare. The terms are fair enough." Alex was happy to add to the excitement.

On the eighth of March, using one of the boatman on the Back Bay, he was able to get word to Washington that Howe seemed ready to order evacuation. The ships would sail within a fortnight.

After that, he stopped going to the Province House, or to any of the coffee houses he had frequented. He packed his finery in a crate addressed to himself in London, and stashed it in the hold of one of the ships that would be used for evacuating civilians. Then he returned home and washed the powder out of his hair. He dressed in brown-linen homespun he'd purchased from a tailor desperate for customers, and disappeared into the crowd at the docks.

He would have left Boston and walked, or even crawled, to the Lower Falls, but John Rowe offered him a paying job. The merchant needed someone he could trust to protect his goods from rioting crowds looting the warehouses on the wharves. He could have refused the job and the money, but the chaos at the docks did call out for someone angry and big enough to throw men out the door. He worked at Rowe's Wharf and in his warehouses, eventually changing his employment from guard to office clerk.

On the seventeenth of March, they gathered as a group and tiredly watched the fleet sail from the harbor out to Queen's Road, the deep channel connecting the town to the sea. The fleet of Naval and merchant vessels stayed there at anchor, for another week. No one knew what they were doing, beside blocking the channel and the harbor to other traffic, but finally, on the twenty-second, the fleet of British vessels sailed for Halifax, Nova Scotia.

John Rowe's clerks returned from the countryside soon after, but it wasn't for another two weeks that Alex could set foot out of Boston or even begin to face his worries about Nina, and how she had fared since she had been shot and had sat bleeding in his arms.

Chapter 24

Wheel and Hammer

It was hours of lying in hazy pain before Nina woke up, and days before she could remember enough to put the story together. She had gone to Boston with the Suffolks to get Maryann, and Josh had shot her as he aimed for Alex. She remembered falling to the floor and then into a daze. She remembered that Alex picked her up and carried her to the wagon.

Nina knew Alex was with her, and that she was on her own bed. She felt heat coming from the fire. She came out of her quiet, safe sleep when Sukie's mother yelled at her daughter to fetch warm water, and ordered Alex out of the room. She felt his warm kiss on her cheek. He had said something important to her, but she couldn't understand him, and when she turned to respond, he was gone.

They cut her shift. She squeezed her eyes shut when they hung the bright lanterns all around her bed. Someone spoke soothingly and poured something bitter down her throat. She was about to object when a wet rag was put into her mouth. She heard loud, commanding voices. She felt cold steel cutting into her skin, and nothing more.

She woke feeling groggy as Mrs. MacAlistair held a cup of something warm and bitter to her lips. She shook her head, trying to dislodge the cup.

"Oh no you don't. Drink this, deary, it will make you sleep." The woman's slight Scotch accent was comforting as she crooned and got most of the draught down Nina's throat.

"What was that, it's horrible!" Nina wanted to remind the witch that she had been asleep before the woman forced her to drink the swill, but she didn't have the strength to speak.

"My own draught for pain. Sleep is what you need, and I intend to sit right here and make sure you don't move beyond the chamber pot for a week, longer if I can stand to be in your room that long, or if that hole takes its time healing.

"That bullet shattered a rib, and ripped those muscles real good." She laughed a little and mumbled something so quietly, Nina had trouble hearing her. Then she tucked Nina back into her bed, checking the thick bandage tied at her shoulder at the same time. She nodded her satisfaction with her work, and moved to sit in a chair by the fire with her knitting.

"When you're feeling better and think you're ready to be up and out, I'll show you the bullet. It will make a lovely charm for a necklace." She chuckled again. Nina gripped the aquamarine bezel that was still safely on her neck. She lifted her head to speak, but then the sleeping draught caught up with her, and she fell into a dreamless sleep. Over the next days she woke only when one of the girls came to help her wash, when Mrs. MacAlistair changed her bandages, or when Mrs. Cotton sat with her to help her eat. Most of the time she slept.

Finally, after Nina had spent days in a stupor, Mrs. MacAlistair stopped the sleeping draughts. She ordered her not to use her arm and to stay as still as possible. Nina took short walks in the early spring sunshine, but most of each day was spent upstairs, in the company of her parlor chairs. Two weeks to the day after Josh had shot her, her head finally clear and the deep ache in her arm fading, she was upstairs napping and was jolted awake by joyous shouting in the stableyard. "They're gone, the bloody lobsterbacks are gone!" Her only thought was that Alex would finally be free to come see her.

Since her injury she had not felt right, the ennui only partially caused by her injury and the sleeping draughts. There were deep changes to herself and her world she needed to confront before she could move on. Soon she would be free to resume her life, as alewife, as tavern keeper of the busy *Wheel and Hammer*. It was expected of her.

During the time she'd spent in the stupor, she was aware of life swirling around her. Everyone came to see her and reported that Martha and Henry were doing well. People said it to help her relax, but she wondered what would happen if they were not doing well. What could she do about it? In contrast, she wondered, why should she return if the young Bigelows were doing well?

When she was well enough to walk through the buildings, she was relieved to see they were. The taproom was as clean and well run as it ever had been. Maria Cotton had hired new helpers, and the kitchen was sending out good food. To her educated palate, the ales were a bit off, but she was sure Martha would learn in time.

She watched out her window as Martha, Henry and the staff established a new rhythm as the inn once again became part of the busy routes to the Neck and to Brighton. She watched as refugees who had fled out of the Town when the British arrived made their way back, with carts of their possessions, the lumber and sailcloth they would need to repair their houses and small ships. From the vantage point of her window, it looked as though the inn had never been busier. And every few hours, Marty or one of the tap-girls would come upstairs with some food or a bit of news, and tell her that everything was going well, and not to worry, there was no reason to hurry back.

Nina wasn't sure she cared to go back, so she felt uncertain about what to do next. She did not know if she should plan on a life with Alex, or without. He had not come, and as time passed she had less reason to believe he would or could. As hours turned into days, and days into weeks, she began to worry that he might have been forced to sail with the British in their evacuation.

She examined her feelings about life, marriage, separation from England and the coming war. She had been around strong feelings all her life. New Englanders were never afraid to express them – at town meetings, the market square and most especially at a public house. As the inn and tavern keeper, she was well acquainted with every point of view, from those of the most loyal Tory to the ideals of the most radical Patriot. Opinions had always swirled at the *Wheel and Hammer*. Certainly that was the way of all taverns, and she had never hidden from loud discussions, but she was careful not to participate.

Over the past few years, the arguments had grown in intensity, and the larger world seemed to move closer to her life at the Falls. Last winter, there had been the death of John Peddleman, which left her alone, the sole person in charge of running the busy inn and raising her son. She hadn't minded, staying focused on what needed doing, and doing it. Being Mistress of the *Wheel and Hammer* during the years of blockaded harbor, battles and siege meant that she had been responsible for finding hops and malted barley, new barrels, and food for the inn. Finding supplies during the shortages brought the outside world and its problems closer than any arguments in the tavern ever could.

The last straw had been Josh. Her one helper had

certainly proven himself to be no friend. That betrayal had been the deepest hurt. She flexed her arm in memory.

There were no longer any fixed stars in her firmament. Independence from Britain had now become more than drunken talk. People clamored for war, for separation. But what would be left after such a war? Would there be someone or something to replace the King as the fixed star in every Englishman's sky? If Alex returned and left with the army, would she find herself the widow of another war?

The wheel at the forge turned. Nina watched out her window as the water spilled over, turning it unceasingly. She had spent ten years like the center of that wheel, the center of the inn and her son's life, a linchpin holding all the turning parts in place, impossible either to move or change direction, stuck in her place, out of love and out of necessity. Would she like to leave? Was she tired of endless brewing and serving? Was she tired of being the linchpin that held the whole?

It would be good to lean on someone, to leave the wheel and jump into the stream, to see what time and fate had in store. Everyone said Martha and Henry were doing well. Did she want to return?

Jack wouldn't grow to want the inn. She knew that. He might help for a day or two, even stay for a year, but he would never have the enthusiasm that Martha and Henry brought to it. To watch them greeting and serving the guests, mimicking the energy of their grandfather - certainly they out-paced her own efforts. Their ale was the only exception.

What might Alex want, assuming he came? Would he want to travel? Would she go with him, could she move far away? She had a house full of strange things brought to Boston on ships from far-away lands, but they had been purchased at a marketplace not seven miles from her home. She loved her strange collection of dolls, dishes, pillows and fabrics, reveled in them, in the safety of home. She didn't think she would like to go far, to meet entirely new people in a strange place.

Mrs. MacAlistair had calmly changed her silk sheets to linen without a nod or a wink, certainly not a word. Was she like her carefully made bed with its outward coverlet of comfortable and familiar knitted squares and a grandmother's faded patchwork? Underneath, was she silk or linen? She suspected Alex would accept linen, but he would gleefully embrace silk.

The men returned to the forge from their break, and the trip hammer interrupted her reverie with its banging. Yes, she would be happy to move in a new direction.

Chapter 25

Within days of the St. Patrick's Day evacuation, John Rowe's clerks returned from the countryside. Alex was happy to see the town come to life, but he was anxious to leave. He didn't care which route he would take, south by the neck or on the tidal river west to Watertown. He was heartily sick of Boston, but having shipped all his clothing to London as a ruse, he wanted to appear at least mildly prosperous before he appeared at Nina's inn, so he took his pay from John Rowe and had new clothes made. A few days later his new clothes were packed, and he was ready to go. On his way out to the river ferry, he stopped to bid farewell to his neighbors.

The Danns were a family of quiet patriots who had needed to stay in Boston in order to protect their shop. They had been kind to him, even as he played the foolish loyalist. Alex thought they might have suspected he was not what he seemed, probably because he allowed Andrea, the beautiful Mrs. Dann, to see the physical and emotional exhaustion he hid during his interactions with British officers and refugee loyalists.

The window curtains were closed, but the door was unlocked when Alex approached the house at the back of their shop. Alex put his head in and called out. He was answered by Robby, their six-year old.

"Mr. Peele, up here. Ma and Poppa are sick and Davida don't look good."

Alex ran up the stairs two at a time. The sight did not frighten him. He had been inoculated when he was little older than Robby.

"Robb, how long has everyone been sick?"

"I was sick first. Momma took care of me. She tried to keep Davida away, but she came to read to me when the fever was bad. I'm better now. See?" He pulled his shirt open to show Alex the healing pustules. Lucky for the boy, they were thinly scattered over his neck, face and chest. Clearly his disease had taken its course, and he would heal with good food and rest.

Alex knelt down to check the boy's parents and thirteen year old sister. They lay on hard mattresses on the floor under thin blankets. Each wore a thin nightshirt with the sleeves sewn together at the hands to prevent scratching of the itchy pustules.

"Andrea?" Alex gently shook her awake. He was impressed with how well she had prepared for the family's illness. So much trouble was caused when a patient's fingernails spread the pus while scratching. "I'll stay till you are better, all of you." He pulled the curtains closed against the bright light, speaking soothingly as he moved around the room. He checked Robert Senior and Davida. Both already had pustules, but neither seemed to be so covered with the red blisters as to be stricken with what doctors called "the confluent type" of the disease. "It looks to me like you all have a mild case. Now rest. You'll hear us in the kitchen for a few minutes, but Robb and I will be right back."

"Alex, there's calomel and laudanum in the cupboard over the stove." Andrea's voice was hoarse, and she spoke very softly.

Alex hunted in the kitchen for the medicines and herbs he wanted. There were no cures that he knew of, but things that would cool the hot bodies of his patients would speed their

273

healing. Right now all he could do was to keep them cool and let them sleep until their bodies demanded food and a cozy bed, the signs of healing. He made tea and let it cool to room temperature. Then, with a bucket of cold water and piles of clean rags, he and Robb went back to the sickroom.

He showed Robby how to give his patient a drink by dipping a clean rag in the water and holding it to his mouth. He showed him how to wipe the patient clean with cold water, clearing away the matter from the weeping pustules and cooling the patient at the same time. Then he made a thick broth for the recuperating boy and sent him to bed in a clean, aired room.

Alex washed the bucket and rags in hot soapy water and began the entire process over again. He cursed his bad luck at having to stay in town, but at the same time he was relieved to have been here to help his friends. He knew others were similarly infected. It was even suggested that the arrival of the contagious disease among his army was one of the reasons for Howe's decision to evacuate – that Washington's stand at Dorchester Hill only fixed the date to make it sooner rather than later. Whatever the larger causes of military maneuvers, Alex knew he wouldn't leave until these good people could take care of themselves.

His patients all survived. Luckily, Andrea and Robert Sr. had been inoculated when they were children, so although they contracted the disease, it had been mild, and they had healed quickly. Young Davida had a harder time, but she would heal. With luck she would not be too badly scarred. Right now, a good soup bubbled over the fire while the family napped upstairs. He would call up as he was leaving. Andrea assured him, now that the contagion had passed, her mother would come help her cook and clean. Alex wondered how an older woman might have missed becoming exposed all those years, but it was not his problem now that the Danns were feeling better.

He did not leave until the next day, not until his clothes were cleaned and dried in the bright sun. It was instinct to get rid of the smell and sweat of working with the sick, but doctors had written about the contagious nature of smallpox, and that simple washing of hands and clothes would stop transmission. He didn't know if the disease had become an epidemic in the countryside, but he wouldn't be responsible for spreading it.

Tuesday, April 23rd Alex woke early and jumped out of bed, eager to be on his way. The tide was coming in, and he intended to find a boat and ride the surging river to Brighton, maybe as far as Watertown, where tidal influence ended. He had few enough things to pack since his fine London clothes were long gone. All the new clean shirts, waistcoats and breeches fit in one sack, and not a very big one. He didn't care - he was ready to move on. He grabbed the one thing that mattered, nestled in its small velvet box, and pushed the box safely into his coat pocket. He pulled his cloak over his shoulder against the moist April morning, hoisted the sum of his possessions onto his back, and bid the Town of Boston farewell.

In its own way, it had been good to him, and he felt some small pride in helping the town throw off its occupiers and blockade. It was a pleasant morning as he crossed the Common to the river. The field sported a few cattle, but it would take at least a summer of rain before the grazing lands recovered from British encampments. All around him was the sound of hammering and sweeping, as buildings were repaired and front steps swept clear of the long occupation's debris - the healthy noises of a town coming back to life.

People did not smile at him. He thought, a bit wryly, that he understood their reaction perfectly well. He was one of the unknown. He had stayed in town during the occupation, living and drinking with Tories and Loyalists. Then he had done the unthinkable and not left with the refugees. He would not, could not, talk about it, or explain why he stayed behind. In fact, most of these people desired no explanation. There might be British spies left behind to watch the town. Perhaps these good folks deserved their unease, but he would no longer count such things among his problems.

He joined the commercial traffic heading upstream and was let off at the landing above Brighton, the place with the Indian name, Nonantum. It was the site of the old Indian village, where John Eliot had first converted his Praying Indians. Alex had once seen Eliot's Indian Bible, a prize possession of a friend at Yale. It had been translated into the Algonquian language with the help of two Massachuset assistants and published in 1663. Even his friend had not let him touch the pages without using a special stick he'd carved himself. The village was gone now, moved west to Natick and dissolved over time, following the path of so many utopian attempts.

For a moment he dreamed that the key in his pocket and the papers in the case on his back would solve all his problems. It began with a man who was leaving on transport to Nova Scotia. The man had sold him the key, along with an address for a connection in Canada. Alex had given him what money he could, and promised to find a buyer, or purchase the property himself. It was the same story with so many others who had sold their livestock and moved away before the local Committee of Safety could confiscate their house and lands. Alex had not been willing to explain to the man or his wife that he did not share their staunch loyalty to the Crown, but as an honest man he would do what he could. Perhaps he would love the land or make a profit in the transaction, a sort of reward for his months of duplicitous ennui.

He turned south at the Corner and began to climb the steep hill, following the road away from the river. He recognized the area from that summer day at the wedding, and dreamed of that warm sun-kissed afternoon when he danced with Nina, drank what he discovered was her fine ale, and watched, unobserved, as his lovely blonde daydreamed in the rose garden. Now he had a ring in his pocket, and was on the way to discover if he could create a life she would want to join.

He hadn't known the farm was so near the village of the First Church. Maybe, if there was time, he would find a few minutes to talk to Dr. Tyrie. Since Nina was a widow, there was no legal reason to talk to her father. But it would be polite to say hello since he was so near their home.

He wondered if her parents' support for their marriage would help him convince Nina to leave the *Wheel and Hammer*, or have the opposite effect. He understood that Jack was the heir to the inn, but there must be some way for the boy to return to the work of the inn as a man - if he wished. Alex simply could not see himself as caretaker for another man's inn and brewery, no matter how good the food or excellent the ale. He clung to the hope that with good will and optimism, he would find a way.

He followed the directions the man had left him, realizing

that his route was bringing him near the farm just past the church. His map said to turn west on a small track, but he stopped to look around. He let the recollections of that summer day nudge out months of dreary loneliness. He hadn't expected or imagined that the damsel in distress under a collapsing table would be the same delicious blonde at the shipyard. Things like that only happened in the novels his sisters read. That he would get to know and love her, and that she would have become such a part of him, was nearly unbelievable. Even these past months apart had done nothing to quell his desire, or his interest in melding his life with hers. He ran his fingers over the small box in his pocket, dreaming of putting that ring on her slim finger.

The morning was late when he stopped to sit on a boulder to rest. He rubbed his aching leg. He hated to admit it, but the wound had been a strange gift. If it had healed well, instead of turning into a lingering muscle pain, he would have sought a commission and would now be slogging through Connecticut on his way to fight what was certainly going to be a long war. But limping he was, and General Thomas was right. He would be of more use to the world as a teacher, and with luck a husband and father.

Carts loaded with people, headed south to the town center for some sort of celebration, headed past him. He thought he recognized one of the groups and hailed them.

"Dr. Tyrie!" He called to the gentleman sitting beside a younger version of himself. A number of women and children sat in the back with baskets of food.

"Well, isn't it Mr. Peele? We are headed to the center for an anniversary celebration for the battles of Concord and Lexington. You must come along."

"Alex! Sorry. Mr. Peele!" A gangly ten year old, a good five inches taller than the lad he had met late the summer before, scrambled over the side of the wagon and fell into step. "Grandfather, there is no room in the cart. Mr. Peele and I will walk."

He turned to face Alex. "I hope that's okay, Alex, I'd rather hear how you have been than listen to my uncles." He started formally, but they soon fell into deep conversation. Twenty minutes later, they moved ahead of the cart-clogged road onto the town green, already full of people.

Day of Thanksgiving and Prayer for the People of Boston so recently liberated from their long blockade, and for the soldiers of the Continental Army as they move south from here, to defend us and create a new nation. On the Anniversary of the battles at Concord and Lexington, April 23, 1776. To be held on the town green.

Nina read the notice that had been posted the week before. She sat in the back of her beer wagon with the tavern girls. She'd been ordered not to drive the team, so Sukie and Maria Cotton sat on the bench, the others sharing the wagon. All the men from the *Wheel* had ridden their own horses earlier in the day. Nina was proud that her tavern would make such a good showing.

She had awakened that morning with the clear head of having slept well, her malaise and depression lifted. The lovely aquamarine bezel, warm against her body, caught the morning light. As always, it moved between her breasts, doing what it was designed to do, reminding her of the man who had given it to her. Whatever it was that was keeping Alex away, she felt deeply that she would see him soon. After all, his reappearance at irregular intervals had been the only constant in this strange love affair. Whether he would stay with her, that was the uncertainty.

Up earlier than expected, she used the few minutes before they were to leave for the celebration to see how things had been without her help. She let herself into the brewhouse and instinctively counted barrels, making sure everything was as it should be. It was, nearly. Some barrels were neatly labeled and arranged, but others were not. Much of the room showed signs of the work having been rushed. Nina understood, and no one could blame the young Turners for that. They had just started to learn the craft when she was felled by that bullet.

She was genuinely pleased at Martha's and Henry's success. It was pleasant to have the running of the inn in someone else's hands, a relief not to be the center of the maelstrom that was the tavern and inn. But what of her real work, the brewing? From the looks of it, and what the tavern girls had let drop, Martha had not fallen into that role as easily as into the others. Yet, she had done well, and the ale was passable. But it was not great. It was not ale that made a drinker stop and sigh, as John Peddleman's had, as Nina's had begun to do.

It had taken her a decade of hard work to learn the alchemy of temperature and ingredient, a decade of reading those old books and watching, listening, smelling mash and yeasts, a decade of asking questions, and listening to her

Father-in-law tell stories about the ales he had made and the brewers he had known. She could pass on that knowledge, but nothing could be learned without time.

The *Wheel and Hammer* had a feature few brewhouses could claim - location at a waterfalls. Its consistently-cool fermenting room was below ground, under the workspace, the watertable from the river keeping the ales at a steady cold no matter the season. It was special and unique. Could she leave it? Did she want to?

What if Alex never came back? Even if he did, he had no land and no home to return to. It would be foolish to give up work that pleased her. Perhaps in years Martha and Henry, or even Jack, might take over the brewing, but meanwhile? She looked around at the room, admitting to herself that she would be sad if she left it all behind. Perhaps, she thought, she had better reacquaint herself with the art of brewing.

She walked from the dark brewhouse into the warm spring sunshine, welcoming the sun on her shoulders. She needed to be a brewer! The knowledge gave her a burst of energy she had not felt since the discovery of wet hops and a leaky roof the previous fall. She laughed when she realized that she would not yet throw off the title "alewife."

She grabbed two apples from a barrel to give her twin Suffolks. Yes, being healthy and ready for the next phase in her life was a good thing.

The day wasn't the anniversary of the battle, but the April Tuesday was a traditional day for the spring thanksgiving, and a good a day for the town to gather on the town green. Nina sat back in the wagon to enjoy the half-hour ride. She looked up into the trees. The sky was blue and birds sang. Swamp maples had their red tinge and the oaks had pale green tips on each branch. It was almost time to plant corn, but not quite yet. The oaks were late, not quite leafed-out into their tiny mouse-ear sized leaves, due to the late winter storms.

Tradition held that the size of an oak leaf was the sign to plant. The delay meant more people could enjoy a day together with family picnics and grand oration continuing until late in the afternoon. The center was crowded with wagons, horses and happy people .

Sukie pulled to a halt in a line of wagons, and slowly edged into the field behind a row of stores. Nina instructed as Sukie led the team to a water trough, and then tethered them to the back of the wagon, their feed bags filled. They pulled sailcloth over the baskets of food they would return for later, took the baskets they wanted, and walked toward the crowds.

A group of men in front of the public house on the green shouted and whistled their approval, drawing attention to a group of pretty women in light spring muslins alighting from a wagon and walking across the road. One or two blushed at the compliment. The others took it in stride, and Mrs. Cotton, old enough to be everyone's grandmother, turned and thanked them for noticing while she swished her skirts. The men's comments changed to appreciative laughter.

***

The youngest member of the group was Maryann Bickerstaff, the little cinder girl, who had come to live at the *Wheel and Hammer*, just a week before.

"Colonel Bickerstaff, what can I do for you?" The man was ushered into Nina's main parlor, his young daughter in tow. At that moment, she looked smaller and younger than Nina remembered from the month before. She had a memory of little Maryann doing something that probably saved her life, but she could not get it to form. She rose and motioned for the

Colonel and his daughter to sit.

She could not imagine what more she could do for the army at Cambridge, especially with her head woozy from the draughts, and her arm in a sling.

"Mrs. Bigelow?" the large man was clearly uncomfortable having to ask a stranger for help. "Ma'am, I have a favor to ask of you. I know it is very irregular of me, but Maryann insists I try, so here I am."

"Please." Nina nodded at the man and turned a smile to the girl. Maryann smiled back. Nina's genuine warmth put the man and his daughter at ease. He continued.

"As I am sure you are aware, we have orders to go south. I am Maryann's only parent since her mother, God bless her, left us last year. We - she and I - were wondering, could she stay here with you till I can come back for her? She seems to think you would be a better choice than her grandmother or her aunts."

"There are too many children at the Aunts, Papa, I told you that. It's not that I don't love them. No one could fit me, and grandmother is so terribly old."

Nina was sure the woman would not like the description, but she nodded her understanding. The child's eyes were glassy with tears at her father's leaving. There was nothing Nina wouldn't do for such a child.

"Colonel Bickerstaff, of course she can stay with us. My son, who is just a bit younger than your daughter, will return soon, and they will have a great summer." She turned to the girl. "Maryann, would you like to work? The tavern girls are lots of fun and everyone pitches in. We are a busy, bustling inn with lots to do. Another pair of hands is always welcome. And we will discuss school in the fall."

She stood and held her good hand out to the Colonel,

who looked as though he might collapse with relief. Nina could see he would be far more at ease with a shoulder against the plow, or leading men into battle, than asking a stranger to foster his daughter. "We will take good care of her sir, I promise." Nina excused herself, and left father and daughter alone for a few moments to say their good-byes.

***

Now Maryann led the way past the stores and stares toward a bit of grass, where she and the other girls spread their blanket and unpacked rolls and jam. She had adjusted well to the busy inn and quickly made friends with the other girls. If she worried at night and cried in her sleep, she kept it quiet. Mrs. Cotton was sure that given a few more weeks, she would have an easier time.

Alex and Jack were just nearing the Green at the end of their short walk when they turned to a commotion from a group of men on their right. Alex blinked when he spotted Maryann Bickerstaff with the group of young women who had attracted the men's attention.

He started, jumping and turning sharply when Jack shouted out, "Ma! You're here!" The boy ran full speed over to the group of women, putting on his brakes so as not to knock Nina over.

On closer observation, the ladies were Nina's tavern staff. Alex placed them on his second glance. He might have wondered about Maryann, but all rational thought fled when he spotted Nina, her good arm around her son.

The day was improving steadily. He had come to the town green almost accidentally, and Nina was here, on the same soil, under the same budding beech tree. He caught her eye. She smiled that amazing smile at him. His breath caught in his throat as all the months of isolation fell away. He felt the good of boundless possibility. He fingered the little box in his pocket.

"Ma!" Jack pointed to Alex standing not five feet away. "Did you see who I found near the Tyrie farms? Hey Alex, come here and see my Ma." His pleasure at seeing his mother up and around again was obvious. People nearby smiled at the boy's enthusiastic shouting. Nina kissed his cheek and spoke a quiet word or two. He hugged her hard, and ran off to introduce himself to the new member of the group.

"Hello Nina, I am so very sorry I took so long to come back." Alex had rehearsed his first words until they lost meaning. Now he spoke softly, feeling as though he should fall to his knees and beg her forgiveness for being away so long. He simply took her hand, and led her to a spot beneath the big tree. He took the blanket she was holding and spread it on the dry grass. He lifted her hand to his lips and kissed her knuckles. It was a gentlemanly kiss, but his lips lingered a moment too long. He sighed silently, savoring the feel of her skin beneath his lips, a sense of relief coming over him. "Will you sit with me?"

Nina swallowed tears. She nodded silently. She sat on the wool blanket and fixed her skirts, making room for him. She moved incrementally closer, linking her left arm with his right, leaving no space between their shoulders. She let her head rest on his shoulder for a moment.

He breathed her in, feeling like he could finally release a breath he had been holding for months, or was it years? It was Nina. He would know that feminine scent for a lifetime. It lacked the flowery essence of hops and barley. Of course, since her injury, she had stopped working in the brewhouse.

285

He wondered, fleetingly, if she missed brewing. Was it a phase of her life she could leave behind?

He spoke quietly. "I should begin by explaining that I know that I am terribly late. I would have gotten word to you, but there was no way to do it. There is no post, and I am very sorry to have kept you worried for these weeks. I know precisely how that feels." He gently touched the thick bandage under her right shoulder, letting the vision of carrying a wounded and limp Nina back to her rooms gently roll away.

"Neighbors of mine, good people who were my friends in spite of myself, got very sick with small pox. Because I know I am immune - I was inoculated as a child, and suffered a minor episode a few years ago in Italy - I had no choice but to stay and care for them. Fortunately, they are happily recovered."

"Alex, you had a choice, and you did the right thing." Nina smiled that he should continue.

"It was only yesterday the mother was well enough to call for help from her family. I left on the first boat." He touched the bandage gently. She held her right arm carefully against her body. "Your arm?"

"Is almost healed. My caretakers insist I do nothing, and must not move my arm. I'm afraid I have lost all will to work."

"Then I will find a way for you to become a woman of leisure." There was a twinkle in Alex's eyes. No good New Englander pursued leisure, and they both knew it. "I know this is sudden, but I bought the ring in January. Nina, will you marry me?" His right hand had been clenching the little box in his pocket. He pulled it out and opened it. Inside was a thin ring with a pale blue-green sapphire in an intricate bezel. It was similar to the beautiful stone that lay heavy and hidden between her breasts.

"Yes, of course. One caveat. Alex . . ." He put his finger to her lips to quiet her, but with no effect. "Alex, I have spent weeks thinking about this, so don't stop me."

He nodded solemnly. He wanted to shout with joy, but he kept his head down.

"The caveat is that we, um you know, before we announce anything, so that if I cannot" she made a face to finish her thought, "you don't have to marry me."

"Nina, I would wait forever for you. You don't need to make any rules." Alex thought of all the arguments he could use to prove such pronouncements were unnecessary, but only action would work.

"Hmmm, if you insist." He put his arm around her shoulder and pulled her against him, his hand nonchalantly teasing at her hip and beginning to run slow circles over her neck and back, pretending all the while to listen to the town meeting member who was speaking on the importance of the day.

Nina felt his hand slowly move up from her back into her hair. She had been trying to remain involved in the speaker's words, but all her concentration was focused on that hand as it moved over her body.

Working one handed, Alex had un-pinned Nina's long hair, letting the thin plaits fall down her back. Back under her white cap, his fingernails gently teased at her scalp, making her jump and giggle slightly. His hand moved over her neck and down her back, slowly drawing circles. He felt her breathe beneath his fingers, her breath catching as she fought to maintain an outward composure he was working hard to disintegrate. He took her hand and touched and massaged one finger at a time. Nina lost all ability to think, nearly overwhelmed by the gentle sensations coursing through her body.

As people stood to applaud the speaker, he took advantage of their being unobserved and kissed her. It was a quick kiss, but deep and powerful. The crowd stayed standing as music played and people moved to stretch their legs and backs. A few children started dancing in a circle.

Slowly Alex moved them backwards out of the crowded Green. Once away, they turned, and as they walked Alex pulled Nina's hand to his lips for a kiss. He sighed her name, and pulled one finger into his mouth, suckling and nipping gently. He heard her breath hitch, and she stumbled into him. He held her tighter, barely in control of his own arousal. If this hadn't been a busy town, he would have taken her against the milliner's shop they had just passed.

They walked between two shops, both closed for an hour or two so the shop owners could hear the speakers. Once completely out of sight of the crowd, Alex pushed Nina against the brick wall and kissed her, covering her body with his. Just for a minute. Gathering his wits before he shamed them both, he took her hand and they resumed their walking.

She put her hand in his and moved his fingers between hers, separating and teasing as they walked further and further from the crowd.

Alex spotted Nina's Suffolks tethered to the back of her wagon. A sail cloth made a small tent over the food and cloaks left behind.

"Will the girls mind a little company?" Alex helped Nina up and climbed in afterwards. He sighed as he pulled her into his arms and kissed her.

"I wish I hadn't hidden the wolf cloak behind those rocks at your brother's farm. I have dreams of lying you back on it, but that will have to wait." He gently lay her back onto the pile of ladies' cloaks, and untied the laces on her old-fashioned waistcoat. His hands cupped her loose breasts, his thumbs teased her nipples. He kissed them one at a time, careful not to get carried away and leave a wet patch on her chemise.

Nina didn't care. She was lost in the wonder of sensation. She couldn't have turned away from Alex if she had wanted to, or cared that her chemise was wet. Her only desire was to open to him, to consume and be consumed. She shuddered and moaned as she lifted her hips to him, and he entered her, filling her warm body with his hard strength. His mouth covered hers in a devastating kiss. She moved under him, matching his thrusts with her own and exploding with him. Gentle tremors rocked the wagon, but they made as little noise as possible, moaning into each other's shoulders, Alex covered Nina's scream with a kiss, catching her passion in his mouth.

"I'm afraid anyone walking by would know what we just did." She said as she caught her breath a while later, lying loose and languid in Alex's arms.

"I guess that's why we should wait a while until we climb out. But I warn you, if we wait too long, it will all happen again, and we will have the same problem. Alex pulled her onto him so her head rested on his chest. He kissed her hair. "You have to marry me now, you know. My ring is on your finger and we 'umm did it', quote un-quote." Nina hit him gently. She peeked out, and started to fix her skirts.

"I think we should get back." She looked into his deep gray eyes. He looked inordinately pleased with himself, yet gently concerned with her.

"Nina, are you happy?"

"Oh yes Alex, very happy." She kissed him hard, jumped down and swished her skirts into place. She retied her boots, hiding the rosy cheeks and sly smile that slid over her face.

Caroline Tyrie had watched the glee with which her grandson had greeted Alex Peele, whom she had met and liked at the wedding luncheon. She observed as they walked up the hill deep in conversation, and noted the care the man took to listen to the child. Now she watched Alex lead her daughter back into the throng at the town Green. She had never before seen Nina so happily connected with anyone but her young son. She stared openly as Alex pulled Nina close and kissed her. Caroline Tyrie sighed with joy. She got up and walked to Nina's blanket, where Alex was still busily kissing Nina. He was trying to pretend no one could see them.

"Anyone who kisses my daughter like that had better be prepared to marry her!" Caroline had intended to sound like a tyrant, but she giggled. Nina waved her ring finger in her mother's direction.

"You will wed after the hay is in. No rushing this time Nina, I'm going to give you a pretty wedding from your father's church. Spend the rest of the day. I will pick you up at the *Wheel and Hammer* after breakfast. No complaints, I have it on good authority that they have been muddling along without your help.

"And Peele, we will expect you tomorrow afternoon to speak with me and my husband." Smiling behind her handkerchief, she walked back to her group, whispering something in her husband's ear.

"I don't suppose she thinks we were just taking a walk, and won't insist on me marrying you, if I didn't want to." Nina lifted her head to look into Alex's face.

"No, I don't think your mother is that stupid. You look well tumbled, and I am not sorry. Do you suppose it is too late to claim the wager? We could use the coin."

"That stupid thing. Do you think Wythe didn't tell me about it? He threatened to kill you if you tried to win it."

"Well I did win, didn't I? Much more than those fools could have imagined. I desperately love you Nina." He took her hand and spoke into her aqua eyes, reflected in the stone that had escaped from her bodice, and the one that glittered on her hand.

"Oh Alex, yes." She tilted her head and kissed his cheek. "I love you too. I think I have since that summer morning. My gallant hero with the wonderful hair." Her hand played with the waves of his queue.

Speechless, he blushed.

Chapter 26

Later that afternoon, Alex walked with Jack down the hill from the town center. The boy pointed him to Seth's paddock, where he found Thorne happily grazing the fresh grass.

"It's been a real treat having the gray here." Seth Tyrie walked over while Alex watched the horse.

"I'm glad he's been useful." The beautiful, elegant and skittish stallion would have only one use on a working farm such at Seth Tyrie's, but even that was important, and could make a man with a few mares rich.

"Yep, we've got at least three mares who've just come into season this month, and a few on a neighboring farm. As I said, he's earned his feed."

Alex had no comment, but also no complaint. The gray looked well content with his life. He whistled for Thorne and was happy that the horse remembered to come. He excused himself, telling Seth he would see him soon. Then he and Thorne went into the barn where Jack had blanket, saddle, bridle and reins polished and ready.

"Thank you, Jack." He felt as though he barely deserved such careful treatment, and was grateful beyond words. Alex put his sacks and fur cloak into his old saddle bags - which Jack or perhaps Nina had somehow found. He mounted; the motion was unfamiliar and yet automatic. "Jackie, I will see you tomorrow and we will have lots of time to talk. I promise." The boy smiled and waved, and Alex and Thorne headed down the steep hill toward the river and west to the Falls, following the main road.

He stabled the horse with a young man he had never met. There was something of Jack in his face, so Alex assumed he was one of the cousins. He paid his penny for the hayloft and a clean sheet, and put his few belongings above Thorne in the stable. He threw his cape over his shoulders and went into the familiar tavern.

Nina returned to the Falls in the wagon. She excused herself, explaining that she would be in for dinner, and went to dress. The evening was cool, but she pulled out the gown she had worn that first night the men had ridden over. It was one of her more daring, with a low neckline and narrow shoulder pieces. She left off the fichu she usually wore with it. She brushed and fixed her hair, reliving those moments that evening when Alex had pulled out the pins and let the plaits fall down her back.

When she was satisfied with herself, she worked on her room, changing the sheets and setting things back the way they had been before Mrs. MacAlistair and her helpers had cleaned and straightened. Then she set candles to mark the path, and went to the taproom for dinner.

Alex sat at his favorite table in the corner, sipping ale and waiting for Nina. He knew what a wonder the *Wheel and Hammer* really was - a busy and wonderful inn, full of life, good food and stories. Did that mean he would be happy for his wife to be its mistress, and he the working proprietor, waiting for a stepson to step into his role? He knew his own wishes, but he had never asked Nina what hers might be. As much as he'd love to postpone the discussion, he could not.

He pushed all unpleasant thoughts out of his head, and concentrated on his blonde who had just walked into the room.

He chuckled, and she looked up, but he shook his head as he stood and moved to meet her.

His blonde. He had thought of her that way for what would soon be a year. In candlelight, he could see she wore a gown he'd memorized from that summer night when she had sat with the men from camp and listened to their stories, adding commentary of her own and matching wit for wit, combining humor with what he now knew to be her natural gentleness.

The night, he had realized that his lovely blonde from the shipyard and wedding was the biting wit in Wythe's alewife tales. Funny how little families understood one another.

Pale green. It reflected her aqua eyes, and brought out the glow in her skin and the layers of blondes in her hair. A pink wool shawl draped over her arms, but she had not bothered with a fichu. The mounds of her breasts showed enticingly, forced upward by the boning of formal stays and the low-cut gown. Only a small bandage blocked the perfect view.

She had gotten a bit of sun that afternoon at the town green, and her nose and those delicious mounds were just kissed pink. The sun might be first, but he had every intension of being second, and doing a far better job. The few minutes together in the wagon had been delightful, but a sip of wine does nothing to quench the desire for a glass.

Nina had contemplated this first dinner, and the night that would follow, for hours, days and weeks as her arm healed. She hadn't expected it to come after such a whirlwind - what did he call it - "tumbling" in the wagon. But that only served to remove her anxiety and increase her genuine curiosity. She could now admit it, longing for more. The strange sleeping draughts had caused her to have strange, vivid dreams, and long hours alone in her bed led to memories of long kisses on a damp, cold night. It hadn't taken long simply to turn the dreams into daydreams. Over the weeks in her bed, she'd learned to appreciate the feelings the dreams had brought and, finally, to crave the closeness she had experienced so fleetingly.

She greeted him, putting her good arm around his waist and her head on his shoulder, just for a moment before they would announce their news to the inn. She held him close and breathed him into her lungs. Her body recognized his essence. It seemed unlikely after so long apart and so few hours together, but the reaction was undeniable. Alex gently kissed her cheek, and pulled out her chair, giving them both a moment before they faced Nina's long-term staff.

Dinner was served as soon as Mrs. Cotton saw that Nina was sitting with Alex. The inn was not crowded, and no one noticed that the couple by the window got better food, fine wine, and faster service than anyone else, but if there were complaints, the glare the cook gave in return would have the patron quietly returning to his chair.

There was so much to tell about the last few months. It hardly mattered that she had been to Boston during the winter to spend time with him at Christmas, and again for the disastrous day at the beginning of March. Neither of those trips had allowed for any kind of visit, let alone intimacy. It was as if he had been another person."Of course you know Josh left for Boston and never returned." She nodded her head and rolled her eyes, as a way of explaining that it was the story told here at the *Wheel*, and more, that no one knew it was Josh who had shot her. Alex nodded. He understood the message - Joshua Peddleman's disappearance was unexplained. He most likely he left for Canada with the other refugees.

295

"You've spoken to Jack?" That was easy, since Alex had walked with him to the town green. They must have talked if not actually caught up. "He told you that my father tutors him daily? Last week when they came to visit, he announced that he won't move back until you're here and ready to teach him Greek. He explained Grandfather's Latin is stronger than his Greek. But my guess is that the Ancient Greeks make Father blush. I didn't have the heart to tell him I didn't know where you were. I'm glad I didn't.

"There is something else. He's been safer at Seth and Alcea's. Too many people have been interested in the inn. First it was Josh's friends who wanted you, then it was Martin Jewett and the Committee."

"The committee?"

"Committee of Safety. Mostly the committees have done a good job replacing magistrates and sheriffs and keeping the peace, but a few have gone overboard and harassed good people just because they are less passionate for the cause of liberty.

"At the corner, near the first parish, the Committee is made up of sane men trying to maintain order. My brothers are members. Even they, I believe, may have overstepped now and then. But the Committee here feels they have the duty to enforce political will. They want everyone to swear to support independence, even if they are not ready or want to be left alone.

"Martin Jewett is their leader. He even punished children for praying for the King. As if youngsters could give up their catechism overnight. Mr. Jewett also thinks I am a lax parent, destroying the moral health of my son. He offered, or should I say threatened, to whip Jack for me. He called it an offer. After that, it was just safer for him and Thorne to live with my family. I sent him away. That's why you found him there. But I think, as much as I would love to spend the summer with him at my parent's, if you are to be here, it will be best if he spends the time with you. We'll say it is for the Greek."

Alex listened carefully to the warning about the Committee of Safety. He hadn't met any yet. Certainly they would not have been working in Boston while the British held the Town, but he could imagine that someone with a thirst for power could become overzealous when given an important task, such as keeping the town safe.

"I understand what harm a tyrant can do, even a petty one. It's a shame to throw off one oppressor, only to accept another. As for teaching Jack Greek, I will look forward to discussing Zeus's multiple lovers and Medea's faithlessness." His laugh was lighthearted. It felt good to talk honestly, even if not all the news was happy.

"Nina, you might wonder how I happened to see Jack and collect Thorne from Seth. You see, I accidentally stopped by there this morning. I was looking for a piece of land." He pulled out the deed from his coat pocket. "I hold here the deed for Theodore Robinson's farm. He sold it to me before he left with the others for Nova Scotia. I wanted to see if I should hold on to it or sell. Do you know it? What do you think of the Robinson land? You grew up near there."

"The Robinsons? If the sheep are still on it – keep it. I loved those sheep when I was a girl. I used to pretend I was a shepherd watching the flock, my muzzleloader by my side, ready to shoot a mad dog or wolf. The Robinsons must have thought *I* was mad."

"You have always been fierce, haven't you?" The thought made his body warm and tighten. He was so delighted he would have that passion in his life. He smiled at the image of young Nina as a resolute shepherd. "Sadly, the family was forced to sell the animals. But would you be happy growing vegetables? I might get the fruit trees back into production, something all the students could work on. I believe studies should be broken up with hard physical labor, and growing food gives a good purpose."

"You mean to start a school?"

"Yes, but maybe not right away, and only if you will do it with me."

"It seems such a big decision, leaving my house and the inn. They are not connected, by the way. I own the house outright. I suppose I could insist Marty and Henry buy the house, but they won't need it. Their parents live very near here, just below the last of the falls, around the bend to the north."

This was new information to Alex, and changed the way he thought of the Robinson farm. "Marty and Henry? Jack mentioned them as though I should know them."

"The cousins. My niece and nephew, Johnny's sister Miriam's children. They are right over there." She pointed out brother and sister who were working at the front of the room. "They came after the hurricane in September, and have been in charge here since I was laid up in March. They are doing a wonderful job. The *Wheel and Hammer* would have closed without their help." Nina sent up a silent prayer that Alex would not suddenly express a desire to manage an inn. She looked the question at him, but he stayed still, listening.

"Alex, this has to be said. I don't know how you feel about the inn. I've known for a while that Jack will never have the passion for the place that those two have. He has no interest in brewing ale or hosting travelers." She shrugged. "Now that there is someone else to do the work, I can admit that I don't like greeting guests or counting sheets. If I had anything to do here, it would be solely as brewer." She made a mildly dismissive face at her tankard of ale. "Marty is learning, and she gets better. I had a decade of working with John Peddleman. You see, I love brewing, the mix and challenge of getting it just right, but running the kitchens, stables and inn was something I had to do, had to excel at, for the good of my son and staff. I think I did it for Jack's future, for his grandfather, for duty, and maybe for Johnny's memory."

Alex waited a respectful minute, and then spoke, "Jack's interest in Greek and algebra had me concerned he might not have an interest in the family business."

"I will leave running the inn to Martha. It should have been hers to inherit if interest could be considered. Hmm, and you? Alex, are you sure you are ready to leave the army? You could teach in a few years, when this is over. I would wait for you."

"You don't have to wait. My war is over. The leg slows me down too much for infantry work, and my espionage days are finished. I am well known to the three generals and their staffs, well enough to be identified by any one of dozens of them. They all lost money to me, you see, more than once. I'm afraid that fixes a man's face in one's memory. It is supposed I accompanied my clothes to Nova Scotia and London."

He swallowed some ale, remembering his conversation with General Thomas, "I was told by a wise man that I should teach. He reminded me, just as there was a cause worth killing and dying for, there had to be a nation worth living for when the war is won. He seemed to believe my use as a soldier was less than my use as a molder of young minds. That you might be with me, help me in that task, that is my very good luck."

He smiled and sighed at his good fortune.

Nina lifted her head. "Oh, I nearly forgot. Speaking of young minds. Maryann Bickerstaff has moved in with me here. She came when her father left with the army's move to New York. She has the room next to Jack's in the attic."

Alex nodded. He remembered his young friend from his time in Boston. "Our first half-orphan then. I thought I would open the school to children of soldiers in similar situations. It seems that fate has begun my enrollment ahead of time. It was wise of the Colonel to leave her with you. She is too young to follow the drum without a mother. She will miss her father, but Maryann is bright, and knows as well as anyone the importance of this war.

"She is a remarkable girl, and might be recognized, so it is good she will be safe here in the countryside. If the British aristocracy have only one fault it is their notion of human behavior. Maryann used their preconceptions about the young, the stupid Americans, and foolish servant girls against them. They never looked hard enough at her to see beyond the cinder girl, never thought she might be the one leaking their information.

"And you? Did they ever think to look at you?"

"Me? No, I never did more than leave my hat on top of Maryann's work. Sometimes her foolscap scribbles were picked up with the hat, but I never did more than that. Couldn't afford to. I'd have been caught in a second. Mine was to listen and, when it was possible, to smooth the way. Make the British comfortable with their decisions, and get word back through channels what those decisions were.

"But Maryann and I are more than colleagues in espionage. I met her just before the battle at Bunker's Hill. We had some wonderful conversations, along with her father and the other children in camp. She went into Boston just after I did, to stay with her aunt and get work at the Province House.

"That day in March, after I left you, she and I made it to Cambridge before the worst of the weather, but it was very cold. I got her out of that barrel about a quarter of a mile east of here. I couldn't do it sooner. There was no way to guess which of Josh's old friends might be watching. He had just shot you. But, by the time it was safe to take her out, she was chattering badly and nearly blue. Poor waif, we rode with her tucked neatly inside the fur cloak, her little feet tucked under me." His sigh explained more than his words. "I'm relieved to find both of you here and healthy. Close as thieves we all are.

Nina put down her napkin. "I wish she were happier. She is not having an easy time. The girl lives for her father's letters. If they don't arrive regularly, she goes into a deep pout, sometimes if one is only a week late. I don't know what we'll do if he gets seriously hurt or" her voice dropped expressing the inevitable worst, "can't write. Maybe it will be better, having her old friend here, someone her father knows."

Alex nodded, expressing understanding. "Jack and I will have to find some project to distract her." With a smile he wiped away the dire maybes, and pulled them back into the here and now.

As he sat back, he took Nina's hand and looked into her bright eyes, dancing excitement. She was happy to see him. She looked really happy. It was a heady feeling, making someone happy simply by arriving. He turned her left hand palm down and touched the ring he had slipped on her fourth finger earlier in the day. "I would ask again if you hadn't already answered. We are connected in so many ways. I am so happy to be here. With you." Alex smiled at the ring and then at her.

Nina looked down at her hand, knowing she wanted to take this step with Alex. It was only last summer that she had taken off the little wedding ring Johnny had long ago slipped on her finger. She didn't remember if that was before or after that strange encounter with the grey-eyed soldier at the shipyard in Braintree. She had worn that little ring, as much to announce to the world that she was *not* hunting for a new man as to remind herself that she had once been married.

This ring - she stared at her left hand - was not like the one she had taken off and hidden in the back of her drawer. It was not small or innocuous. It was pink gold, set with an almost perfect, miniature copy of the aquamarine with the intricate bezel. As always, when she thought of the stone she could feel the pendent move against her body. She shivered and looked up into Alex's deep gray eyes. He raised her hand to his lips and kissed it.

He rose and pulled out Nina's chair, helping her to her feet. He draped his warm cloak over her shoulders against the chill, and ushered her out the door into the early evening light. "Lets walk." Nina took Alex's hand and led him away from the inn's buildings, further down the lane toward the river. They stopped near back of the stable, at the smaller of the two falls.

As always, the rushing water blocked out the sounds of the world. The spring evening was already turning cool, and Nina absorbed Alex's heat as she turned into him, resting her head on his shoulder. "I never get tired of it, the falls. The constant roar, and the mist rising around the rocks. I suppose I will miss it when I leave." She stopped for a moment to listen. "Not irreparably, but I will miss it. I have lived here so long." She let out a deep breath and sighed. She tilted her head and looked toward Alex, checking that he understood.

He did, more than he could explain. He also had fallen in love with the sounds and smell of the churning water. He pulled her against him. Resting his chin lightly on her head, he kissed her hair, breathing in the smell and essence of Nina, noting again that he missed the scent of hops and malt. But as delightful as it was to have a women who smelled of good ale, it was of no consequence. On the other hand, Alex understood security and change - especially, what such things meant to Nina, whose responsibilities had always been met head-on. He lifted her face to his, he feathered kisses lightly across her cheeks and lips. She held his gaze, opening her lips, welcoming the kiss. Alex sighed and covered her mouth with his. He felt in many ways this was their first kiss - not of relief, or good-bye, but a kiss of honest passion.

Their separations had never been of their making, and he had missed her. Almost before he had learned her name, he had missed her. He deepened the kiss, entwining their tongues, feeling as if they entwined their souls. His hands loosened her plaits and played with the soft, long strands of blonde hair. He teased them from their pins. He couldn't wait to see it loose and flowing over her sumptuous and naked body.

He was glad they had already had their tryst. It took all the worry away from the night. Now he knew he wouldn't lose her. He had long wanted to see Nina loose and sated with pleasure, but he'd never had any intension of tricking her into it. It was important for both of them that she join him willingly, not out of fear of losing him, not even from seduction.

Their moment was interrupted by the sound of horses coming hard into the lane. Nina immediately reached to fix her hair and jacket, but Alex pushed her behind him.

"Who is it?" Alex wanted to curse.

303

"It's Jewett and the Committee of Safety. They must have a reason to be here so late. Usually they come for dinner and stay too long. I must go and see to it."

"No Nina, I get to take care of this. Go in by the kitchen door and stay out of sight. I'll come to your house when Jewett leaves."

He walked her through the kitchen door, seeing her seated and continuing on into the taproom. Nina was surprised at how easy it was to let Alex deal with the unpleasant situation. She sat with Mrs. Cotton and watched through the peephole she'd had built to watch the room.

Martin Jewett and the other three members of his committee sat at their table, tankards already served and finished. Three of the men looked like they wanted to leave, and were in the process of standing and moving toward the door. The fourth man, Martin Jewett, showed no interest in leaving, now that his ale was finished.

Dodi had been their waitress, and now he gripped her by the arm, yelling into her face. She looked frightened, even faint. With Jewett holding her so tightly, there was no way to tell if she was stable or ready to fall over. The other staff huddled near the front of the room watching, too shocked to move. The tavern had not been busy, but since the arrival of the Committee, most patrons had either left or moved away. Among those that stayed sitting, there was general interest in the unfolding events.

Alex took it in. It wasn't hard, he knew this type. Weakness only fed his ego. Jewett gripped Dodi by the upper arm and was holding tight.

"Dodi," he had obviously asked her before, "you must know where Peddleman has gone. He has had weeks to contact you. Don't lie and say he hasn't. A man doesn't leave a pretty girl like you behind without a word."

"Mr. Jewett, Joshy, I mean Joshua hasn't written a word to me. I promise, I have no idea where he might be." She tried to squirm away, but Martin Jewett held her tight enough to cause pain.

It was time to stop this nonsense. "Jewett! The girl is clearly telling the truth. Leave her alone."

"Who the hell are you - interfering in the work of the Committee?"

"Alex Peele, lately of General Washington's and General Thomas's staffs in Boston, Roxbury and Cambridge. Mustered out due to a battle wound." He held out his hand but was ignored. "I assume you are Jewett. What is it you want of Dodi?"

"The girl is carrying Peddleman's child and I want his location."

"Mr. Jewett, are you sure the child is male? But no matter, I think his or her location is obvious."

"Not the baby, you idiot! Peddleman." Martin Jewett started turning red, uncomfortable with Alex's attempt at humor.

Alex pulled himself upright and drew out his words as sneeringly as possible. "Mr. Jewett, if the young lady says she does not have the man's location you should believe her. Being enceinte does not give her any sort of divine knowledge about Joshua's whereabouts. As for his contacting her, he would not be the first man to abandon an expectant mother.

"Furthermore," Alex tried to move between Jewett and Dodi, but the other man held firm. "I believe you have harassed this inn often enough. So let me give you a few proposals. First. Move your meetings elsewhere. The town has

305

many fine establishments, and if you need help choosing another location, I will personally find you one." He happily noticed that the other members of the Committee had moved away from their leader, rather than moving closer to prove their allegiance. "Second. Leave Dodi and the other girls alone. They know less than you do about loyalists, the activities of Josh Peddleman, or his friends."

"*You* seem to know something about Peddleman and his friends - care to enlighten the Committee?"

"No. There is nothing I have to say to you. All pertinent information was given to General Washington weeks ago, but I will tell you that Peddleman was in Boston, and preparing to evacuate at the beginning of March when I lost track of him. As for the men he considered his friends, they are your problem." Alex turned to Dodi.

"Miss Smith, is there someone who can walk you up to your room to rest? I think this has been enough of an evening's work for you." Alex walked to Jewett. The man dropped his hand from Dodi's arm, and she ran to the other girls who rushed her through the kitchen. Alex stalked to the rear and opened the door to the tavern, waiting for the Committee members to go out into the evening. "Good night gentlemen, I hope not to hear of your meeting here again. If I do, I'm afraid I will have to mention it to Hancock." He looked over his nose at them as if he had known John Hancock for years, rather then having a chance meeting, one time, in the General's anteroom.

Alex waited until the four men rode off. He spoke quietly to the staff, feeling eyes on his back. Not knowing what else to do or say, he went out the front door and simply walked down the lane. He took a deep breath, shaking off the angry mood of the taproom.

Nina sat in the tavern kitchen watching the scene through the hole she used when she was busy with ledgers, in awe with how well Alex handled Martin Jewett. She could fully understand how valuable he had been for Washington. She imagined Alex in the tense, occupied town, soothing all those frayed nerves, preventing bloodshed and God knew what else. She spent a moment just staring at him after the Committee left.

"Gad, girl, if that man didn't look at you like you were a linzer torte, I would grab him myself." Mrs. Cotton was shooing her out the back door. The cook was right. It was time to go home.

As she undressed and pulled on her robe, she replayed the scene in the taproom. She had hardly noticed, but this Alex had looked different than she had seen him before. Tonight he wore the plain homespun clothes of a laborer or farmer, a linsey-woolsey waistcoat, and linen shirt and breeches. He had changed from the traveling leathers he'd had on earlier, those she had seen before, when he was a courier. Those few times she had seen him in Boston, he had worn his London clothes, what he'd called his disguise - silks and fine brocades.

But even in plain linen, without anyone knowing who he was, he took command of the tense, almost explosive room and soothed frayed nerves. He had even confronted Jewett and made the man back down. So that was the Alex that Washington and Thomas had relied on in Boston.

He had a vibrance, an energy and focus she had never before noticed. Maybe she had met him too soon after the Battle at Bunker Hill, when he was still recovering not only from his leg wound, but also from the military loss and shock of battle. Next, she had seen him in Boston, where he had pretended to be something he was not. Tonight it was as if all that camouflage had fallen away, leaving behind a man in command of his world. She was surprised that such a man had ever been obedient to anyone. It spoke volumes that General Washington could command not only the obedience of such men, but their full respect.

She stared again at the new ring on her finger. She would have insisted that she knew Alex. They had talked deeply, and of important things, during their short respites together. She had seen his intelligence, passion, kindness and gentle humor, his patience, certainly his patience.

This was a man of strength. She wondered why that should surprise her. She simply had not considered it since they had become close, perhaps because he had been so kind to her. It would be new, having that strength by her side.

She had lived a strange kind of independence at the *Wheel and Hammer,* never trusting anyone to help or let anyone too close. She had been in charge of her world, but with so much, so many, dependent on her, it had weighed on her, far more than she'd been willing to admit. Loving Alex would require surrendering that brittle independence, the shell that was the alewife. She would have to trust that he would not hurt or leave her.

She trusted him. Hadn't that been part of the strange promise he had made to her? Real trust was that and more. Truly trusting and loving such a man would require all the strength and faith she had. She knew she was going to have to bite her tongue until she got used to it.

***

Nina lit the candles leading from the front door and up

the stairs to her little parlor. She felt a kind of energy, a dizzy feeling that started deep in her gut and radiated to her extremities, making movement almost difficult. She opened the door to her room. The fire was laid, and the few candles on the dresser were already lit. She took off her robe and put on the nightrail she had saved especially for this occasion.

Alex breathed the moist night air, letting the tension leave his body with the exhale. Inside Nina's little house, he was met with a row of candles leading up the front stairs and down the short corridor to Nina's room. He followed the lights, carefully snuffing them as he went. He entered Nina's little parlor. He sat and pulled off his boots and waistcoat. Draping his cape across the top of the door, he entered Nina's room.

It was dark but for a small fire. The windows were open to the brisk wind. Those opulent cushions, remembered from the day he had carried her, bleeding and weak, into this room, were scattered on chairs and the floor near the hearth. Oriental carpets hung from the walls and covered even his own traveling box. The room smelled of woodsmoke, and was that sandalwood? The whole was most unexpected and delightful.

Nina sat cross-legged on the bed. What she wore was extraordinary, almost beyond explanation. Cut like a chemise, it seemed to be made of deep turquoise silk that shimmered in the firelight. It was painted in greens, browns, and vivid reds, with two dragons whose tails clashed over her breasts and shoulders. Both paint and silk were translucent, meaning that Nina's lovely body was as exposed as if she wore nothing. No, Alex just stood there taking in the astonishing sights and smells, less than nothing - it was if all her loveliness was emphasized. He sucked in a breath. It was almost a gasp.

Pulling off his shirt and breeches, he was at the bed in a

step and pulled her into his arms, the silk moving between them as if it had a life of its own.

"A guest left it behind. She had stayed a few days with a man who was not her husband." Nina pushed out the words between kisses.

"Poor husband, he never knew what he missed." Alex feathered kisses over her lips and neck, while his hands moved over the silk on her breasts and hips. Watching the dragons writhe as Nina moved beneath him, his desire was nearly blinding. Leaving a hand on her hip he kissed her breasts, pulling the silk covered nipples, one at a time into his mouth, as if fighting the dragons for control of his damsel. He kissed her down to where the beasts protected her sensitive spots and added his mouth to their attempted consumption of his blonde.

Nina moaned, totally consumed with sensation. It seemed as though the silk was stimulating her senses, each painted dragon trying to best the other by making her cry out in her need.

"Alex!" There at least she hadn't screamed for a dragon. And he was there, kissing her soothing her, teasing her, entering her, filling her. She rose to meet him and shuddered, matching his rhythm and pushing against him, again and again. She felt one with the motion, one with Alex until she shattered into a million pieces, as he reached his climax, pouring himself into her in deep shudders, and collapsing, gathering her in his arms.

Chapter 27

"Aunt Nina!" The voice on the other side of the door had been quietly and politely trying to nudge her out of well-deserved sleep for a few minutes. It had been a long and wonderful night. Nina wondered at her own fears, the ones she had clutched to herself for safety. How could she not have understood?

She lifted her head, trying to catch the meaning of the knocking sound. She put her feet on the rug beside the bed and tried to stand. Alex mumbled something that sounded like "mumph" and pulled her back. The door opened. Nina forced her eyes wide, only to see Martha staring across the room, a look of shock on her face.

"Aunt, that is a man in your bed." She shook her head. "I mean there is a *lady*," she emphasized the word, "in the taproom. She doesn't want anything to eat, she just insists we find you."

"Martha, that's my mother. This is Alex Peele. Alex, my niece, Martha Turner."

Alex sat up and offered his hand. Marty bravely shook it. "Lovely to meet you." She turned an adorable shade of pink and fled the room.

"Tell my mother that I'll be right down." Nina called after the fast-moving girl who was already half-way down the back stairs. She got up and washed in cold water left over from yesterday. She reached for a clean chemise and stays, wishing that Marty had lingered long enough to help. Strong hands reached for the chords at her back and pulled them gently into a knot. She felt warm lips on her neck.

Nina reluctantly pushed Alex back toward the bed. "I am going to see my mother. Don't come down, please. Stay in bed, go back to sleep. I'll send her off to David's and tell her to come back for me at lunch."

Nina put on a skirt and work jacket. She fought her tangled hair until it told no tales of the long night, and pushed it under a cap. She drank a glass of cool water until her teeth and breath felt fresher. Then, assured that there were no telltale signs that might interest a mother, she went down to the taproom and joined her at the table.

The room was fairly empty. It was a slow time after the forge workers' breakfast, with only a few travelers in the room. Bright morning light came through sparkling clean windows, and the floor shone with a new coat of wax. Nina made a note to tell Marty and Henry that the room looked wonderful. "Mama, you are early. I have had no time to pack."

"Well Nina, it was such a lovely day, I thought I would take the carriage out and see if you needed my help packing."

Nina was shocked. Warmed and surprised by the kind offer, she could not let her mother see Alex in the bed or the tangled sheets, or even get a whiff of sandalwood. "Mama, there are a few things I'd like to see to first. Why don't you go and see David, Natalie and the kids, and I'll pull out some bags and start. You can help me when you come back."

"Nina dear."It was clear that Caroline Tyrie was about to say something to her daughter, something she wouldn't want to hear. But being a good mother she stopped her words and left.

"Two hours, Nina. I will be back in two hours."

Two hours and fifteen minutes later, Nina and her mother

were in Nina's room going through gowns and underclothes to pick out what she would need for a month or two away.

"You are going to need new clothes." Her mother threw another jacket into a pile for giving away. "How did you meet Mr. Peele? I know he was at the wedding, but you must have seen him since."

"He was among the men Eliphalet Wythe brought to the tavern during the encampment at Cambridge. We talked then."

"Well, being a friend of Eliphalet is no great recommendation, but your father remembers an excellent conversation with him, and of course I take Jack's endorsement as high praise."

"Mama!"

"Shh, Nina. I have been thinking. The wedding will be in late summer. The banns will be read and Alex must write home. Where is his home?"

"In the mountains of New Hampshire."

"I'm quite sure we've sent a minister of two in that direction."

"Yale."

"Hmmm. Well, either way. He must write home and have the banns read there. August will give everyone plenty of time."

"And if I want to marry sooner?"

Her mother stopped her constant motion and turned. "Nina, you are my last wedding. And you were the first. Ten years ago you barely asked, just rushed off to the Lower Falls and married that boy. I want to do something nice for you. I like Alex, and I want to tell the neighbors and cousins that I do."

Nina just nodded. It was clear she needed to do this for her mother, and a pretty late-summer wedding, with berry pies and wild flowers, would not be a burden.

***

"No roses, no daffodils." Alex had already talked to her father, her mother and both of them together. Then all four of them had weak wine and talked for another hour.

"I like asters and golden rod." He walked her out the front door of the elegant white house and down the drive to where Thorne munched on some grass.

"You did follow about the dowry, a large dowry?"

"Of course I did. We would be fools to look away from that."

"You sound so dispassionate. You would give me up for money?" The twinkle in her eye told Alex she was kidding. "You are right, even I can wait. I already know how patient you are."

Alex rolled his eyes, but it would truly be foolish to rush and be denied a large dowry, money from Nina's grandfather who had owned an indigo plantation off the coast of South Carolina and left money for his daughter's children. He kissed her hair through the demure linen cap. It seemed so quiet after what they had done during the night, a night that they would have to wait to repeat. "I'd like to be able to say, damn the dowry, and your mother's plans. But we have to acquiesce, and not just for the money. Your mother needs to do this for you. Allow her to mother you, and marry from her house. It's nearly May, August is not so far off."

"Well, I would disagree that it is a short time." She tilted her head and felt the now-familiar thrill as his lips touched hers. "Promise me I will see you often." He murmured as she let her head fall onto his shoulder.

"Picnics by the river?" His gray eyes teased as he whispered into her lips. "It sounds delicious. Nina, if you have

314

no objection, I'd like to undertake some repairs on the inn. I walked around after you and your mother left, and there is quite a lot that needs to be done."

"I'm sure the *Wheel* can support you. It's a great idea and I'm sure it's fine, but talk to Henry I don't want to step on his toes."

"And since I am sleeping in your house, may I sleep on your silk-satin sheets?" He put his arms around her waist and pulled her close against his body. "I just want you to know, patience isn't easy for me either." Gently, he let her go.

The morning had not started as easily as the afternoon had ended. Dr. Tyrie had jumped right in, confronting him on his prospects. If he had been a minister, it would have gone more smoothly, but an aimless scholar had fewer paths. "I know that as a widow, the father has no real say in Nina's future, but I would like to hear from you what sort of life you can offer my youngest."

Alex tried not to squirm. "I admit to having little at the moment. I was teaching at the Indian College in New Hampshire when the alarm came to join the army at Cambridge. As I'm sure you remember I am a scholar, so I assume I will teach again, perhaps found a school."

They talked for a while about tuition and where students would come from. When that was finished, Alex asked about the Robinson land. "Dr. Tyrie, I wonder if I might ask about some land near here. The Theodore Robinson farm?"

"Yes, his place was just down the hill, west of here. The Robinsons fled with the British. What business is that of yours?"

"I am not at liberty to explain how it happened, but in Boston before he sailed, Mr. Robinson sold me the deed to his farm with the assurance that I would try to increase the price and send him the difference."

"You would do that for a man labeled a traitor and a Tory? The Committee wanted to seize that land and chase him off. He sold his herd and fled at the last minute."

"So he explained. I simply promised that I would see the land well used, and get money to his relatives if I could."

"I'll have Jack show you down the hill, I know he's been anxious to visit with you again."

"Thank you, sir." Alex looked up to see the older man almost smiling at him.

"Mr. Peele, Mrs. Tyrie - Caroline - is right. I think you will be very good for our Nina."

Alex bowed out of the room, thanking Dr. Tyrie again for his time and blessing. That was before the other meetings. Now Jack came around the corner to find Alex and his mother at the end of the lane.

"Hi Ma, Hi Alex." Nina rolled her eyes but did not correct her son. It would be easier for him to change "Alex" to "father" than "Mr. Peele." But knowing Jack, it would be a simple "Pa."

The men walked due west down the hill, and Nina stayed behind to visit with her sister-in-law and drink some of the hot steeped herbs Alcea served instead of tea or coffee. She waved them off.

Jack matched his stride to his idol's until Alex slowed down. "Alex, did Ma tell you how Thorne and I got to stay over here?"

Alex had a pretty clear idea what had happened that night, but he was interested in what Jack knew. They were in the field crossing to the road. "I know some, but why don't you

316

tell me?"

"Thorne came here when I did, last winter." It was a longer version than the one he had imagined. An awful stew made up of Josh's friends waiting at the inn stable, those infiltrators at the camp, and Martin Jewett and his crazy idea that he could punish another man's child, even if that man no longer lived. Alex pulled Jack to him for a wordless hug. He tussled his hair and they continued their walk.

"None of the fellows believed my Ma got to meet the commander. Then another time the commander and Mrs. Washington came by the inn to ask Ma to do something for him. I don't know what that was, but it must have been big, because she came home shot up."

"Yes, Jack, it was big. They asked her to help get Maryann away from the house the British generals were using for their headquarters. She lives at the inn now. I think you two will get along."

"A girl? But you said she was working inside the Generals' headquarters? Like a spy?"

Alex nodded. Jack thought about it for a few minutes, then seemed to think that was a fine idea.

Alex left Jack to mull through his thoughts, and concentrated on his own. It had been a terrible year here, as disruptive for this family as it had been for so many others. Jack had been well treated, no doubt spoiled, living with his grandparents, but he'd barely seen his mother since she had been shot in early March. Nina had told her son everything except that it had been Josh who had fired that gun. As for that night in December, he had perfect recall that he picked up that rock. Now he discovered from a child's storytelling that he had stupidly created a problem while solving another, sending Nina

317

straight to Josh's friends at the inn. Lucky for all of them, she had found a solution. Her quick thinking was one more reason he adored her, Alex doubted her ten year old wanted to hear such blather. "I hope Thorne hasn't been too much of a problem. He can be a bit of a high-strung rapscallion."

"Oh he's much better now. And Uncle Seth says he has more than paid for his feed."

Alex walked over the grounds of the Robinson farm. The land was pleasant but rocky, better for grazing than tilling, but useful nonetheless. The house and outbuildings had been abandoned when the family fled, and looked it. The main house had been burned from one side and would have to be demolished. The newer addition was small, but it could be useful. He was sure he could get someone to buy the land for grazing, but if it was to be a homestead, the buyer would have to start from the beginning. It wouldn't be him. He couldn't imagine dragging Nina away from the rushing water for this.

They raced each other back up the hill, away from the eerie quiet of the abandoned farm. He was saddling Thorne to ride back to the inn when Nina broke his reverie. "Seth wants a quick word before you go." She let out a sigh and Alex turned to her. She put her hand over his on the back of horse. "You're not sorry at any of this?"

"No. Well, I am sorry I've somehow forced you out of your house, into your mother's."

"I actually think it might be a vacation. I will probably begin to act like a sixteen year old."

"In that case, you won't mind that I take Jack back with me. He has become my translator for this life in the world outside."

"I'll miss him, but I suspect my mother and I would fight

over him. He will be better off getting to know you better. As I said last night, it will be good for both of you."

"Alex?" Seth walked into the barn, joining Alex as Nina backed away silently to the tackroom, giving the men room to talk. He absentmindedly patted the horse's neck. "I heard from my Father that you hold the deed to Robinson's land. No good buildings there."

"Yes, I noticed that. Do you know anyone who would like to buy the land?"

"Uh'huh, but truth is, we'll give you a better price if the buildings are gone. Too dangerous for sheep - they'll wander in and break their skinny legs, probably strangle themselves. I'd pay not to have to fill the holes myself."

"So if I remove the buildings and fill in the cellar holes, you and your whoever will buy it?"

"Yup, My brother, and my brother-in-law. We have our eyes on the grazing over there. Want to raise sheep. We each have a few, but to increase the flock we need the extra land. The Town has removed the tariff on home-raised wool, so we thought we would give it a try. And who knows, thanks to this fellow, I might have a horse farm too. Come over after Meeting on Sunday. I'll make sure the others are there and we can deal."

"Seth, that sounds fine. Thank you. I'll see you then." He put out his hand and Seth gripped it, sealing the agreement. Nina walked into Thorne's stall, checking to see if her brother had left. "I heard Seth. I'll make sure he gives you a fair price."

Alex nodded. He had no doubts she would, his alewife, but it was time to go if he wanted to settle in before dinner. He lifted her hand to his lips for a gentle kiss, then pulled his newly, officially affianced, pretty blonde into his arms. It was a good-bye kiss, but for the first time he could remember, there was no sorrow.

In one swift motion, he mounted and rode out to find Jack and his bag waiting for him in the barnyard. Nina waved them off.

Chapter 28

They rode into the lane and stopped. They had talked during the ride, and Alex felt he already knew Martha and Henry. He'd told how he had come to know Maryann in Cambridge and in Boston.

"That's Henry at the stables!"

When they were all caught-up and introduced, Jack brought Alex to the house and soon disappeared into his room.

"Does Nina own the land? I know she owns the house, but what about the land it sits on?" Alex had ridden to the Upper Falls after telling Jack he was going to talk to his Uncle David. They were sitting in the kitchen, sharing a meal with Natalie and their three children.

"No, she doesn't, and it has concerned me since she built there. Not that I believe any of them would be so mean spirited, but legally the Bigelows could throw her off the land. If they did, she might have to leave the house behind. I have been trying to convince her to get them to sell since she built."

"I have a better idea. I'd like to buy some land as a wedding gift, and move the house. Do you know any that might be for sale? It would have to be near the falls."

"I think Turner is ready to sell. There is a field just this side of his place. A hill with a rocky incline sitting over the river. Nice for a house, has a good view of the river. But it's not good for much else. Dirt's too thin to farm, and most of the piece is too steep for grazing. Dumb beasts would fall into the river given half a chance. He'd have to fence the whole thing.

Now with Henry at the *Wheel*... I'd wager he would rather sell."

Alex shook David Tyrie's hand and thanked him for his help.

" Peele, if you decide to go that route, I know a fellow with a team of oxen. He moves barns and houses for a living. My mill hands work for him sometimes. Let me know, we'd all love to help, for Nina."

Alex nodded his thanks and went home.

The next morning Alex and Jack walked over to the Turner farm and store to talk to his aunt and uncle. It was a satisfying meeting, and the Turners did indeed want to sell.

"I'll have the promise of coin when I pass the deed to Seth Tyrie. That should be Sunday after meeting, but I will have to improve that property before I can buy this one." They were marking the best spot for the foundation, and the well that would have to be dug.

"Peele, that won't be a problem. Miriam was pretty adamant that I sell to family. I was saving the piece for one of my kids, but I'll be honest, the farming on this spot is difficult and it won't work for grazing. Mimi adores her little Nina, as she calls her. If selling to you will keep her happy, I'll welcome you as our new neighbor."

Alex was greatly relieved. Abe Turner was exactly the honest, hard working man he seemed to be. If only military enterprises worked as smoothly, he might not have been wounded, and the Americans would not have to battle their way across Long Island in the heat of the summer.

And so with his platoon of laborers and carpenters, Alex became commander. First they dug a well at the new housesite. Once assured of good water, Alex and Abe Turner measured for the new foundation. After securing the new location for Nina's house, Alex and his team, which of course included Jack and Maryann, moved east to the Robinson Farm. There, they tore down buildings and filled in cellarholes. Alex looked up at the work as they finished the first day, and announced that all fieldstones would be collected and moved to the new site. These would be used for the new house or the planned brewhouse. The work would clear the site considerably, and new stones would not have to be found. Alex had already chosen the small building they would move west. It was empty with well-built storage bins and windows. When the oxen arrived, they would have the man and his team for the week.

"Alex, these trees are small enough to move. The sheep will nibble them to the stump." The row of young trees looked likely, and would make the beginnings of a lovely orchard at the new house. He set Jack and Maryann and the other interested children at the task. Unlike dirt and rock moving, the trees were moved by the Suffolks with Jack driving the team. The holes for the young trees were dug and watered. When Alex came by to inspect the site, behind what would be Nina's vegetable garden, he found it exactly right.

Jack and Maryann were excited to be part of this unusual enterprise, but insisted that it stay secret from Nina. Alex was not so sure, especially when her beloved Suffolks were carting an orchard from one side of Newton to the other, but they swore Alex to secrecy.

"You seem unusually tired. Are they working you too hard repairing the inn?" A few loose shingles had been Alex's excuse the first time he had fallen asleep on Nina's shoulder after dinner.

"I'm sorry, that really is a sorry excuse for my

exhaustion. I'd be honest, but I am sworn to secrecy. And for the sake of my future, I am loathe to break that vow."

Nina looked in the direction of Alex's gaze at her son and foster daughter. She laughed. "I could be angry at all of you for plotting some devious riddle or something. But I will behave and not beg for clues. Just please get some sleep."

Alex knew that Nina was concerned about his health. He had looked ill during the winter, and she must have worried after that Christmas debacle. He felt terrible lying, and dutifully promised not to let whatever they were doing prevent him from resting.

The truth was that he was tired, but less exhausted than he had been in years. The hard physical labor in the summer sun, swimming in the river in the afternoons, and Mrs. Cotton's good food, had brought back his strength and health. He even forgot about his leg, sometimes.

It was important to get all the work done well before the wedding in August, and it was up to Alex to remind his helpers of their small and big tasks along the way. If the house was to be moved, Nina's things had to be safely packed. That work fell to the tavern staff, who boxed Nina's shelves and carefully stacked them in sawdust in Nina's beer wagon. While that was happening, the foundation for the new site was dug, and fieldstones and wooden beams were laid nearby, ready to receive the house and the shed which would follow and be attached at the site.

When all of that was done, the moving crew was called. The man and his skilled crew, accompanied by two teams of four oxen, arrived at dawn on what promised to be a hot summer morning. The men began by digging out the foundation from under the structure. When the stones were removed, ditches for six enormous beams were dug beneath the house, and the long posts pushed through. At the command of the chief, in groups of two or three at the ends of the long beams, one hundred men from the iron forge, the saw mill and local farms, who had come to help, lifted the beams onto small flatbed wagons. Strong ropes were attached from the flat wagons to the ox carts.

The men from the moving crew ran from one beam to another, keeping the house steady, the carts facing the right way and the oxen moving. To prepare for the move, the team leader had already checked the width and strength of the road ahead, cut the trees and branches that were in the way, and then a small bridge had to be built over a rut in the field they needed to cross.

Slowly, the crew moved the house across the road, over a flat field and up a small hill. It was at the top of the hill that they turned the house and let it down into place. Then all the workers, listening carefully to orders from the crew, repeated their work in reverse, and set Nina's house onto its new foundation.

Alex had hired a mason to check the big central chimney and hearths, in case the mortar had cracked or bricks had broken. He left the man with Dodi, Sukie, and Mrs. Cotton, who had volunteered to unpack Nina's treasures and put them back where they belonged. Then, he and many of the morning's volunteers rode to the Robinson Farm to move the small shed. The process was essentially the same, but with no cellar or chimney the relocation took very little time.

It was late in the evening when Alex and the children returned to the house on the hill. He and David had stopped to talk to Seth Tyrie. There was obvious strain between the brothers, but even David said afterward that it had been nice to see family. He nodded his approval when his older brother handed the money for the land over to Alex. He was relieved to be rid of it. The entire process had begun with a lie, and ended with hard work. He needed the money Seth and his partners paid him, but he would make good on his promise to Mr. Robinson when he could.

They got back to a nearly finished, and quiet, house. Neighbors had completed the fieldstone foundations for both buildings, which now stood as one. The tavern girls had rehung the pictures and Nina's things, and books lined her shelves, though the order might have been reversed here and there. The smell of fresh mortar from the repaired brickwork hung over the house, but it would dry. Bricks in the kitchen and parlor fireplaces had shifted in the move, but all repairs were finished sometime before Alex returned.

Alex sent his young charges to wash and find food at the inn. He watched the sunset from the front yard, imagining where Nina would put her kitchen garden and the flowers she would grow along the front path, now that she would have time to weed and water. He set his busy mind to planning the new, expanded, brewhouse that Jack, Martha and Henry insisted they needed.

He marveled at the good friends they had - that Nina had people who had put their work aside to help move her house, to give Nina a new life, near to the old, for the friendship and security they needed from her, and she from them – but gently separated, so she and her new family could grow. Alex knew this was the most amazing wedding gift anyone could offer, and he felt humbled that he had come into such a warm community.

He wondered for just a minute that he'd tricked her into loving him, that he was not nearly as good a person as the honest men and women who had come to help. He prayed he was worthy of Nina's love, but as the sun faded into dark night, he chalked-up those feeling to needing sleep, ran cold pump water over himself, and climbed into bed.

***

The first weeks at the Tyrie farms hadn't been terrible. Nina had gardened with Alcea and learned much from her about the healing herbs she grew. Nina especially enjoyed watching and learning about drying and concentrating various plants into tinctures. After she had told her sister-in-law about Mrs. MacAlistair's cures, and how she wished she knew more, Alcea had helped her build a medical kit for her new home. She was sure she wasn't ready to treat the very ill or badly wounded, but a few weeks with Alcea gave her an excellent beginning.

Mostly she planned the wedding, insisting that the dress be homespun and made by a local modiste. She wanted the new dress to be a variation on the dress she had worn to the picnic, and she was pleased that the dressmaker made a lighter, more frivolous version, yet kept it recognizable. Her mother scoffed at the simple dress, wanting Nina to insist on French silks or Italian velvets, but Nina knew what happened in late summer, with heat and storms and sticky bodies, and stuck to her original idea.

There simply wasn't much anyone wanted her to do. She knew the children wanted her far away from the work on Robinson's farm, but she didn't know why. It was not like her to leave a mystery unexplored, so one day when everyone was busy elsewhere, she dressed in country linen and took a trail over the hill, through the woods to the farm. It was a long way around, but she was able to watch the work for a while without being seen.

It was a surprise. The workers all seemed very pleased with themselves. David and some of his men were there, as were some of the forge-men from the lower falls. She couldn't see why, but they were laughing as they moved heavy stones to a flatbed and filled dirt into holes. There seemed to be a big mountain of dirt for this task. She wondered where that much dirt could have come from. Of course, since the whole affair was a secret she couldn't probe, but she was curious.

Alex saw her before she spotted him. He climbed to her spot and pointed to a bird in a tree or something, trying to distract her from the work. "I have orders to distract you away." He took her hand and led her over a path to the back of a small storage shed. He opened a door and let her precede him into the room. The little building stood upright, but it was without a floor or foundation.

"Alex, I don't want the children to condemn you for talking to me. I really didn't know I'd find you here and I'm sorry, I certainly didn't mean to intrude."

"You don't mean a word of that." Alex's eyes teased her; he pulled her close and kissed her hard. Cupping her breast through the linen vest, he pulled off her neck scarf and kissed down to replace his hand. He felt that familiar ache, a muted yearning he had come to associate with Nina. For a night it had seemed he might banish that feeling, but it had returned when she moved to the Corner, leaving him alone in her bed.

He'd had enough of yearning, of tamping down his desires. She was so here, so lovely with the dirt on her cheeks and her hair loose from her walk. He did need to distract her away from their project. He pulled her closer and lifted her onto the grain bins that were built into the wall, lifting her skirts up over her knees.

Nina felt cooler air rush up her legs, but it did nothing to cool her. Alex ran his hands over her naked thighs, first slowly on the outside, and then teasing, menacing the tender skin of her inner thighs. She considered that she should worry that someone might walk in, but abandoned the fear as a rush of desire overwhelmed her.

She let her head fall back against the whitewashed wall and heard the loose chips of whitewash fall to the floor. Alex untied her bodice and put his lips to her breast. Moaned pleasure escaped from deep in her throat as Alex pulled her down the slanted grain bin, her legs open as she slid onto him. He filled her completely in that moment and she wrapped her legs around him, pulling him in deeper. She writhed as he pounded her against the wooden bins. The small shed wobbled in the dirt, but did not collapse.

Alex shook off his release, and carefully dressed, but Nina still lay in a daze of dust, chips and desire, her bodice and legs open in a wanton pose.

It was not the afternoon he had planned, to make love to his lady here in the half-destroyed shed. He covered her mouth with his. She was still wound up and needy, responding to every touch. He wished he had all day to tease her to pleasure, but to leave her like this would be cruel. Alex took Nina in his arms and lifted her back onto the flat of the bin. He kissed her breasts, and lifted her skirts and kissed her thighs, one and then the other, carefully working his way to her delicate center.

He kissed her and she moaned. He nipped and it made her jump. He did it again, reveling at her reaction. He made murmuring, soothing sounds as he teased with his tongue. He used fingers and entered her wet shaft, simulating loving her, though his cock was beginning to object to missing the game. Finally, though it felt too soon, he suckled at her nub until she came, muffling her pleasure as she shattered. Alex held her close to prevent her from shaking down the small building.

He gave her only a minute, then pulled her upright and fixed her bodice, fichu and skirts. He pulled her into his arms, feathering kisses over her cheeks and lips.

"Nina, only twelve days to our wedding. Living without you is the greatest torture. Now leave the back way and don't look, or Jack will pout." He spoke into her hair. "I don't want to surprise you, so much as to please you, and I'm afraid if I give away the secret, you might tell me to stop. I can't or I won't because I believe this strange project will make you happy." She lifted her lips to his to shush his speaking. The kiss was long and satisfying.

They fell into normal conversation as they left the small shed into the clean outdoors. Nina tried obediently to look away from the work, but Alex quickly put a hand over her eyes and his arm around her waist to lead her away from the site. "I'm walking Nina back home, I'll be back soon." There was some growling behind him that he was shirking, but laughter followed them up the hill.

Alex took his hand from her eyes, but kept his other arm around her waist. She leaned onto his shoulder, enjoying the closeness. "I've been meaning to ask if you mind traveling this summer to meet my family. If we wait, it will have to be another year. I won't subject you to a White Mountain winter."

"Of course we can take a trip north, and I can't think of anything more pleasant than a trip to the cool mountains after this summer heat. Write and tell your mother we will leave as soon after the wedding as we can." They arrived at the Tyrie home. Nina shrieked, and covered Alex's eyes.

"What now?"

"My project and you can't see it. The wedding dress is in the window, its purple silk cover fell off."

"But I did. It looks wonderfully like one I remember very well." He seemed to drift off for a happy moment.

"Shhh, no you didn't see it. My sister says that is bad luck."

"In that case, I absolutely, positively did not see it." He kissed her gently and ran off – up the drive and down the hill. Nina smiled, watching him. A summer of sun and work, and his leg was much stronger, his body again the familiar one she had memorized from that moment at the shipyard.

Chapter 29

August 24, 1776

Saturday of the wedding, Alex dressed in clothes he'd stored in the wooden box. They were his best and would be for a long time. He'd acquired the suit during his travels and declared the fabrics too fine and the colors too dull for the Alex who had lived in Boston during the siege. The silk breeches were from Italy, the brocade waistcoat was French, and the linen shirt was the finest the London shirtmaker could produce. All of these things were out of place and out of date.

He woke early and dressed slowly, so by the time he walked over to the inn stables, his horse had been borrowed by Jack and Maryann. The tavern girls and the inn guests had been invited to join the family at dinner, which would be served in Seth's cow barn. So he borrowed one of the inn's new horses from Henry, reminding him not to be late for the early dinner.

Nina had eaten dinner at the tavern during the week, and apologized to the staff for not having a wedding they could attend since they would not marry in her father's church. Although her father would have performed the new ceremony if she had insisted, she'd chosen tradition, unlike her cousins who had all been married inside the church. Tradition meant her uncle, the magistrate and member of Town Meeting would preside, while her father, much higher in rank in the opinion of many, would not officiate, and would attend merely as father of the bride.

Alex and Nina had met with her parents and signed the

formal contracts. Most were traditional - the requirements and expectations of economic commitment and marital fidelity. The others explained the way Nina's inheritance from her grandfather would work. She was to maintain control of the money. It was available to him as her husband as long as the marriage lasted, but if the marriage ended in divorce or death, control was to return to her and her issue. Of course, that would include Jack and any children they might have together.

Alex did not understand why Nina did not have control of the money prior to her marriage, since the will gave her almost total control later. It was probable that it had been her mother's idea, a way to control her wayward daughter. Of course, it was too late for that.

With Nina's permission, Alex had borrowed against the money for the land and construction of Nina's new house. She would retain ownership of that also. He signed the documents thinking he was marrying quite a wealthy woman. At least he would be allowed the use of the house during their lives, and the income in the unhappy event that she predeceased him.

He could not help thinking that modern marriage laws, with the assumption that all wealth belonged to the husband, sanctified by church, minister and God, were somewhat simpler, but Nina and her parents were rooted in traditional New England ways. He could see the advantage should a marriage fail, and there was little difference in a long, happy marriage.

It was at that meeting that Mather Tyrie told him that he had a letter from the minister in New Hampshire to whom Alex had written earlier in the summer, requesting that banns be posted three times, as required. He had not expected a return note.

"Mr. Peele, the Reverend Johonot writes that he sees no

impediment to your marrying. He does however have one requirement that he requests me to enforce." Alex looked at Nina, who shrugged her shoulders. She hadn't heard anything about another requirement.

"Papa, what is it, please?" Nina knew her father. When he got in this serious mood, he could drag out the most mundane thing forever.

Dr. Tyrie harumphed. "He merely asks that I make known to you, your mother's insistence that since she cannot travel at this time, there being a harvest, lambs to tend and cows to milk, that you leave here to go there as soon as is possible. To that end, I have hired a coach which will meet you at Newburyport in four days."

"How do you expect us to go from here to Newburyport?" Nina could see various traps in her father's plan.

"You can stay here and we will bring you north the Monday after the wedding."

Nina inhaled sharply, and let out the breath. She had agreed to the old-fashioned wedding in her mother's parlor, even if her good friends, and none of Johnny's family, could fit in the room, but now it seemed she was to be ushered into her wedding bed by her sisters and mother. Some habits should be left in the seventeenth century. She looked at Alex for help.

Alex winked at Nina and took a breath. "Dr. Tyrie, thank you for offering your help, but that is a very long drive. Nina and I will go to Boston and take the packet north. If we cannot sail to Newburyport, we will find transport from Salem to the carriage. It is much closer by water."

Nina's father knew when he had been bested. He gave a subtle shrug in his wife's direction, as if to say he had tried, and then he rose, declaring the meeting over.

Nina looked out the window at the hazy hot day. It was hot and was going to be hotter, the type of heat that would only be broken by a big thunderclap and merciless rain. It had been hot like this for days, and the bits of rain had only increased the humidity. There was no indication today would be any different.

Nina had prayed all week that the heat would break and the fresh air would pour in from the north with an autumn wind in time for the wedding. It had not happened. "Pull it up and out of my way. I no longer care what my hair looks like." Nina looked back at the mirror, and up at her sister Verity, who was trying to fix her hair in an elaborate style.

"It looks like rain." Nina's cousin Tateen, who had been paying no attention to the others, pulled the curtain back and pronounced.

Nina nodded, but even that was a mistake, since it caused her sister to poke her with a hairpin. "Ouch, stop. Verity, my hair cannot be improved."

"It's these darn pins. They are bent and there are none in the stupid stores."

"I'm sorry my wedding has inconvenienced you. You know pins are on the list of non-importables. Until manufacturing improves, we must cope."

"Yes, your Patriotic-ness." She went back to trying to unkink the pins.

Finally it was time to dress and go down to the parlor for the simple ceremony. Nina, Verity and Tateen made their way downstairs. Her parents were talking to her Uncle Seth Tyrie and Tateen's mother and father. Jack and Maryann were obediently sitting in their chairs, silent in the still heat, but

Alex stood alone, expectantly watching the doorway.

He looked up when he heard the three women cross the front hall. Nina looked radiant. Her aqua eyes glowed with sheer happiness. The bezel, on the outside of the gown, looked as though the whole had been designed around it. Again, Alex felt as though he had wandered in under false pretenses, but then, if anyone knew the truth of him, it was Nina. He forced himself to look at the dress he had been ordered to ignore two weeks before. He recognized it immediately as a copy of the gown from that summer picnic, the day he had fallen in love. Had it been that simple?

The modiste had done a masterful job translating the simplicity of that summer gown into the elegance required for even a simple wedding. But as lovely as the gown was, in her eyes was an expression of pure joy. He would kill to keep that look in those eyes.

"And so with the power granted by the Province of Massachusetts, I pronounce you man and wife."

Alex took both Nina's hands in his, leaned into her and kissed her. Nina lifted her face to his, wanting to claim him by running her hands through that wonderful hair, but the kiss was brief, barely satisfying. Alex stepped back, separating them slightly. It was after all, her mother's best parlor. He put his arm around her waist holding her, and together they signed the magistrate's book and the town record, making their marriage contracts legal and recorded.

Nina thought later that if she hadn't just gotten married with cousins, parents, sisters and brothers, and friends who were on their way to the beautiful wedding dinner, she would have noticed that her son and foster-daughter looked upset. As it was, she only hugged the children and moved onto the next person in line. She had leaned over and chatted to the children, who were now inseparable after spending the summer together, but they hadn't expressed anything more than their discomfort in the heat. The excitement they were barely containing she attributed to the surprise they had been working on for her.

The afternoon wore on, heavy with promise of the brewing storm. The wedding party adjourned into the barn and luncheon was served. Soon a fiddle came out, and the younger crowd started to dance. Alex led Nina out onto the dance floor for a country dance. She felt his eyes on her as though he moved his fingers over her body. She felt flush and a little heady as lines formed around them, everyone wanting to say what a wonderful day it had been and how glad they were to see Nina so happy. She wanted to scream.

It had been a long summer being Caroline Tyrie's daughter, and now the day seemed to go on forever. She wanted to go home, to begin again where Alex and she had left off, the morning her mother had come to collect her at the Falls. She hadn't wanted to move here, although there were good reasons to spend time back with her family. It was now over. The marriage lines had been signed and the settlements agreed on, the dinner eaten and dances danced. She wanted to leave and hear the Falls.

Nina needed to tell Jack that he and Maryann should ride back to the inn with Dodi and Sukie, Mary, and Mrs. Cotton, but when she went to find him, he was explaining in elaborate detail the importance of the ninety degree angle and why it was called "right." The other boys were spellbound, and Nina did not want to interrupt. Maryann was equally occupied. It was so rare to see the girl happy that Nina did not have the heart to disturb her conversation with one of the other young girls. She found Mrs. Cotton and explained. Satisfied that she would see the children in the morning, she allowed herself to find Alex and motioned that they should leave.

Seth had nearly convinced Alex to use his carriage and leave Thorne at the farm when Nina walked outside.

"Hi, we should go home before someone else wants my attention." She leaned wearily into Alex. He slipped his arm around her, kissing the top of her head.

At that very second, the storm that had been holding off all afternoon, with lightening and thunder in the far distance, roared over the hill. Lightening split the air, followed immediately by a thunder clap. Seth's horses, already in the carriage traces, reared in fright. Alex grinned at Nina, grabbed her hand and they ran across the field to where Thorne was calmly waiting. He helped her mount and jumped up behind. They waved at the shocked well wishers who had gathered at the barn door to see them off.

"Nina, are you ready for a wet ride home, my adventuress?"

She laughed into the wind. "I haven't adventured nearly enough, but, yes Alexander, I expect nothing less from one who conquers lands." She leaned back into him, warm in his arms in spite of the driving summer rain. She turned as much as she could and lifted her face for a kiss. They were at the Falls by the time the first the storms moved out.

"Where is my house?" Nina stared at the stone structure where her little white house used to be.

Alex just grunted, and turned the horse toward the Turner's.

"Alex, no one is home over there, they are back at Seth's; where are we going?" She was genuinely confused as Alex

338

brought them up the little hill. A bright yellow house with red shutters greeted them. Nina blinked the rain out of her eyes as though they were cloudy.

"Jack said you would love the colors. I had no choice but to believe him. Was I right?"

"Yes, I love it." Nina was overwhelmed with the work they must have done to accomplish the move and the changes. "He and I always wished we could have chosen the color of the house, but John wanted it to match the inn. You moved it here? How?"

"David, as much as anyone. He knew how it was done and found the man with the team of oxen. He is also the man who said I should buy the land and move it."

"I'm sure he was right. He's been worried about my house being on the inn's land." They dismounted and Nina studied the house, running to see it from different angles. "Tell me what you've added, it's very different." She was excited.

"We changed only two things. The rest just looks different from the outside. Let me show you." Alex led the way into a small lean-to shaped stable attached to the back of the house. There was room for a few horses and dry feed. "I thought we might need temporary shelter for one or more of the horses here, when weather or time prevents us from using the stable at the inn. I expect to build a real stable back there when we can." He pointed past the laid out garden area. "Here is the other change." After they fed and toweled off the horse, Alex opened a door to the small side storage room that now connected to the kitchen. The pump sat in the middle of the room, shelves and bins lined the wall.

"You've put the pump indoors. Oh, such luxury - thank you!" She turned to kiss him. "Do I recognize this room?" She looked hard at a grain bin, and suddenly found herself lifted

339

into Alex's arms and carried from the little storage room with one interesting memory, into a very familiar room and up wonderfully familiar stairs, to her own parlor and bedroom.

"I confess to being slightly nervous," Alex sat down on the small boudoir chair with Nina in his lap. He kissed the back of her neck.

"You nervous? Why ever for?" She cocked her head and turned to look into his face.

"I've never been married before."

"You don't want to hear about my other wedding night?" Nina almost giggled. The memory of two awkward children seemed so remote.

"No, I doubt that would give me confidence." Alex leaned Nina forward and began to untie the wet ribbon that held her gown together at her back. He didn't want to cut the silk, but the drenching had turned the fabric stiff, and he was ready to use his knife if frustration warranted."Not at all," he gritted his teeth in concentration.

The knot finally gave way. Alex loosened it by pulling the eyelets away from the stiffened ribbon. Once it was loose enough, Nina stood and let it fall to her feet. She pushed it away and turned to untie his equally wet and stiff cravat.

It took longer than it should have to remove wet linen and silk, but Nina insisted that this first time they shouldn't be half dressed or even covered in silk dragons. Alex understood and persevered. He even refrained from using his knife to hasten their efforts.

***

It was late. The windows opened hours ago to let in the wind from the storm, energy almost as wild and free as Nina felt with her arms and legs wrapped tightly around her love, now let in the cool dry breeze she had been praying for all week. Slowly she climbed out of the bed, careful not to wake Alex. They had only just fallen asleep, and it would be unkind to wake him so soon. She found the soft quilt that was usually draped over the foot of her bed. It was neatly folded on the corner of her dressing table. She spread it over the bed and climbed under the worn, quilted linen. A feeling of joy, so deep it nearly overwhelmed her, came into her as Alex reached for her.

Later, as she spooned into him, his arms holding her safely against him, she laughed at herself for holding on to her fears for so long, but she was happy that it had been Alex Peele, not some nameless man who had come into her life. Nina allowed only a brief moment for that thought, before falling into a deep gentle sleep.

They were awakened by rattling pot and pans in the kitchen, and smells of coffee and maple syrup. Nina poked Alex in the side to wake him. Kissing him awake had already proven to produce results that had not led to climbing out of bed.

"Alex! Wake up, someone has made us breakfast."

"What time is it? Feels like dawn."

Nina peeked at the glass clock in her parlor. "It's nearly ten. I don't think I have ever slept this late. At least not without Mrs. MacAlistair's potion."

"Come back, it's chilly with you out of bed." He leaned back on the pillows, his bare chest proving to be an interesting temptation.

Nina stopped herself. "Silly, there's coffee." She checked her clothes press, hoping to find something suitable for Alex's new wife. She settled for one of her better "inn gowns." She nudged Alex again so he could tie her stays. Then she went downstairs to see her son and friends. She was followed just a few minutes later by Alex, who undid all the effort Nina had extended in those minutes to make it seem as though nothing in her life had changed, by announcing that he had missed her, sitting and pulling her into his lap, and kissing her soundly in front of the tavern girls, Maryann, and Jack, who looked slightly perplexed but not unhappy. Nina turned beet red. Laughing, she hid her face in her hands.

Chapter 30

"I'm worried about Maryann." The well- sprung carriage had been waiting for them in Newburyport and they headed north. "She is always one letter away from tears and now with the news so bad, I hope she can withstand the waiting."

It had not been long since news had reached them of Continental losses. The Americans had been chased across Long Island toward Manhattan. Alex knew it was nearly inevitable that the British would capture New York City. He could only imagine what the residents would do to the town as they abandoned it. The city had a long history of set fires. The coming conflagration and subsequent looting wouldn't be the first, nor would it be the last.

Knowing there was nothing they could do about military losses or Maryann's worrying about her father, so Nina set her mind on enjoying the trip. Certainly the scenery was obliging.

She had gone to Salem by ship a few times, and by wagon after the port of Boston was closed, but she had never gone around the Plum Island peninsula to see the Merrimac River. Rivulets and streams gushed into it, in seemingly endless fashion. If they hadn't had a destination and days in front of them in a carriage, Nina would have taken off her shoes to play in the sandy streams.

"I am going to play in those sand bars on our way home."

"Like child, like mother. I seem to remember a blond boy playing in the waves at Braintree. Maybe we can spend a night in Newburyport on the way back and spend some time on the

343

beach." Alex was as happy about letting his toes feel the cool water as Nina was. He hadn't felt relaxed - not this relaxed and happy - since he was a small boy. He shook the reins and smiled at Nina, hoping the posting inn had a comfortable bed and good food.

It took four days and four teams to get them to the north side of the mountains. Nina stopped remarking on views of tall peaks, the occasional bright red tree - even though it was only the very beginning of September - or the way the clouds seemed to turn into mountains and mountains into clouds. She was sure Alex noticed her gasp in awe at the majesty and beauty of the scenes in front of her. Beyond the gasp, she was without words.

"Alex," they were still heading north through the river valleys, "what is it like here when it snows?"

"Winter." He seemed to think a while. He steered the team over a small stream and through a covered bridge before he answered. "It's unspeakably beautiful, crystal clear air, snow, ice. But dangerous. Travelers die if they are caught out in the storms. We stay home, isolated by town or county until spring. Everyone attends church and that helps, all children make their way to school, and then spring always comes ... sooner or later."

"Even us southerners know about the sooner or later part." Nina looked around, imagining the valleys filled with snow instead of the mountain green around her. The gray granite peaks must simply blend with the bare trees and the white snow, creating a monochrome. She shivered. Alex put his arm around her and pointed.

"Ahead, that next farm is my folks.' You'll see it when we round the next bend." He had explained at the last inn that they would keep the team at the farm and return them at the end of their trip. The innkeeper had no trouble taking money to give his horses a week in fresh grass.

"Ma! We're here!" Alex called across a field at a youngish woman, surrounded by sheep, a dog at her side.

"Ma? You too. I will never get him to call me something respectable if you're going to be his father." Nina mumbled as she jumped down from the carriage and ran after Alex into the field of black-eyed susans. The sheep bleated and scattered. Nina was gathered into her mother-in-law's arms, and led back to the substantial farmhouse she could just see from the pasture. The dog moved the herd into the gated pasture, and a young boy swung a gate closed.

"My grandson Noah." She told Nina, and then turned to Alex, who was standing still, looking up at the mountain. "If we don't get his attention, he will stare up there all day, that is till he starts to climb." She turned back to her son, "Alex, bring the team to the barn. That way you can unpack Nina's things." She tuned back to Nina. "He can let them graze tomorrow in the lower pasture, won't hurt them to eat hay for a night." She opened the door to the kitchen. Nina was greeted with the smell of fresh bread and a stew of some sort slow-cooking on the hearth. Nina liked her. She let out a breath.

They spent ten days. Nina had not known that walking on thin trails upward into the hills would reveal such a different world. The plants changed very few feet above the valley, the birds seemed different, and even the rocks and trees behaved in ways she had never seen before. Sometimes a tree's roots had grown carefully around a rock, only to have a stream overflow and sweep the rock away, leaving the roots suspended in the air, still hugging the thin soil below them.

"Nina, just ahead." Alex had promised his favorite view

of the valley and a picnic on the mountainside. Her feet hurt from a week of climbing around these hills, but she wouldn't have wished for bad weather or days indoors. No, aching feet were a small fee for the wonderful sights, and time with Alex was worth all the blisters and sore legs.

"Ouch!" She twisted her ankle and sat on a log to rub it.

"I hate to make you move, but rotten logs are terrible places to sit." He pointed to the red bugs crawling over the dead, rotting wood. He bent over and picked her up. It wasn't much farther so she didn't feel sorry for him, and it was so nice to have a ride, happily safe in Alex's arms. She let her head fall onto his shoulder, he carried her to where he had already spread out the blanket and food.

He knelt and let her make herself comfortable. Nina wiggled her ankle, making circles to see where it hurt. "I think it will be okay. I'll make it down." She seemed hesitant. In a few minutes, Alex had carved a sharp tip on a sturdy stick to be used as a walking stick. He put it next to her and took the plate she offered.

"Picnics are special things to me."

"Really? Why is that?" Nina was feeling the warmth of the sun and the wine. She took off her light fichu and let it fall onto the blanket.

"Especially picnics that are in hidden coves, far away from other people."

"What makes you think the nephews won't come this way? They seem to like all your favorite spots."

"Market day in town. No one misses it but visitors who have to spend four hours in a carriage tomorrow."

"I see."

"How is that ankle?" Alex unlaced her boot, untied her stocking and gently pulled it away from the slightly swollen ankle. "We'll let you put that in the icy stream on the way down. It will feel good. I'd best check your other foot."

By now Nina was falling into a familiar haze of arousal. They hadn't had nearly enough time together since they had arrived. There were nieces and nephews and Alex's brothers and sisters, who seemed to be everywhere. There were late nights with not enough time to say everything that needed to be said.

When they were alone, Nina could not relax if she could hear conversations from the hall or through the walls. "I'm sorry I have not been a very giving wife since we have been here."

"No matter." He covered her mouth with his, deepening the kiss; her tongue found his and intertwined with a growing need. His hands and lips found her bodice. He carefully unpinned her jacket, stowing the pins in his hat.

Alex leaned back to look at Nina, lit by the mountain sun, her cheeks pink, her breasts pale, pink nipples matched her sun-kissed cheeks. He kissed her nipple as a bird called to its mate; she trilled in response. Nina sighed a moan, and pushed his shirt over his head. Her hands found his buttons on his breeches and slowly undid them, one by one.

He pushed her back to suckle again, her hands found his hair, she arched, moaned and cried, "Alex" it was breathy and the wispy wind carried it away.

"Please." Nina whimpered, their favorite game, making her beg.

He kissed her, rolled over her and entered her. She rose to meet him, to move with him, as naturally together as clouds and mountain.

The rested horses made the first leg of the return trip faster than planned, so they continued south, shortening the trip by one day. They stopped for a day at the ocean, took the packet to Boston, and the stage to the Falls. They were back in time to see the broadside published in New York on the twenty-third of September, about the hanging of Nathan Hale.

They stared at the paper, but neither one spoke. Hale had been a Yale man, a school teacher from Connecticut. Nina looked at the distress in Alex's face. Had General Howe been so angry at being caught off-guard in Boston that he hanged the young man without any sort of trial?

The taproom was very quiet. Nina expected to be greeted by Jack within minutes of the stage's arrival. They were right on time.

"Marty, where are the children?"

Martha motioned that they were to come into the kitchen. She hugged them welcome and then sat them at Mrs. Cotton's table.

"They've taken Thorne and left."

Nina felt the blood drain from her body.

"Left? Who let them?"

"No one. They left a note. It's on your kitchen table, I thought you would go there first. But I can tell you quickly what was in it.

"Maryann got a letter from someone in Westchester that her father was hurt. The children didn't know where to start. They looked at a map. They are headed for a town called Poughkeepsie."

"When did they start?" Alex had already started planning. He knew which map Jack had looked at. He and the children had been mapping the progress of the Americans across Long Island and looking at cities up the Hudson which might be sympathetic – as if they were military planners. He had thought it was a good exercise in geography, and it seemed to help Maryann worry less. Now he had to use what he remembered from that schoolroom project, to find his students, before they were hanged as spies. He had no doubt that if they were caught by the same men who caught, tried, convicted and hanged Hale in one day, they would be treated just as he was.

"Yesterday before we opened. I found their note on the counter." She pointed to the high table at the front of the taproom.

"Nina, I'll take one of the other horses and bring them back." They were at the table looking over Jack's note and the map he left.

"It won't work. She will just turn around to go to her father and Jack will help her. Alex, they can't go to southern New York on Thorne." Nina put her head in her hands and burst into tears.

Alex was baffled. He stopped pulling food from the pantry and turned to her. "What? Why not, what does Thorne have to do with finding Colonel Bickerstaff?"

"They can't be seen on Thorne, and neither can you."

"Why not?" He stared at her. There was something deeply wrong and he had no clue what it could be. "Nina, tell me!"

"I hadn't, I didn't tell you... well, because there was nothing you could do. By the time I saw you on Christmas, I thought the danger was over." She took a deep breath, knowing it was time to tell Alex what had happened. "It was at the dinner party, the one last December." Alex nodded, remembering. Nina gulped and went on. "Josh had these friends, they spent time with him here at the inn. Alex, those men at Cambridge that night weren't just causing trouble, they wanted you. Specifically you, but they didn't know who you were. They hunted you through me, but especially through Thorne. Someone, probably Josh, told them that the gray would bite and rear for anyone but you. So they convinced themselves that if they found the gray horse, they would have you.

"What if their leader with all his minions, and there may be dozens, what if they are still looking for the gray stallion? Jack and Maryann could be riding right into the worst of it."

"Why didn't you tell me that I sent you from one danger into another one with that horse? Nina, I am mortified. Jack told me about taking the horse to Seth's, but I didn't realize." Alex sat back at the table, his head in his hands.

"No! Don't be. I won't deny it was frightening, but to Jack it turned into a great adventure. I'm sure he told you about finding Thorne in the hemlocks at the Upper Falls, and riding in the dark, over the hills to the Corner." She didn't want to tell him about her frozen, bloody feet, the long ride over the hills above the Second Church to evade the riders, or Jack's getting lost on his way to his grandparents, having to stay off the major roads. Only that, "he was safe by sun-up."

"You're right. We have to stop them before they get near the Sound. They will be riding right into their territory."

Nina pulled her rifle down and started cleaning it and her sidearm, while she spoke. "We can disguise the Suffolks. If we paint their blazes, they will look like any other farm horse."

"I'll take the team. There is no 'we' in this. It is too dangerous." Alex hoped he sounded adamant.

Nina focused her efforts on cleaning the firearms in front of her on the table. She could not stay here alone, waiting - she could not. He would need her, and she needed to be with him.

If the worst happened, if he were spotted, she had to be there, with him, for him, no matter how opposed he might be. For ten years, she had worried that Johnny had died alone in the Michigan forests. Now Alex was going to where it would be most dangerous for him. She had to be there. She said nothing, but simply shook her head.

Alex knew Johnny's death in wilderness, and Nathan Hale's execution, hung over them. He could never compete with or deny young Bigelow, and he hadn't known Hale, but he understood the similarities were too extreme to ignore. He shook his head and looked helplessly at Nina. He knew she would come. He would simply need to keep her safe on the journey. "You're right about Thorne, he is noticeable. You will insist on joining me, won't you? I won't try to stop you. I'm sorry I mentioned it." He moved to leave the room and prepare for their journey. "Think of where they might stop on the route. Where would Jack know to stay once they were at the Hudson?"

Nina heard footsteps as Alex went upstairs to find his things and pack for another long journey. She paused to listen as boxes were moved and opened. She looked down at the table. She hadn't checked the rifle or sidearm since she was shot, but she was no stranger to them. She brought both on every delivery she made. John Peddleman had insisted she know how to shoot, and be willing to do so. She had never fired in conflict, but having the weapons had saved her life, and barrels of ale, more than once. Jack was the better shot and she wondered if he had taken a pistol, but she would have to check at the inn. Hers were still here.

Nina went up to pack her things. The trip to New Hampshire had required pretty summer gowns and a shawl or two. This trip required blankets, warm clothes, for herself and the children, her medicine kit, and the sailcloth she stored in the attic. She was gratified that everything was where she had left it, but also slightly uneasy that someone had packed and unpacked everything she owned. There was no time to think about that now. Maybe she would rearrange the whole house, when everyone was home and safe.

Nina was so tired from traveling she wanted to put her head down and sleep. But the first order of this next trip was to pack correctly and then, using the map and notes, get as close to where the children were staying as possible. It was going to be hard - they had the significantly faster horse. Nina hoped they lacked the stamina to ride for long periods, and would stop when they were tired.

Nina went into her parlor and opened John Peddleman's notes. He had corresponded with inn owners and brewers, many of them only a few towns or Provinces away. She found a notebook that was free of dust, as if it had recently been taken out and read.

"Alex, I have it. Jack used his grandfather's notes. Let's match it with your map, and see if we can get ahead of them. From what Jack had to work with, I think we can make a map of their route, ending with John's friend from his days in London, Pieter van Wijk, a brewer in Poughkeepsie. Alex laid his maps open on the floor of the parlor, while Nina read out the place names from the journal Jack must have used. In a short time, Alex had completed his notes and they were ready to go.

The Suffolks got their passengers to Springfield in three days. Inn keepers on the route had seen the children when they had stopped for food, or in one case to spend the night. Nina tried not to let her fear for their safety overwhelm her. She spent long periods in a brooding silence that Alex did not try to disturb.

Nina had been impressed with the width and power of the Merrimac only a few days before, but even miles from its mouth the Connecticut was wider. It was calmer though, and soon the ferry strong enough to carry the horses and a wagon made its daily appearance, and they were heading south-west to their destination.

They did not stop or slow often. Much of the area was at least nominally controlled by Indians who did not always look favorably on white travelers. Again, there was no word of injured children, nor sight of Thorne and his riders.

The deep forests were now multicolored with the leaves of early autumn. Some held on to summer green, but occasionally a maple or poplar would show red or yellow in a blaze of light. It was as though they were following the fall south. Weeks ago in New Hampshire, many of the trees were red, and on the mountainsides, some were already bare.

Nina would always think of that summer as a time of rivers - her own, small and manageable, and the others, each bigger than the next. The Hudson was the exclamation point to them all. By the end of the week they heard its roar, and headed south into the city of Poughkeepsie.

Poughkeepsie sat on the eastern shore of the river, large even here, almost one-hundred miles from its mouth. All day and night, ships and barges brought goods north from New York City, and returned with crops, lumber, furs and minerals.

They found an inn with a good stable and left their clothes in a pleasant, clean room. Following the directions of the owner, they walked toward the river where the brewery owned by Pieter van Wijk was located.

"Mr. van Wijk, I am Nina Bigelow." She looked at Alex

and shrugged, making a silent apology for not using his name. She wanted to shout out, "Have you seen my son?" But before she could say anything, Pieter motioned that Nina and Alex should follow him to the kitchen.

There, sleeping on the warm rushes in front of the fire, were Jack and Maryann. At the sound of footsteps, Jack looked up. He ran silently to Nina, and as he always had, threw himself into her arms. Alex caught her from tipping over, and they laughed.

"Jackie, I could whip you. What on earth were you thinking, taking Thorne all this way?"

"Ma, I had to. Maryann was going to ask westward travelers if they would help her. Sukie told her she mustn't, but she wouldn't listen. She is that worried about her father. I did leave you a note and clues like Alex said a good agent always does."

Nina glared at Alex, but Pieter was leading them back into the large taproom and pouring ales. He handed Jack a pint of cider and began to speak very quietly, his voice, barely above a small rumble in the big room.

"It was good the children thought to come here. John Bigelow was a good friend and I would help his grandson under any circumstance. But you see, being Dutch I am trusted and distrusted by the English and the Americans. Everyone comes here, and everyone gossips. Lots of chatter comes upriver with the boats. I hear all the intrigue from south of here. Right now, if you listen carefully, you learn that the British are hunting a young deserter. That is of no importance. They will only shoot him if he deserts twice, or perhaps three times more.

Of greater interest is that they are searching for a man they believe is hiding, or being hidden, on an estate about half way from here to New York City. The great British do not know which farm, and they need to be very careful not to anger the Dutch, many of whom have not chosen sides. The area they search is inhabited with very wealthy Dutch landowners, the Patroons. They dare not annoy them. Their own officers have been ordered to tread lightly with the wealthy group. The commanders believe these Patroons might yet agree to aid the regulars, if their lands are not abused.

"My people told me this afternoon that the injured American is hiding in an outbuilding at a farm in the town of Cortland Manor. The milkmaid is American, not Dutch, and she has been caring for him, but she is at risk of being discovered. Her mistress does not know.

"My man said the soldier is mending, but he must be removed before he and the girl are discovered." He put a thin napkin on the table with the dishes his waiter brought out from the kitchen. In moments, Maryann came out the door.

"Don't worry, Maryann. I think we can find him tomorrow." Alex looked at the map drawn onto the silk napkin and pushed it into his waistcoat pocket.

"It would be faster if I took Thorne and found him. Then I would know."

"Maryann," Alex lowered his voice to a no nonsense tone. "It would be dangerous for you to take that horse south, and your father may not be able to ride. Even if you could find him without our help, it would be a foolish, dangerous enterprise. I will hear no more of it. Do you understand?"

"Dangerous?"

"Yes." It was clear Alex was not going to offer more information. Maryann reluctantly nodded assent.

Chapter 31

"If we can push the Suffolks to thirty miles today, we can be there early enough tomorrow to be out of the Hudson Valley and at the old pig-iron quarry before afternoon. Wijk has a man who needs to get to Boston. He will ride Thorne and deliver the horse back to the *Wheel and Hammer*." The group nodded a kind of quiet understanding.

"I'm sure Jewel and Bella can do the thirty miles. They have been resting for the day, and we are not such a heavy load. They seemed to laugh when I put the brown paint on their blazes. The girls are ready for an adventure." Nina had the children laughing as they traveled south, parallel, along the big river. She didn't think she had ever forded more streams, paid to go over more bridges, or taken the team on more ferries. The river might be too big for spillways and water wheels, but the streams that fed it were fast moving and plentiful.

Not only to keep up morale, but to make them look like a local family heading to the local marketplace, Nina encouraged her passengers to sing as they traveled. They made camp in a light drizzle and spent the night huddled under the wagon, with the sailcloth under them against the damp, chill ground. Nina did not know how the children had coped during their journey south, and right then she didn't want to know.

After breaking camp the following morning, they found themselves in the traffic around the City of Peekskill. It was a bustling town with industrious looking people, all of whom seemed to have somewhere to go on the beautiful day. The trees in this region glowed a bright orange instead of the northern red, but they all admitted that the warm color had its own charm, especially against the blue sky of the perfect fall day.

Alex leaned over as Nina passed around fresh buttered bread with jam they had just bought from a street vendor. "Listen, everyone should know what is happening in case one of us gets separated. Charles is being hidden in Cortland Manor. The town is just east of here. We should be there in under an hour." He opened the map and pointed to the estate. "Once he is in the wagon, we go upland to an abandoned iron camp. It's a good seven miles northeast from the Manor, and we can only hope Bickerstaff can make the trip, but I see no choice and neither did Wijk." Everyone nodded. Singing resumed, but it was slightly forced. Maryann seemed ready to run away and solve the problem herself, but she had begun to realize that such behavior was foolish.

***

It was at the next crossroad. Nina was sitting on the bench next to Alex. A kerchief covered her hair from the dust. She hoped she looked like a farmer's wife and not like herself. Weeks of travel had removed the last of her sickroom pallor and turned her nose and cheeks pink. She was concentrating on the signs marking the side roads when she looked up and directly into the face of one of Joshua's friends. In fact, it was one of the two who had been at Cambridge that night looking for Thorne.

"Alex, listen fast. That man will recognize me. Not you and not Jack, you are safe. I have to go. I have the direction. I will go to the manor and, if you are gone, I will find the camp. Don't come back for me, that would be foolish. Worst thing happens, I will see you at the *Wheel and Hammer*!"

She hissed furiously as she slipped backward off the bench and into the bed of the wagon. She ripped off her kerchief and bonnet and handed them to Maryann. She quickly kissed Jack on the top of his head, as she moved back and jumped off the wagon gate. She smiled at the aplomb Maryann showed as she, almost magically, put on kerchief and bonnet and climbed onto the bench next to Alex. The familiar man looked up, shook his head in disbelief and walked away.

In seconds, Nina's hood was pulled over her pale blonde hair and she headed east, away from the river. She patted her canvas sac with her pairs of warm socks and her fire-starting kit, pleased to have it and her warmest cloak. She kept her head down, trying to ignore the road behind her, when she felt something fly by her head. A basket landed next to her. It had a tea towel in it, ready to receive bread or eggs from a local farmer or bakery. One of her clever family had thrown the basket to her. She would look so much more like a countrywoman upon an errand carrying the large country basket. She hooked it over her arm, ready to fill it with whatever might appear.

Nina knew that the team would have to follow roads, heading east into the farmlands that surrounded the large town, but she did not. Having spent her childhood ignoring fences, and outrunning rams and bulls too full from a summer's grazing to bother with more than a passing glance and grunt at a trespasser, she had no trouble getting to the estate before late afternoon.

She was on the lane leading up to the farm when a British soldier stepped in front of her. "Miss, excuse me. There has been some trouble in the area. If you don't mind telling me where you are going?" The soldier looked as though he was the model for what a man in uniform should be. He was impossibly tall and his eyes shot blue ice. He was not the sort of man she would want to know, even if he were not wearing a red uniform.

Nina wanted to say that actually she did mind. But at least this fellow was in regimentals and was not the fellow she recognized. "Not at all, I was just getting some special eggs from this farm. You see, the French hens are setting, and my mistress wants some of these French chickens." She was sure she should be hanged on the spot for inventing such a stupid tale. She hurried into the back yard of the estate, hoping to see the one person who might help her. The man followed her. "Sir, I'm sure you don't want to disturb the chickens, you know how flustered they can be."

She walked past, and away from the big house toward the outbuildings, trying to look like she had been here many times before. She hoped she looked convincing, but her heart was pounding, and her hands were shaking. She realized she had been feeling this way all morning, ever since she had seen that man in town look up at her. Feelings from that terrifying night came back. Suddenly, she was sure she would never find a way out of this.

She wouldn't be sad. Alex would care for Jack. Hadn't he done that all summer? He would make a wonderful father and do a wonderful job. An enormous wave of sorrow came over her that she would not be there to share parenting with him. It nearly drove her to her knees. The tall soldier's footsteps matched hers, she felt his shadow on her shoulders.

"Did I hear you say you came for the French hens' eggs?" A new voice, cheery, female, and young brought Nina back to the present.

"Yes I did, for my mistress. I believe she spoke to someone here."

"Come with me." The young girl ignored the redcoat. She must be used to them, this far south. He hovered right outside the chicken coop, not sure if he should keep following this quarry, or return to town and find another. They heard him enter the coop, gag from the unexpected smell, and flee outside.

"You seemed to have been telling the truth, thank you, sorry to have disturbed you." The man stumbled over his words as he gasped in fresh air. He stayed listening for a few more minutes, making no effort of move off, but the noise from the chickens more than drowned out the voices of the two women.

"You're Nina?" Nina nodded in surprise. "The man with the two kids told me to expect you. They left with the wounded man about an hour ago."

"You're the person who has been caring for Charles? Thank you from all of us. I know how scared you must have been. It's frightening to care for a wounded patient under the best of circumstances. Have soldiers been here before?" She motioned with her chin to the man standing just outside the coop.

"No, luckily today is the first. They have been questioning people in town, and my mistress has asked me if anyone might be hiding in one of the outbuildings." Clearly being questioned was distressing, but that appeared to be over now. Nina took the girl's small hand in hers and gripped it. The girl smiled at her. She began gathering eggs into her apron, walking up and down the rows of setting hens. When she had collected all she could find, she put them carefully into Nina's basket. "I'm sure you will use these. No one here will miss them. Just pretend they are all French hens." She laughed, as she pulled some bread and meat from her pocket and put them in the basket with the eggs.

Nina looked at her basket of food. "I don't know how to thank you."

"Don't. I'm just happy it will be over. It is over, I mean." She took a deep breath. "The track you need leads straight north from here before it goes east. You'll find it from the back lane. It leads away from the barnyard." She pointed out the door. Then she opened a back window, and helped Nina out, handing her the big basket as she got both feet on the ground. "Stay down," she whispered. Nina heard her walk in the opposite direction, toward the front of the chicken coop.

"Well, Miss. You wouldn't have anything unusual going on around here besides French hens, would you?"

"No sir," she smiled up at the handsome officer. "But you are welcome to help me muck out the stables. I'm expected to have it done before dinner, and if you are going to tag along, you really must help." She made a half-handed wave at Nina as she spoke to the man, and picked up her pitchfork. Nina expected that she had already finished putting the hay Charles Bickerstaff had been lying in onto the muck pile. The poor British spy-catcher never had a chance.

She headed north up the road.

As the day waned she saw a barn. She was tired, but not yet exhausted. Much of her anxiety had eased, and the sense of adventure with which she usually attacked her problems had returned. It wouldn't hurt to see what was in the empty building. Luckily, on a window sill, under a thick layer of dust, was a barn lantern. Its enclosed candle still had hours left to it. The lantern was small, but since the candle wasn't much burned, she left behind a few shillings. The shielding, which kept sparks from lighting the hay and setting the barn on fire, would work just as well for walking in dry woods.

Once she was well off the road, she cleared a small area of twigs and leaves. Using steel, flint, and more tries than she would admit to, she lit the char-cloth and her tow. By lighting a few twigs, she had a nice neat flame for her candle. It seemed a lot of work just to light one small candle, but there was little choice if she wanted light. She closed the front of the lantern and stomped the embers into the dirt. The old track was clear enough even with only pale candlelight, and she set off, watching the sun drop into the hills over her left shoulder.

The October night closed in fast. She pulled her hood over her head for warmth, feeling what she was certain was unnecessary fear. Alone in the dark woods with only a circle of pale light for company, the moon a distant crescent that barely cast its light onto the forest floor, Nina counted her footsteps crunching in the dry leaves.

She felt eyes on her, but quick glances to left and right revealed nothing. She quickened her pace, hoping to reach Alex and the camp before whoever was following her caught up. She alternated – dismissing the feeling of being watched, convincing herself over and over it was only the tiny circle of light, fooling her into feeling afraid – and being absolutely certain she was being followed.

The map had said it was ten miles, but she felt she was making good time. The hill leading to the camp was not steep, and it was not hard to follow the old tracks and the recent ones of her beloved Suffolks. She laughed as she remembered carefully painting their blazes, worrying about Alex and Thorne, only to be the one recognized.

She held her little lantern in front of her to light the path, pushing herself to go one step at a time up the hill and not rest until she saw the campfire, although it would take much of the night. The path had taken a sharp turn to the left to avoid a steep incline when she heard footsteps and breaking twigs just behind her. She left the trail, blew out the candle, and ran deep into the brush that grew along the long unused road. Nina gripped the pistol she kept in her pocket under the cloak, knowing she had primed it and loaded it hours ago. She hoped it would fire.

But not like that. She tripped and fell. She would have blacked out in the fall, but the sound of a gunshot jolted her right back awake. She lay back to assess her pain, trying to discover if she had shot herself. The fear was almost worse than pain. She lay perfectly still.

Swift footsteps came closer and Nina cursed herself for giving away her location with the gunshot.

"Stop! I have another pistol and it's aimed right at you." Nina knew right away that was a stupid thing to say. She couldn't see the nose in front of her face, let alone this assailant.

"Missus, are you a'right?"

The voice was young. Hands took her lantern and lit the candle, far more quickly than she had done it. "Lady?" A young face, barely older than Jack but clearly wearing a British uniform, stared down at her.

"Y'yes. I am fine. Stunned from the fall, but unhurt."

"Good. I didn't mean to scare you."

"Why were you following me?" Nina was very confused. The British would never send such a young recruit to bring in an American officer.

"Promise you won't laugh nor turn me in?" Nina sat up, motioning for the young man to sit as well, and tell her his story. "I took the shilling and joined, but I didn't like it. It's been one year and I want to go home, but my commander says I owe too much for my uniform, boots and food, and must stay to work off the debt. When we quartered near the river, I jumped in and swam up a stream. That was three days ago; they must a' figured I'm drowned.

"I followed you because you look like an American, all simple and pretty. Normal, country, like my Ma. I thought you might feed me. I promise I won't eat much, and then I'll be on my way."

He sounded sad and lonely, this boy who needed more than a meal. "Let's see what we can do. Can you help me? I think I twisted my ankle." The young man helped her stand. She leaned against him and they started back up the path. "I certainly hope those eggs are unbroken."

***

Alex took the team through the market square, concentrating hard at not turning to watch Nina work her way through the crowd. He schooled himself to have faith that she could blend in. Wasn't the world of commerce her world? She should have no problem being one of the hundreds of merchants or farm women who were in the town square this morning. They drove out of town and headed east. They found the town of Cortland Manor, and stopped the team on a nearby lane. They were greeted by a young woman with a filthy pitchfork on her shoulder.

They exchanged pleasantries until she blurted out. "Are you the people come to claim my patient? I had given up hope you would come before his leg turned green."

Alex pushed Maryann, not unkindly, behind him before she started to cry. He felt her swallow her tears and listen to the girl.

"We heard it was a rib?"

"It was. That's where the bullet grazed him. He hurt his leg running from them. Bruised it badly on a rock or something. I wasn't able to do much for him, but he's healed a bit anyway. This way." She led them to a small tool shed near a growth of trees. She opened the locked door. "I had to keep the door locked from the outside to keep out the curious. I would have welcomed him leaving." She answered their questions about the locks before they could ask them.

"Hi!" The Colonel half sat up. His eyes sparkled when he saw his daughter. Maryann ran to his arms, ignoring his foul smell.

Alex took charge. As they maneuvered the injured man onto a board, Bickerstaff panted in pain even from the short move. Jack walked the team and wagon as close to the shed and the injured man as possible.

"On three we lift." The two children had one end, Alex the other and Charles Bickerstaff, his face white with strain, pushed off with his good leg. "One, two, three" They all heaved the large man onto the back of the wagon. It was clear the colonel had been re-injured in the move, but that could be dealt with later.

Alex walked a little bit away with the farm girl who had risked so much to help a stranger. They spoke a few words and he handed her a purse with small coins, American and British. "Easier to spend and not be questioned. I know. And much thanks." He pulled himself onto the bench, handed Jack the reins, and pointed north down the lane and away from the road and town, up a grown-over track into the hills.

The going was slow, since they didn't want to jog the colonel's leg anymore than they had to. At one point, probably half way up, Alex had had enough.

"Jack, Maryann get out. Follow this trail the rest of the

way and get a fire going at the camp. Take the big kettle out of the back and get water boiling. The girl said it is on this road - at the top of this little mountain. It's grown over now but was a pig-iron camp, so there should be water and a clearing of some sort. I'll get your father there as soon as we can. It's silly to wait till night to get camp set up, when you can be up there in an hour.

Maryann again wanted to object, but swallowed whatever she had been about to say. Alex thought that maybe this trip had finally taught her to follow directions - maybe, but she would never make a soldier. In any case, he was happy that the children ran ahead. The two men let the horses follow the old track, slowly up the hill.

Alex pulled his mind from wandering and kept it firmly on his charge and the trail in front of him. Defiantly refusing to worry about Nina, he engaged Charles Bickerstaff in conversation when the man was awake and in pain, and let him sleep when he could. He kept up that pattern hour after tedious hour, sometime dozing on the bench while Jewel and Bella did the work. Alex woke with the sound of a gunshot from down the mountain. It seemed to come from just below them on the trail. He listened for another, for a scream or at least someone yelling – the sounds of conflict. There was nothing. The noise might have been a branch cracking, for all he knew.

The Colonel was sweating with the strain of the journey, and badly needed to have the leg and ribs seen to. Alex reminded himself that he had promised Nina that whatever happened, he would not go back. Not until Bickerstaff was safe.

***

Jack and Maryann had done a good job of making camp. A firepit was set up, the stones were neatly arranged, and a pot of water boiled merrily. Nearby was a stream of clean water. Alex took a few minutes to clean his face and hands, and was beginning to wash the wound in the Colonel's leg, when Jack shouted and start to run.

"Everybody, get your rifles! There's a redcoat holding Ma!" Jack ran to the wagon to grab his gun, he raised it to his shoulder and aimed it at the man. "Let - go - of - my - mother!"

Alex jumped, spilling bloody wash-water. He turned to see Nina limping into camp supported by what looked like a boy in a red uniform, his arm around Nina's waist. He pulled his rifle from his sac.

The day had been too long. He had been focused and worried, on the edge of outright terror, a horrible combination. He lifted his rifle and aimed it at the heart of the man in the red uniform.

Nina saw determination in Jack's face. He certainly was not her young son anymore. She would cope with that later."Jack put that down! Alex, no!" She held out her hand and stepped hesitantly away from her helper onto her weak ankle. "His name is Gordon Clarke, Gordy. He's hungry and I promised to feed him. The boy is a deserter from His Majesty's 23rd. He's hungry." She turned to Alex. He lowered his rifle and reached for her, took a step and almost collapsed on his stiff leg.

She limped toward him to help. She collapsed laughing into Alex's arms. "I hurt my ankle again. The same one from the mountain." She wiggled it, as if to show that it hurt. "Jack! I said put that down." She had looked to see that her son had not relaxed. She took a step toward him. He shrugged and lowered his weapon. They had come so close to shooting her new adoptee after she had promised him he would be safe.

Gordy nodded a quick thanks, bounded over to Jack and

put out his hand. "Show me those huge beasties you've got there. I love horses." Jack introduced the Suffolks. Nina looked over, to see the boys who were nearly men, in deep conversation.

"Jack, you and Gordy find the big frypan and help Maryann with those eggs. There is bacon in the back of the wagon. We'll see about more food tomorrow." She went to see to the two gentleman, picking up her medical kit and bringing over her small lantern.

She was bone tired, and her ankle hurt more than she would let on. But the real patient had to come first. The ball was out, probably only nicked the rib enough to shatter it on its way, but even these many days later the wound in his side would benefit from a few stitches. Alex held Charles' shoulders, while Nina, using silk thread and stitches every girl learned, sewed up the wound. The bruise in the leg was clean with Alex's washing, she handed him a jar of salve her sister-in-law swore by. She wished she had that sleeping draught of Mrs. MacAlistair's, but their patient would have to get by without. Alex passed him a flask of rum.

That night everyone went to bed early and fell asleep: the newest member of the group, because he was fed and comfortable for the first time in days, perhaps weeks; the patient, because he was clean, and had drunk a good deal of rum; the youngsters, because they had run up the hill, the last days had been scary, and now they were relaxed, comfortable and truly tired.

Maryann slept as near her father as his injuries would allow, as if she might never see him again. Nina was sure that in the morning she would relax, but would be sure to keep an eye on him as she did her chores in the camp. She would not ask her to go far. Jack quickly adopted Gordy as if they were long-lost brothers. At first, Nina listened to their whispered chatter to see if Jack was uncomfortable with the newcomer, but he seemed happy to have this refugee to care for.

Alex was worried about Nina's injury and the long, tiresome day being too much and chilling her. He set up her bedroll near the fire. He would have rather joined her, held her close all night to keep her warm, but he needed to stand guard – there was no one else. Maybe in a few days he could trust Gordon to stand a shift, but not so soon upon his wandering into camp, and Alex could not yet be sure that no one was searching for the young deserter.

"I don't want to sleep alone," Nina whispered not wanting to disturb the others. There had been few private moments these last days.

"I have to stand guard, and you have to stay warm and safe." He helped Nina bed down, gave her a warmed, wrapped rock for her chest and propped her ankle so it would not swell. Then he pulled his cape off his shoulders and wrapped the fur around her. "Good night, my love." He kissed her and grabbed the last of the blankets and went to sleep at the edge of camp by the Suffolks.

Sleeping near the horses gave him the advantage of their natural shyness and a loud whinny whenever a newcomer came near them. He planned on sleeping and letting Jewel and Bella wake him if there was an intruder. He took his own warmed flat rocks, one for his feet and another for his chest, and climbed into his bedroll, arranging himself and hoping that exhaustion and relief would combine to let him sleep.

He hadn't considered he might be awakened by the one intruder the Suffolks would let through the line. "Alex?" It was hours later. Nina had tossed and turned, unable to get comfortable while all around her, the camp slept. The warm stone on her stomach felt heavy. She hoped they were home before there was snow and warm rocks would be necessary every night. The ankle was sore, but she felt fine as she stood and pulled Alex's warm cloak over her shoulders. She walked past the wagon to where Alex lay sleeping on the edge of the trail. "Alex" She whispered just loud enough to break the silence.

She knelt next to him and covered him and his bedroll with the wonderful cape. She pulled off her night clothes and climbed in next to him, snuggling into a familiar, comfortable place at his side. She ran her fingers through his wonderful hair, askew with sleep, and kissed him awake.

Pale firelight glimmered through her hair. He pulled her down to him, mirrored her efforts, unbraiding her long hair, and letting the soft, pale strands fall free. He touched her back and realized that she had already undressed and was naked in his bedroll. He kissed the soft skin of her neck and breasts, feeling her melt for him.

Alex took a deep breath as his hands worshiped the woman lying languidly next to him. They had made love most nights since they'd married, sometimes calmly and quietly like in his parents' house, sometimes passionately with an animal need that seemed unquenchable. It was hard to imagine this beautiful, strong woman was the alewife who had curled away from him and shivered in fear, or the woman he had teased into reluctant pleasure. He couldn't doubt she was the heroine who had rescued his horse, or the angel who had contrived to feed him and save him from abject loneliness on Christmas, already a lifetime ago. He kissed her, their tongues twining as they breathed and drank of each other. It had been an interesting year for them. A revolution of their own, he supposed.

He watched in delight as Nina responded by arching and stretching her arms over her head, relaxed and beautiful in her nakedness. She smiled at him, an open joyful smile he could feel more than see in the half light of the dying fire. She reached up to put her hands in his hair, pulling him down to her, sighing under him, opening to him, putting her legs around his, and welcoming him. The fire popped, and a log hissed as it dropped into place, falling exactly where it was supposed to be.

Afterward

They began the slow trek north three days later. The rains had finally come, but they hugged the coast in Connecticut instead of heading north into the mountains, and were in New Haven, safely at an inn, before the worst of it. Their last act at camp was to burn every bit of red wool they could find. Nina carefully saved the pewter buttons from Gordy's uniform - those could be melted at the forge into new ones. He'd huddled under blankets until they reached a town with a general store selling a few ready-made items.

On the journey north, Colonel Bickerstaff insisted upon hearing everything Private Clarke could tell him about the British Army, structure and camps. The boy did not know anything much new, but it was impossible to say ahead of time what might be useful. The two men spent hours in conversation, with either Jack or Maryann transcribing every word.

The private's long story was finished just as they reached Providence, where the Colonel insisted he be left. "My mother can see to my convalescence. I have enough to thank you people for." He spoke gruffly, but was clearly very grateful. "Maryann, the offer still stands to stay with Grandma." He looked at her quizzically, his leg rested on an upholstered footstool in his mother's parlor. "Grandma, Papa. Alex... Mr. Peele, now that he will be my teacher." She took a deep breath to start over. "Mr Peele has offered to teach, *really* teach me, not like a girl. I'd like to go with them – back to the Lower Falls."

Her grandmother, the somewhat formidable Mrs. Bickerstaff, looked like she might object to a girl who wanted an education, but then pursed her lips and nodded. "Then you must do it, Maryann. Who knows what challenges a girl will face in this new nation?" Maryann kissed her grandmother on her cheek, and hugged her father goodbye.

***

Nina took the reins so that Alex could stretch his leg. The slow journey which had done so much for the Colonel had caused his leg to ache again, and the damp weather did not help. Nina knew he would never say anything about it. After Providence, with no invalid in the wagon, they let the horses run full speed. They arrived at the stable yard at the *Wheel and Hammer* late morning the next day. The children jumped right out to introduce their new stablehand to the tavern staff. No mention would be made of the red uniform or where they had found Gordy Clarke.

Gordy led the Suffolks into their stall. The new boy was wonderful with horses. Henry would be relieved.

Nina stepped away from the chatting, giggling crowd and toward the river. She looked back over the familiar place, letting feelings of home and happiness fill her. She felt a hand on her back, and she leaned into him. He said something that was drowned out by the roar of the falls, and Nina looked questioning at him, but he shook his head. It had been nothing important. He kissed her long, not caring who looked over to see the new brewmistress kissing her husband, loving that he could build a life for them here, in this beautiful spot.

Neither lover spoke, letting the sound of the falls fill the comfortable silence. Arm in arm they turned and walked across the road, toward home, the familiar little yellow house with the new red shutters.

Dear Reader,

Thank you for reading *Beside Turning Water*, the third book in the **World Turned Upside Down** series. If you have read the other two, this story sits chronologically between the other books in the series, *Cardinal Points* and *Fate and Fair Winds*. The books in the series do not need to be read in order. Characters may visit each other's book, but never play major roles twice.

***

The British Parliament enacted the Intolerable Acts in the spring of 1774, a few months after it became clear that Bostonians had no intention of paying for the tea they'd destroyed the previous December. To punish Boston, these laws directed how judges and sheriffs were to be appointed, how town governments could function, and, of course, they closed the Port of Boston to all vessels that were not owned by the British Navy.

Nina's world is not Boston or the Port, but because of the nearness of her tavern at Newton Lower Falls to the large town and the connection along the river to the encampment in Cambridge, her area and the people who live there would have been strongly affected by changes in government and trade. These acts did not bring about subservience in the countryside, but instead brought countryfolk to the Battles at Concord and Lexington, and Bunker and Breed's Hills.

A word about the weather in this book. The story opens at the Battle of Bunker Hill. June 17, 1775 was a hot day. In fact, researchers believe that no date of an important battle was hotter until the Battle of Gettysburg, during the Civil War eighty-eight years later. The Battle of Monmouth in New Jersey, on June 28, 1778 was famous for the heat in which it was fought, but it is believed that the heat at Bunker Hill was worse.

There are two other major storms in this book. One is a hurricane that hit the Carolinas on September 3, 1775. It roared up the east coast, causing damage in every major American city and into the Canadian Maritimes. It is estimated that by the time it ended, four thousand people had been killed by rushing water, tides and building collapses.

On March 5, 1776, a nor'easter helped the Americans drive the British from Boston. The storm provided cover so farmers and soldiers could build redoubts into the frozen ground on Dorchester Heights. At the same time, high winds swirling between harbor and land prevented the Royal Marines from landing and taking the hill. General Howe had known for a year that the British would have to take Dorchester Heights eventually, if they wanted to keep the town. He waited too long, and when he awoke on March 5, he saw sixty cannon aimed at his Men o' War anchored in the harbor. Within days, he asked for terms.

The treatment for smallpox used in the story was taken from Tomlinson Fort's treatise, *A Dissertation on the Practice of Medicine*, published in 1849. The standard of treatment in the eighteenth and early nineteenth centuries, written up by Dr. Fort, was to keep the patient cool, since heat increased itching and redness. When I first began to write about the Danns and the epidemic that hit Boston just toward the end of the occupation, I wanted Alex to get a chicken and make a hearty stew for them. I was surprised to learn, instead, that cool, thin foods, light clothing and blankets was the standard of treatment.

The smocks, sewn at the hands and feet, and the trimmed

fingernails and toenails, I learned of from the *Diary of William Bentley, 1811 - 1819,* who described preparation for his inoculation and week of recovery. Inoculation often lessened the severity of the infection, but only survived illness guaranteed full protection, as Alex explains.

To those readers who might not live in the Boston area, the Upper and Lower Falls of the Charles River in Newton are real. The Upper Falls is the greater drop, at twenty feet. The Lower Falls consists of two separate falls. The first drops sixteen feet, and the second six feet. They are lovely parkland now, and the water flow is part of the USGS survey for the Charles. These falls were among the first industrial areas in America. By 1704, there was a forge and triphammer at the lower falls. A smith shop was recorded there by 1722, and over the century, there was a snuff works, iron works, sawmill, paper mill, and calico printing mills. By 1800, paper was the most important product made at the Falls.

My versions of Generals Washington and Thomas are completely my own, based on outside reading. However, the dates on which Washington received information from "someone in Boston" match those sent by Alex back to camp. The historical events in the book- the Battle of Bunker Hill, the number of check points, batteries and guards on the neck, the occupation, siege lines, and Battle of Dorchester Heights, the storms and the heat - are all described as others recorded them. John Rowe's warehouse was, in fact, looted by British troops as they evacuated.

Dory Codington is a student and teacher of history and sometime guide on Boston's historical Freedom Trail. Her primary interests lie in using historical references and her imagination to understand the daily lives of those who lived during significant periods in history. Dory currently lives in Massachusetts with a husband, a daughter, a son and a tortoise.

Edge of Empire books take place during America's Colonial, Provincial, and Revolutionary Periods. *World Turned Upside Down* is how many people in America and Britain felt about the outcome of the American Revolution. Lord Cornwallis's troops stacked their muskets, when they surrendered at Yorktown, to a song by this name.

Books in the series are:

Cardinal Points
Fate and Fair Winds
Beside Turning Water

Other books by Dory:

Through the Eyes of a Poet:
The Life and Writings of Kate Fort Codington

Visit **DorysHistoricals.com** for the latest news and historical tidbits.